TO THE CAST AND CREW OF
SHADOW AND BONE. ESPECIALLY BEN,
WHO IS ONE OF THE GOOD GUYS.
—LB

FOR DISCO, ROSE, AND GEOFF.
—DP

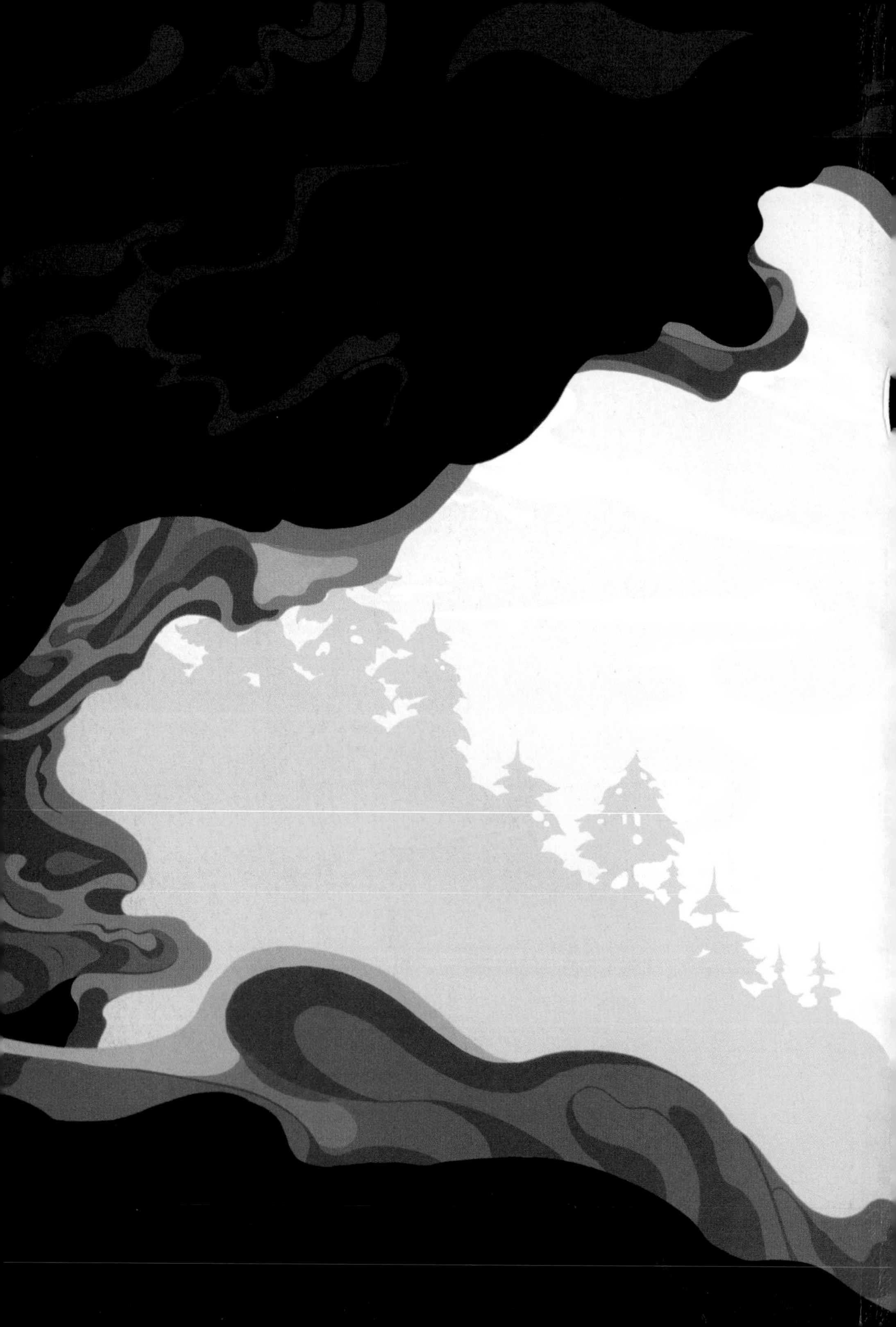

GRISHAVERSE
DEMON IN THE WOOD
A SHADOW AND BONE GRAPHIC NOVEL

LEIGH BARDUGO &
DANI PENDERGAST

ROARING BROOK PRESS
New York

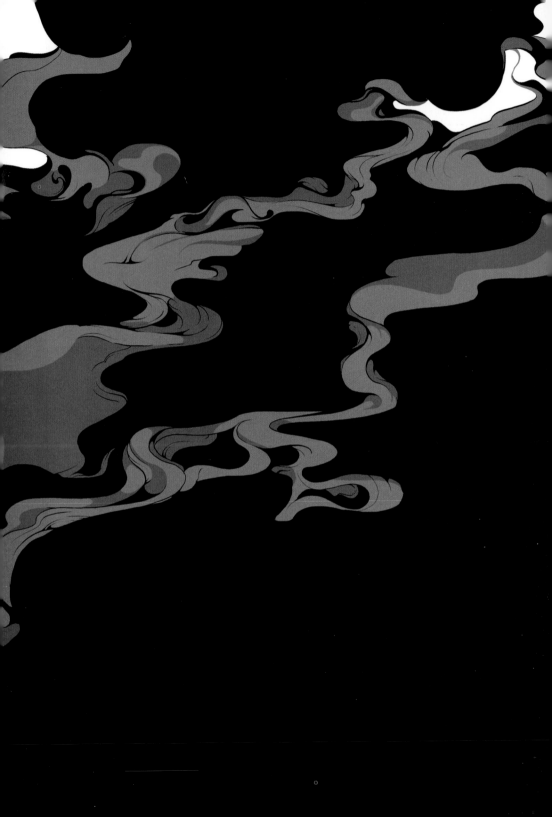

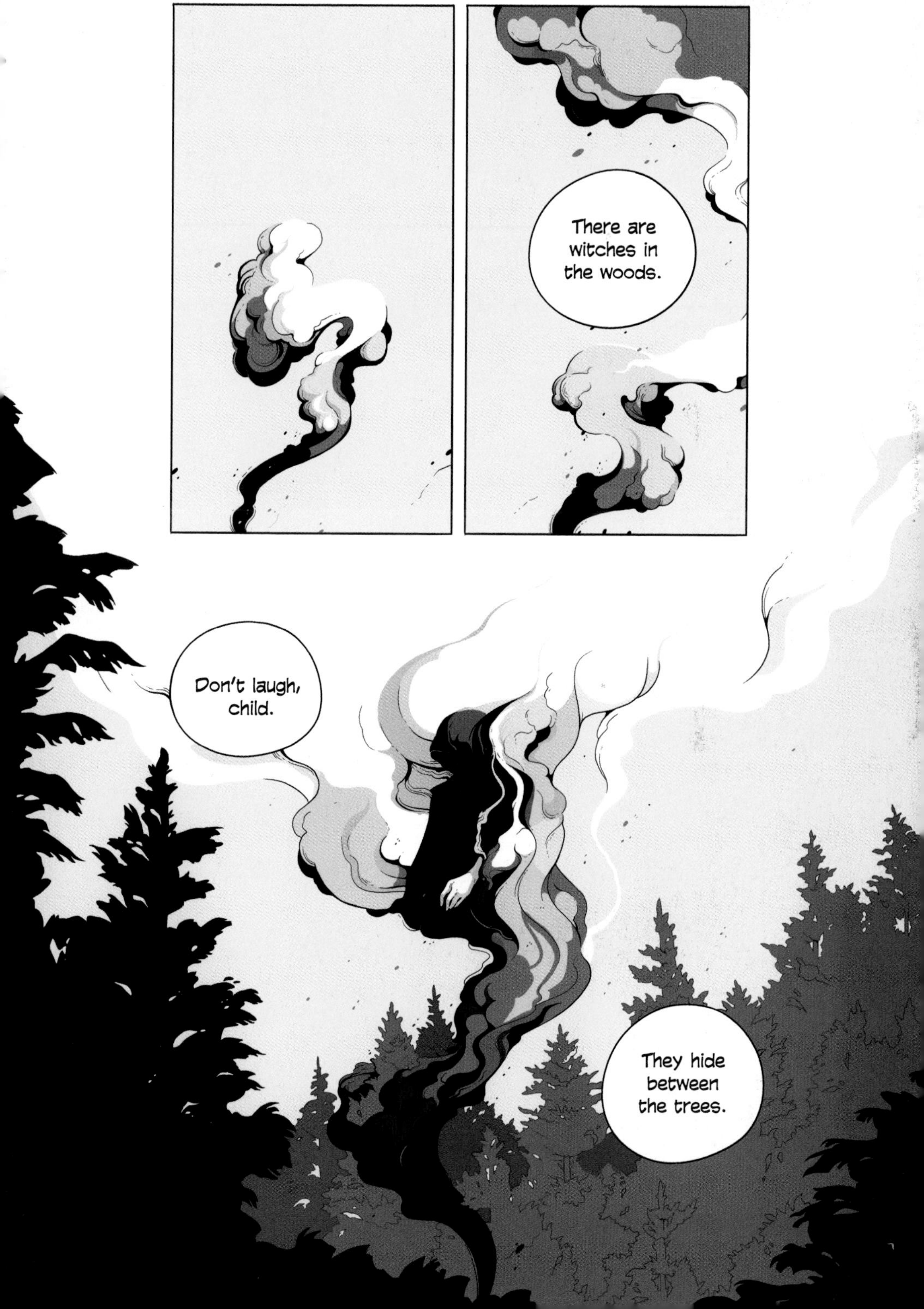
There are witches in the woods.
Don't laugh, child.
They hide between the trees.

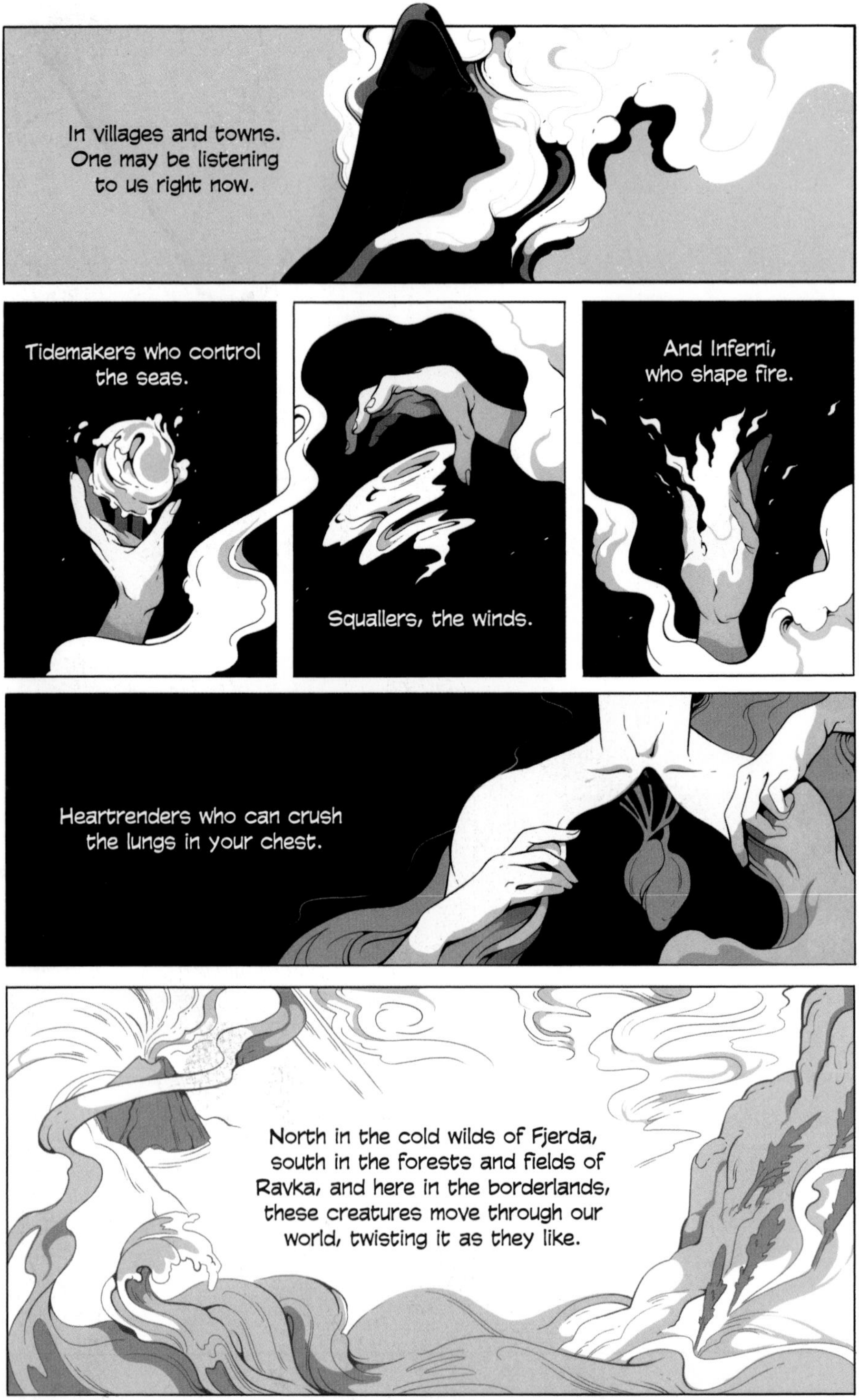
In villages and towns. One may be listening to us right now.
Tidemakers who control the seas.
Squallers, the winds.
And Inferni, who shape fire.
Heartrenders who can crush the lungs in your chest.
North in the cold wilds of Fjerda, south in the forests and fields of Ravka, and here in the borderlands, these creatures move through our world, twisting it as they like.

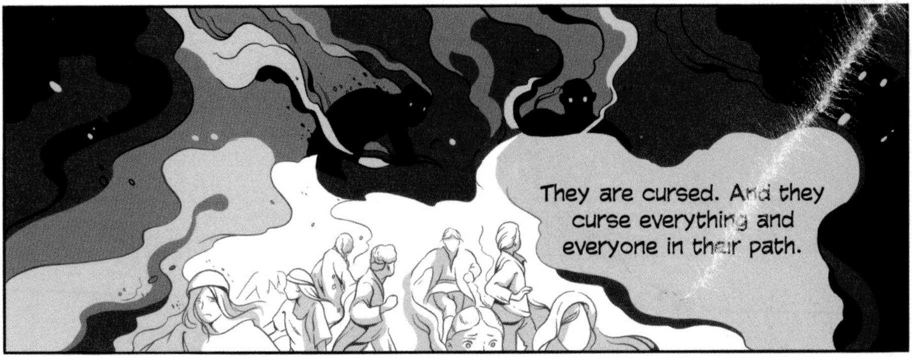
They are cursed. And they curse everything and everyone in their path.

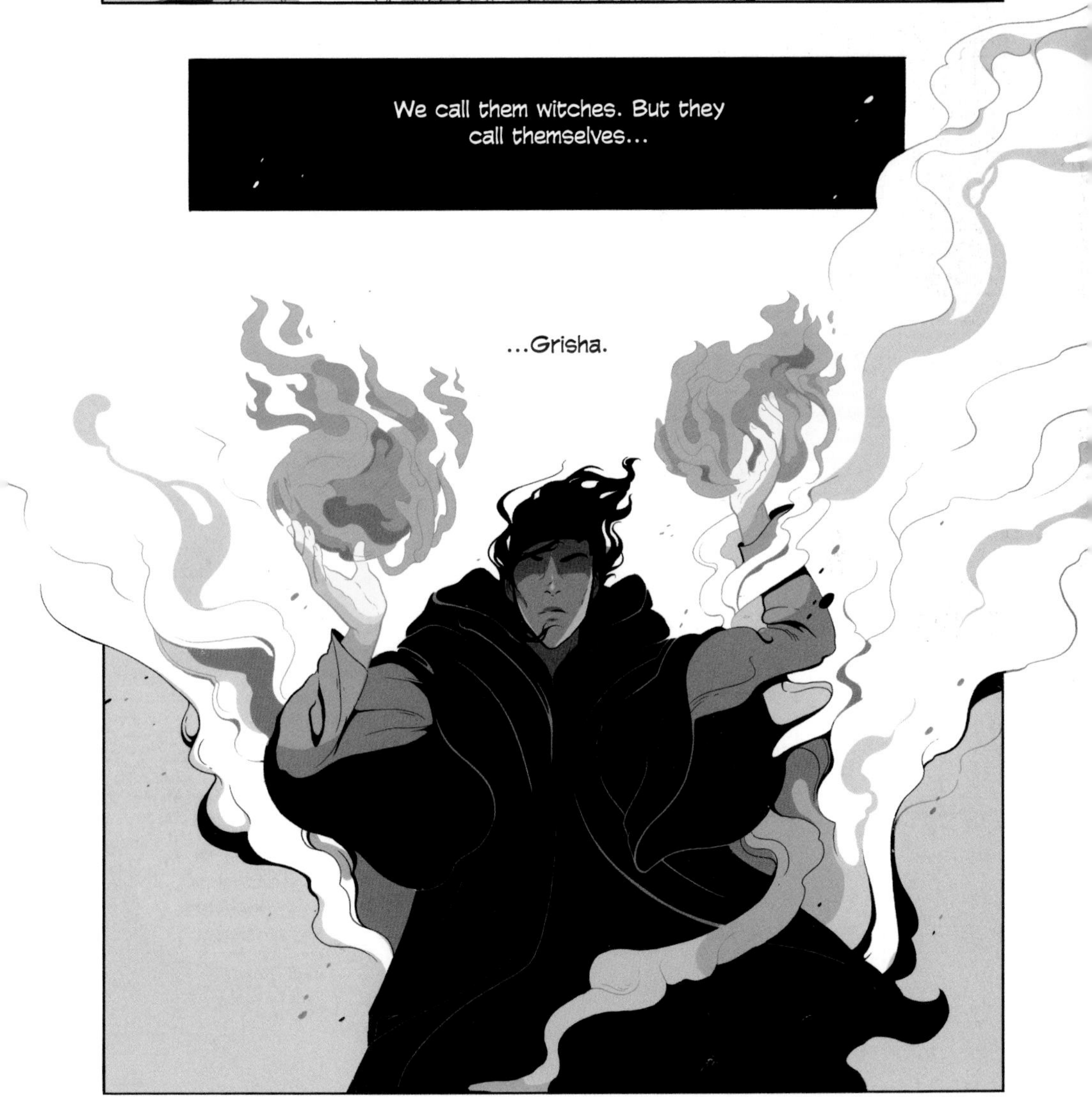
We call them witches. But they call themselves...
...Grisha.

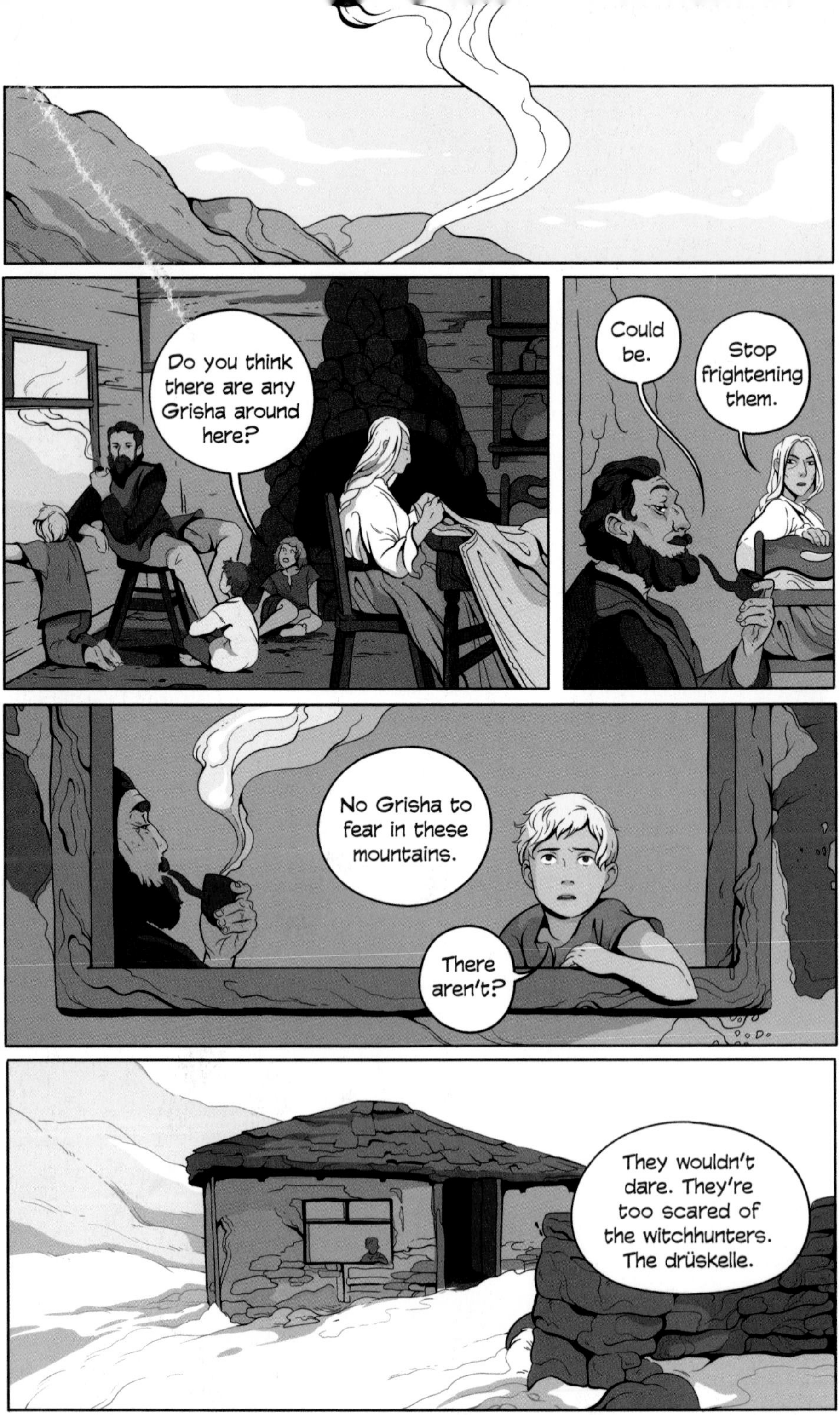
Do you think there are any Grisha around here?
Could be.
Stop frightening them.
No Grisha to fear in these mountains.
There aren't?
They wouldn't dare. They're too scared of the witchhunters. The drüskelle.

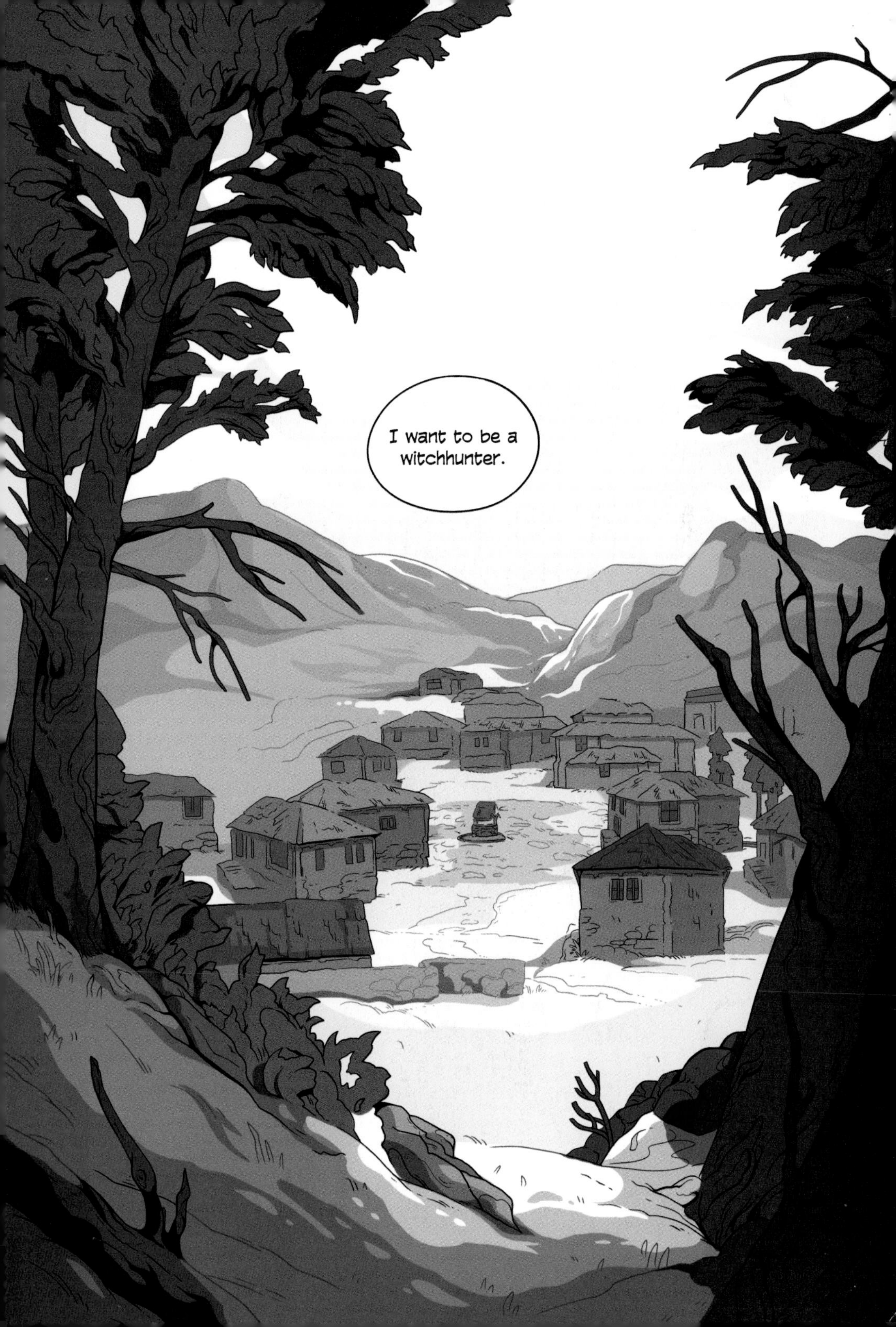
I want to be a witchhunter.

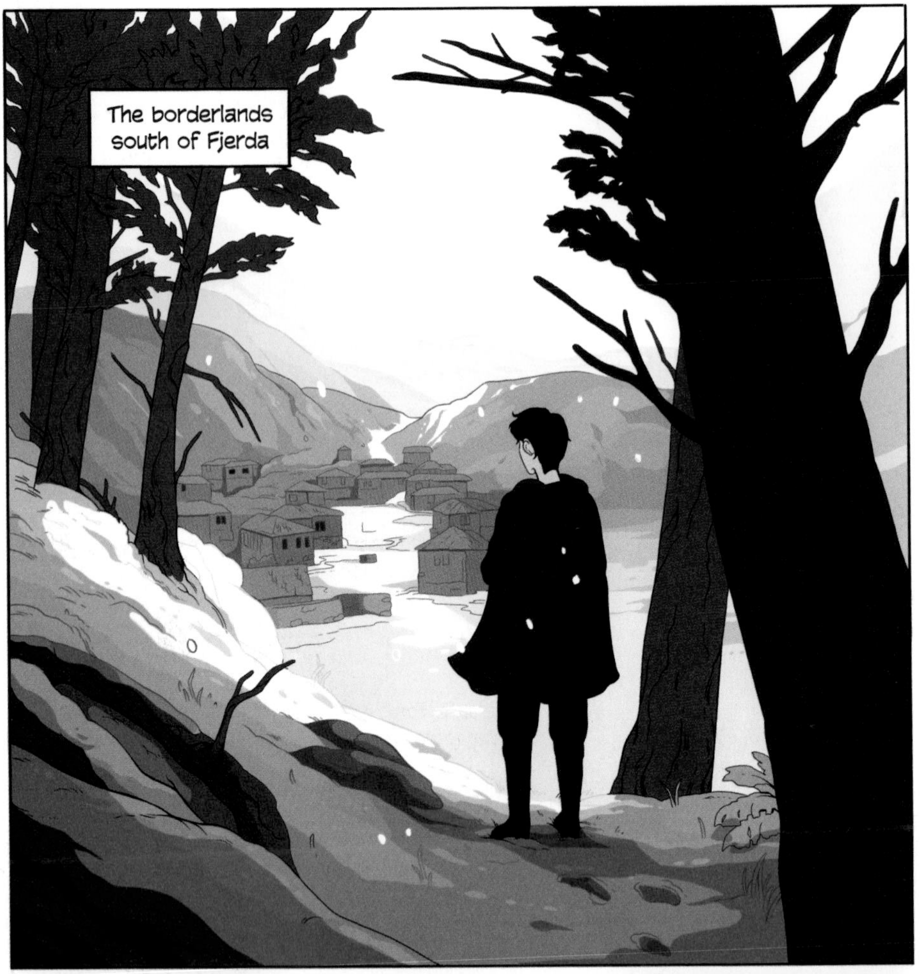
The borderlands
south of Fjerda

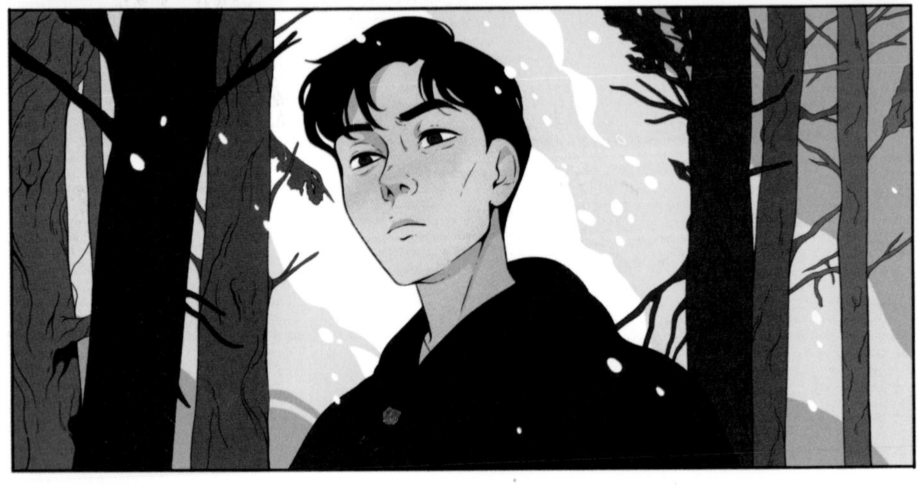

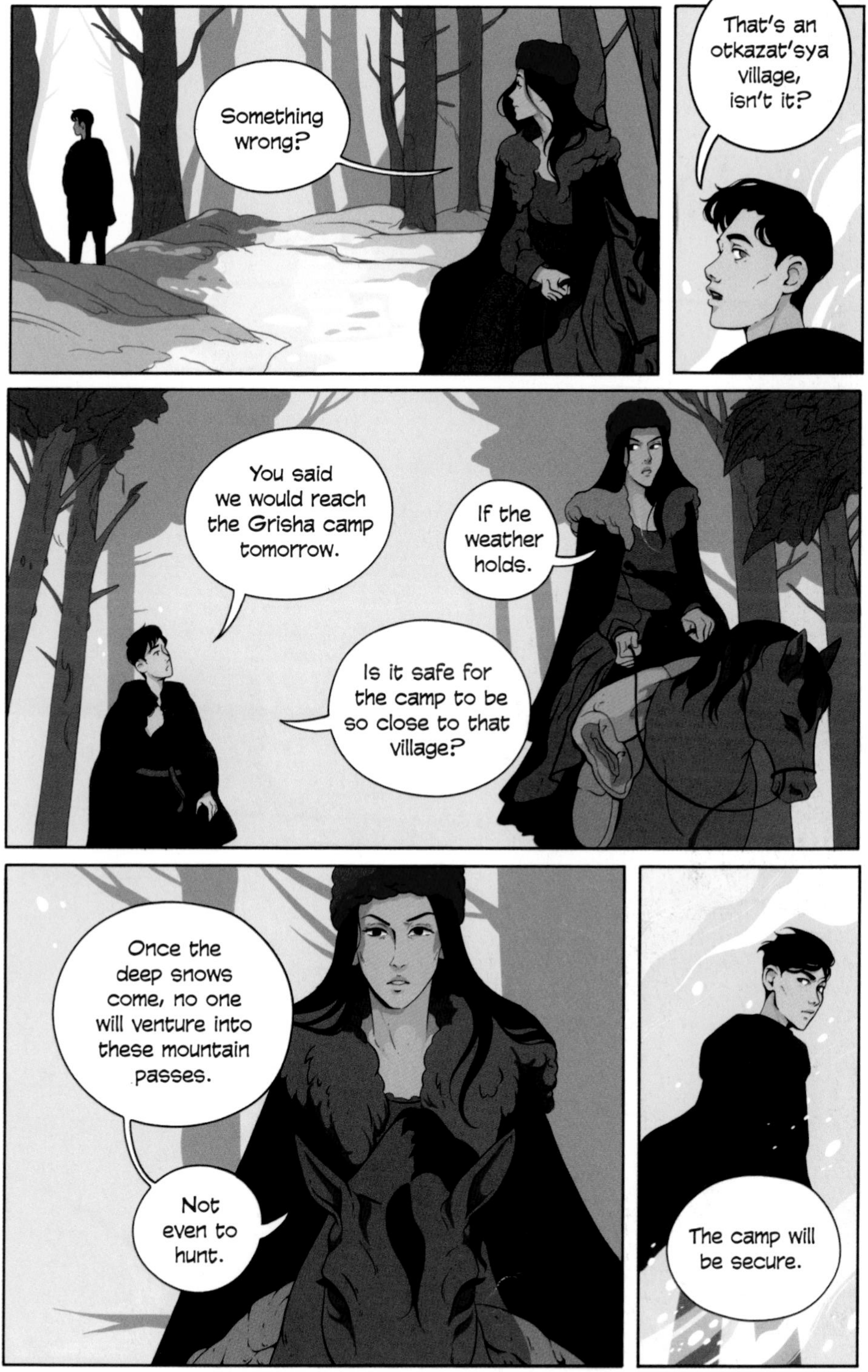
Something wrong?
That's an otkazat'sya village, isn't it?
You said we would reach the Grisha camp tomorrow.
If the weather holds.
Is it safe for the camp to be so close to that village?
Once the deep snows come, no one will venture into these mountain passes.
Not even to hunt.
The camp will be secure.

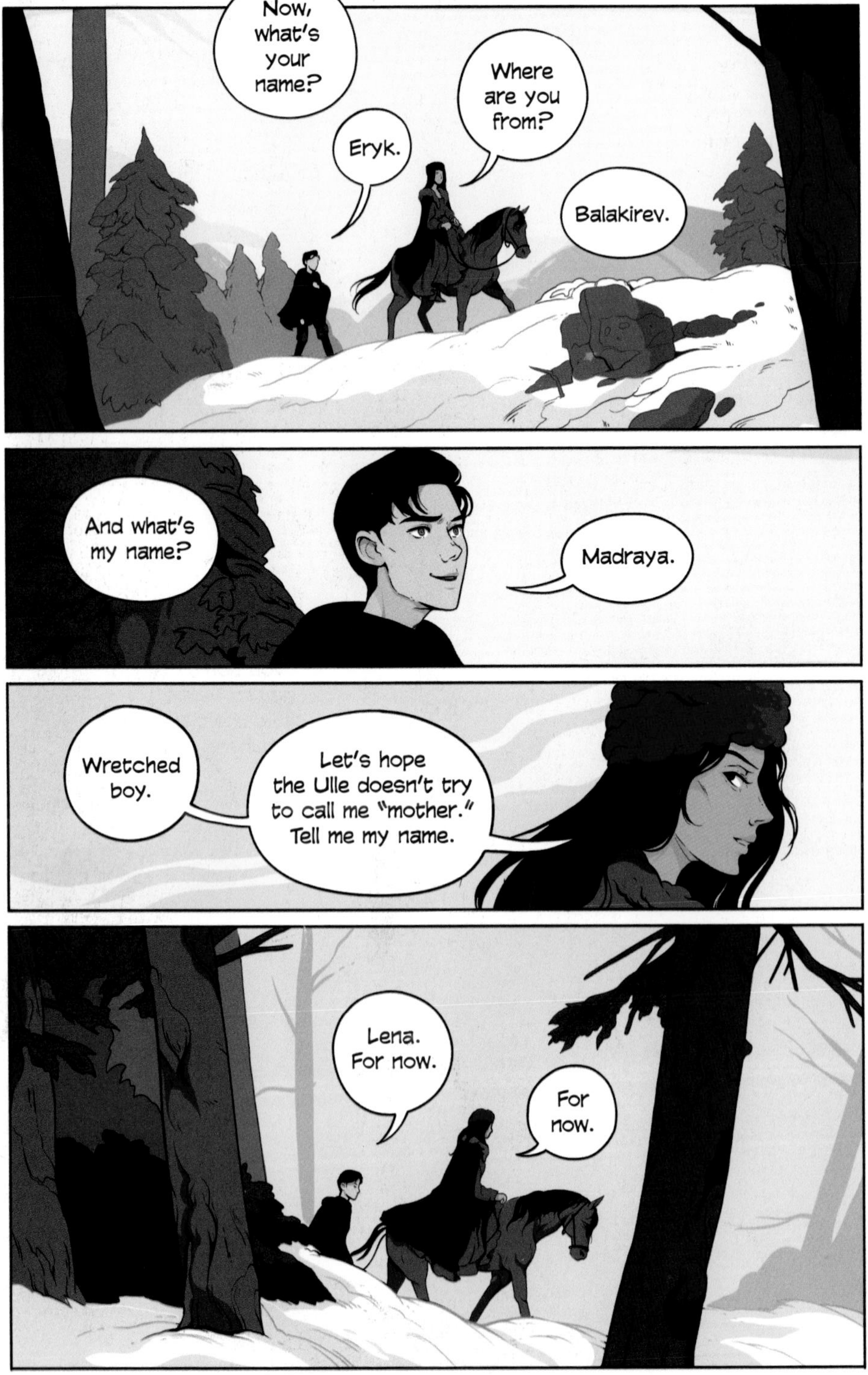
Now, what's your name?
Eryk.
Where are you from?
Balakirev.
And what's my name?
Madraya.
Wretched boy.
Let's hope the Ulle doesn't try to call me "mother." Tell me my name.
Lena. For now.
For now.

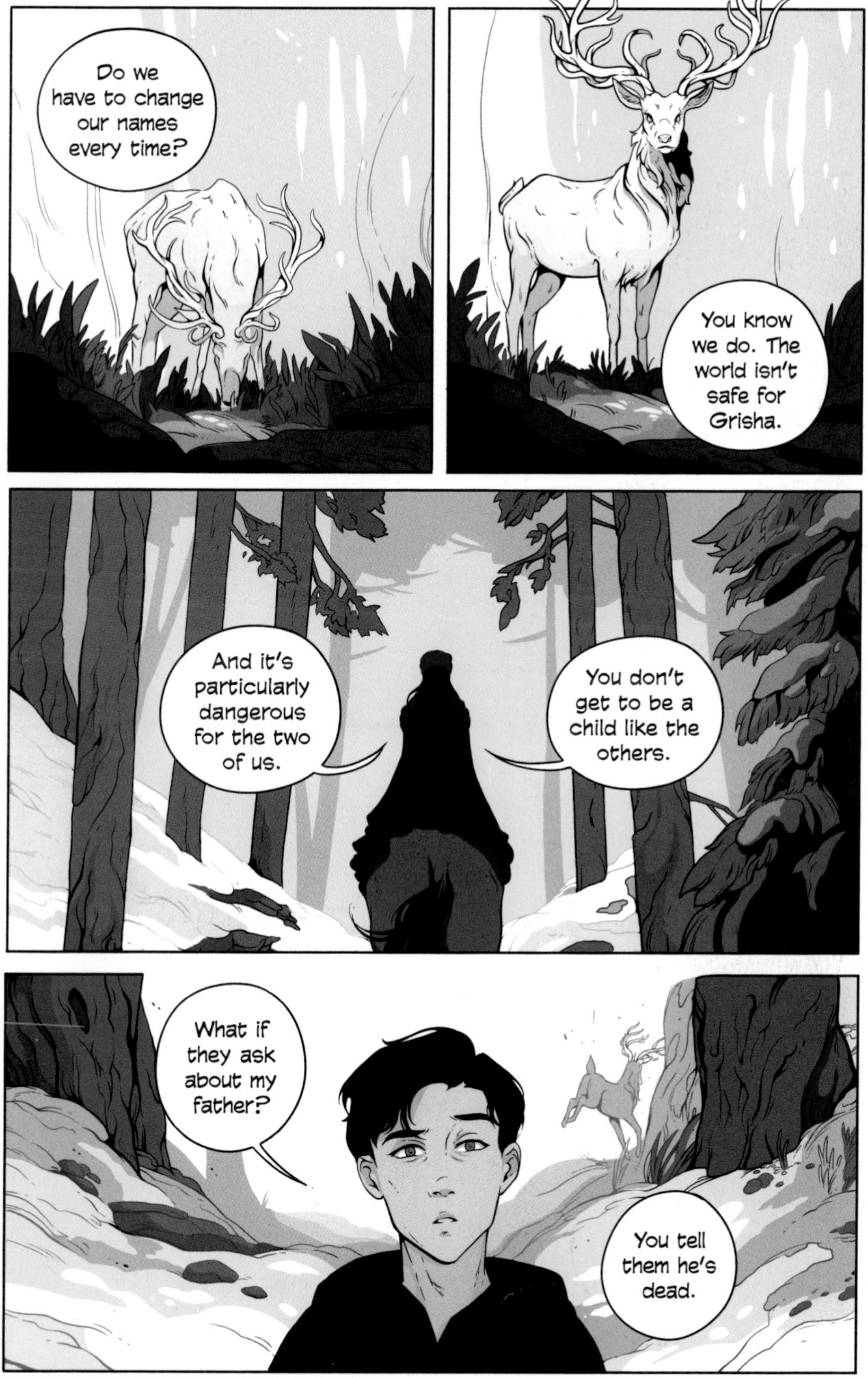
Do we have to change our names every time?
You know we do. The world isn't safe for Grisha.
And it's particularly dangerous for the two of us.
You don't get to be a child like the others.
What if they ask about my father?
You tell them he's dead.

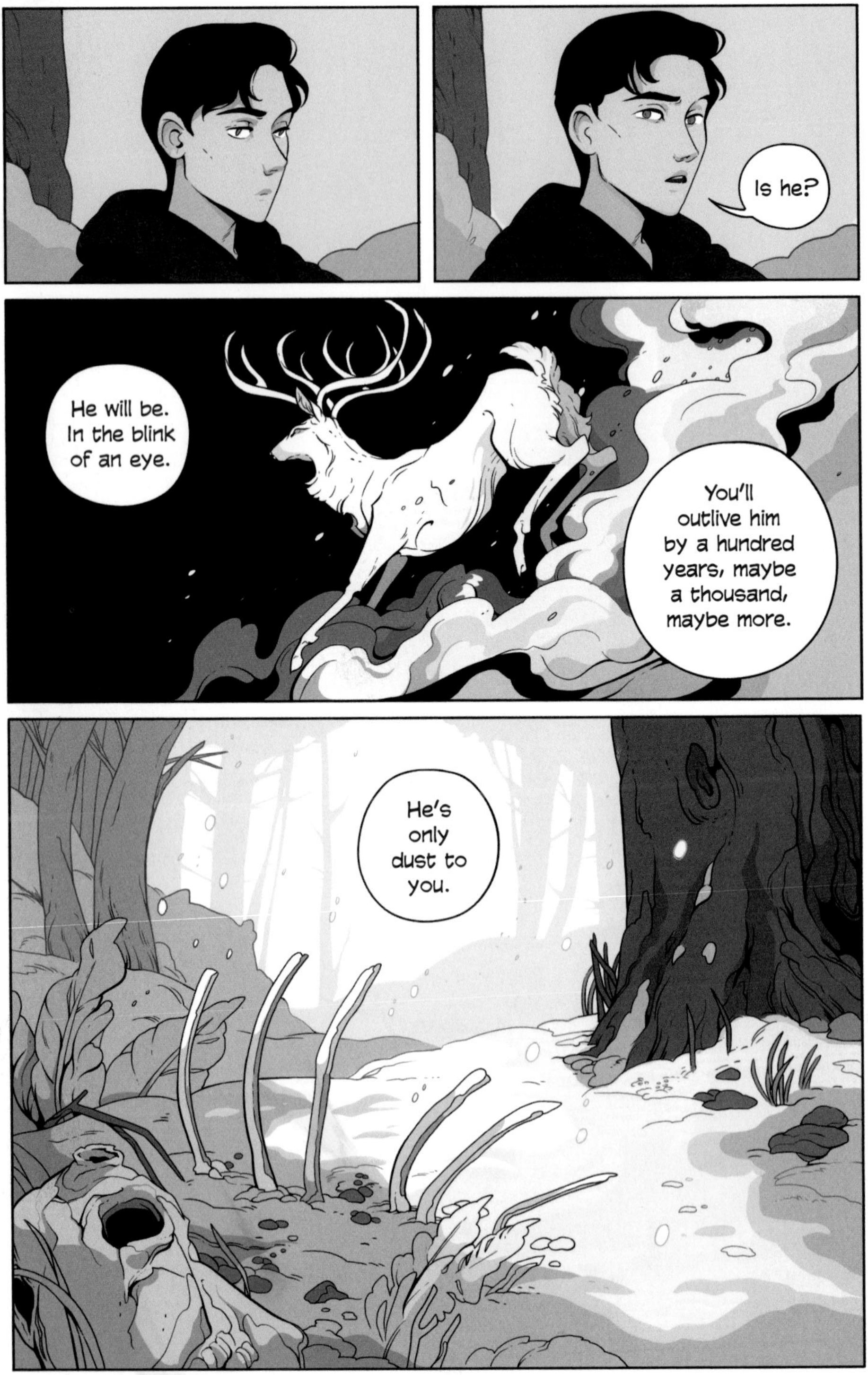
Is he?
He will be. In the blink of an eye.
You'll outlive him by a hundred years, maybe a thousand, maybe more.
He's only dust to you.

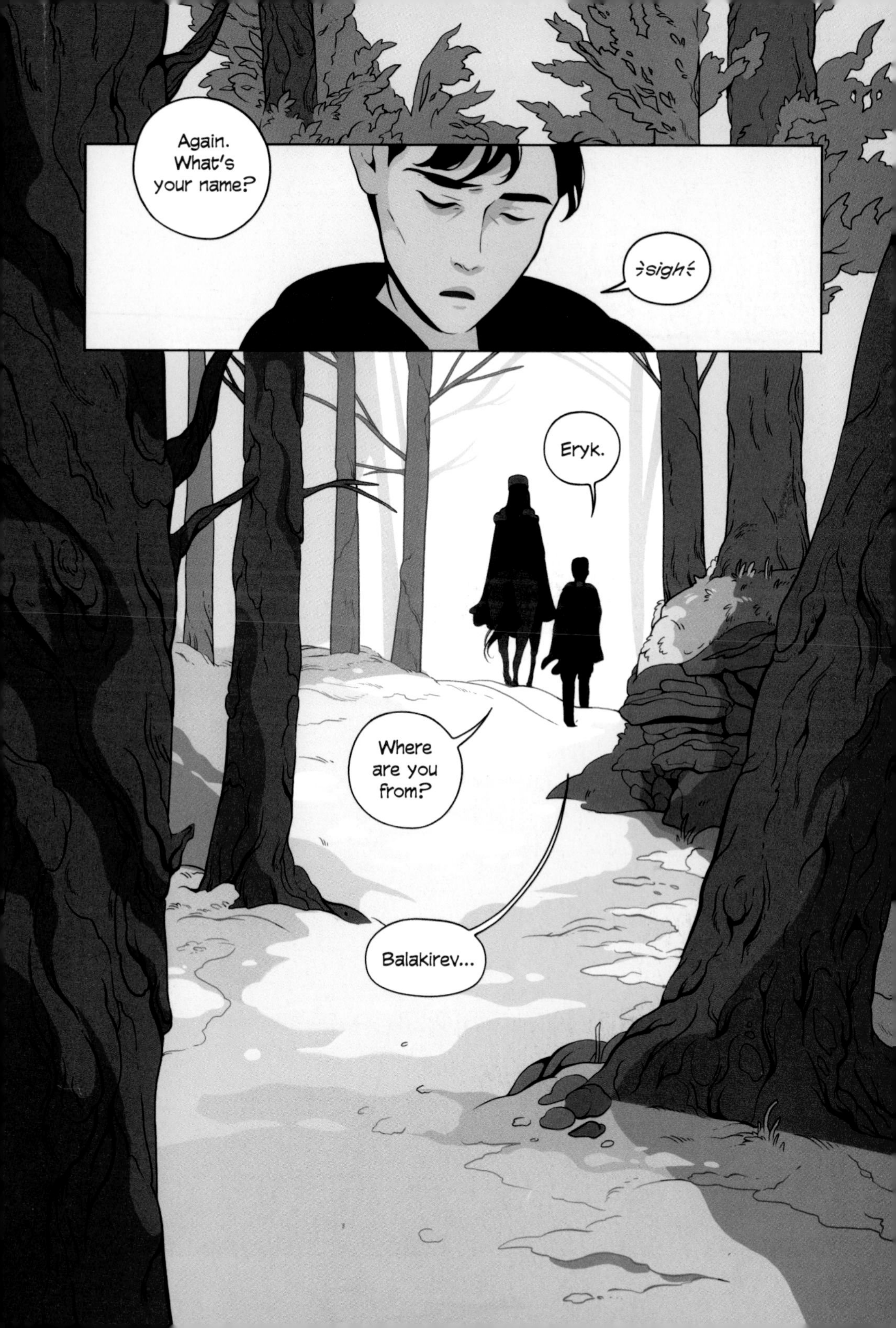
Again. What's your name?
sigh
Eryk.
Where are you from?
Balakirev...

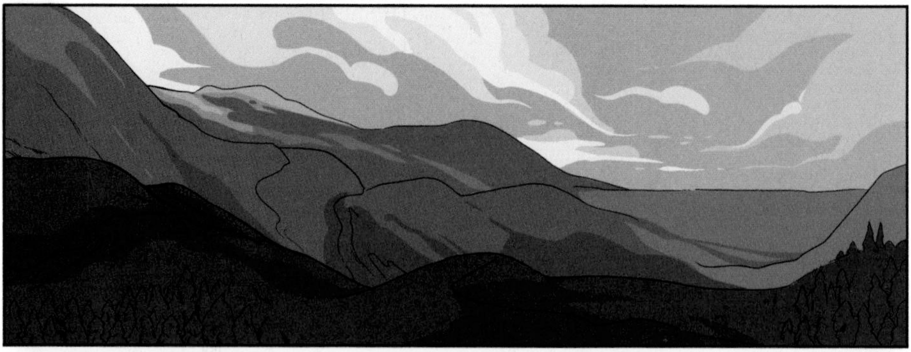

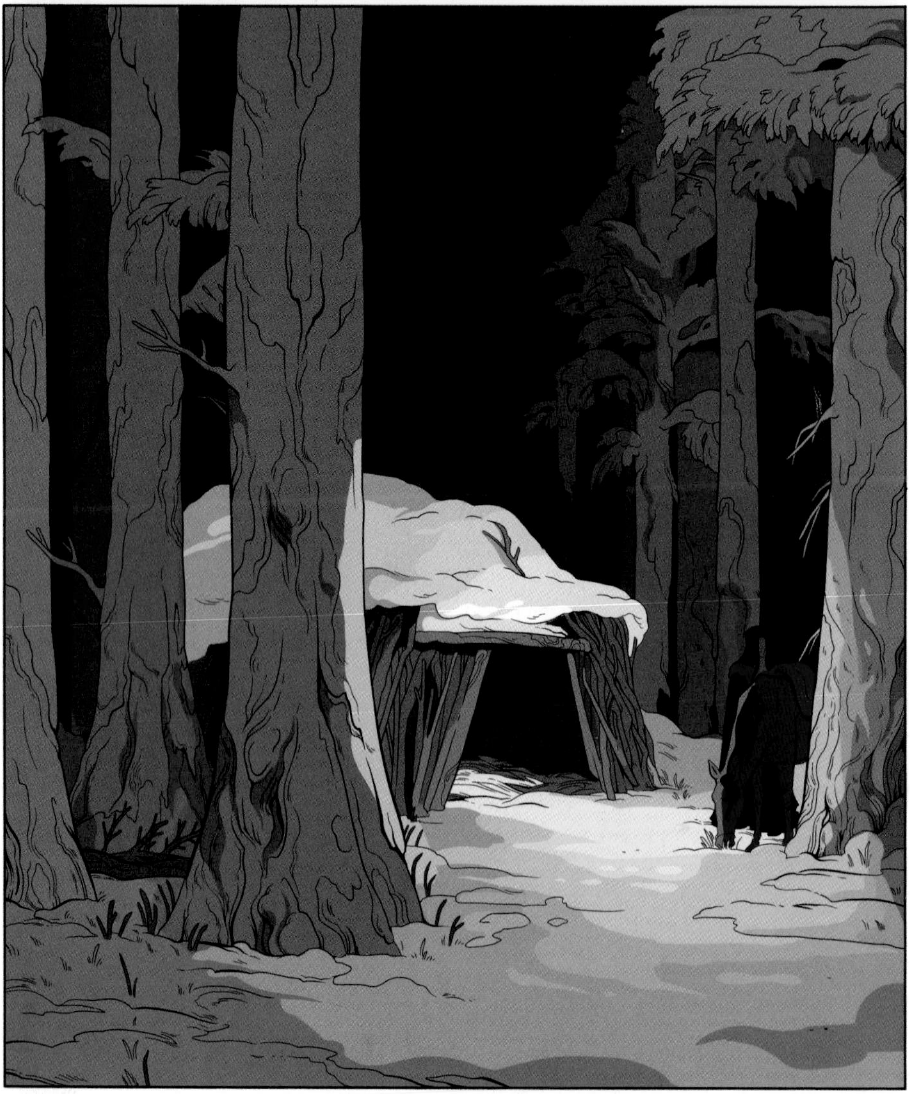

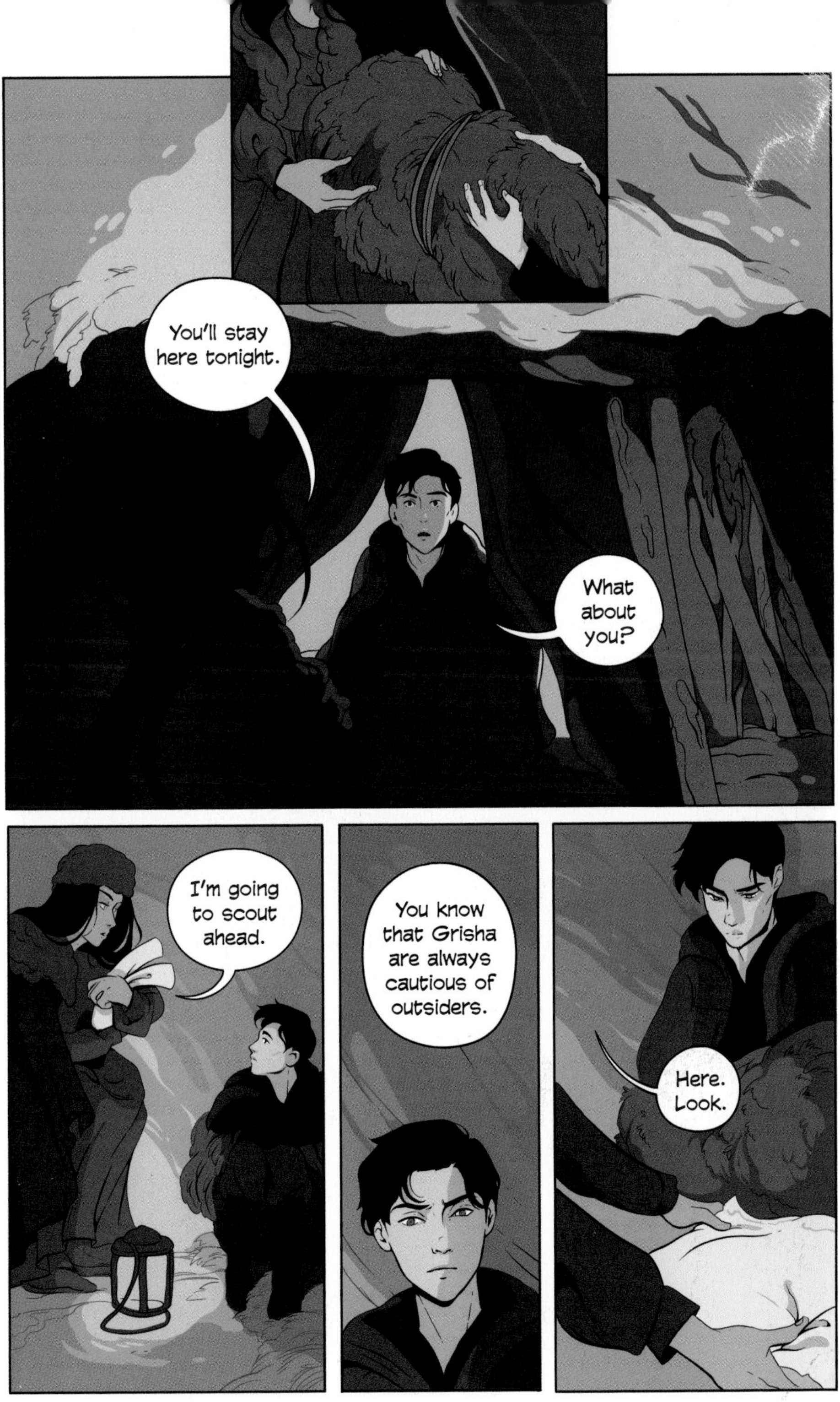
You'll stay here tonight.
What about you?
I'm going to scout ahead.
You know that Grisha are always cautious of outsiders.
Here. Look.

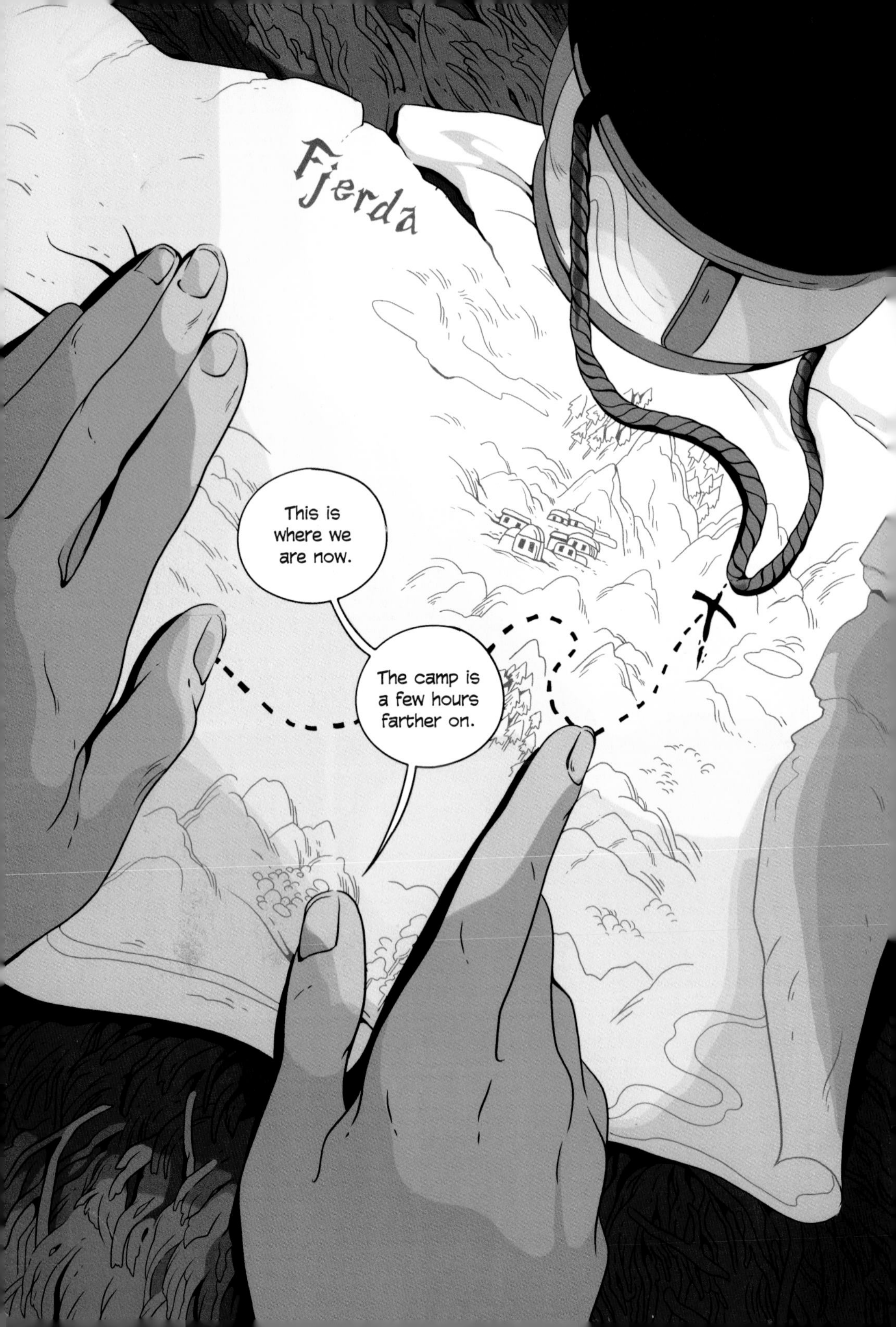
Fjerda
This is where we are now.
The camp is a few hours farther on.

Rye bread. A waterskin. They should last you one night.

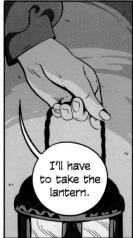

I'll have to take the lantern.

But—

It's our only one.

I know. I'll need it to light the way.

You'll be all right, won't you?

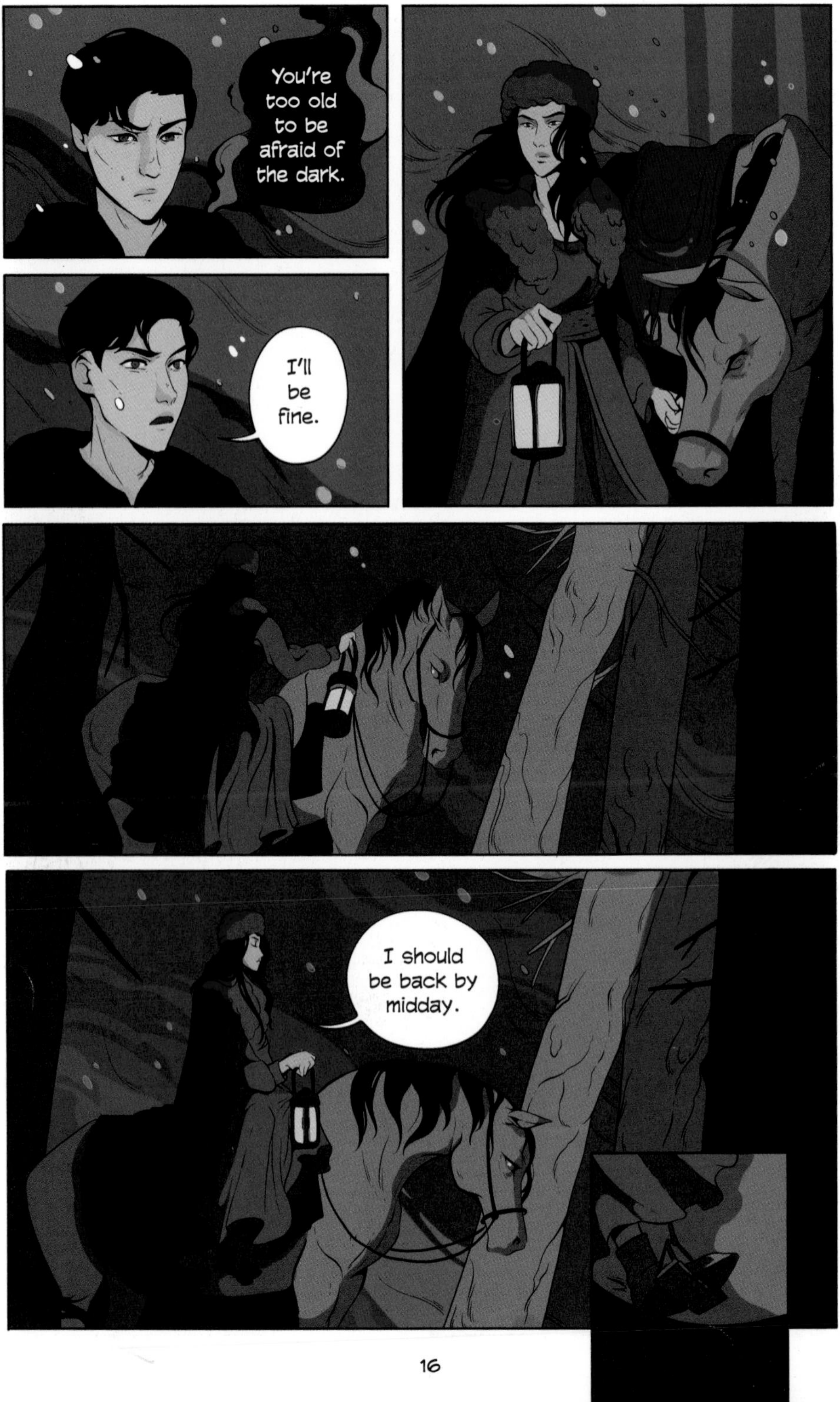
You're too old to be afraid of the dark.
I'll be fine.
I should be back by midday.

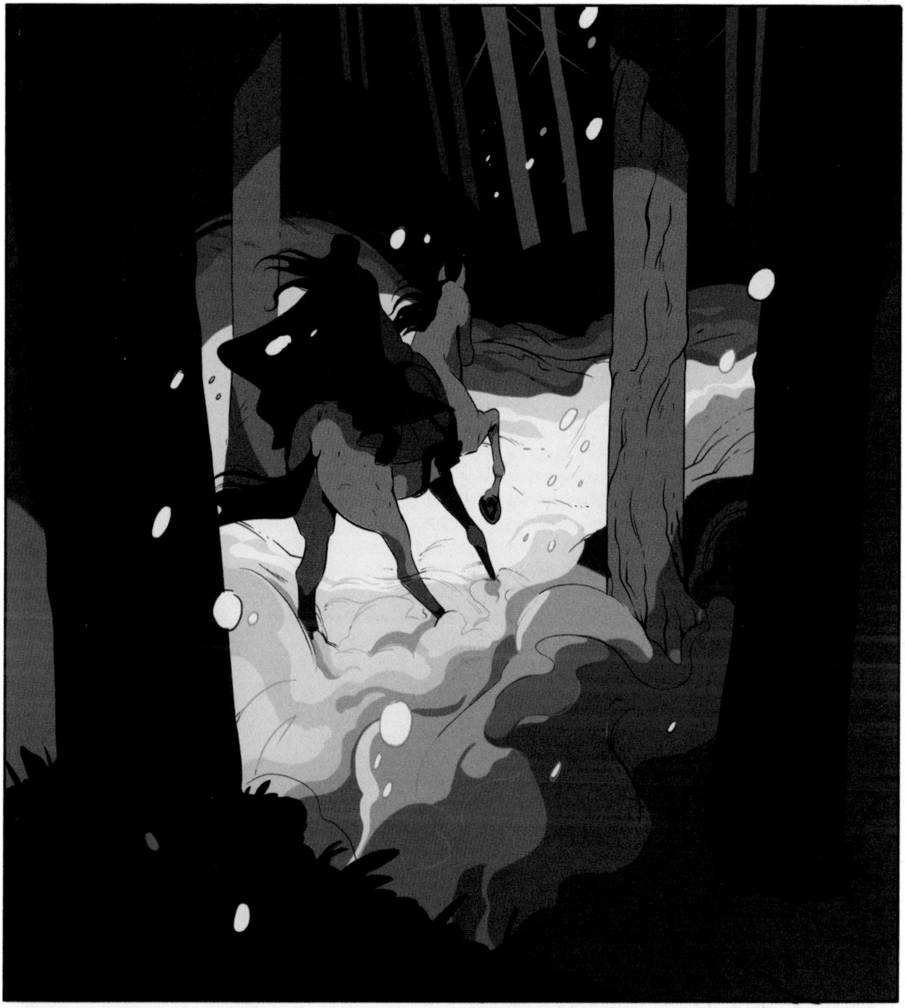

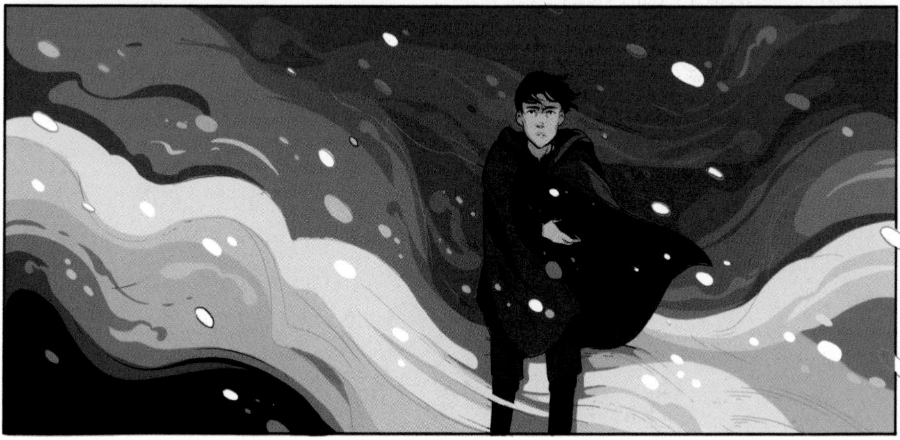

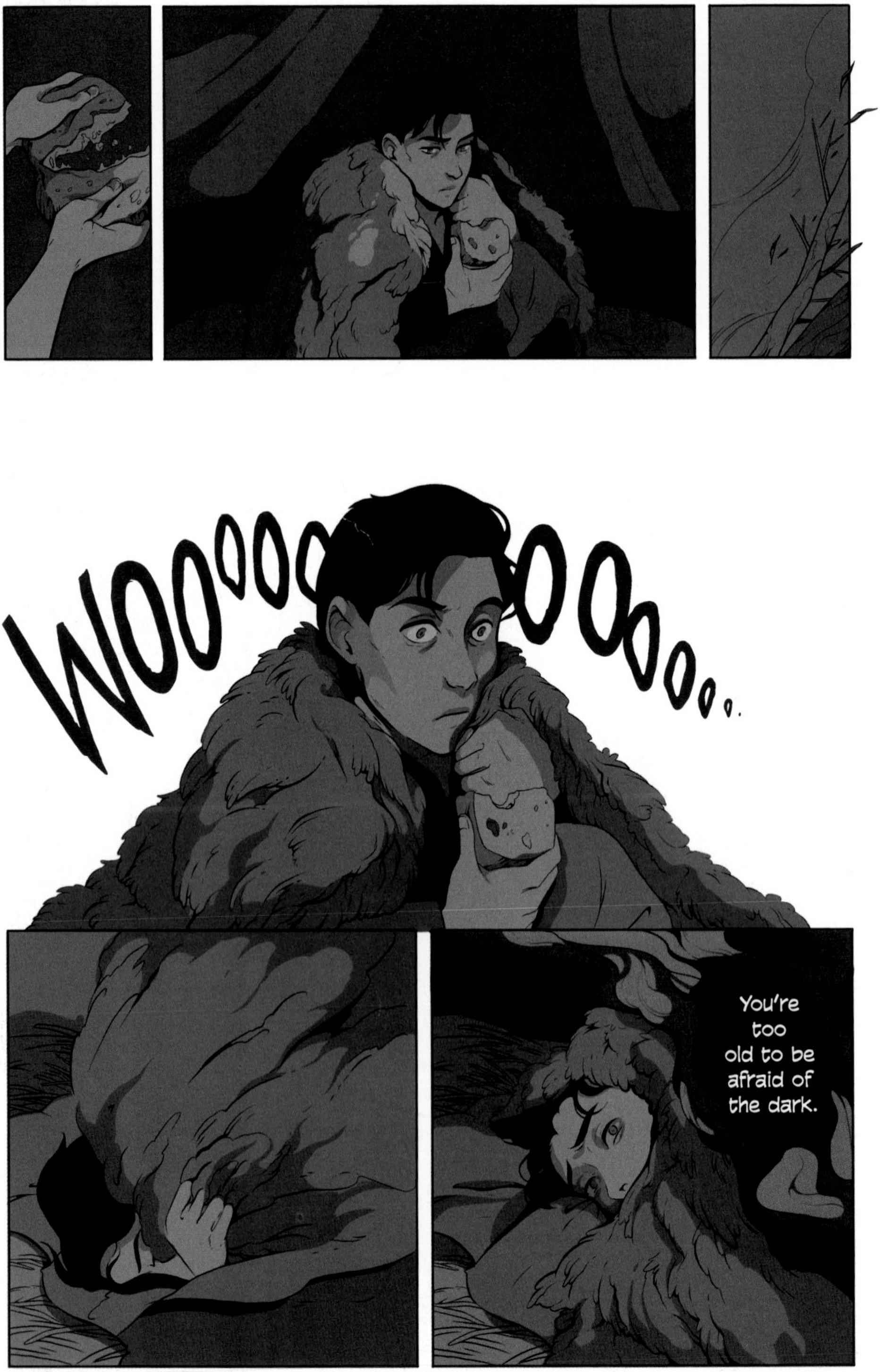
WOOOOOOOOOOoo..
You're too old to be afraid of the dark.

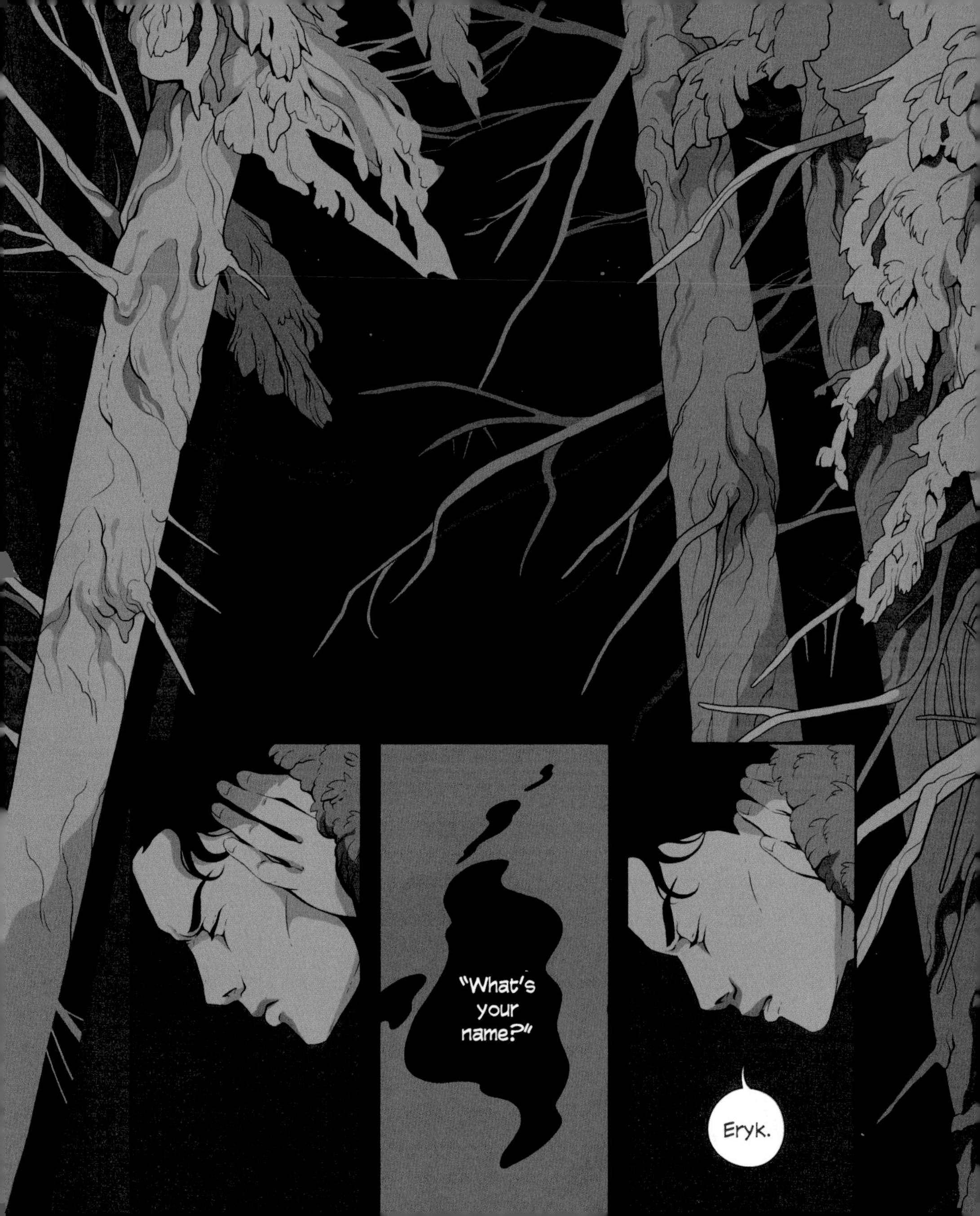
"What's your name?"
Eryk.

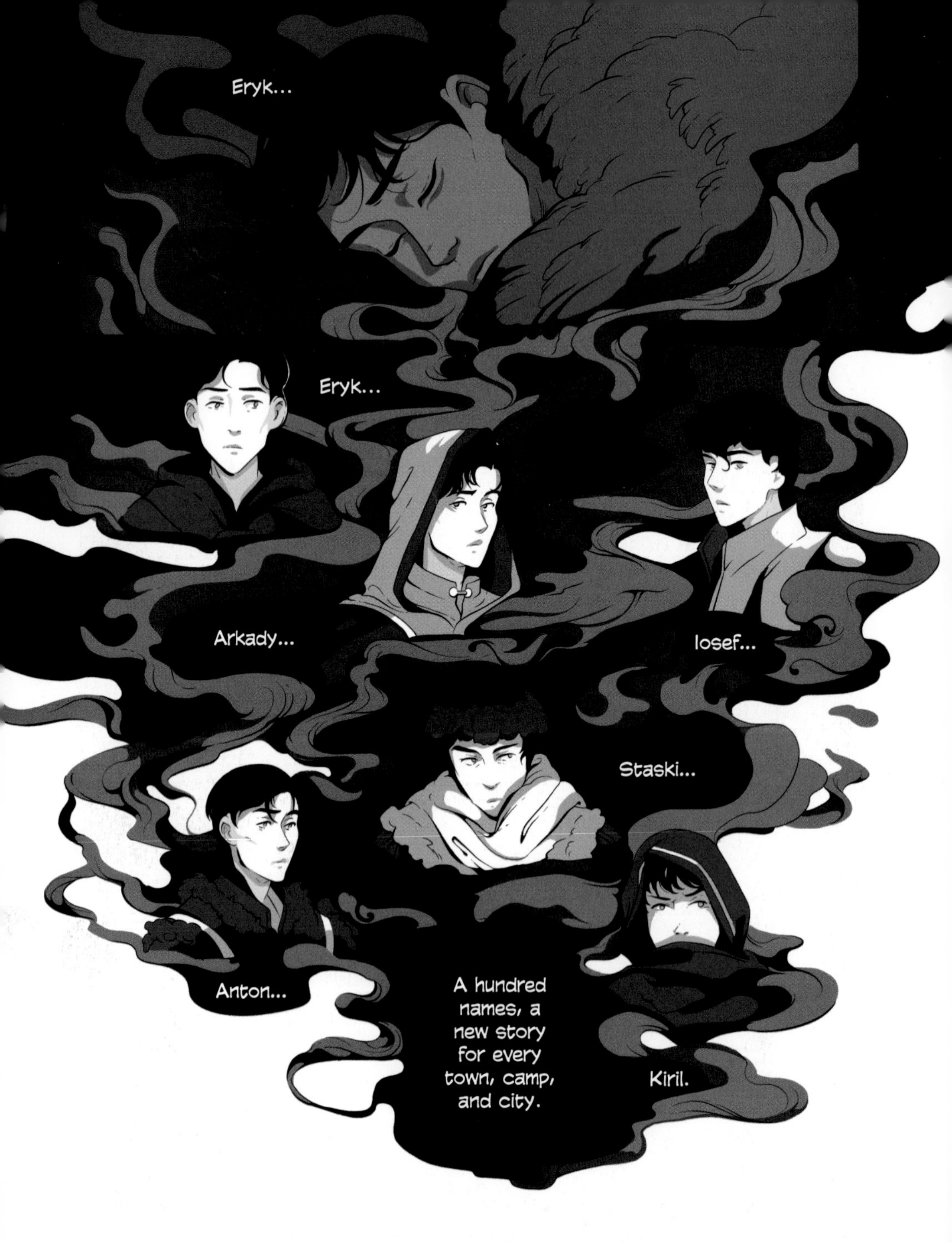
Eryk...
Eryk...
Arkady...
Iosef...
Staski...
Anton...
A hundred names, a new story for every town, camp, and city.
Kiril.

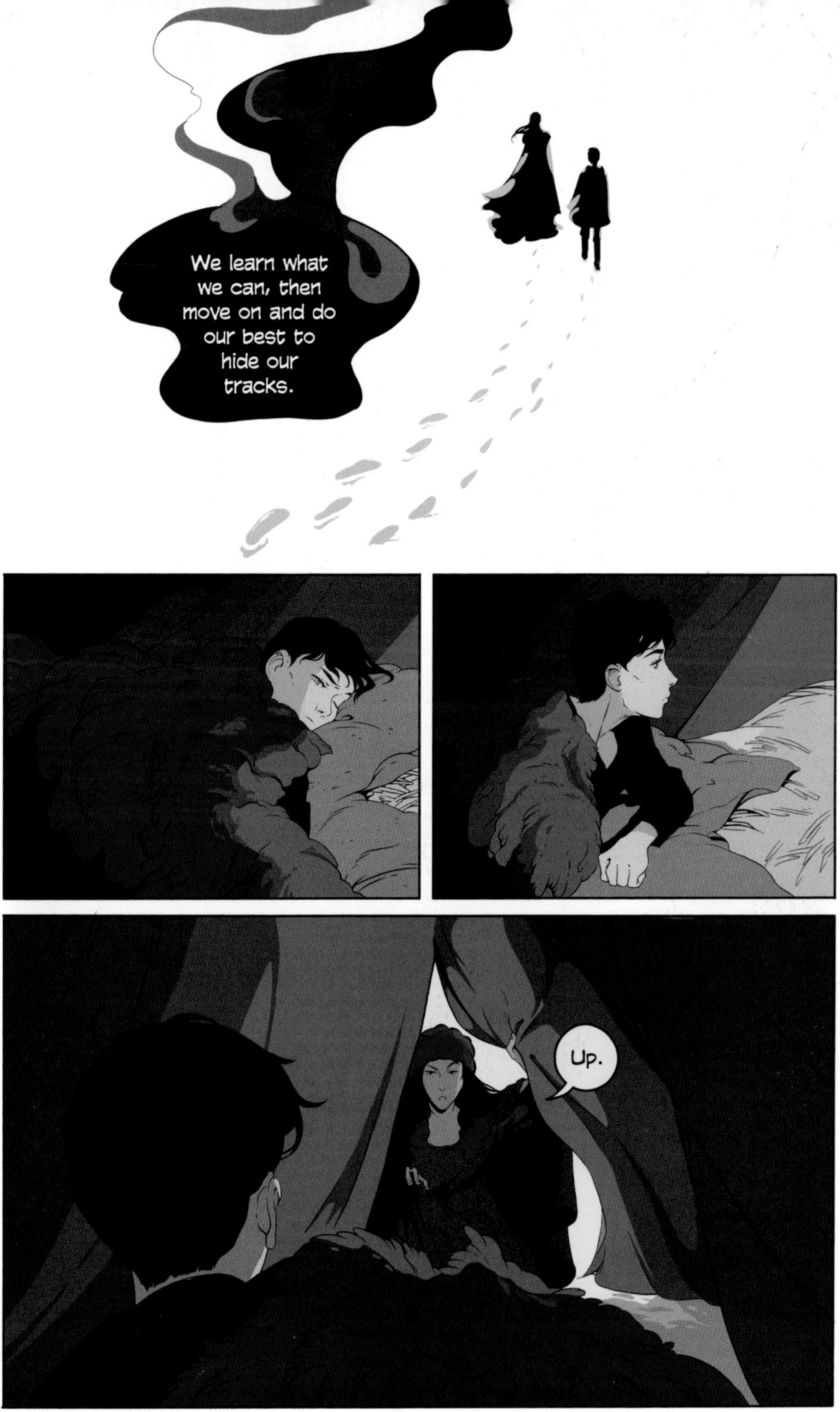
We learn what we can, then move on and do our best to hide our tracks.
Up.

If anything goes wrong, you know what to do.

I know.

Fight.

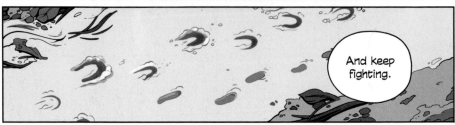

And keep fighting.

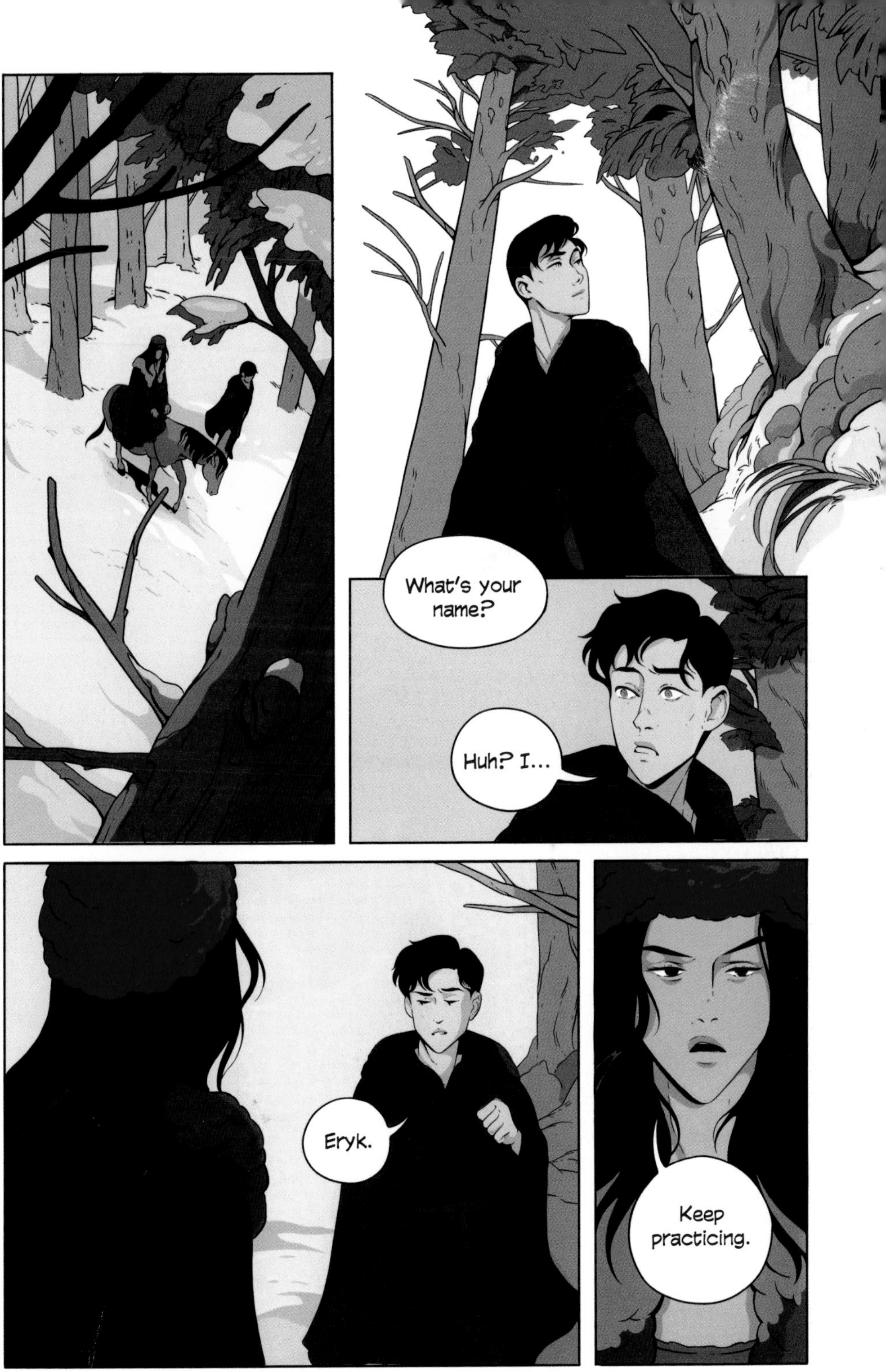
What's your name?
Huh? I...
Eryk.
Keep practicing.

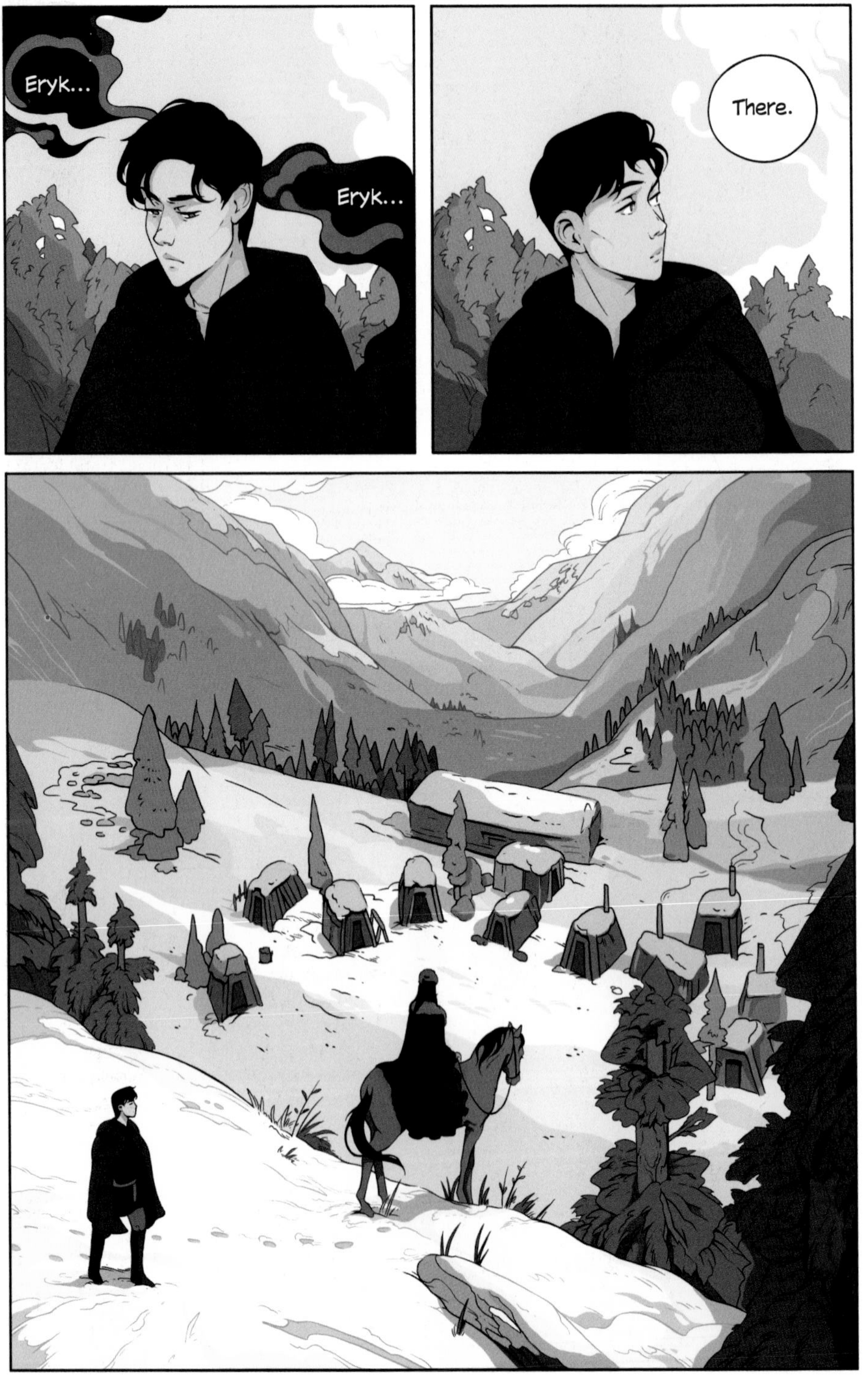

Eryk...
Eryk...
There.

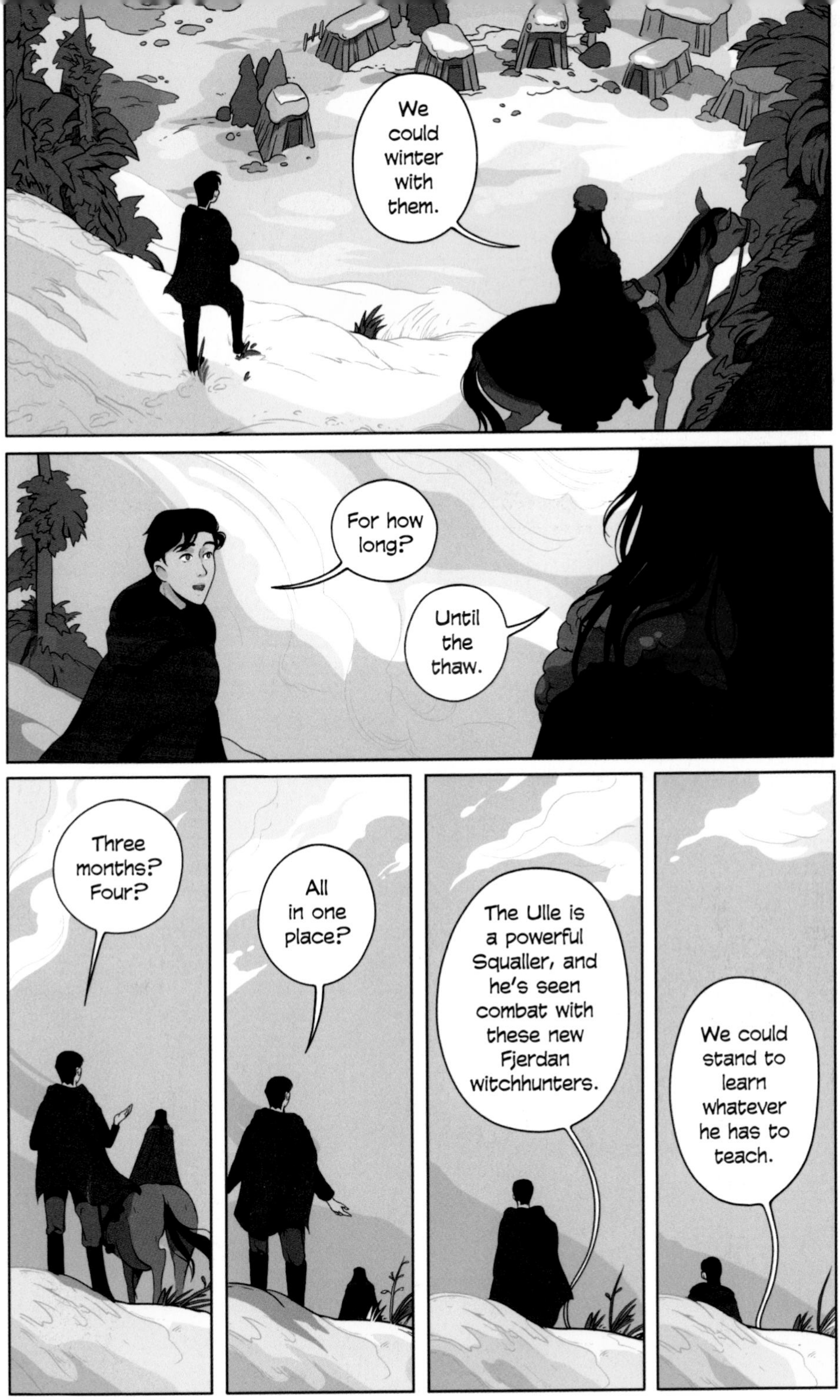
We could winter with them.
For how long?
Until the thaw.
Three months? Four?
All in one place?
The Ulle is a powerful Squaller, and he's seen combat with these new Fjerdan witchhunters.
We could stand to learn whatever he has to teach.

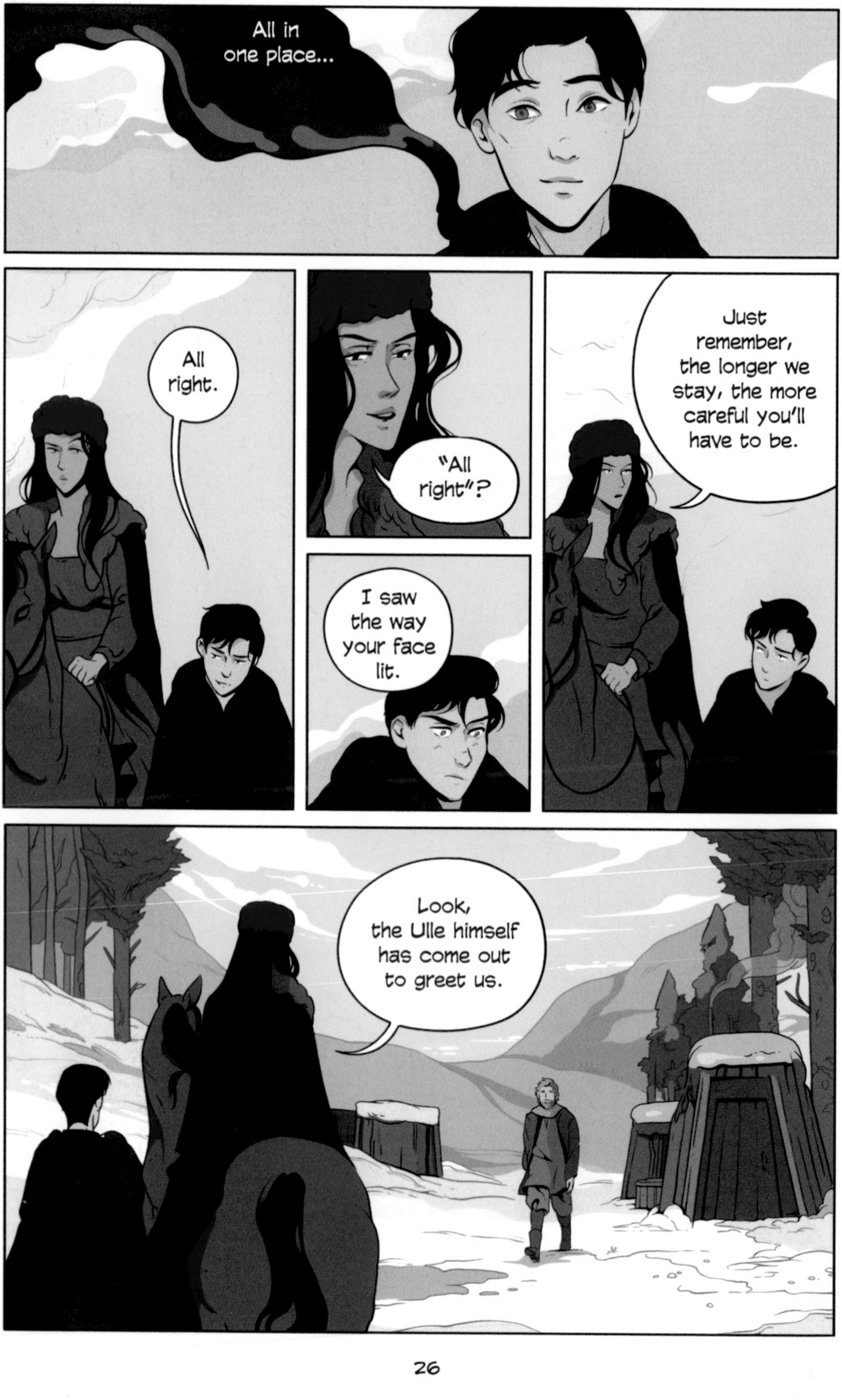
All in one place...
All right.
"All right"?
I saw the way your face lit.
Just remember, the longer we stay, the more careful you'll have to be.
Look, the Ulle himself has come out to greet us.

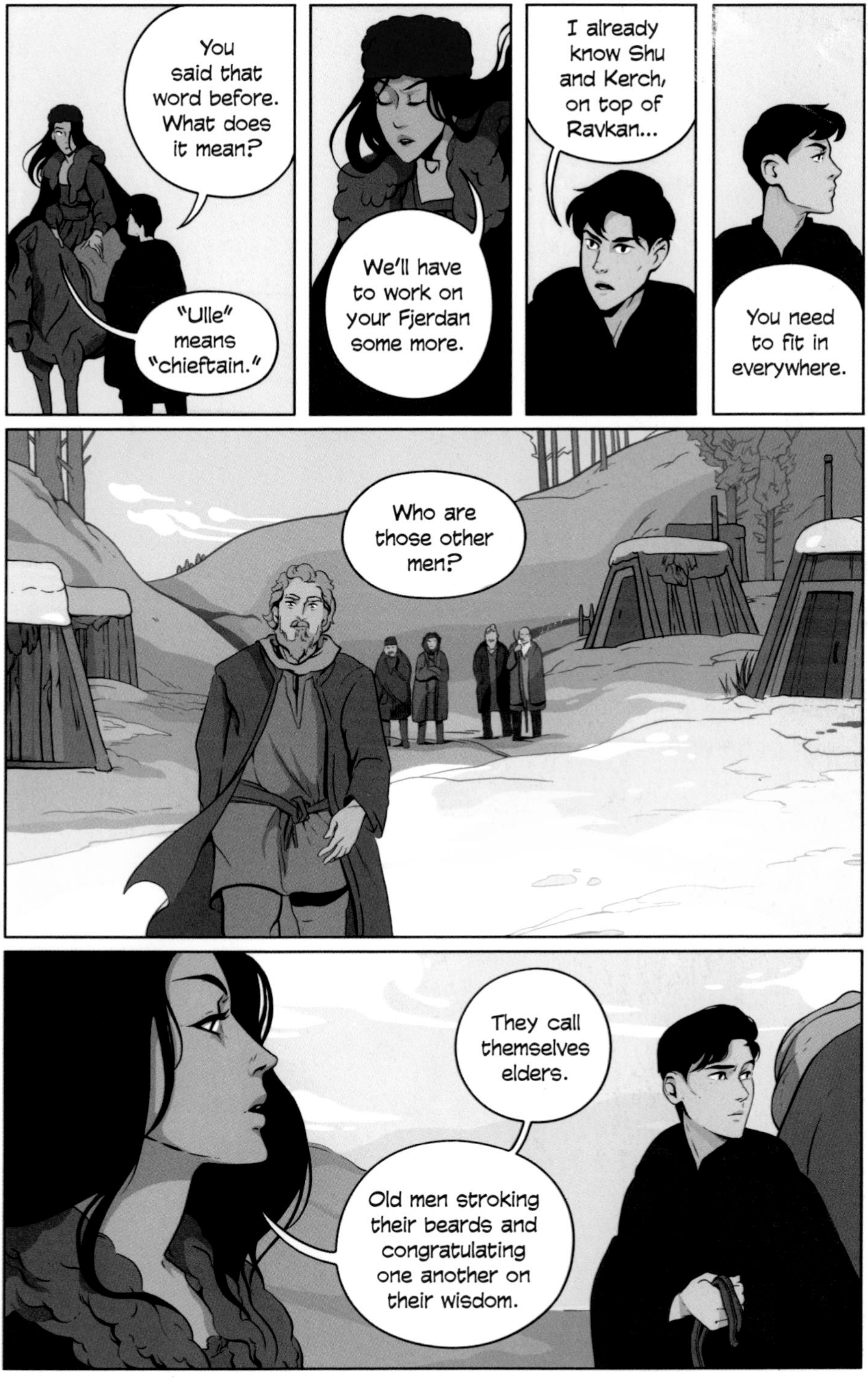
You said that word before. What does it mean?
"Ulle" means "chieftain."
We'll have to work on your Fjerdan some more.
I already know Shu and Kerch, on top of Ravkan...
You need to fit in everywhere.
Who are those other men?
They call themselves elders.
Old men stroking their beards and congratulating one another on their wisdom.

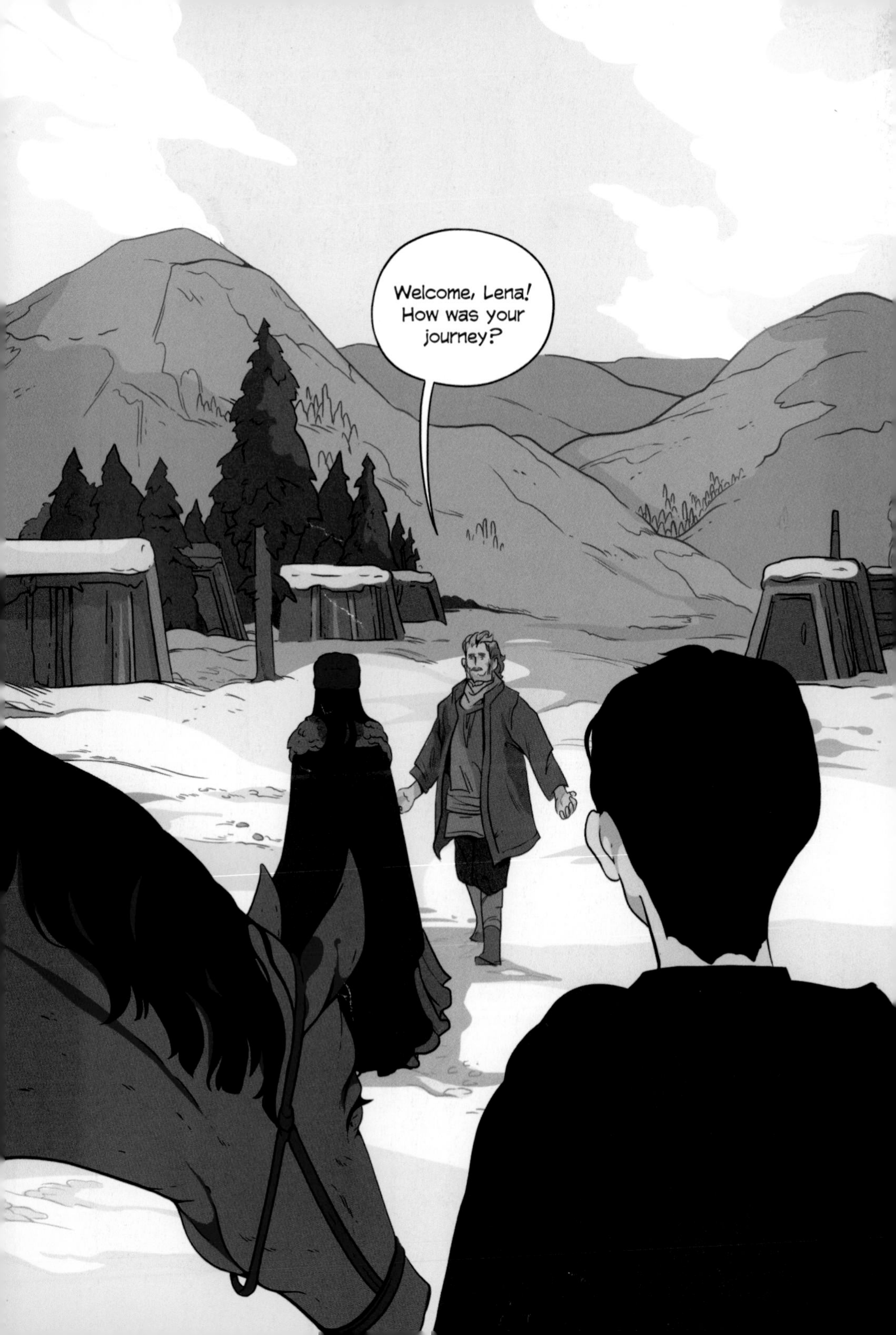
Welcome, Lena! How was your journey?

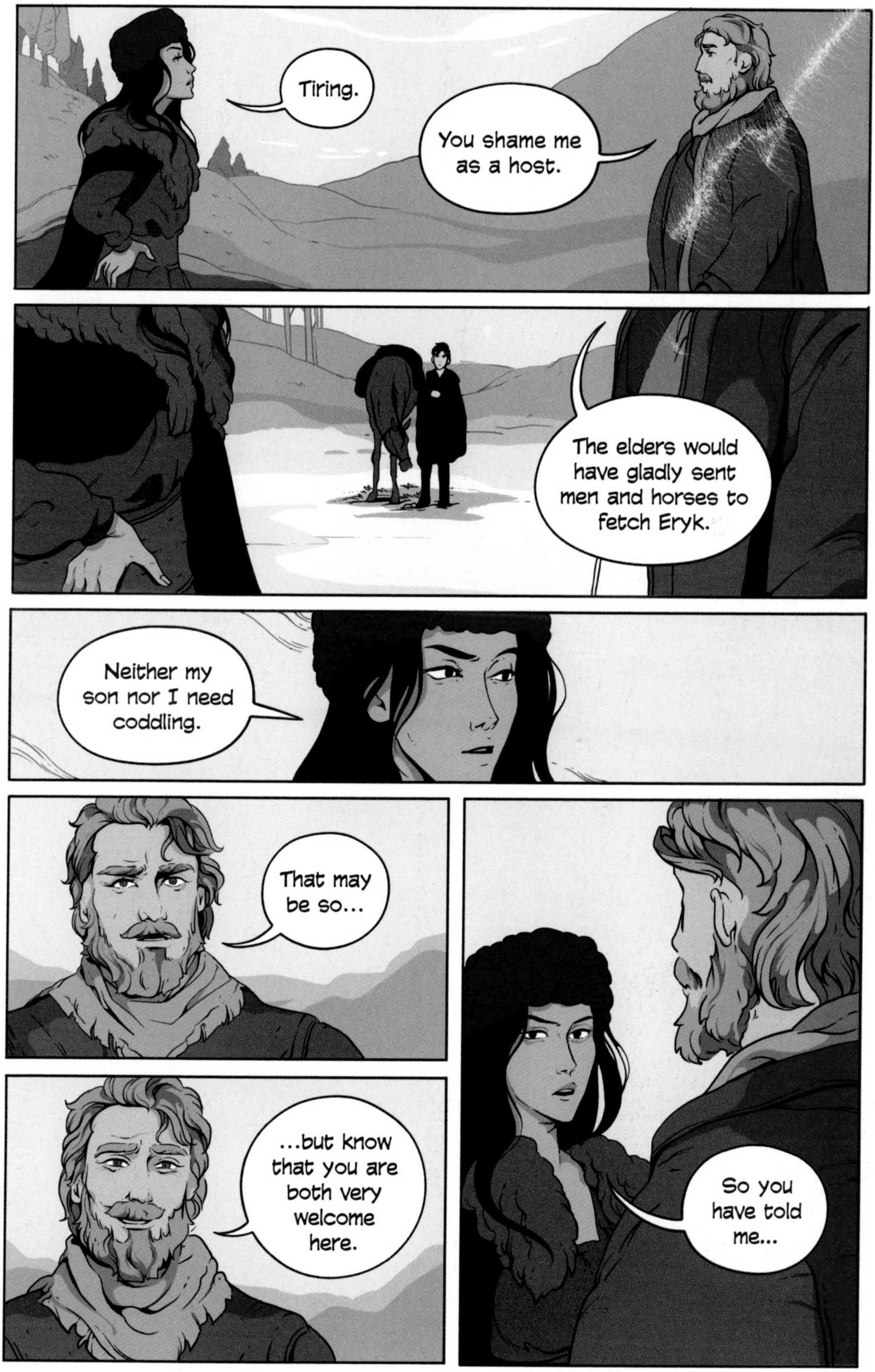
Tiring.
You shame me as a host.
The elders would have gladly sent men and horses to fetch Eryk.
Neither my son nor I need coddling.
That may be so...
...but know that you are both very welcome here.
So you have told me...

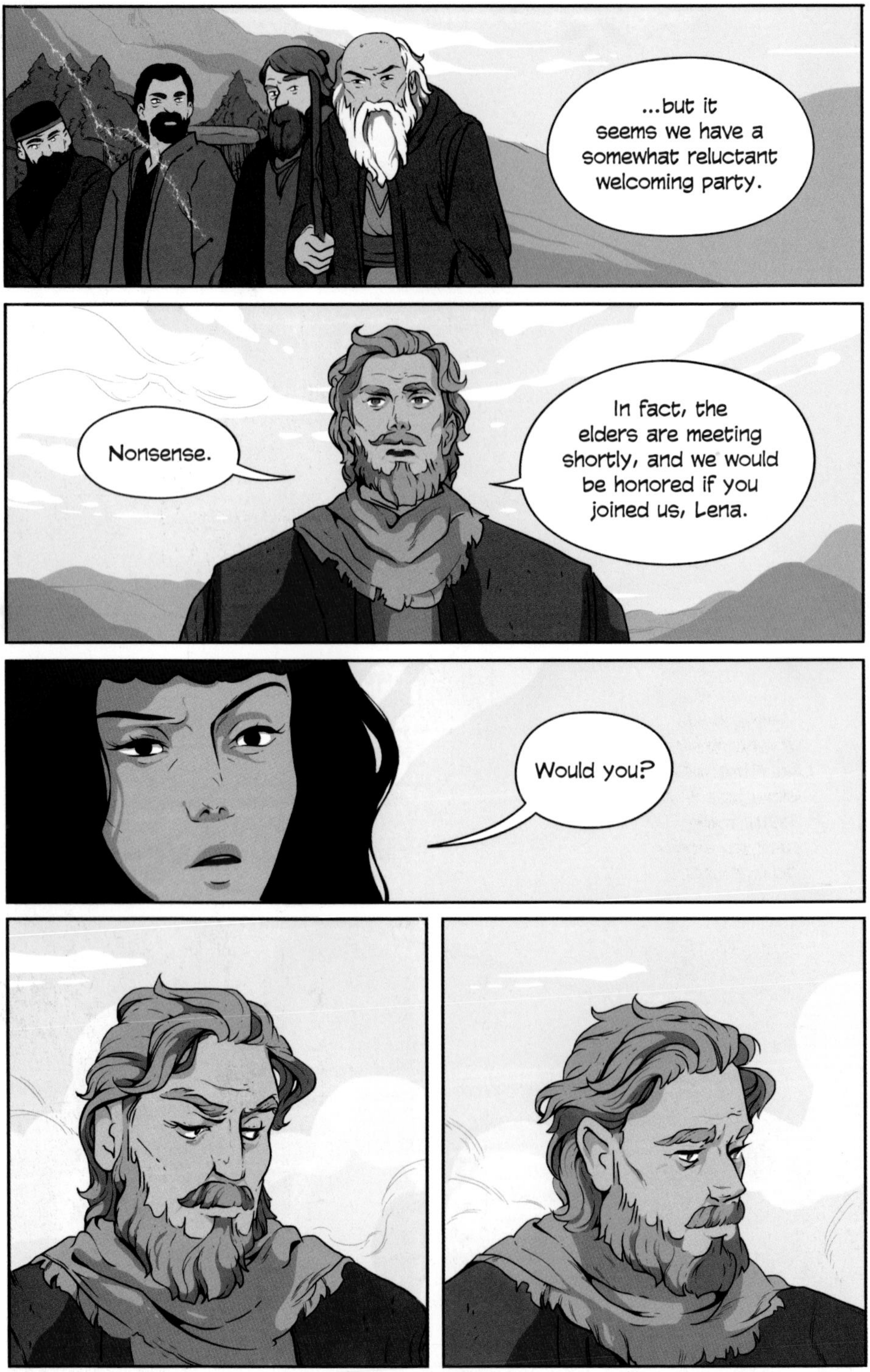
...but it seems we have a somewhat reluctant welcoming party.
Nonsense.
In fact, the elders are meeting shortly, and we would be honored if you joined us, Lena.
Would you?

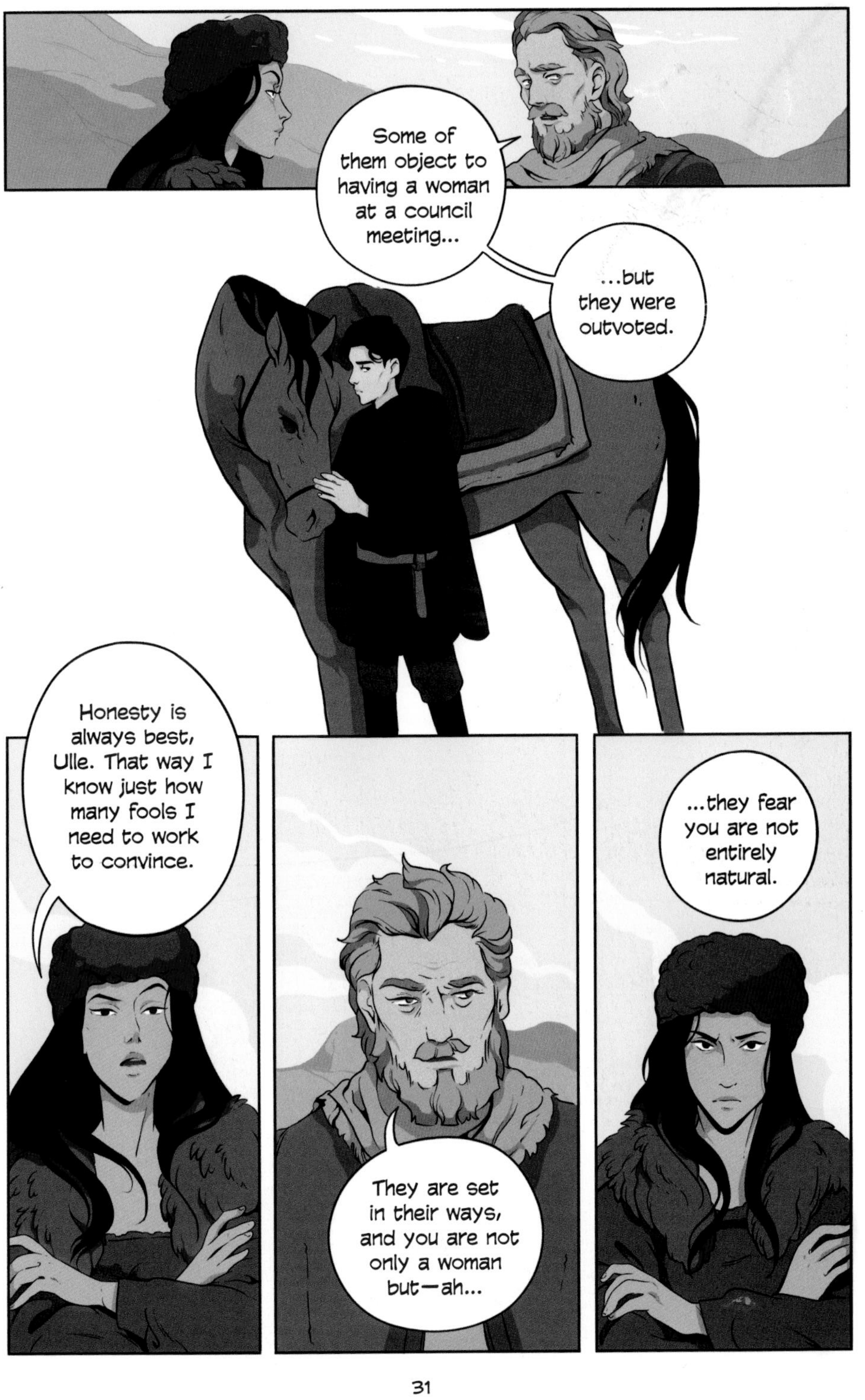
Some of them object to having a woman at a council meeting...
...but they were outvoted.
Honesty is always best, Ulle. That way I know just how many fools I need to work to convince.
They are set in their ways, and you are not only a woman but—ah...
...they fear you are not entirely natural.

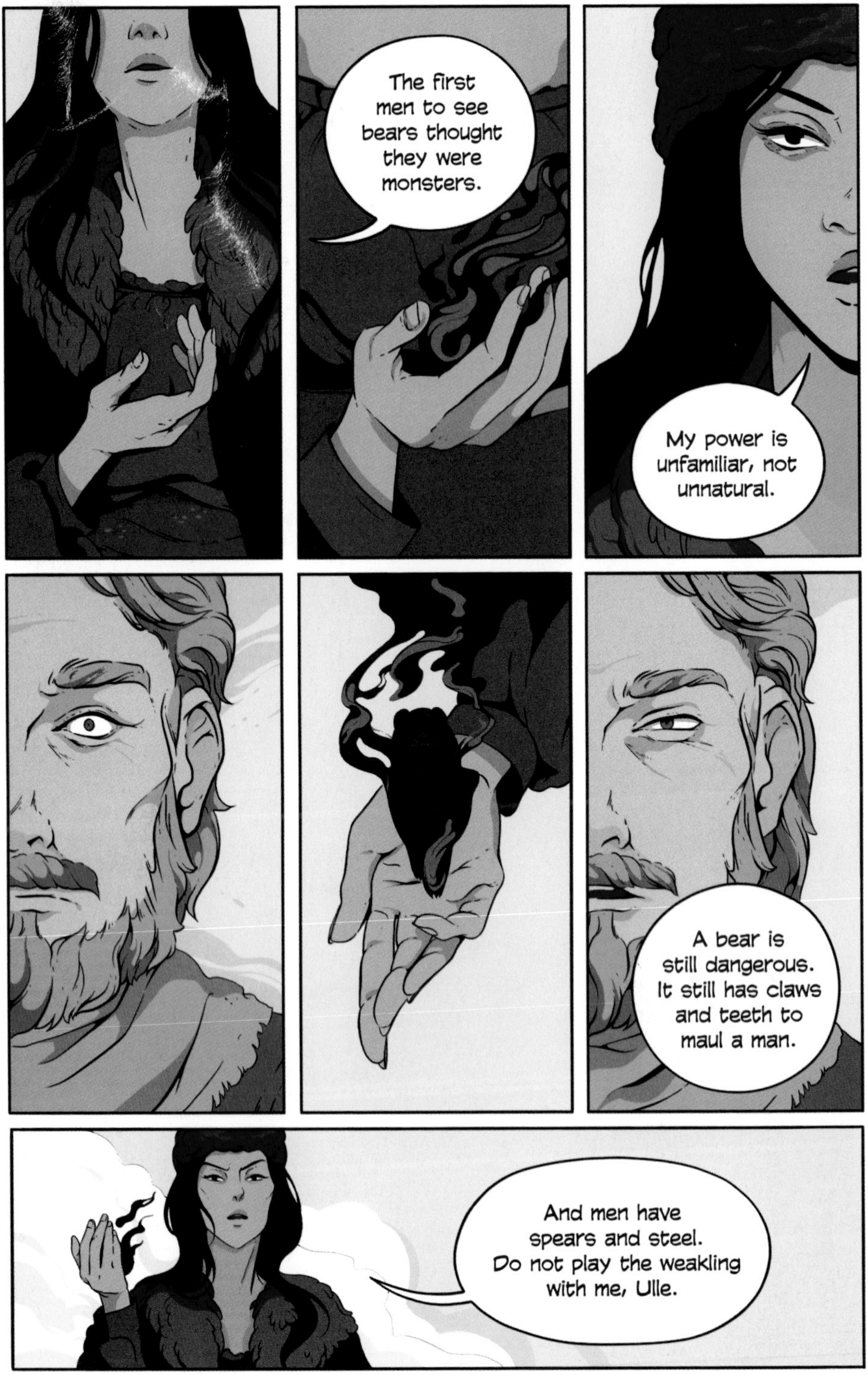
The first men to see bears thought they were monsters.
My power is unfamiliar, not unnatural.
A bear is still dangerous. It still has claws and teeth to maul a man.
And men have spears and steel. Do not play the weakling with me, Ulle.

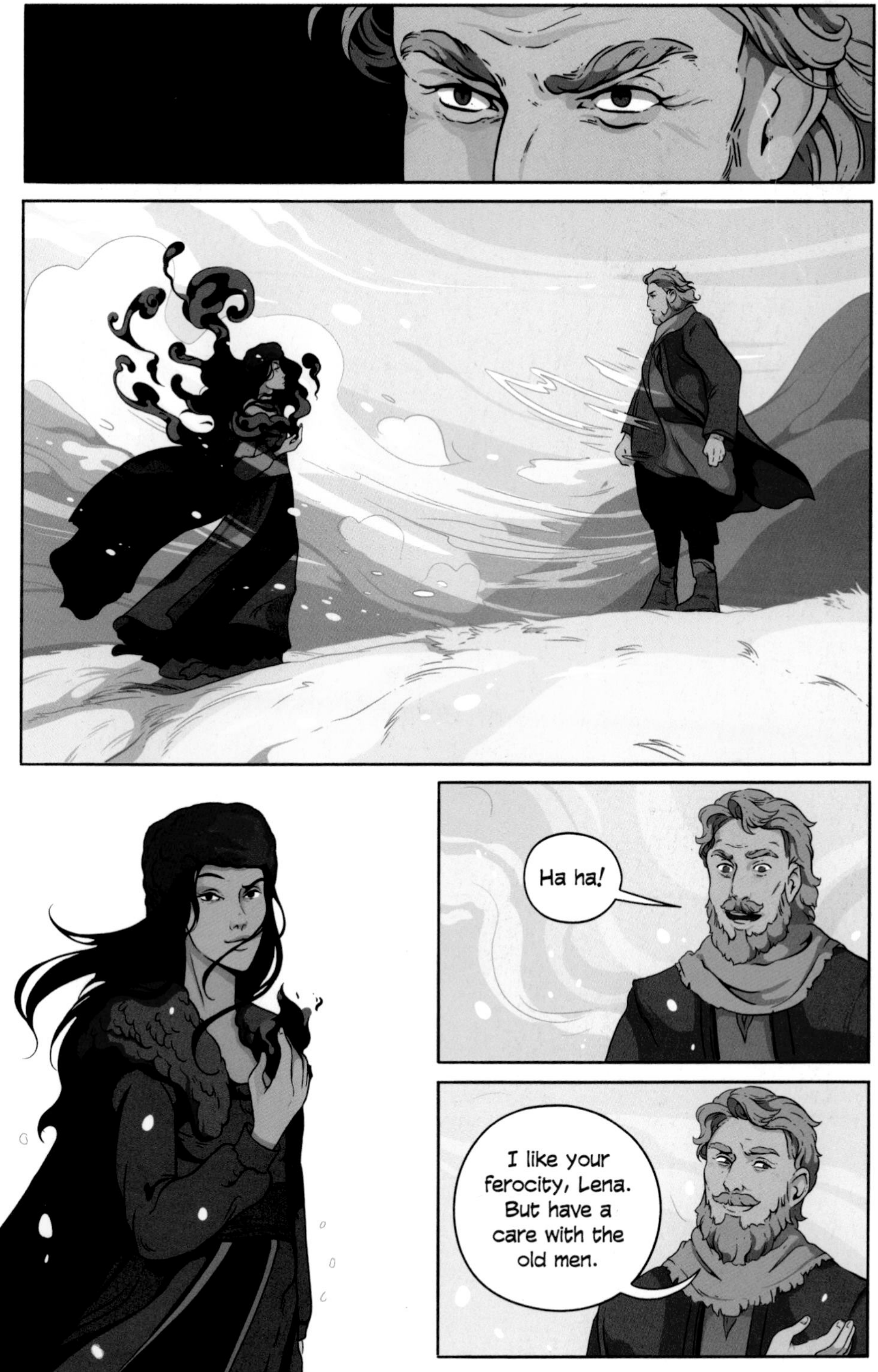
Ha ha!
I like your ferocity, Lena. But have a care with the old men.

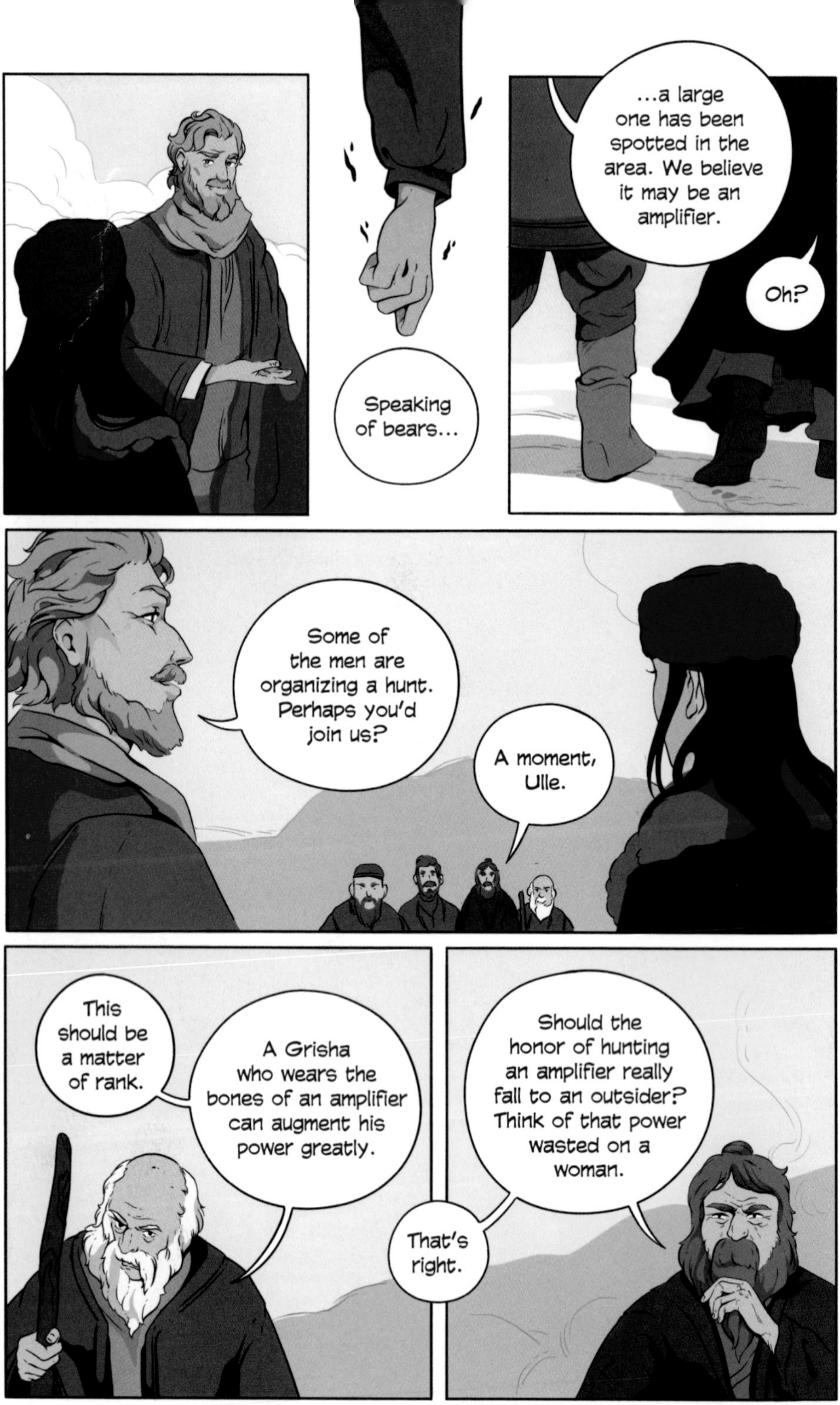
Speaking of bears...
...a large one has been spotted in the area. We believe it may be an amplifier.
Oh?
Some of the men are organizing a hunt. Perhaps you'd join us?
A moment, Ulle.
This should be a matter of rank.
A Grisha who wears the bones of an amplifier can augment his power greatly.
Should the honor of hunting an amplifier really fall to an outsider? Think of that power wasted on a woman.
That's right.

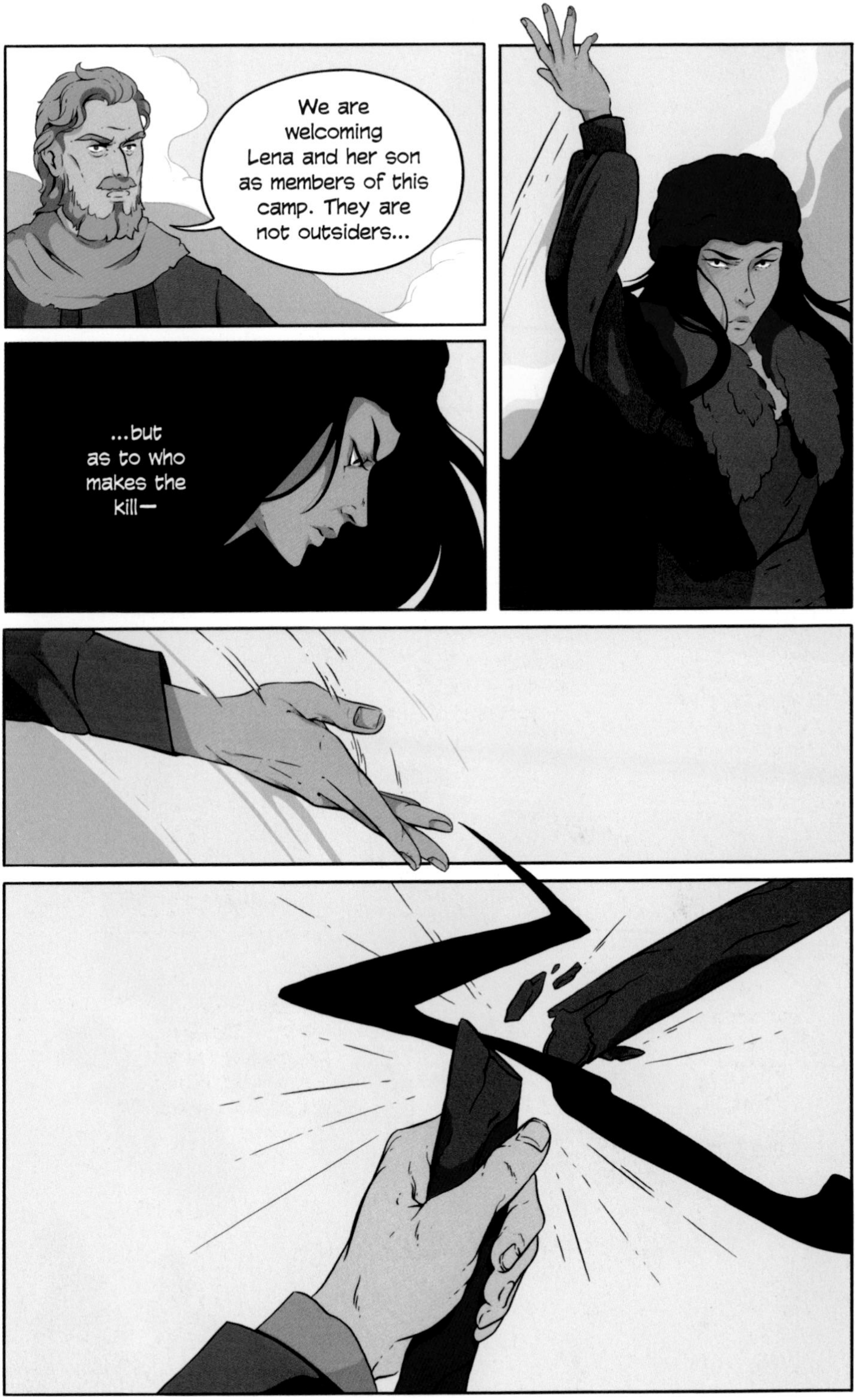
We are welcoming Lena and her son as members of this camp. They are not outsiders...
...but as to who makes the kill—

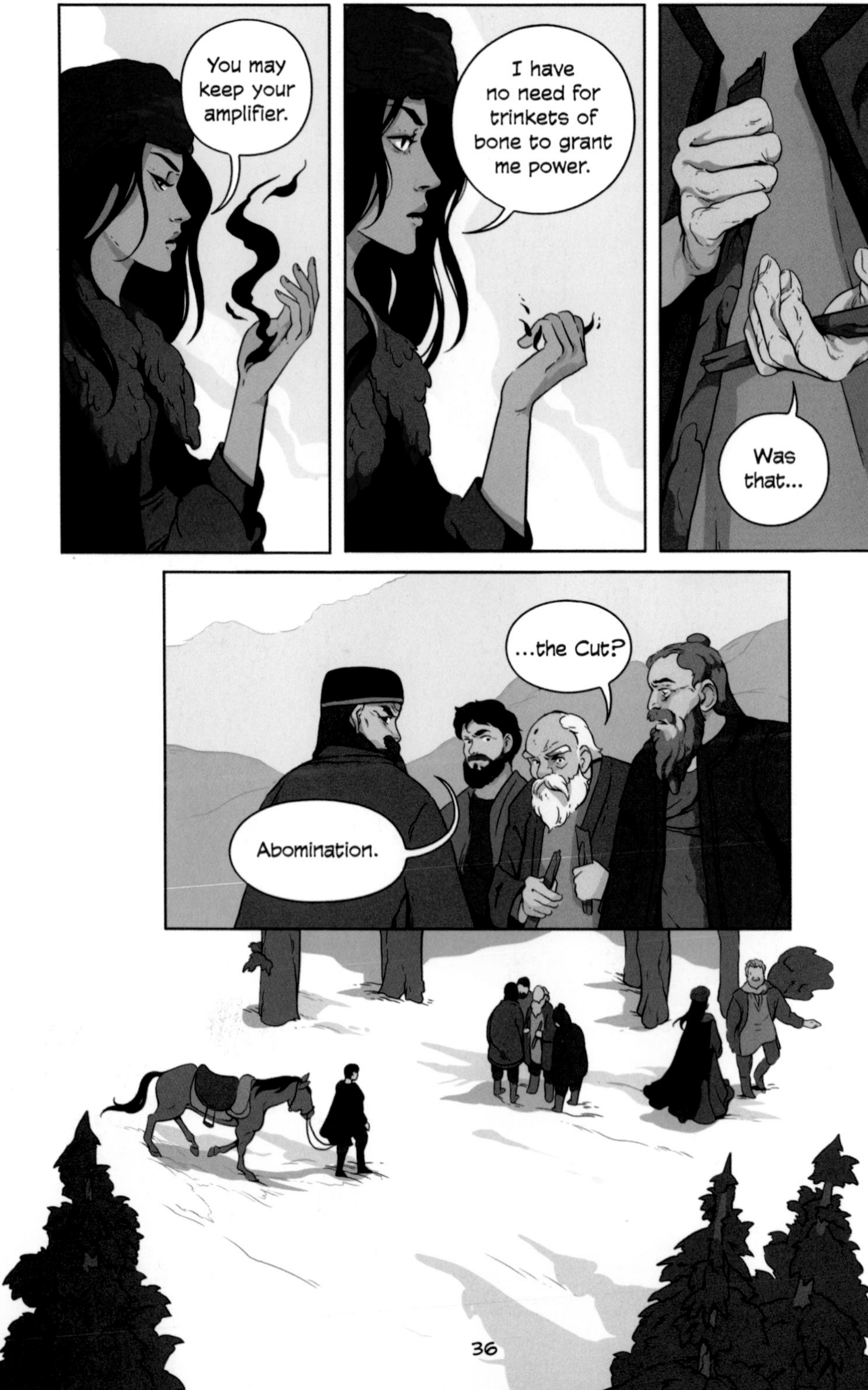
You may keep your amplifier.
I have no need for trinkets of bone to grant me power.
Was that...
...the Cut?
Abomination.

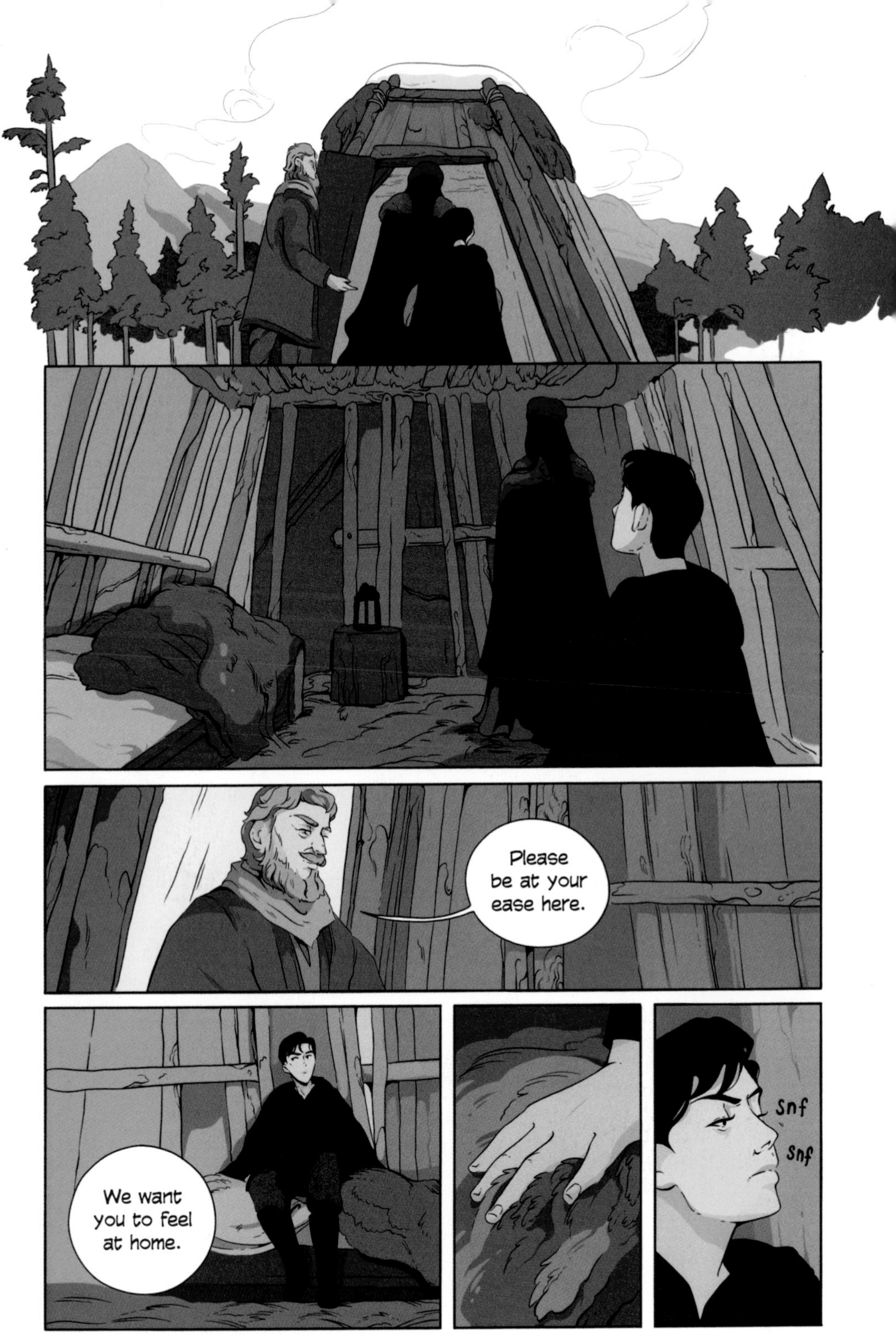
Please be at your ease here.
We want you to feel at home.
Snf
Snf

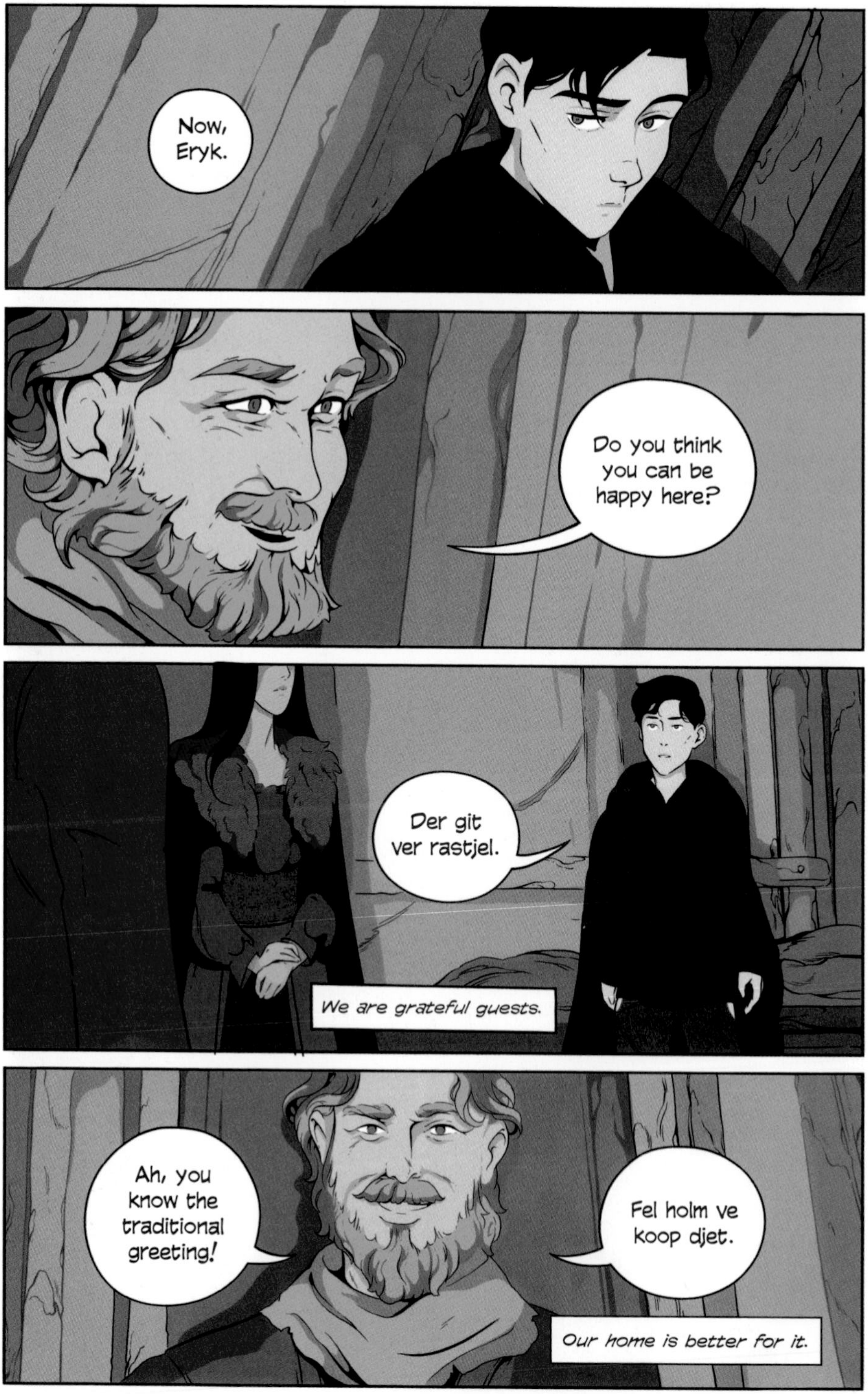
Now, Eryk.
Do you think you can be happy here?
Der git ver rastjel.
We are grateful guests.
Ah, you know the traditional greeting!
Fel holm ve koop djet.
Our home is better for it.

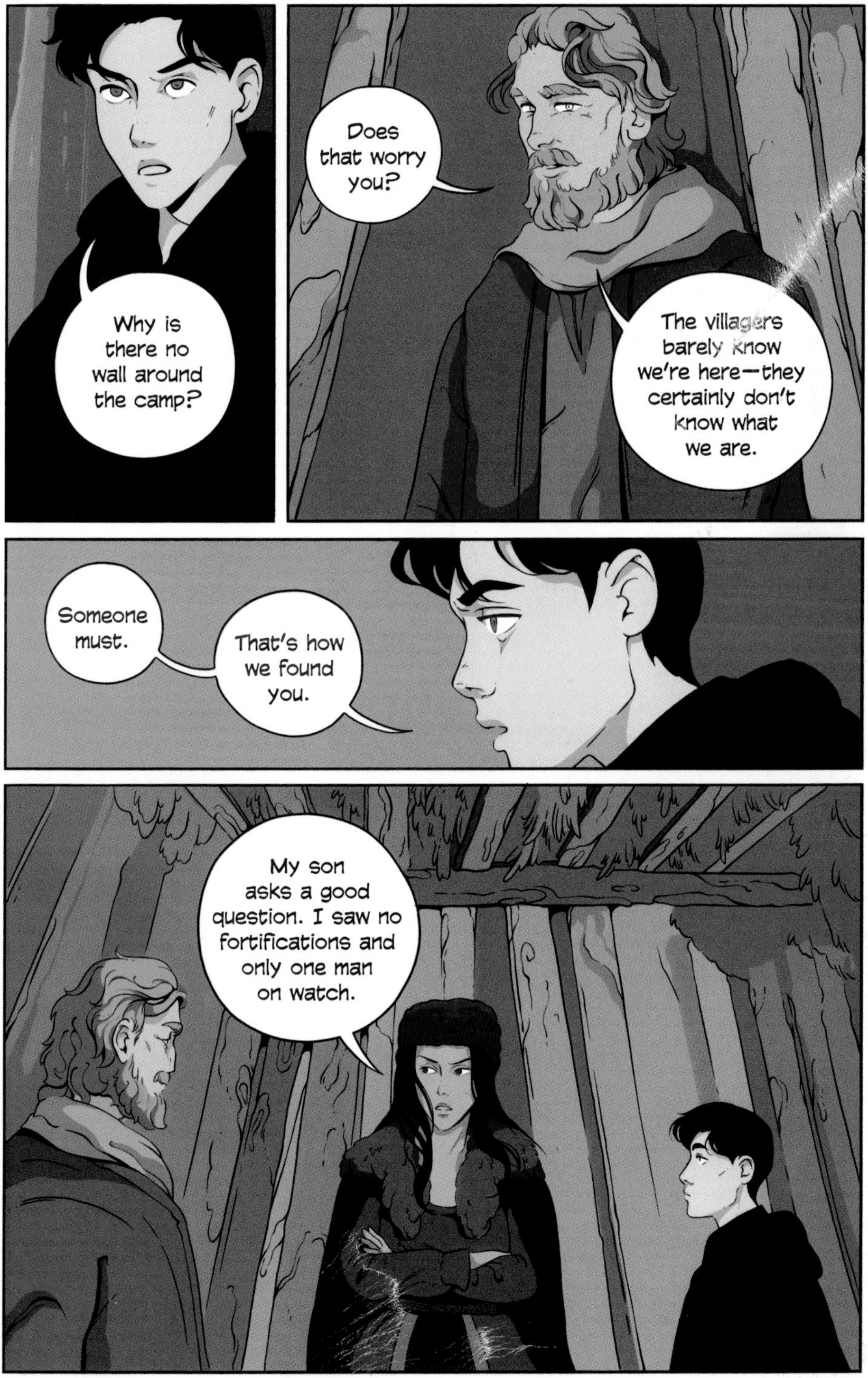

Why is there no wall around the camp?
Does that worry you?
The villagers barely know we're here—they certainly don't know what we are.
Someone must.
That's how we found you.
My son asks a good question. I saw no fortifications and only one man on watch.

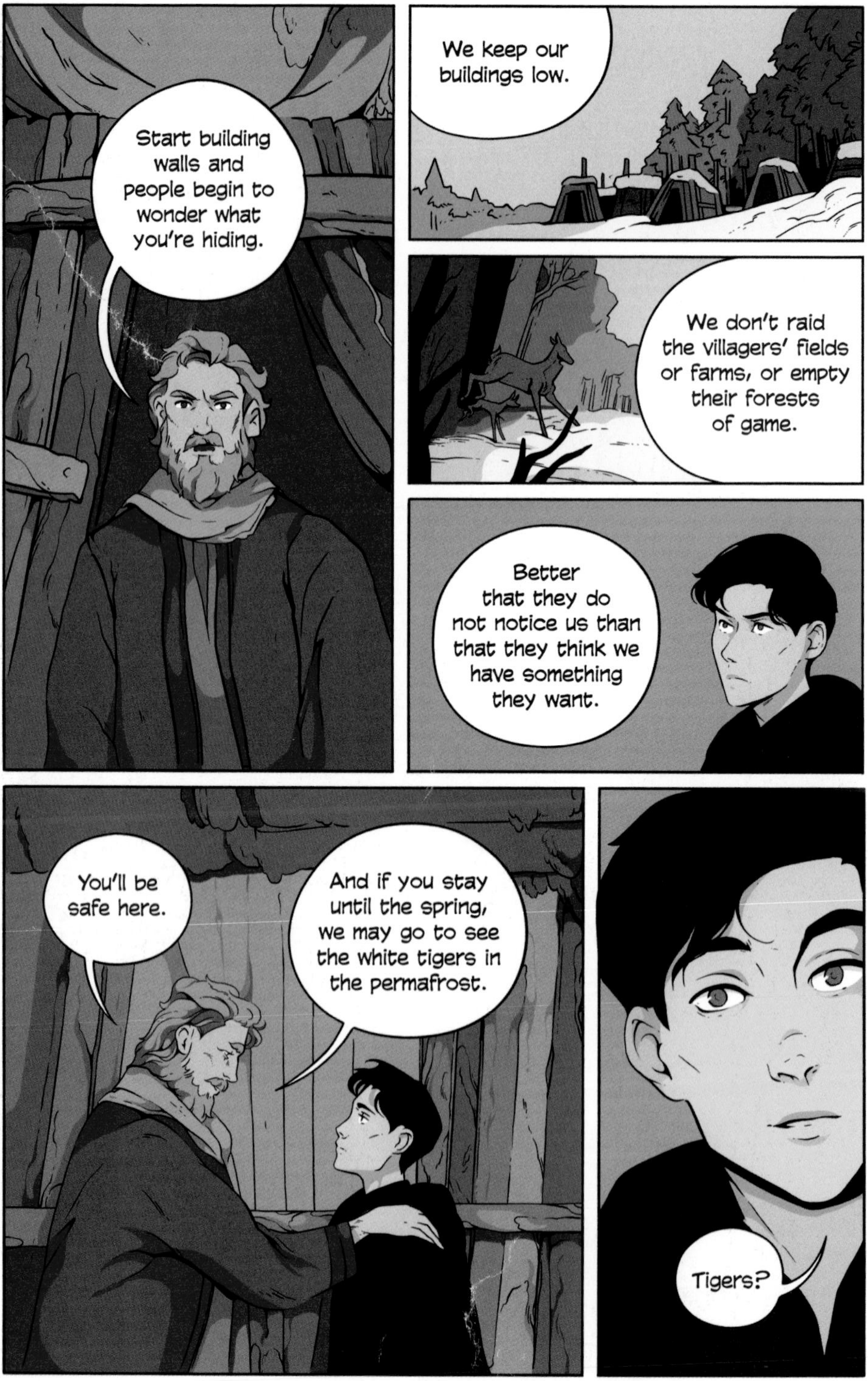
Start building walls and people begin to wonder what you're hiding.
We keep our buildings low.
We don't raid the villagers' fields or farms, or empty their forests of game.
Better that they do not notice us than that they think we have something they want.
You'll be safe here.
And if you stay until the spring, we may go to see the white tigers in the permafrost.
Tigers?

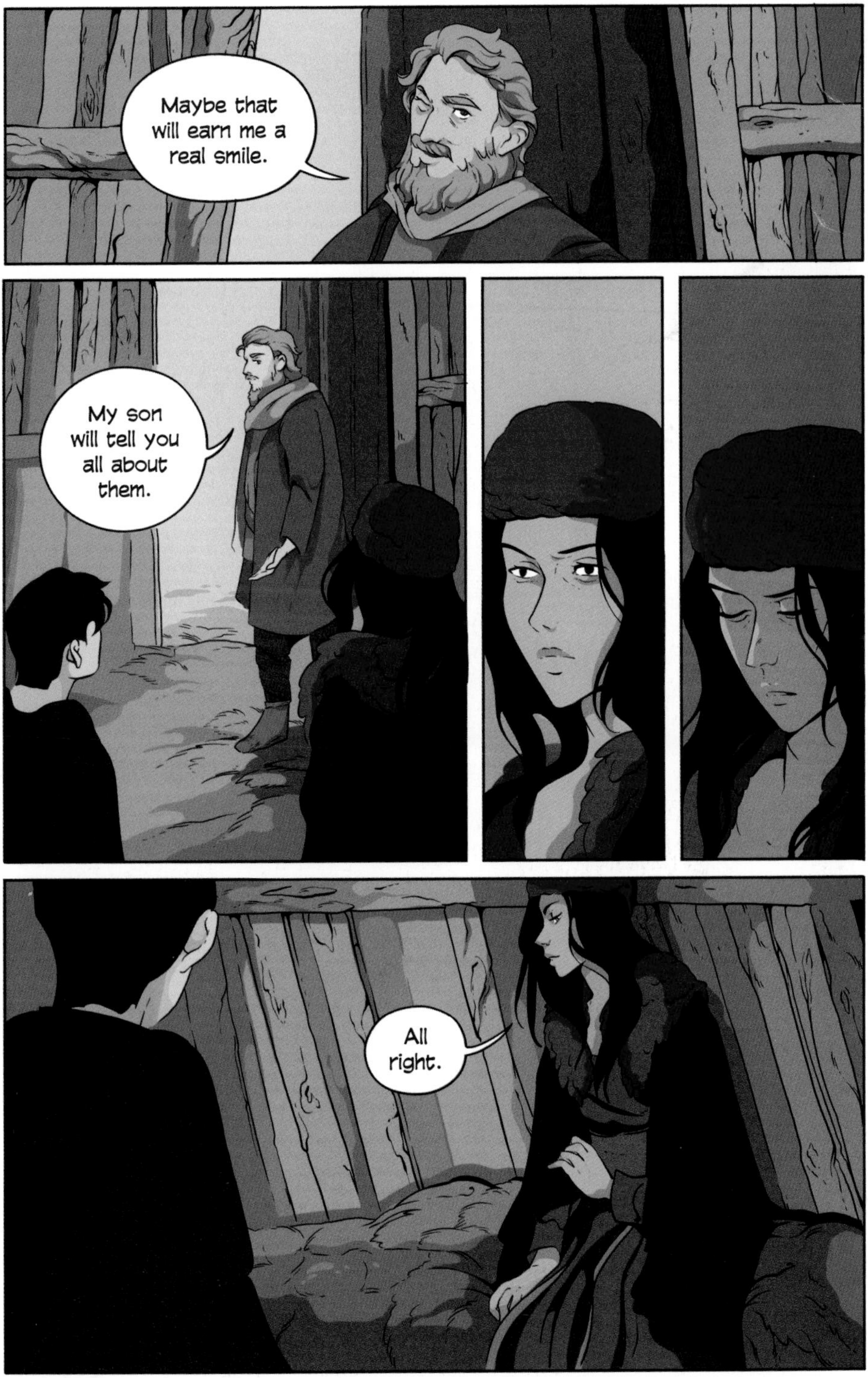
Maybe that will earn me a real smile.
My son will tell you all about them.
All right.

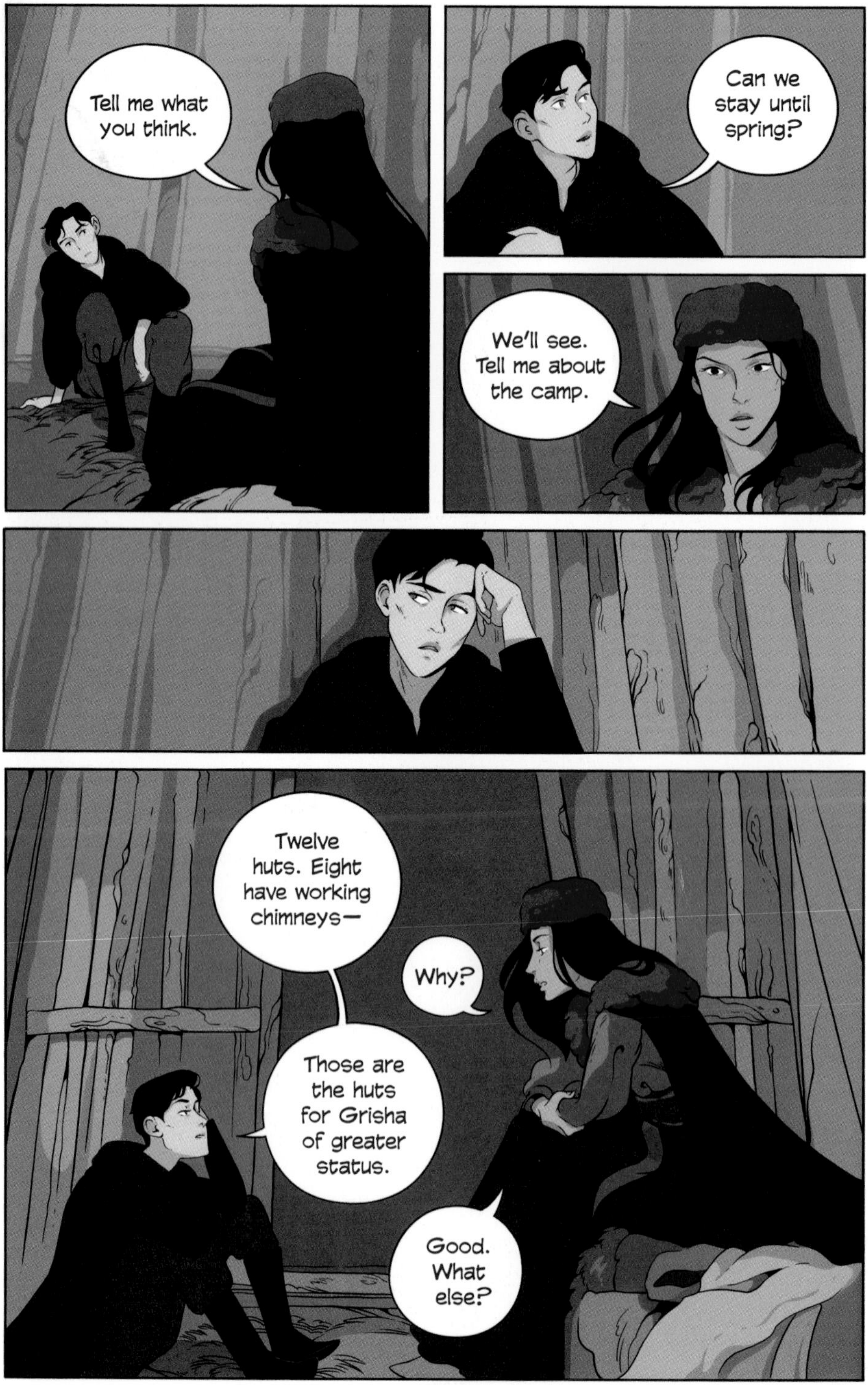
Tell me what you think.
Can we stay until spring?
We'll see. Tell me about the camp.
Twelve huts. Eight have working chimneys—
Why?
Those are the huts for Grisha of greater status.
Good. What else?

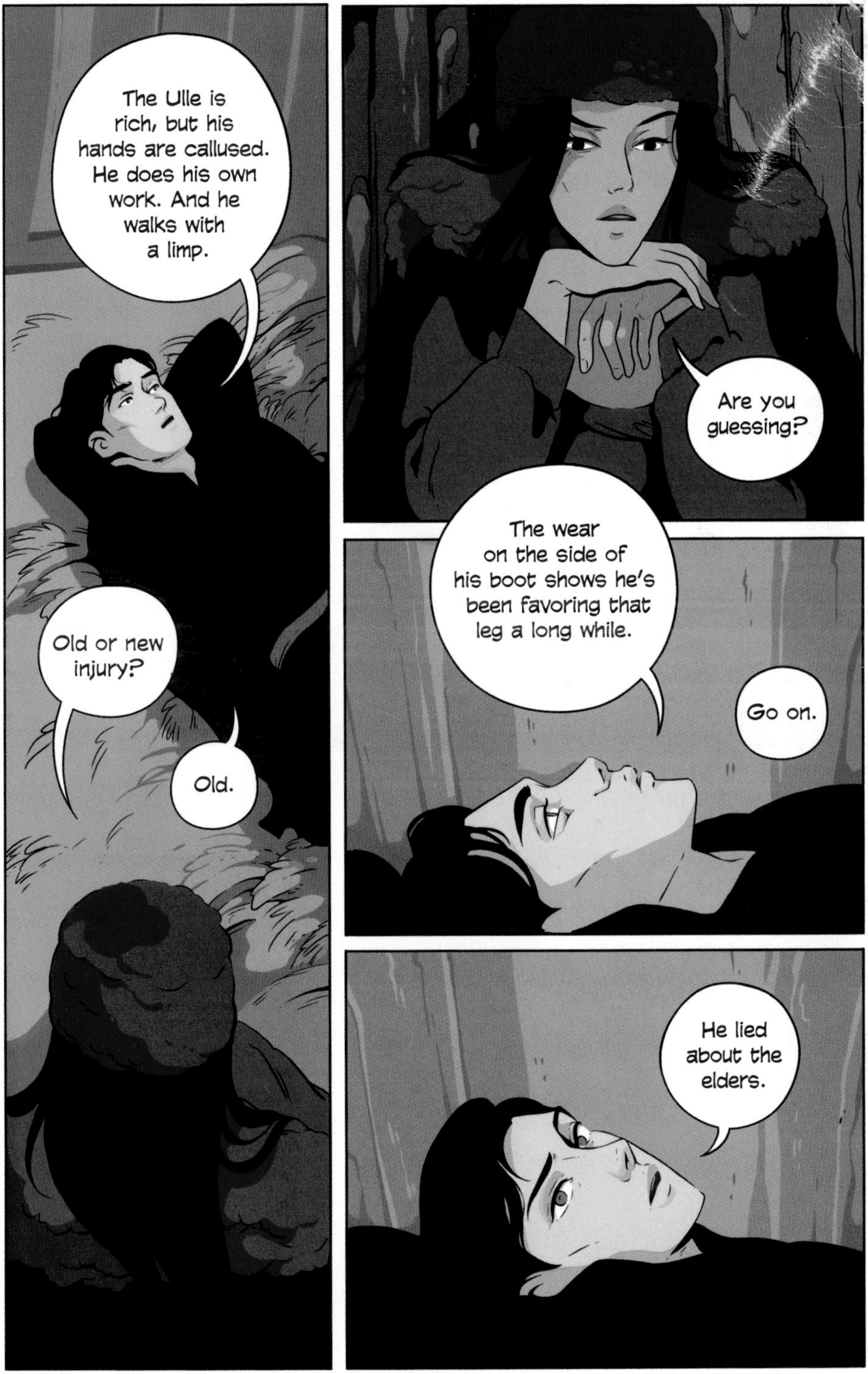
The Ulle is rich, but his hands are callused. He does his own work. And he walks with a limp.
Are you guessing?
Old or new injury?
Old.
The wear on the side of his boot shows he's been favoring that leg a long while.
Go on.
He lied about the elders.

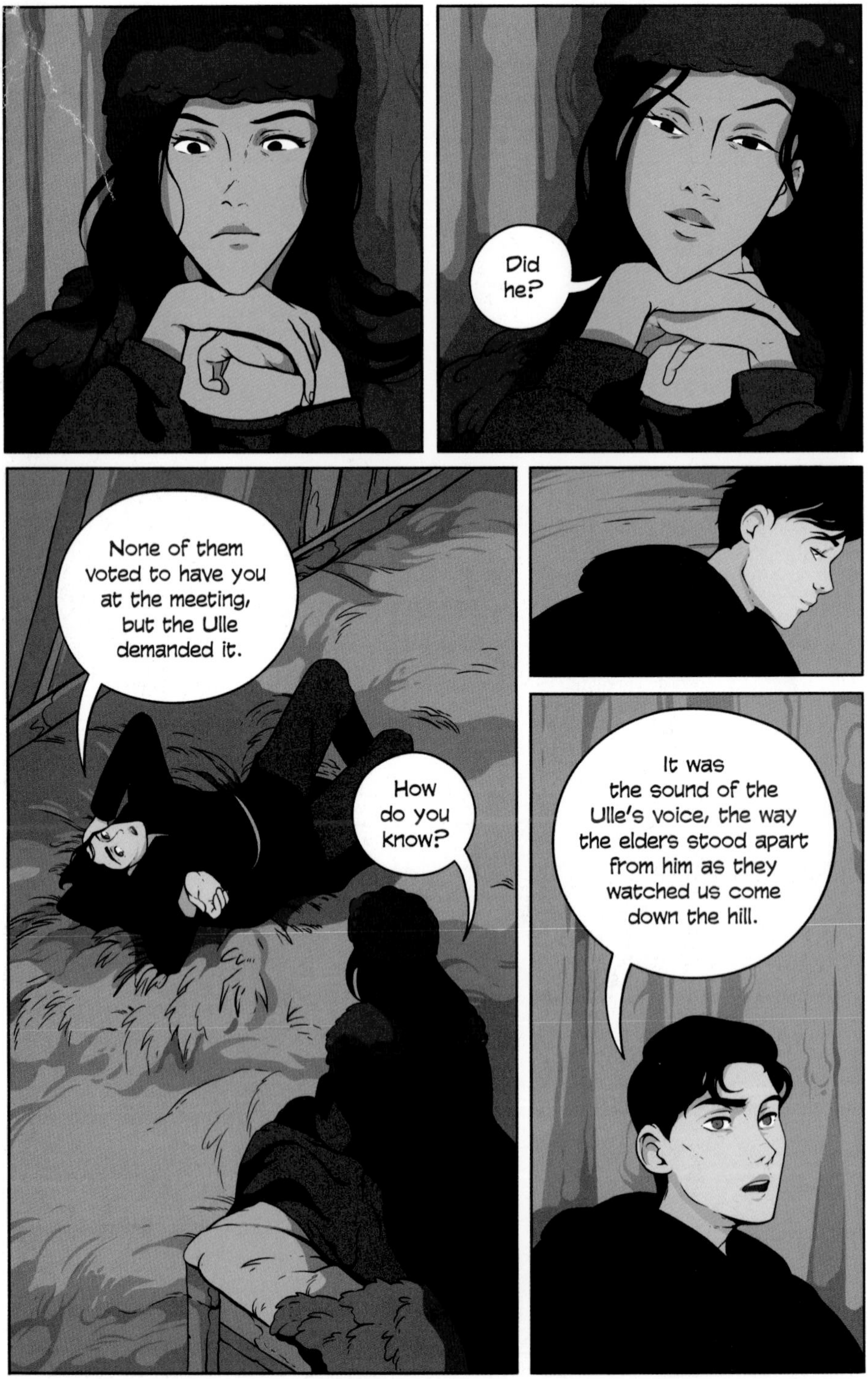
Did he?
None of them voted to have you at the meeting, but the Ulle demanded it.
How do you know?
It was the sound of the Ulle's voice, the way the elders stood apart from him as they watched us come down the hill.

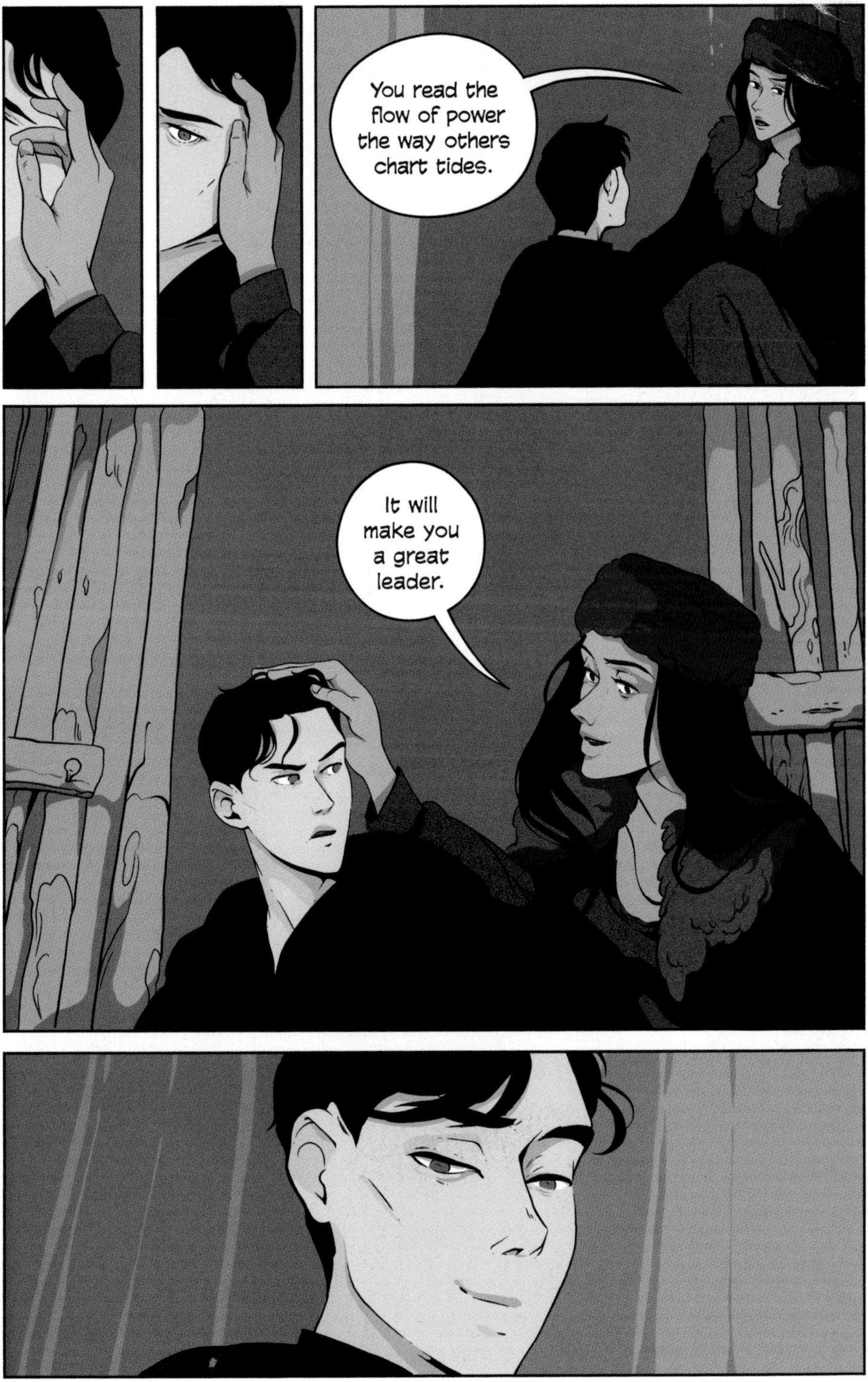
You read the flow of power the way others chart tides.
It will make you a great leader.

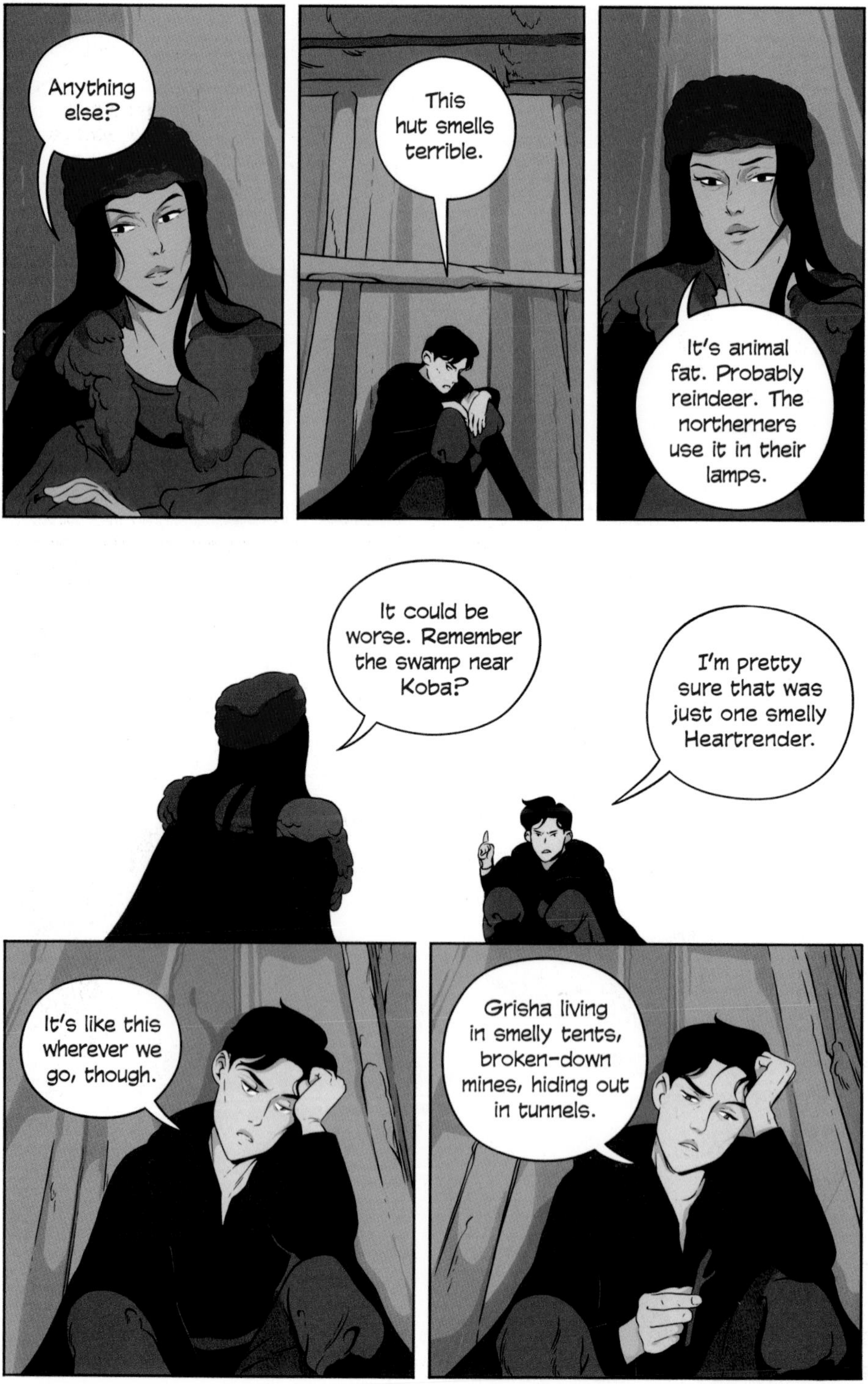
Anything else?
This hut smells terrible.
It's animal fat. Probably reindeer. The northerners use it in their lamps.
It could be worse. Remember the swamp near Koba?
I'm pretty sure that was just one smelly Heartrender.
It's like this wherever we go, though.
Grisha living in smelly tents, broken-down mines, hiding out in tunnels.

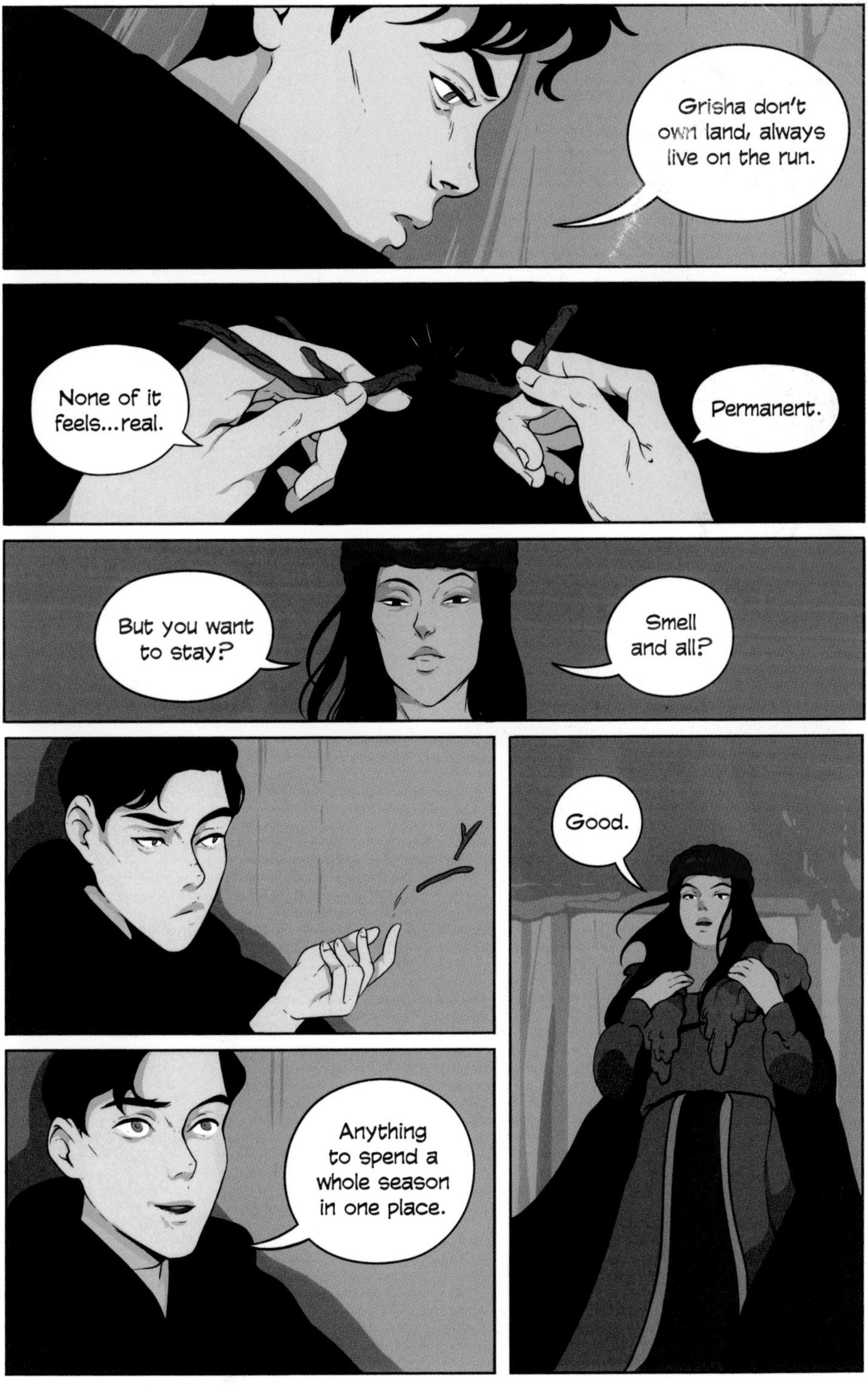
Grisha don't own land, always live on the run.
None of it feels...real.
Permanent.
But you want to stay?
Smell and all?
Good.
Anything to spend a whole season in one place.

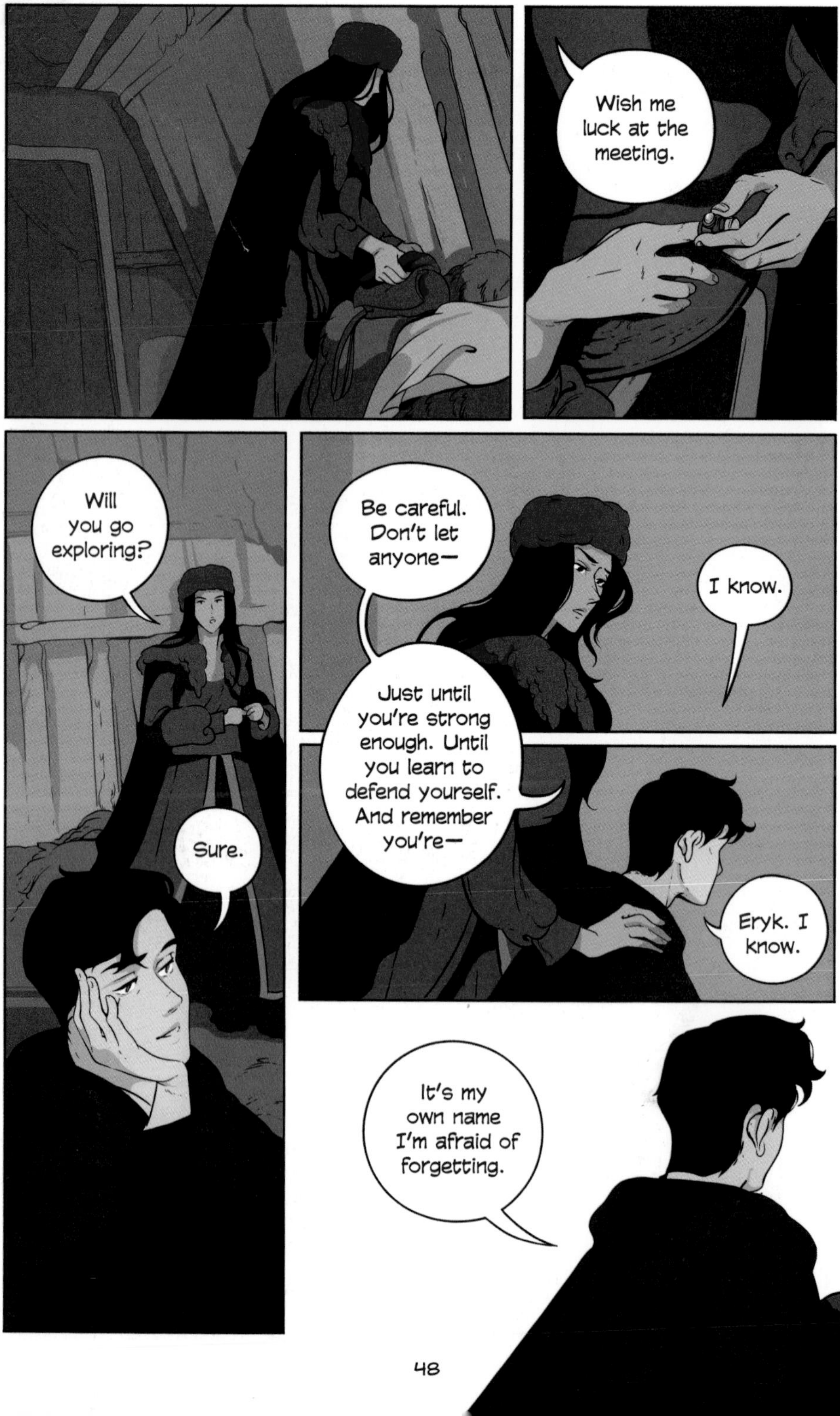

Wish me luck at the meeting.
Will you go exploring?
Sure.
Be careful. Don't let anyone—
I know.
Just until you're strong enough. Until you learn to defend yourself. And remember you're—
Eryk. I know.
It's my own name I'm afraid of forgetting.

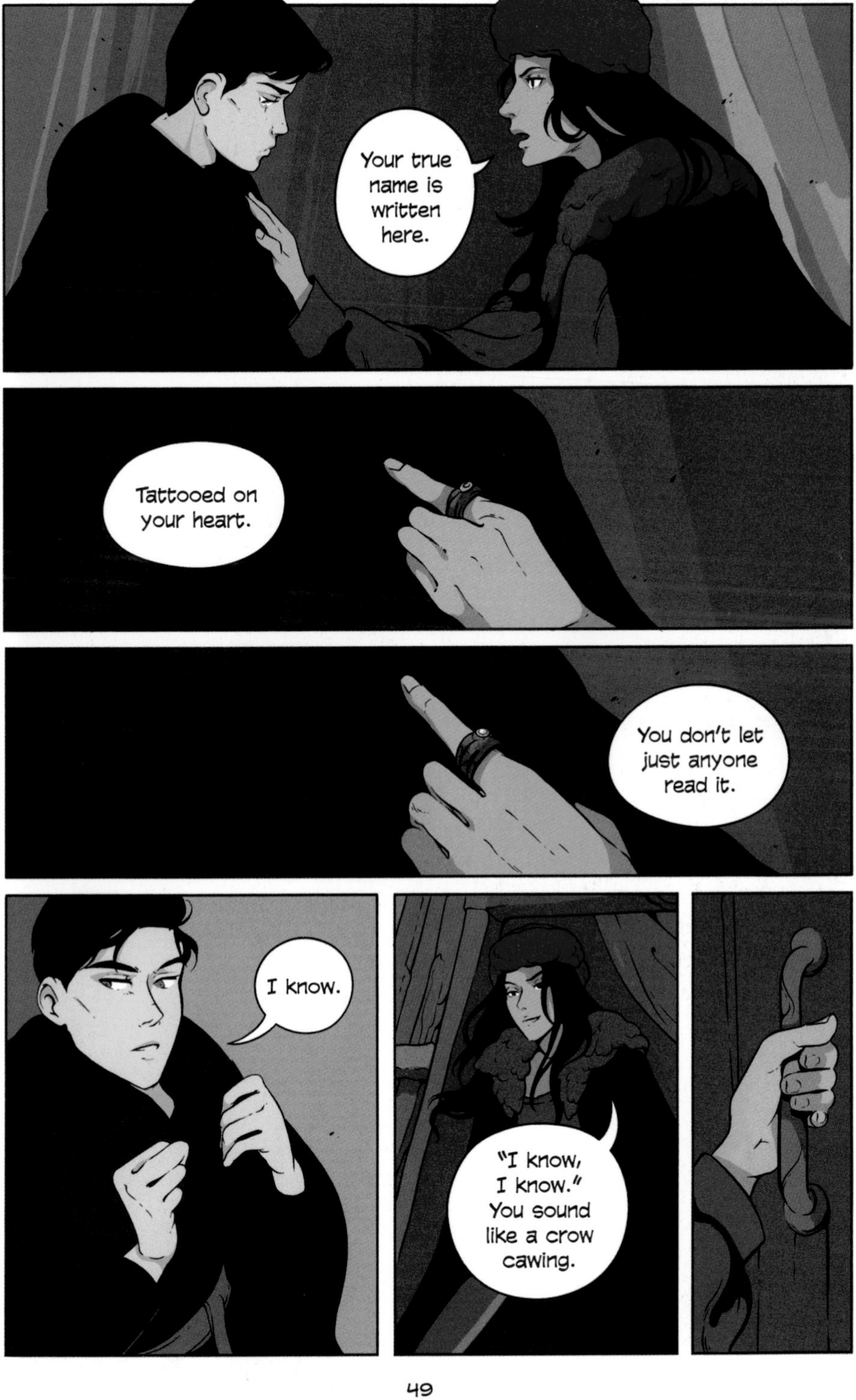

Your true name is written here.
Tattooed on your heart.
You don't let just anyone read it.
I know.
"I know, I know." You sound like a crow cawing.

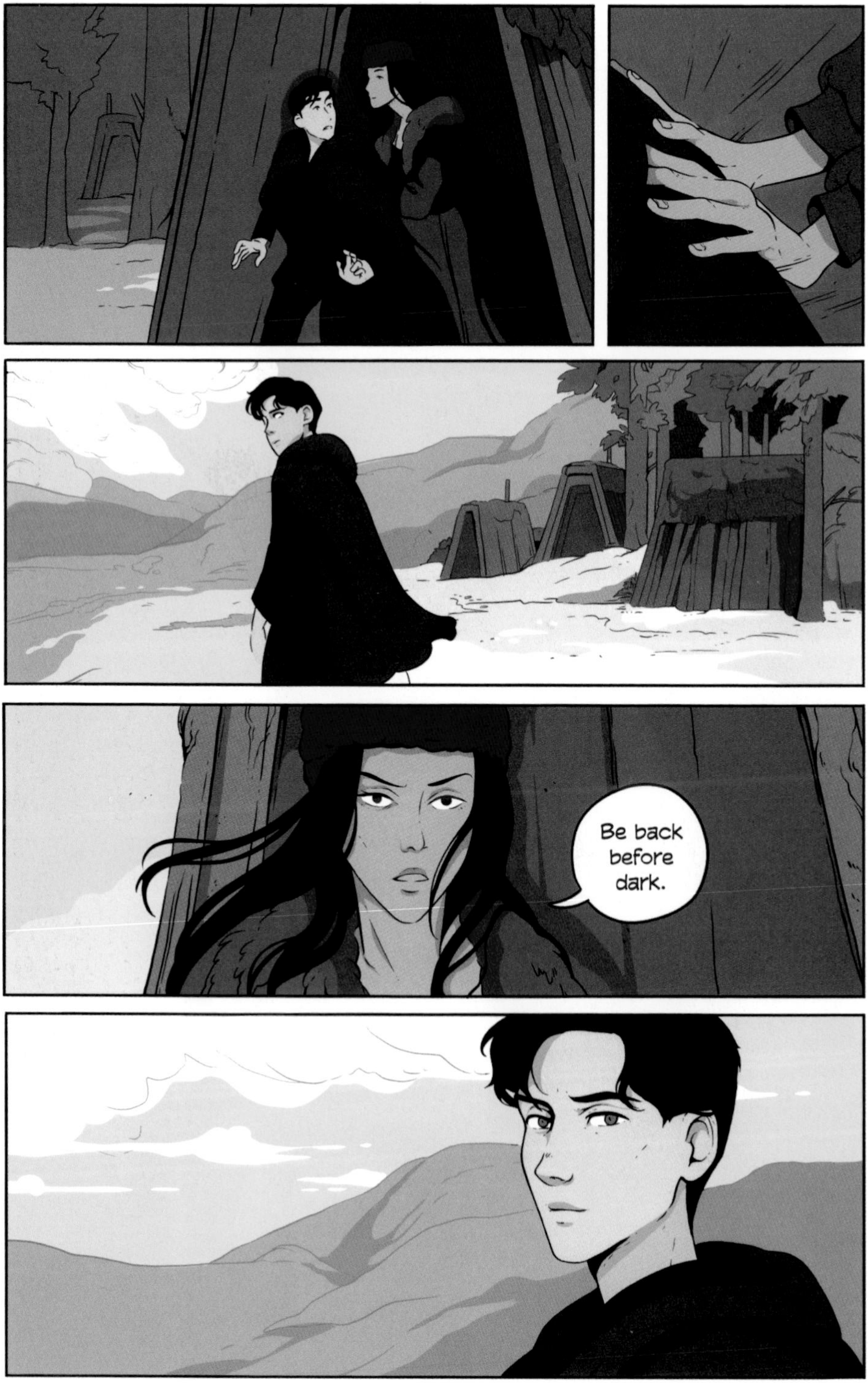
Be back before dark.

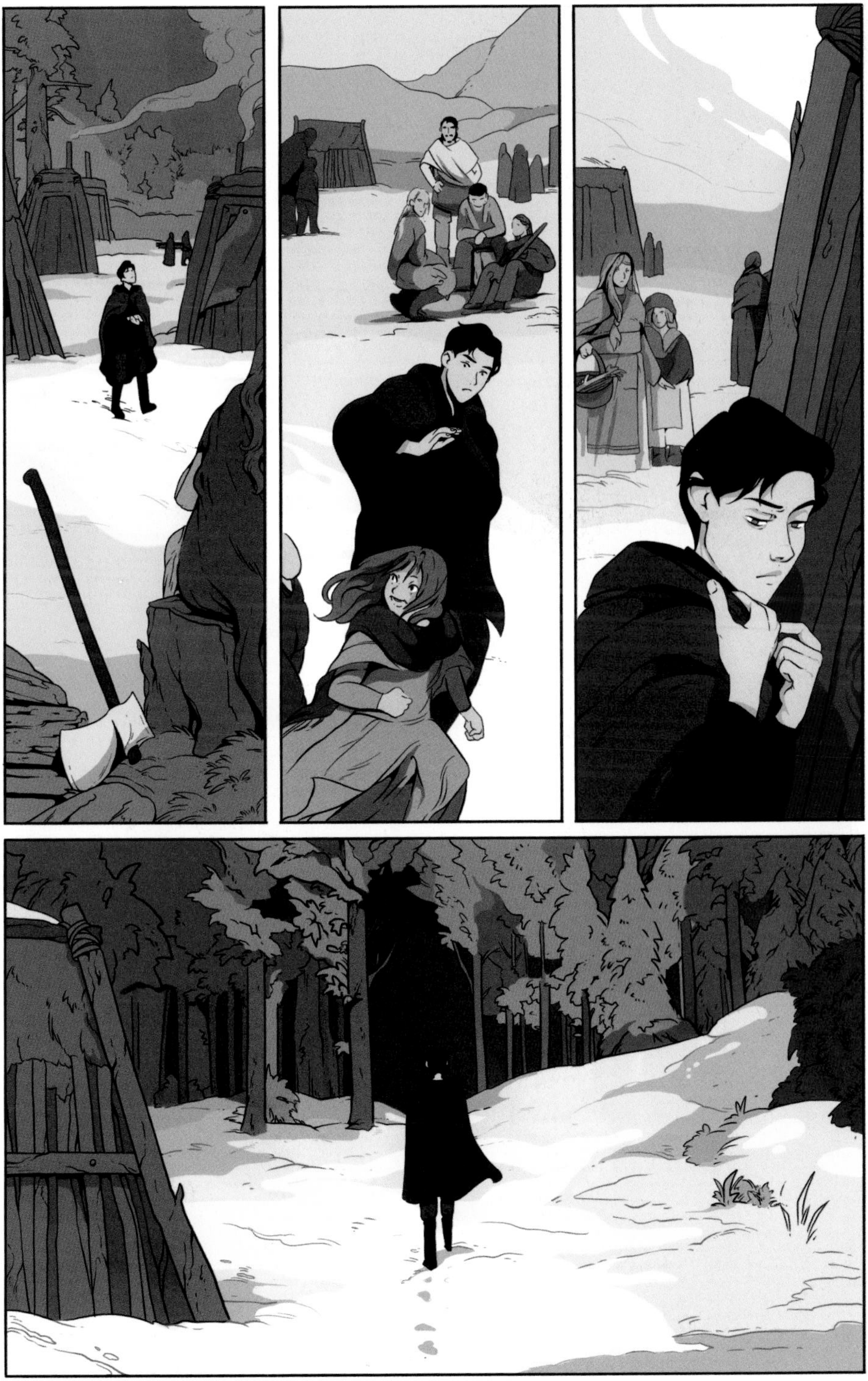

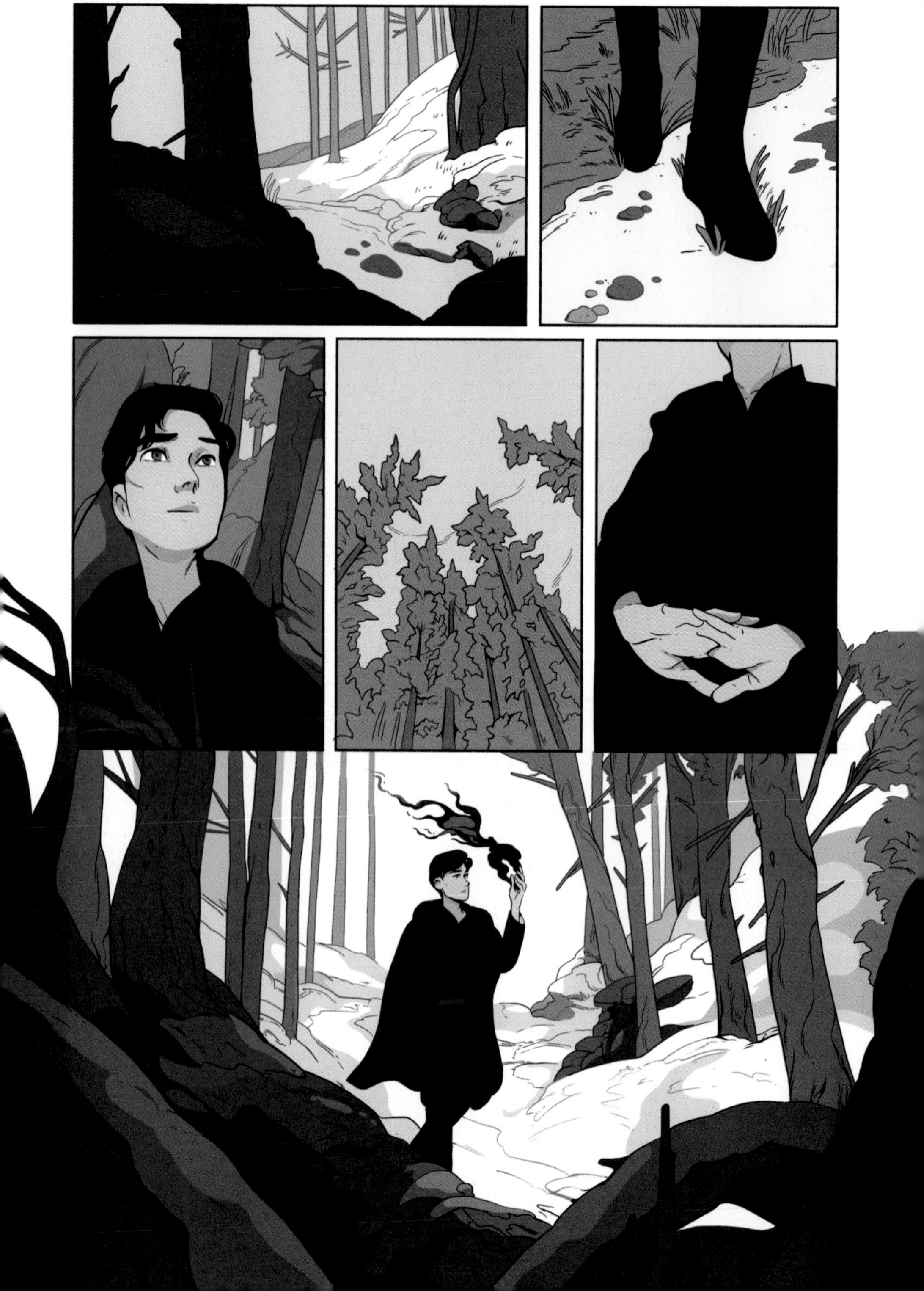

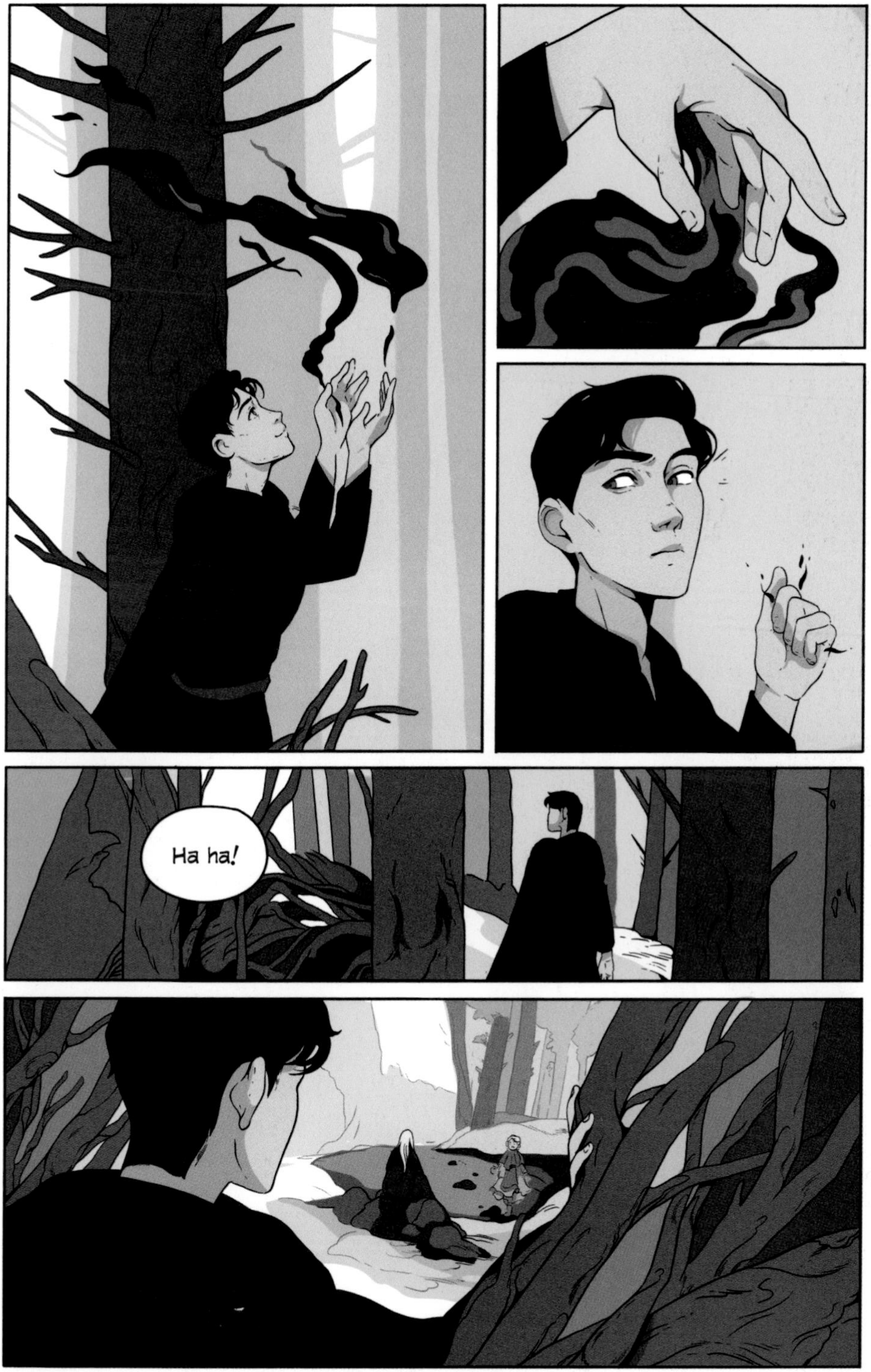
Ha ha!

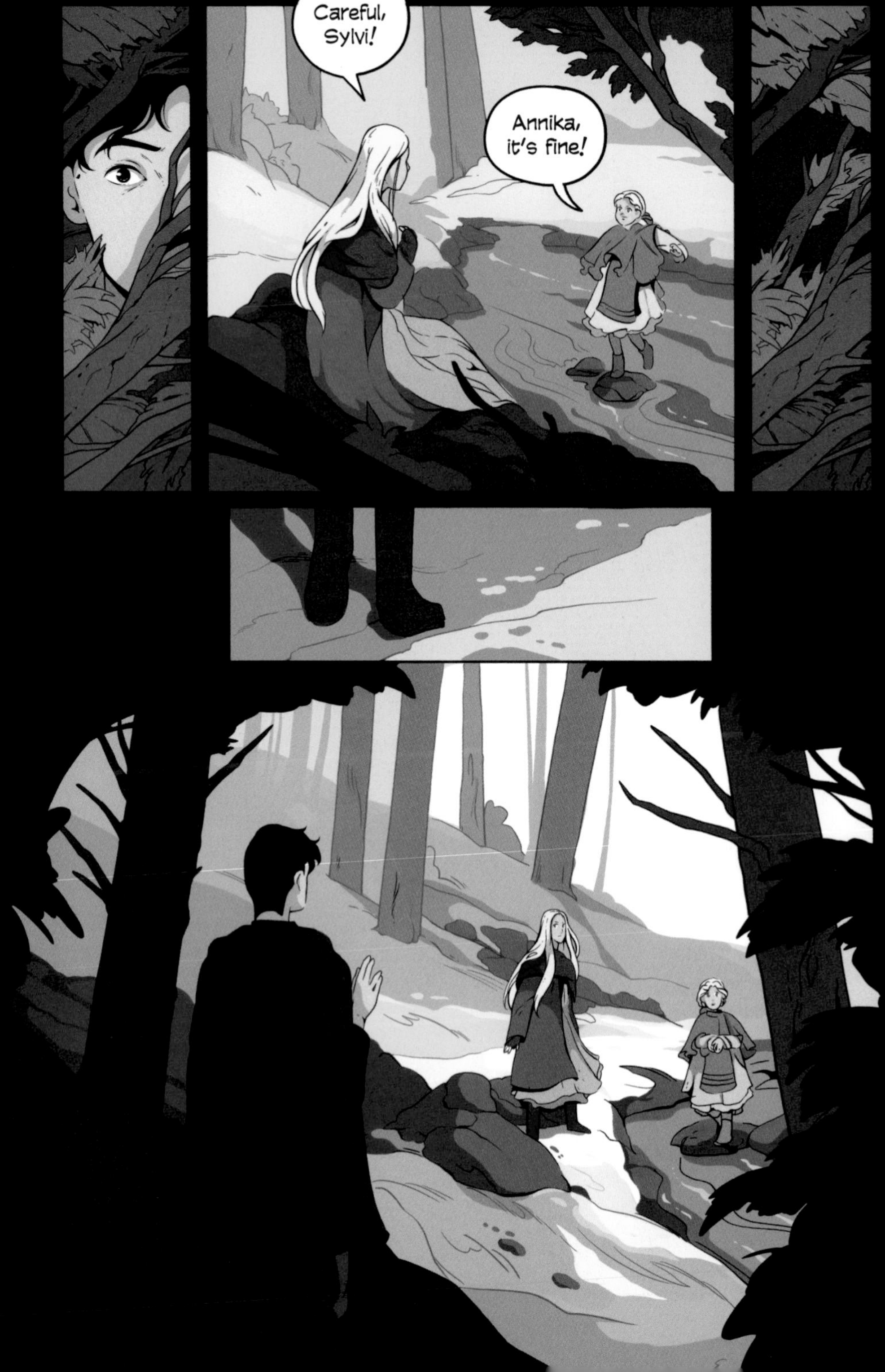
Careful, Sylvi!
Annika, it's fine!

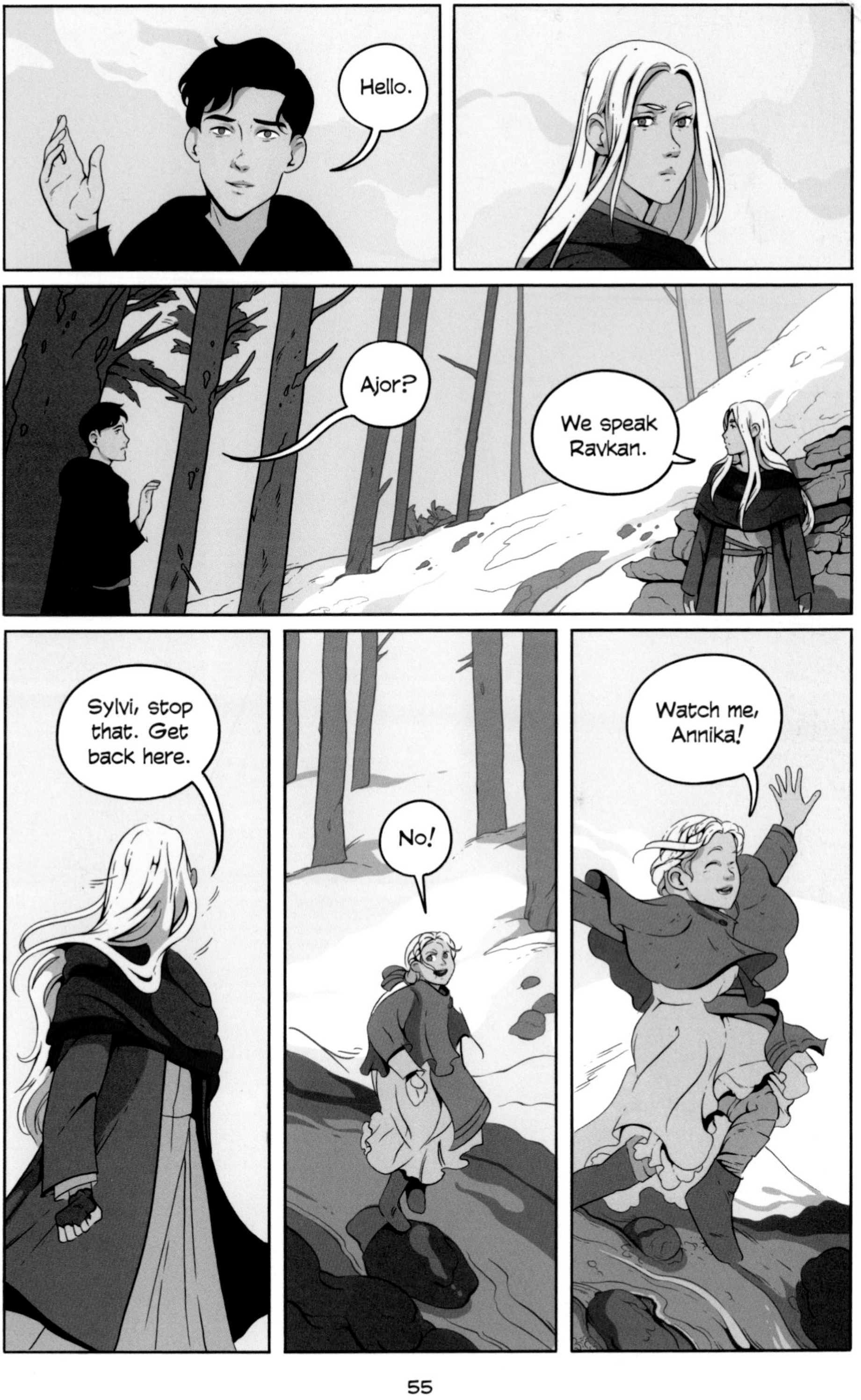
Hello.
Ajor?
We speak Ravkan.
Sylvi, stop that. Get back here.
No!
Watch me, Annika!

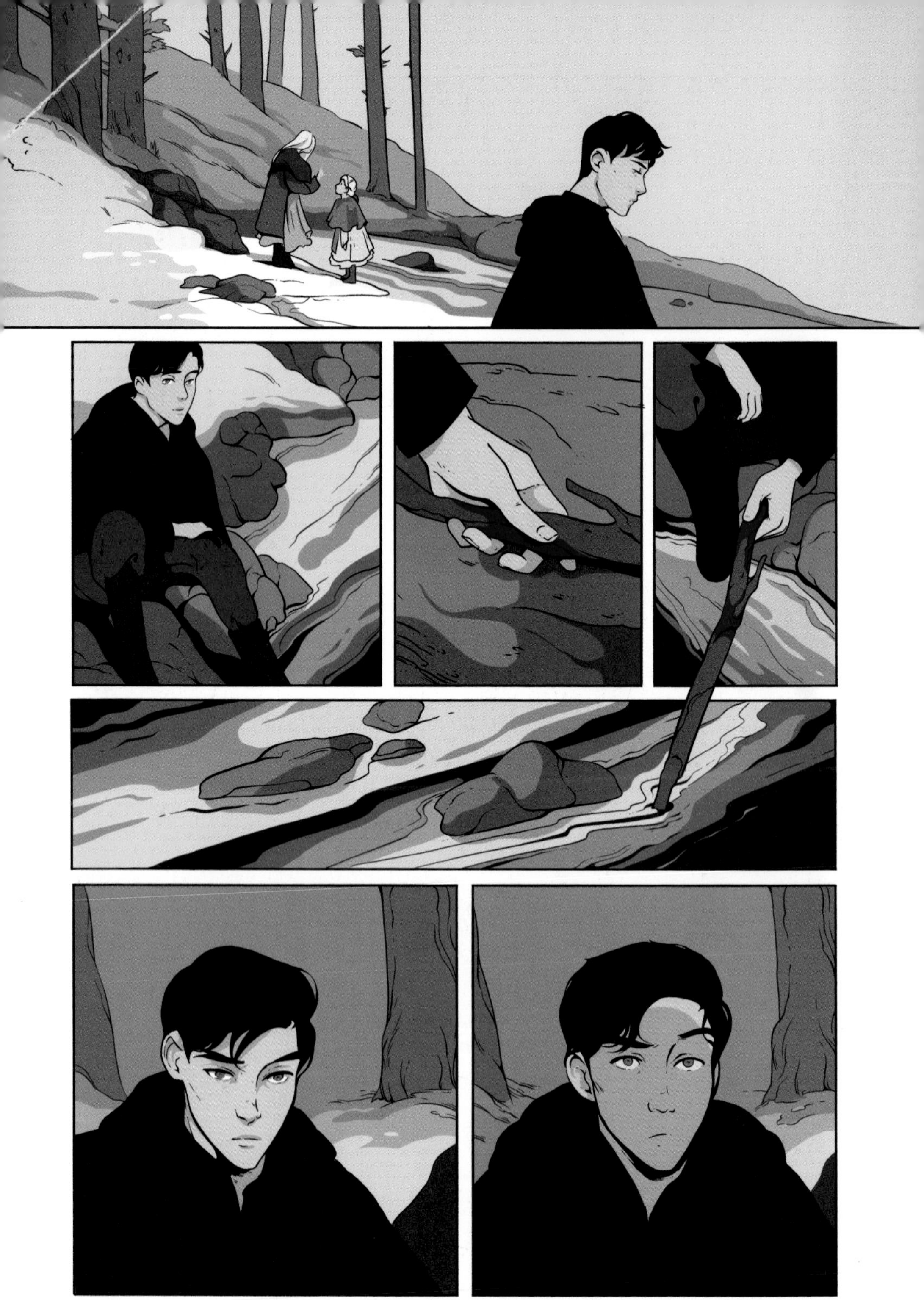

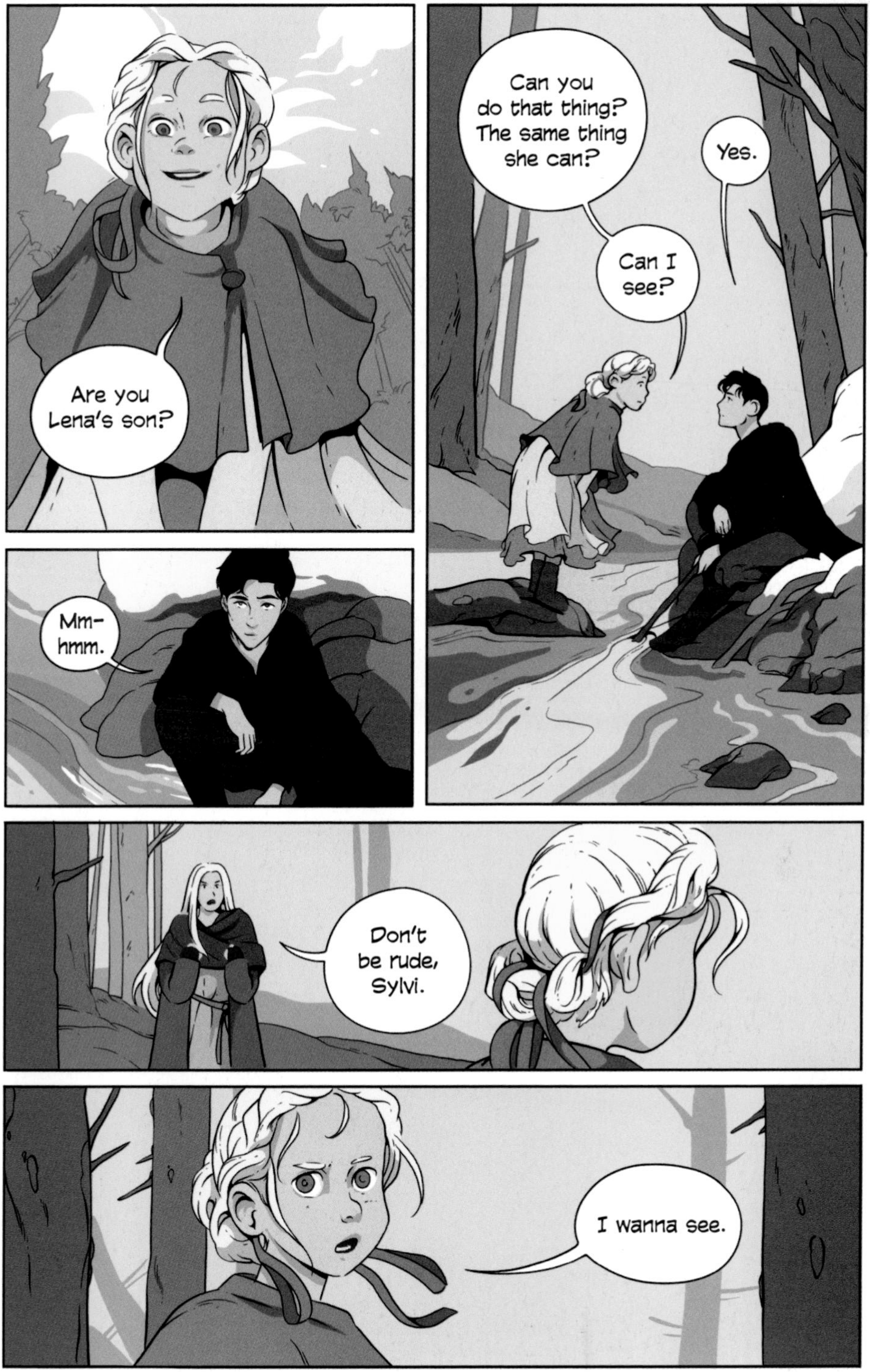
Are you Lena's son?
Mm-hmm.
Can you do that thing? The same thing she can?
Yes.
Can I see?
Don't be rude, Sylvi.
I wanna see.

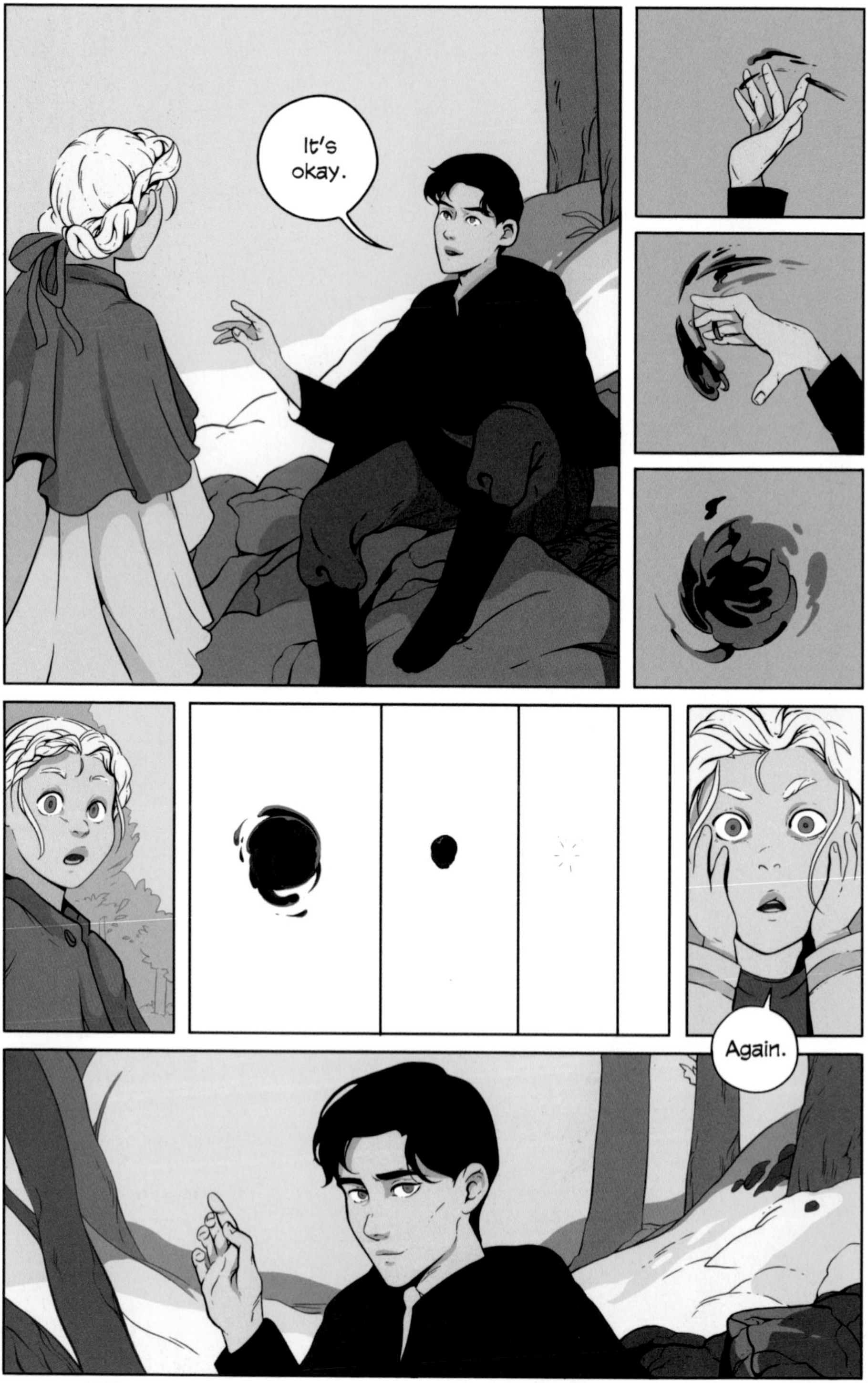
It's okay.
Again.

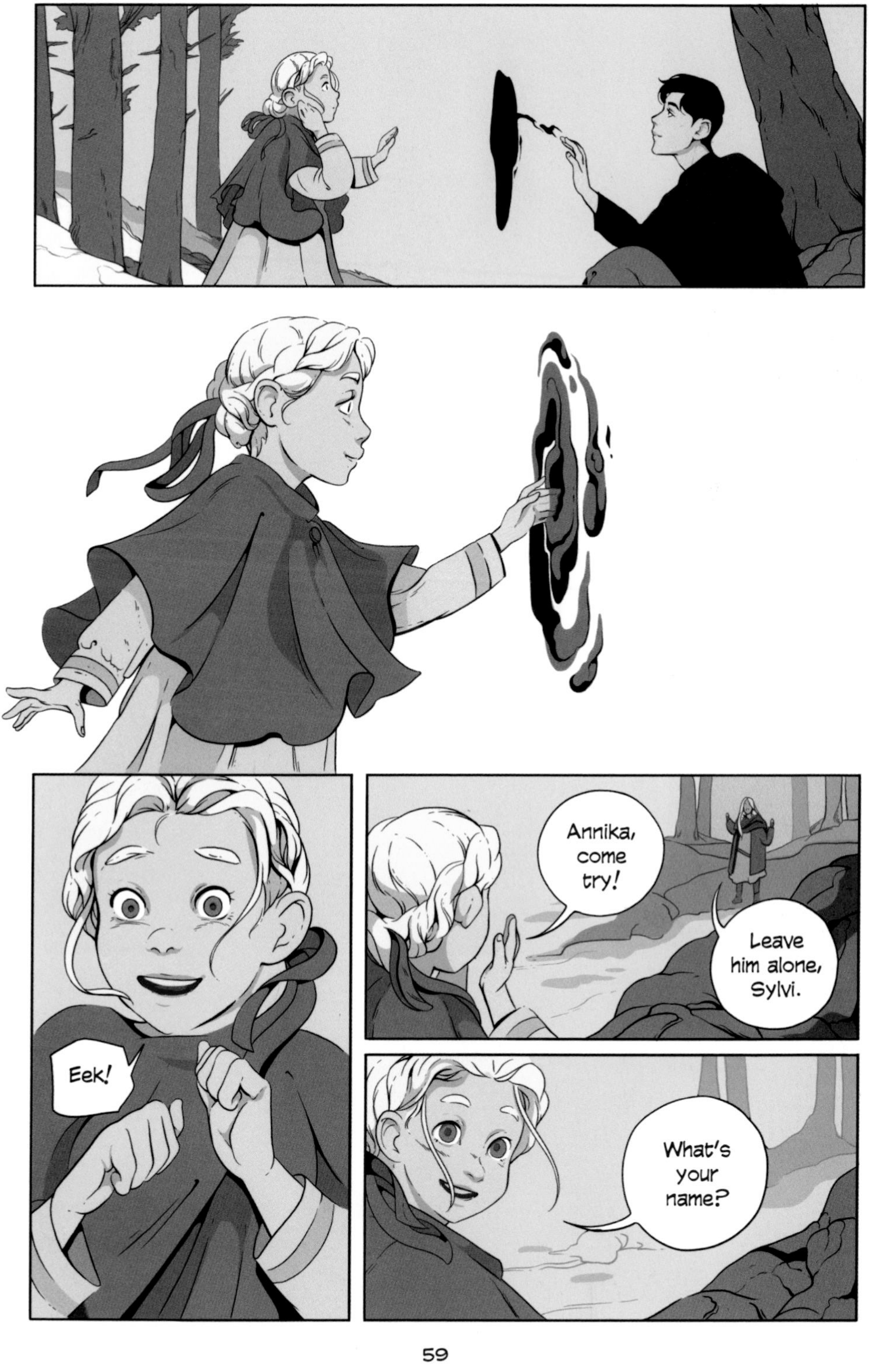
Eek!
Annika, come try!
Leave him alone, Sylvi.
What's your name?

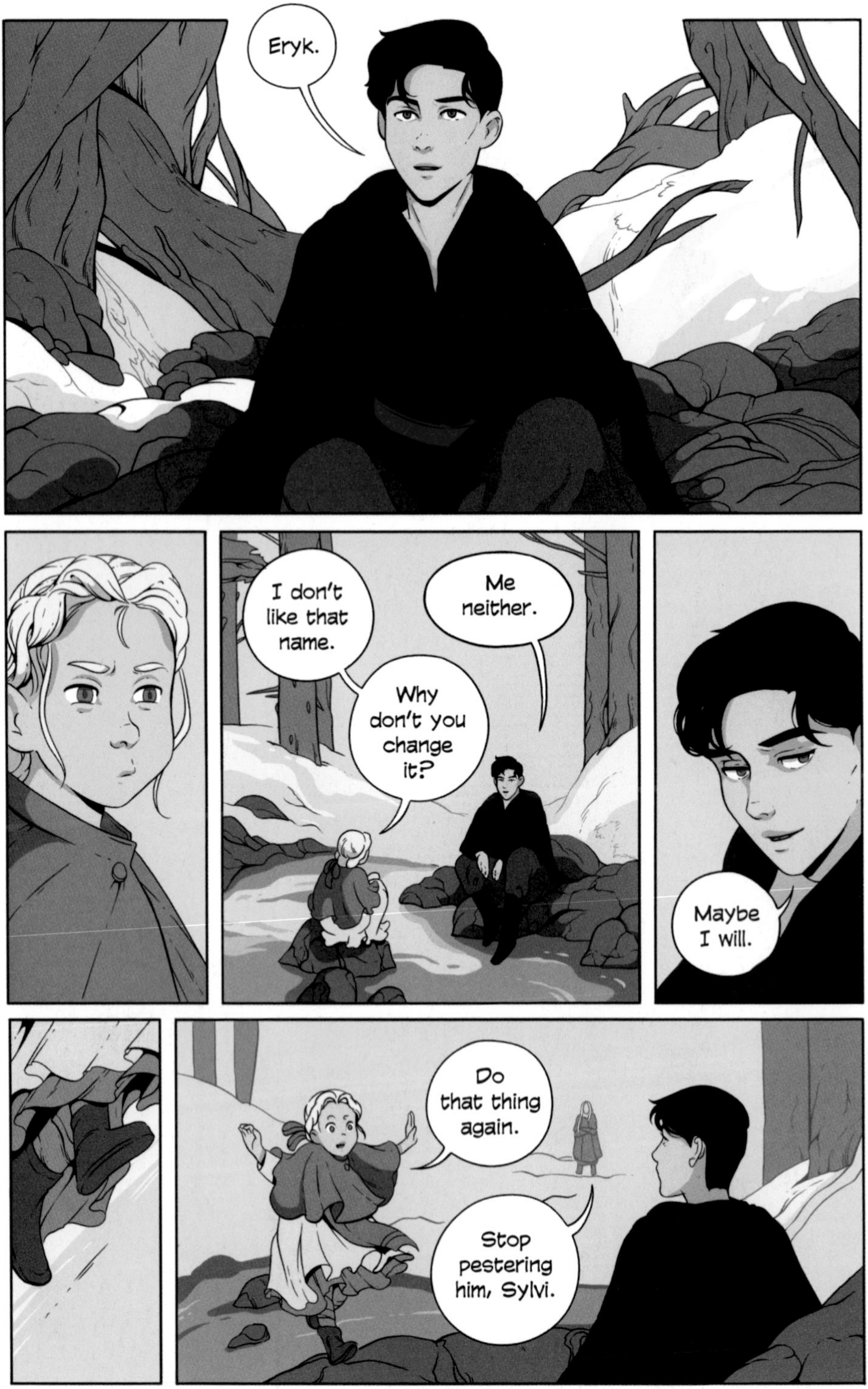
Eryk.
I don't like that name.
Me neither.
Why don't you change it?
Maybe I will.
Do that thing again.
Stop pestering him, Sylvi.

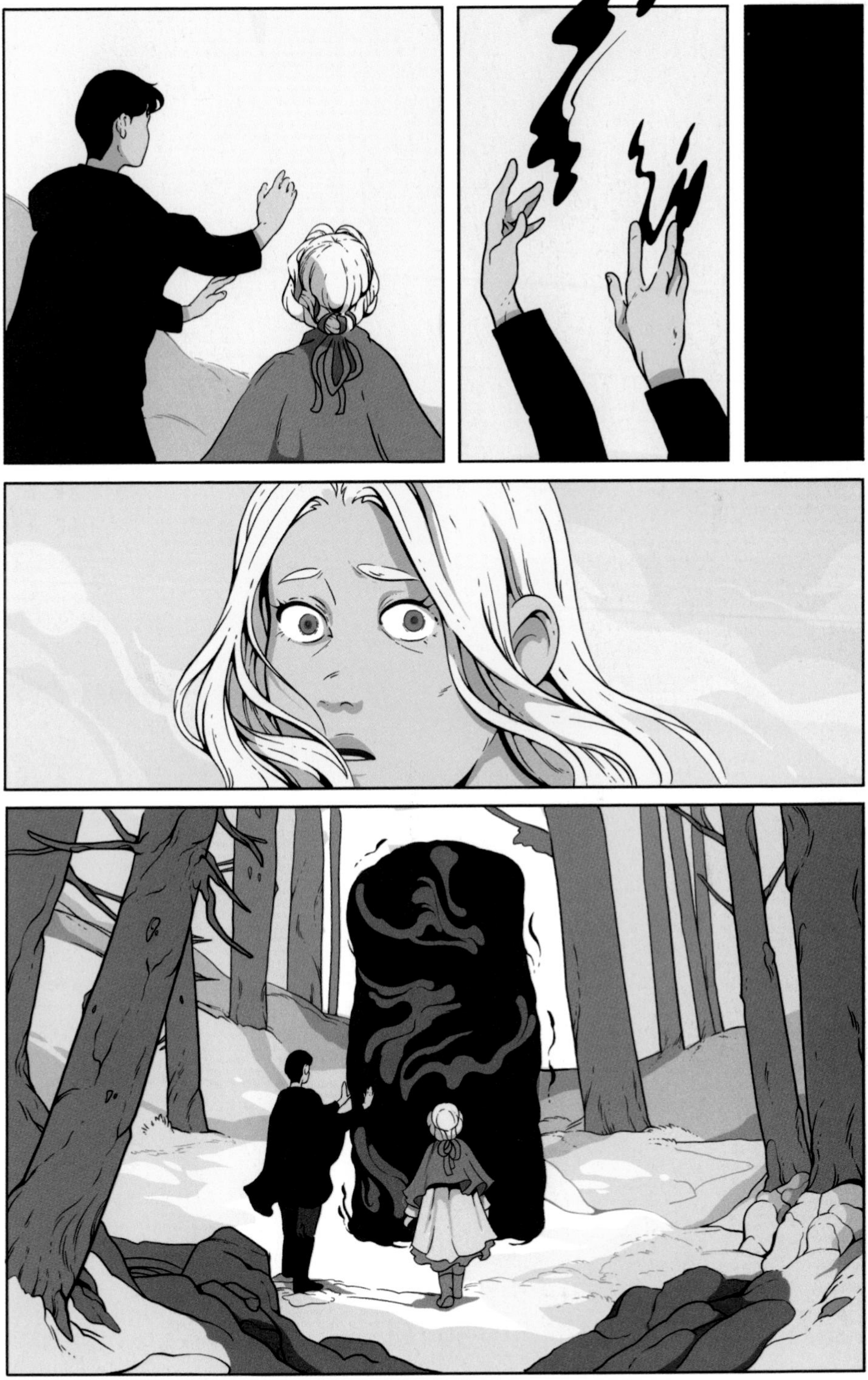

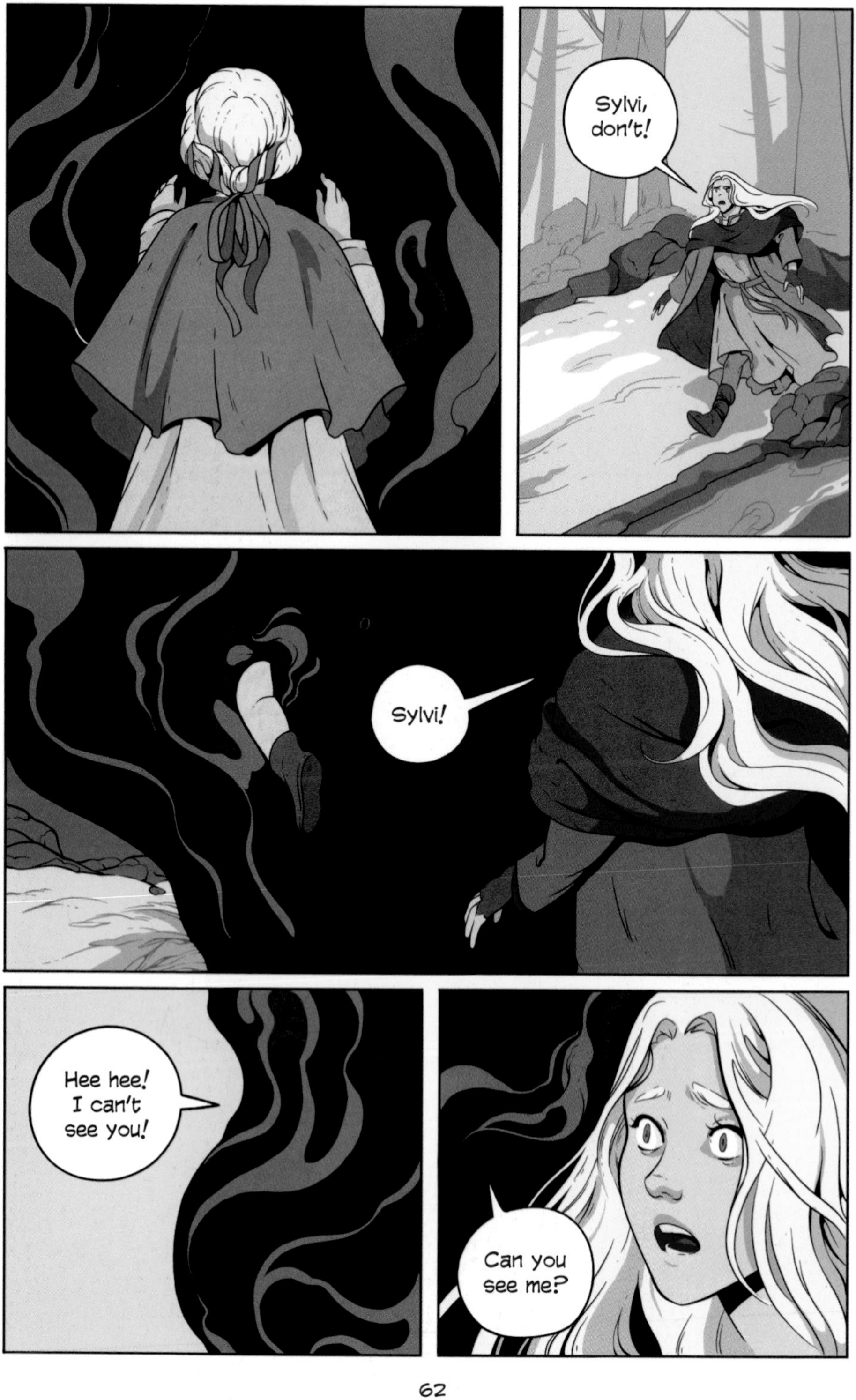
Sylvi, don't!
Sylvi!
Hee hee! I can't see you!
Can you see me?

Bring her back.

She's standing right there.

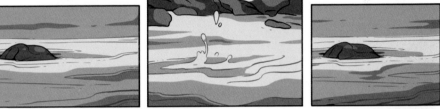

Why'd you stop?

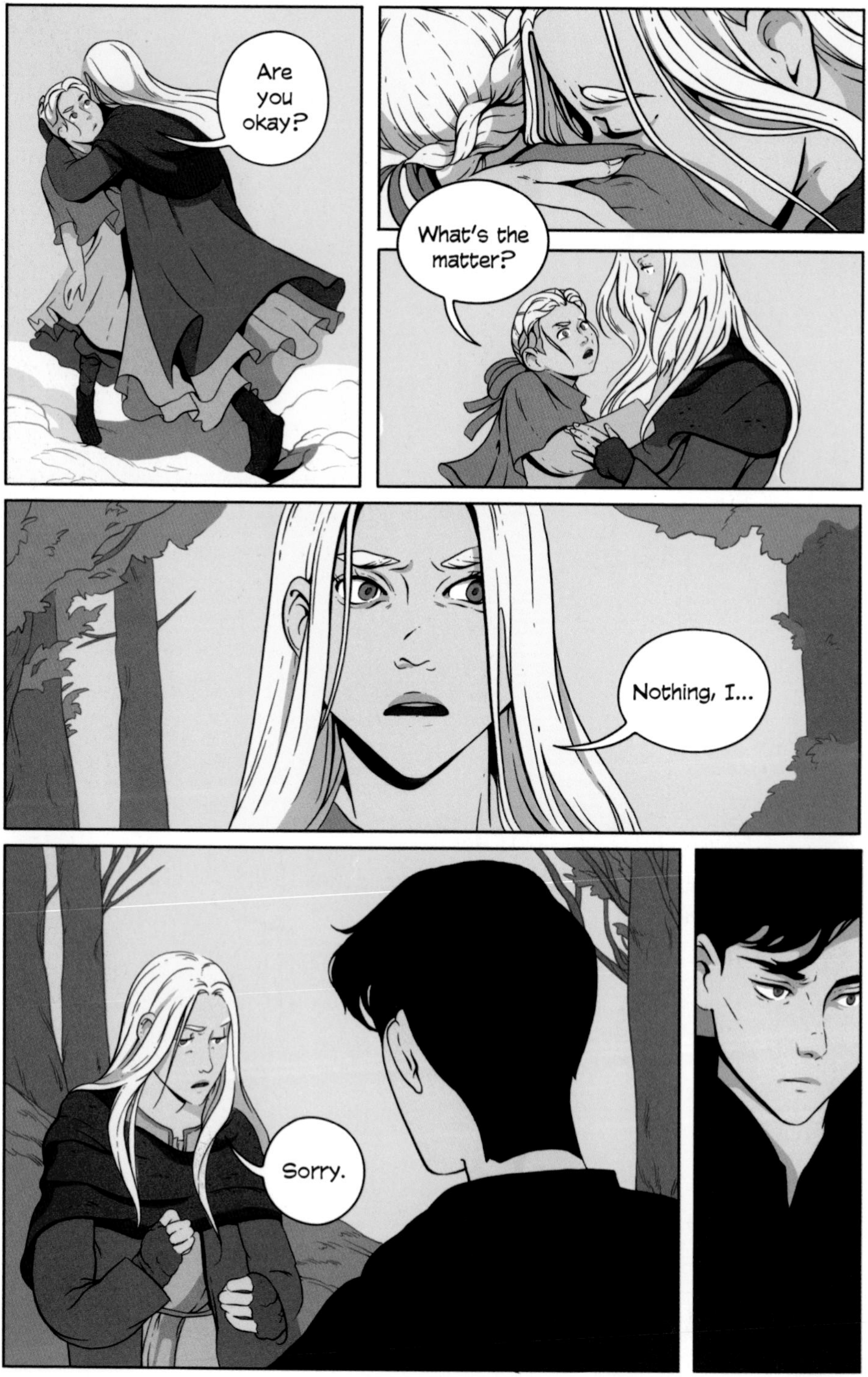
Are you okay?
What's the matter?
Nothing, I...
Sorry.

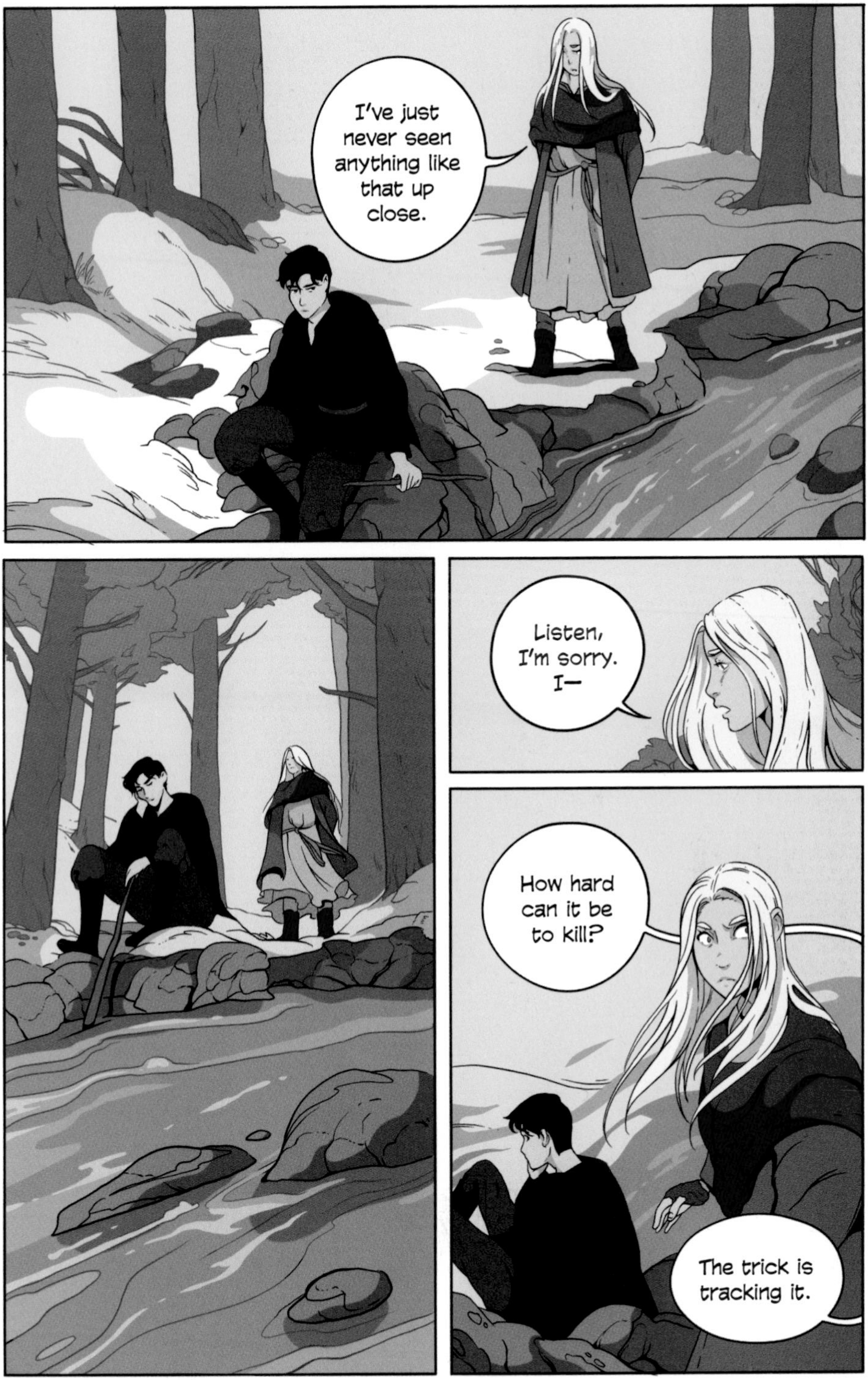
I've just never seen anything like that up close.
Listen, I'm sorry. I—
How hard can it be to kill?
The trick is tracking it.

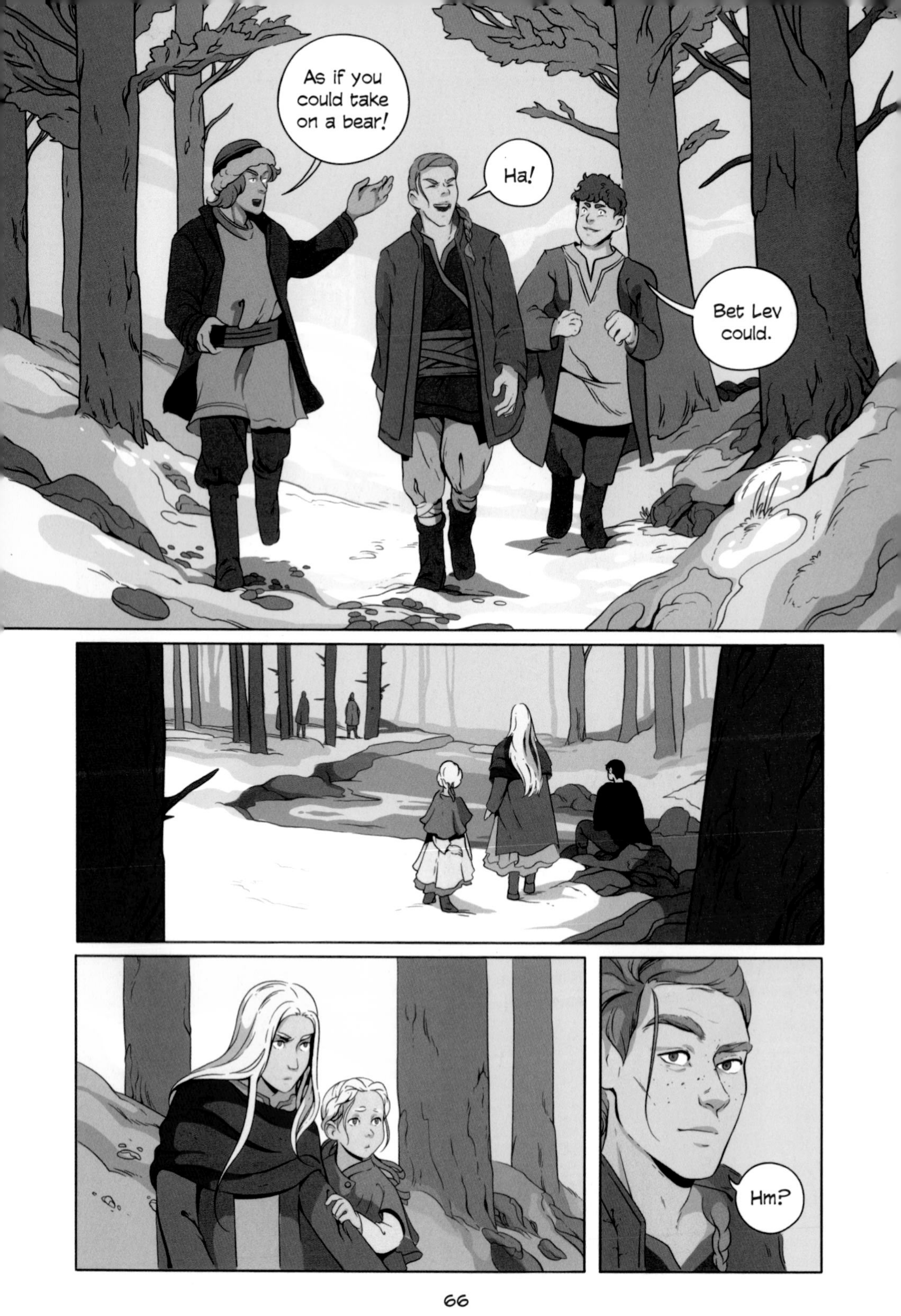
As if you could take on a bear!
Ha!
Bet Lev could.
Hm?

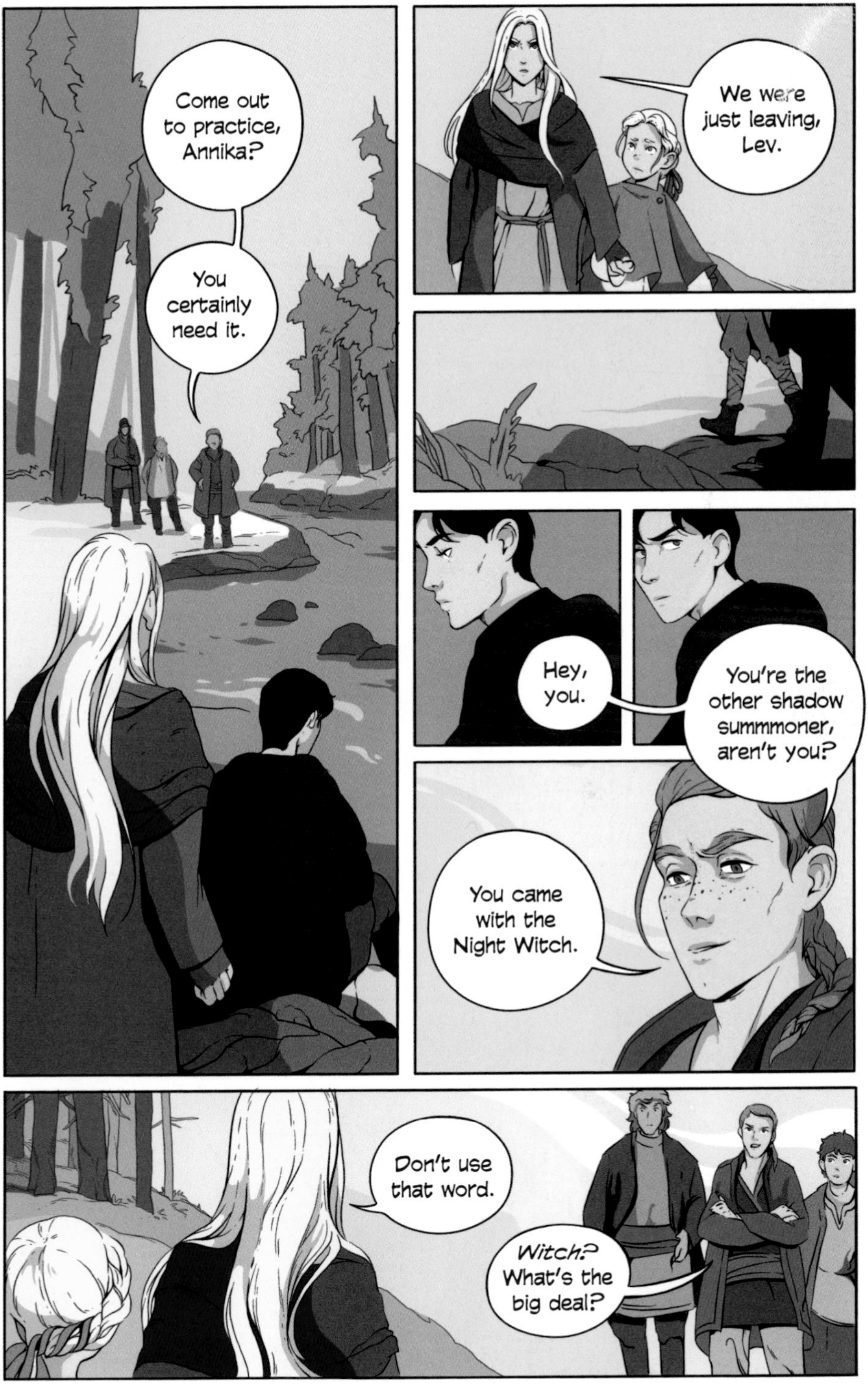
Come out to practice, Annika?
You certainly need it.
We were just leaving, Lev.
Hey, you.
You're the other shadow summmoner, aren't you?
You came with the Night Witch.
Don't use that word.
Witch? What's the big deal?

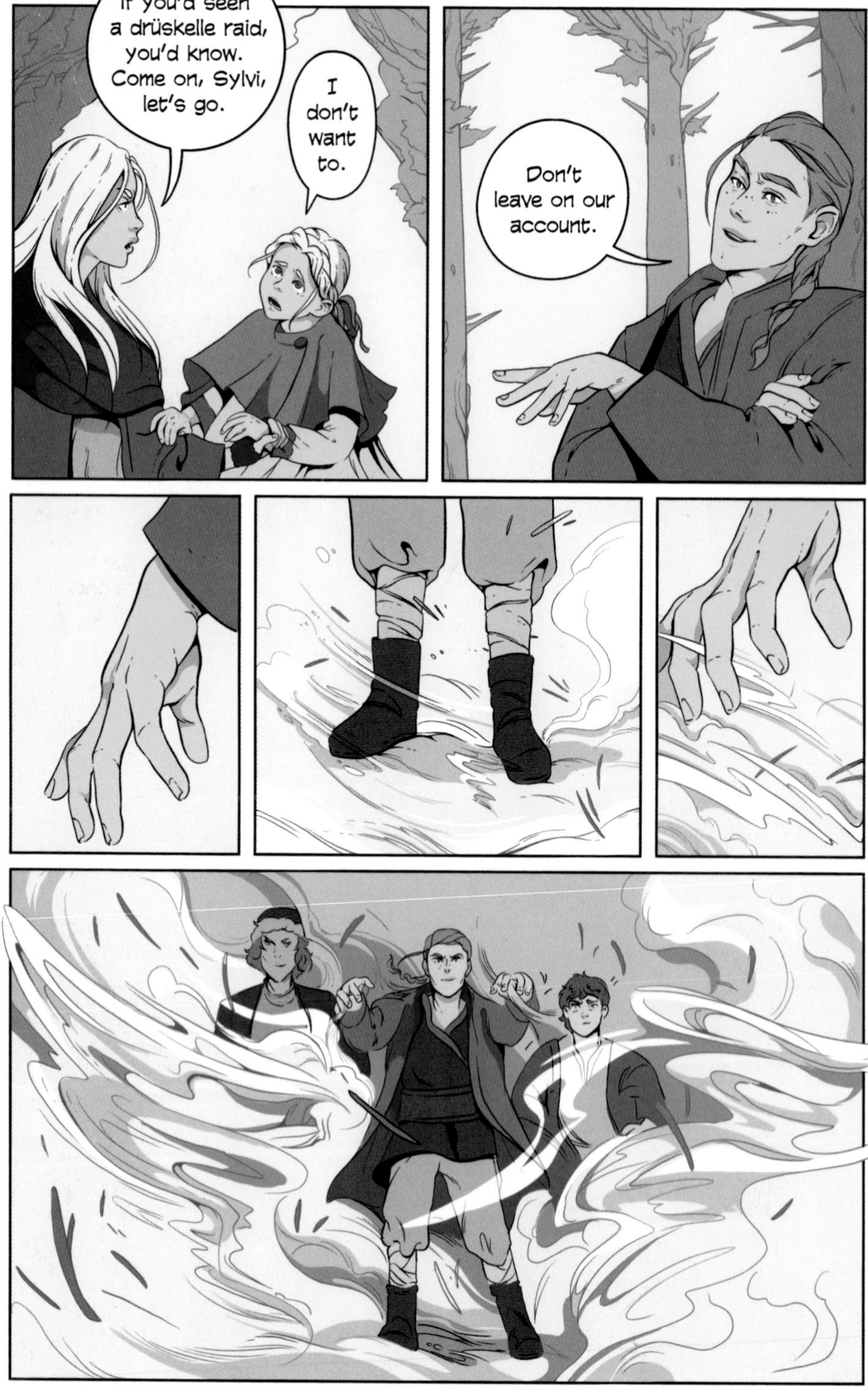
If you'd seen a drüskelle raid, you'd know. Come on, Sylvi, let's go.
I don't want to.
Don't leave on our account.

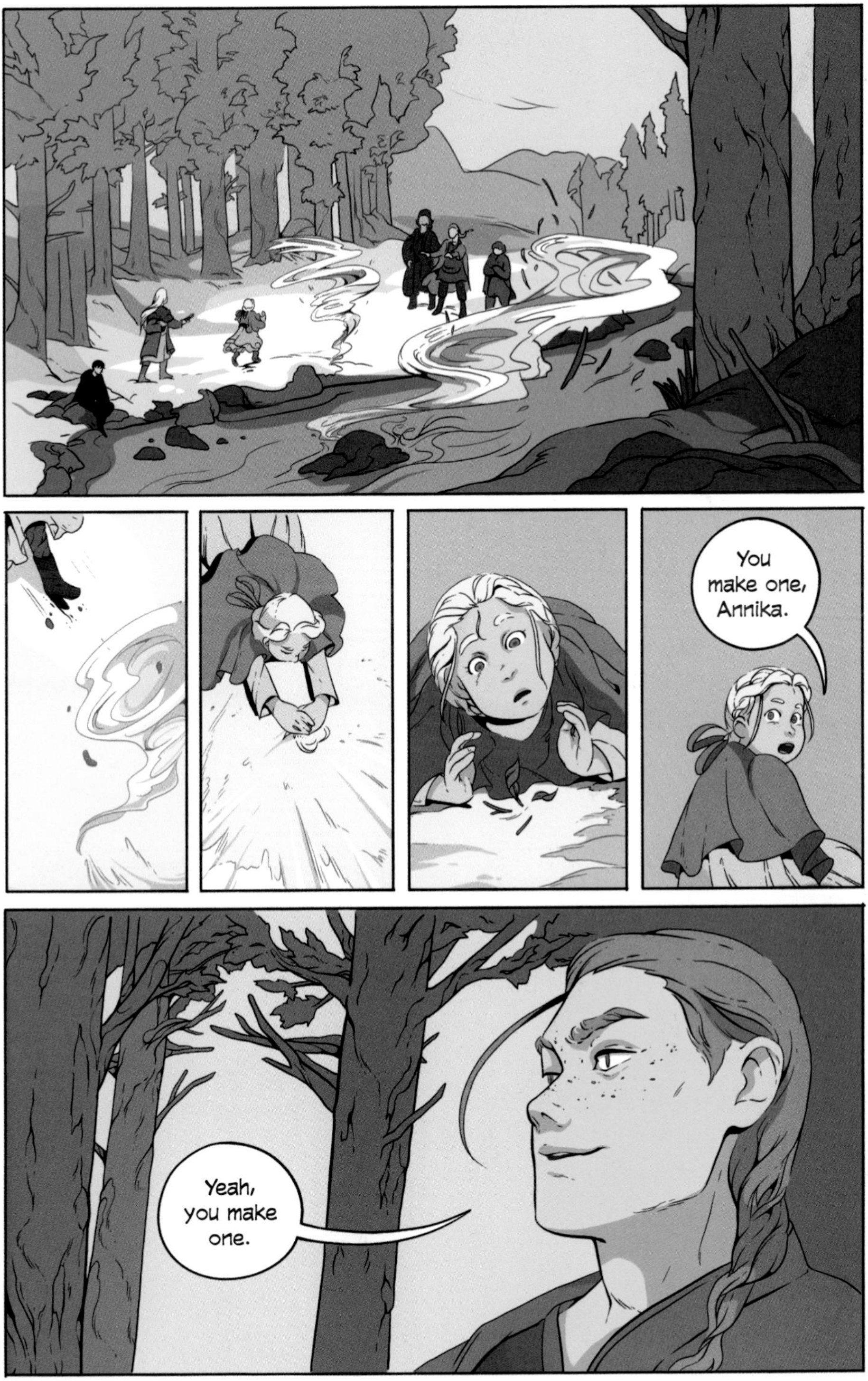
You make one, Annika.
Yeah, you make one.

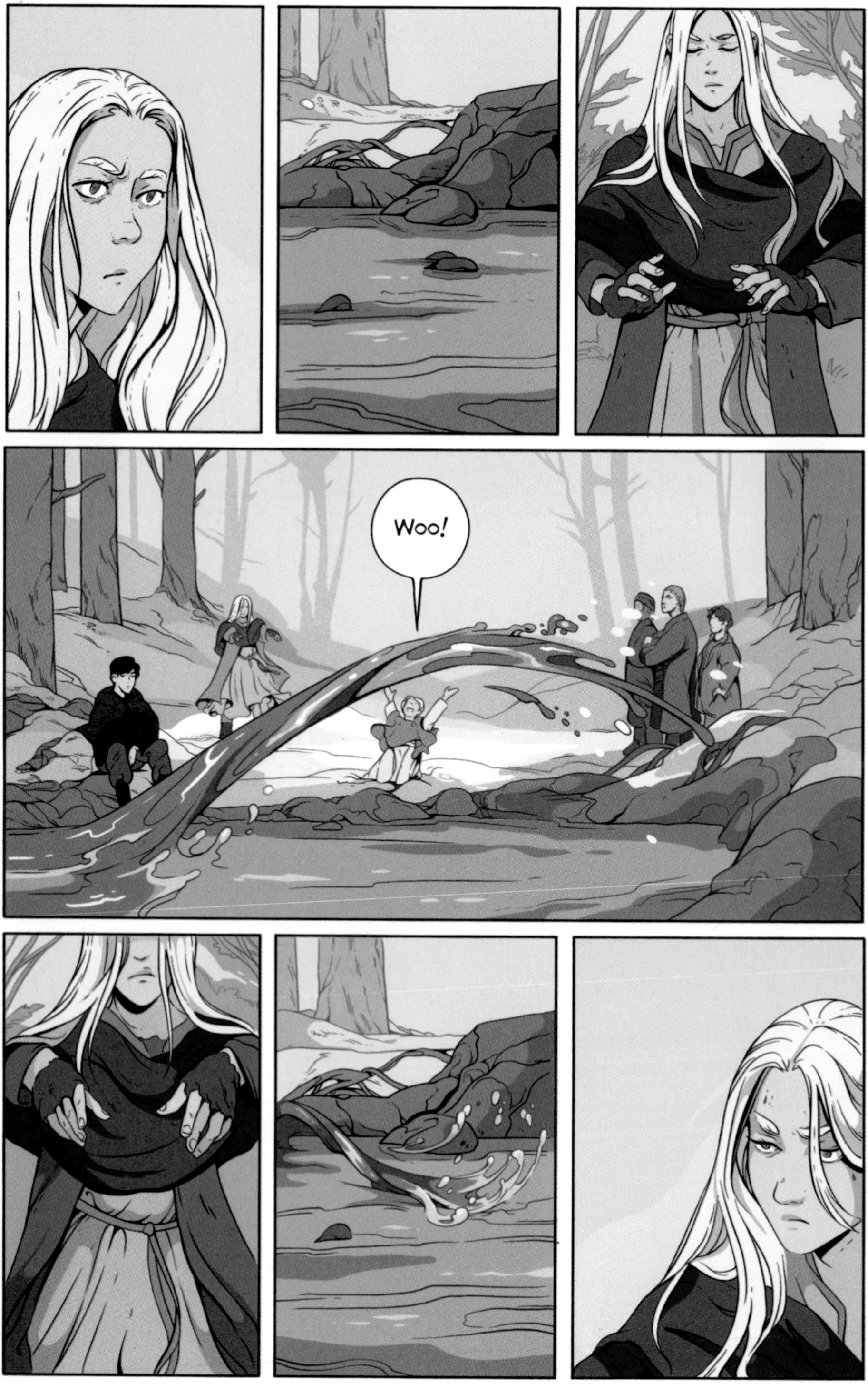
Woo!

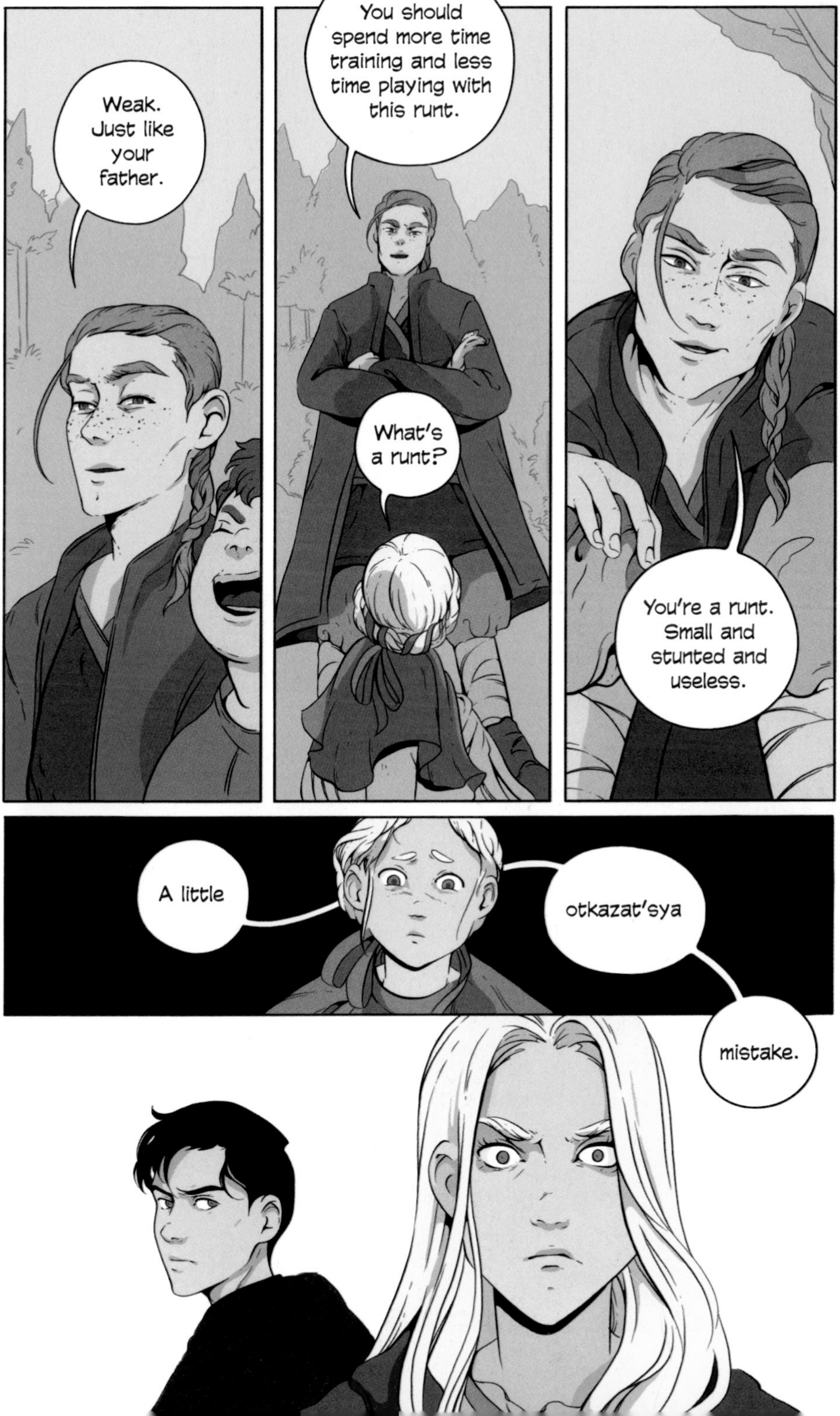
Weak. Just like your father.
You should spend more time training and less time playing with this runt.
What's a runt?
You're a runt. Small and stunted and useless.
A little
otkazat'sya
mistake.

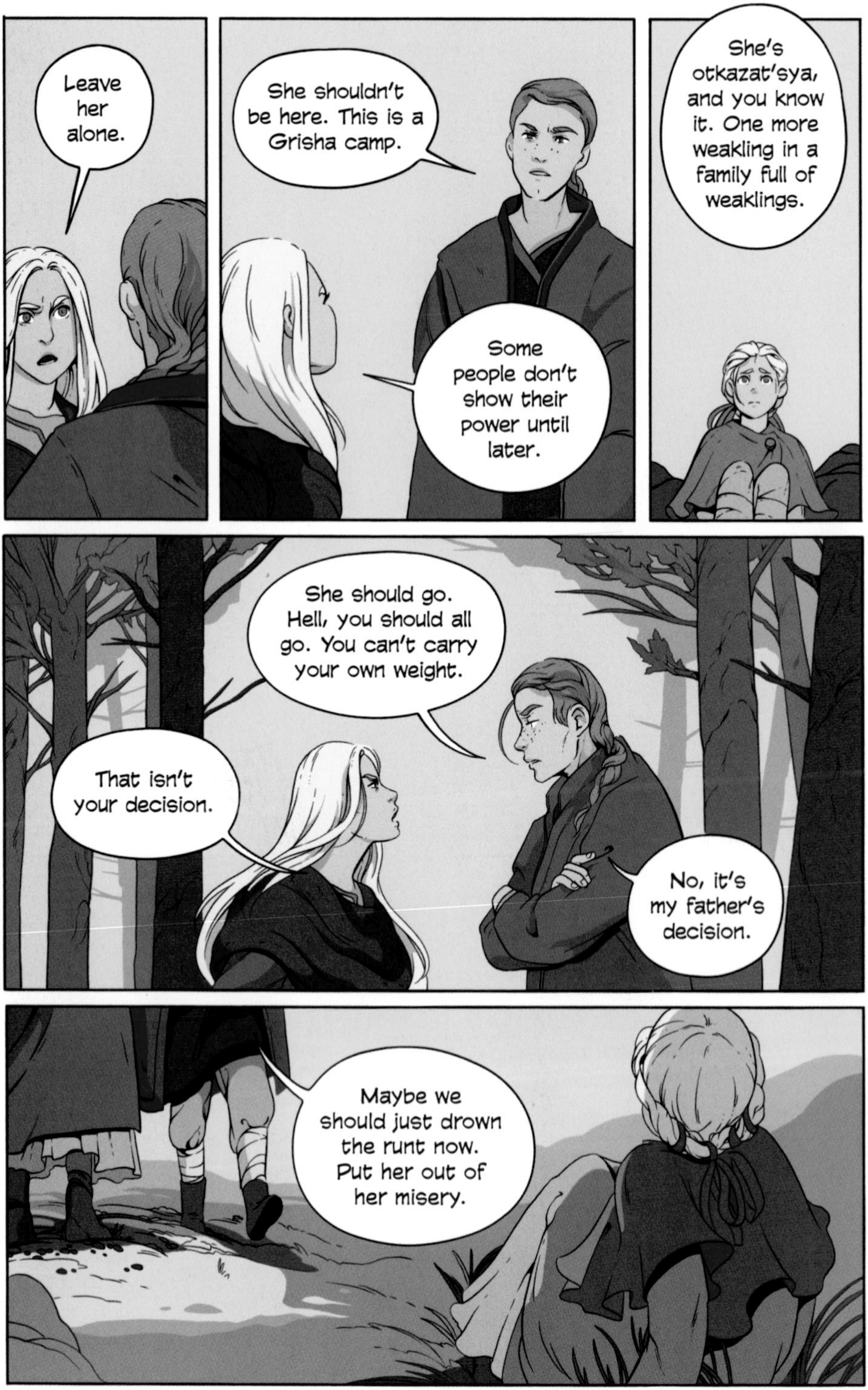
Leave her alone.
She shouldn't be here. This is a Grisha camp.
Some people don't show their power until later.
She's otkazat'sya, and you know it. One more weakling in a family full of weaklings.
She should go. Hell, you should all go. You can't carry your own weight.
That isn't your decision.
No, it's my father's decision.
Maybe we should just drown the runt now. Put her out of her misery.

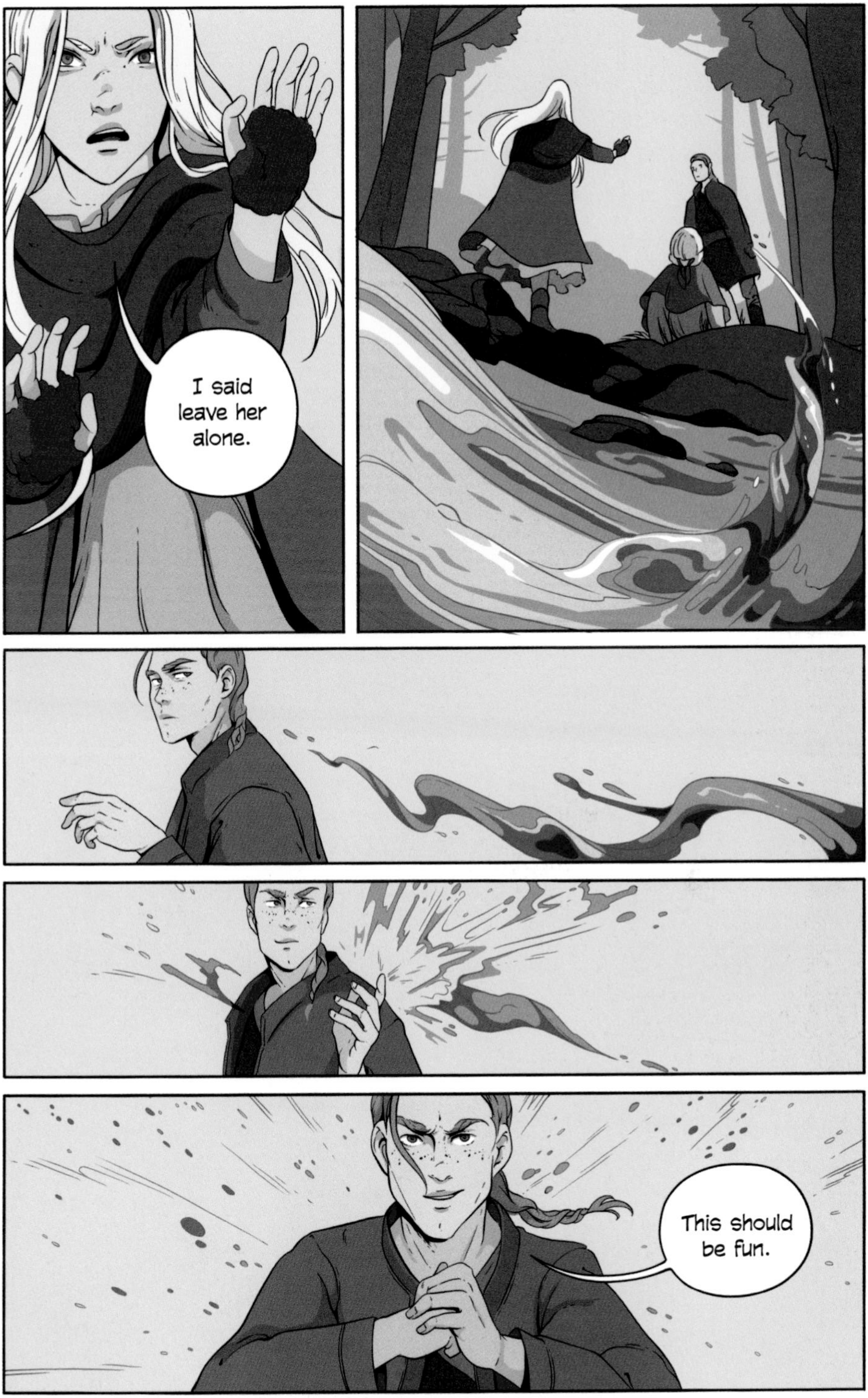
I said leave her alone.
This should be fun.

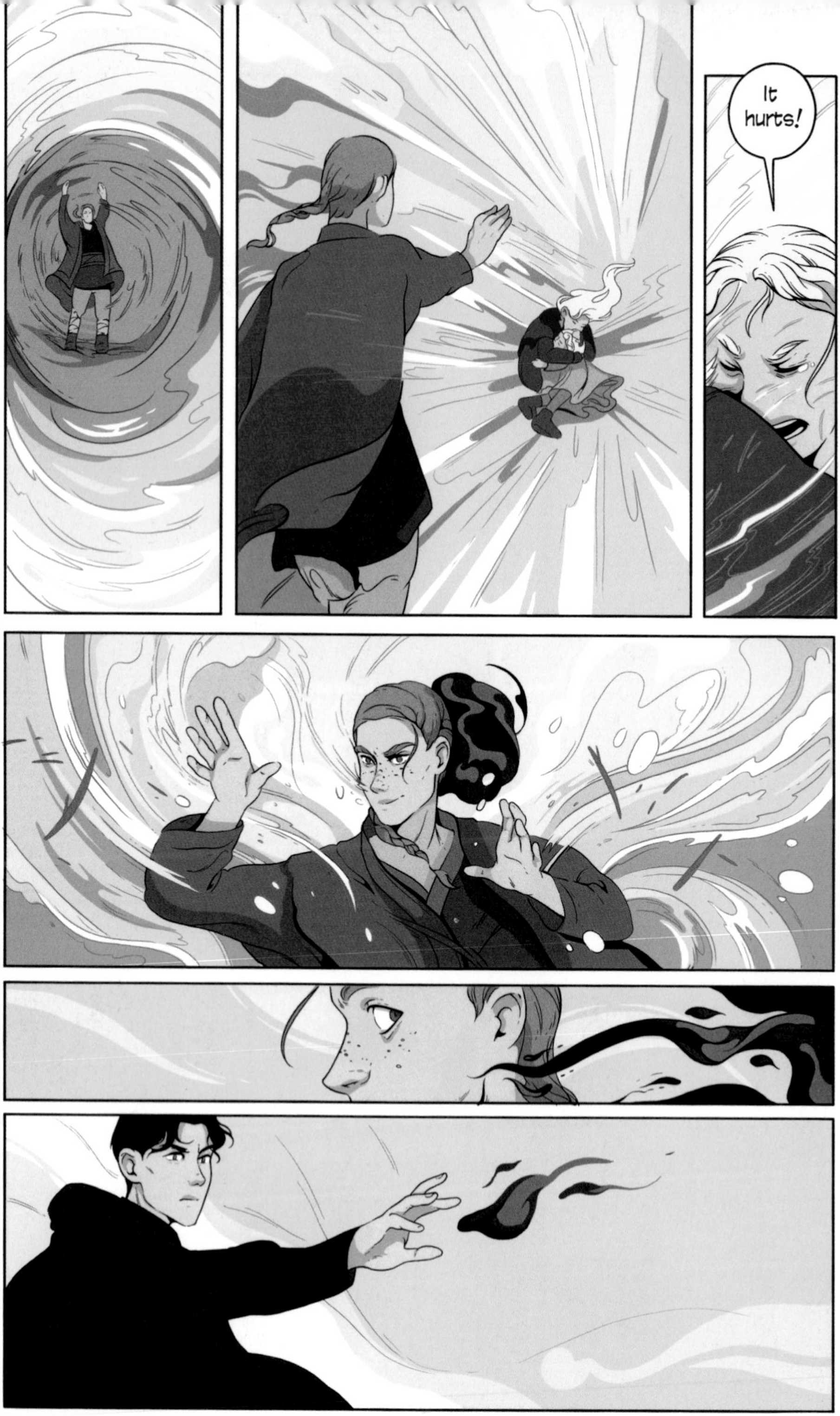
It hurts!

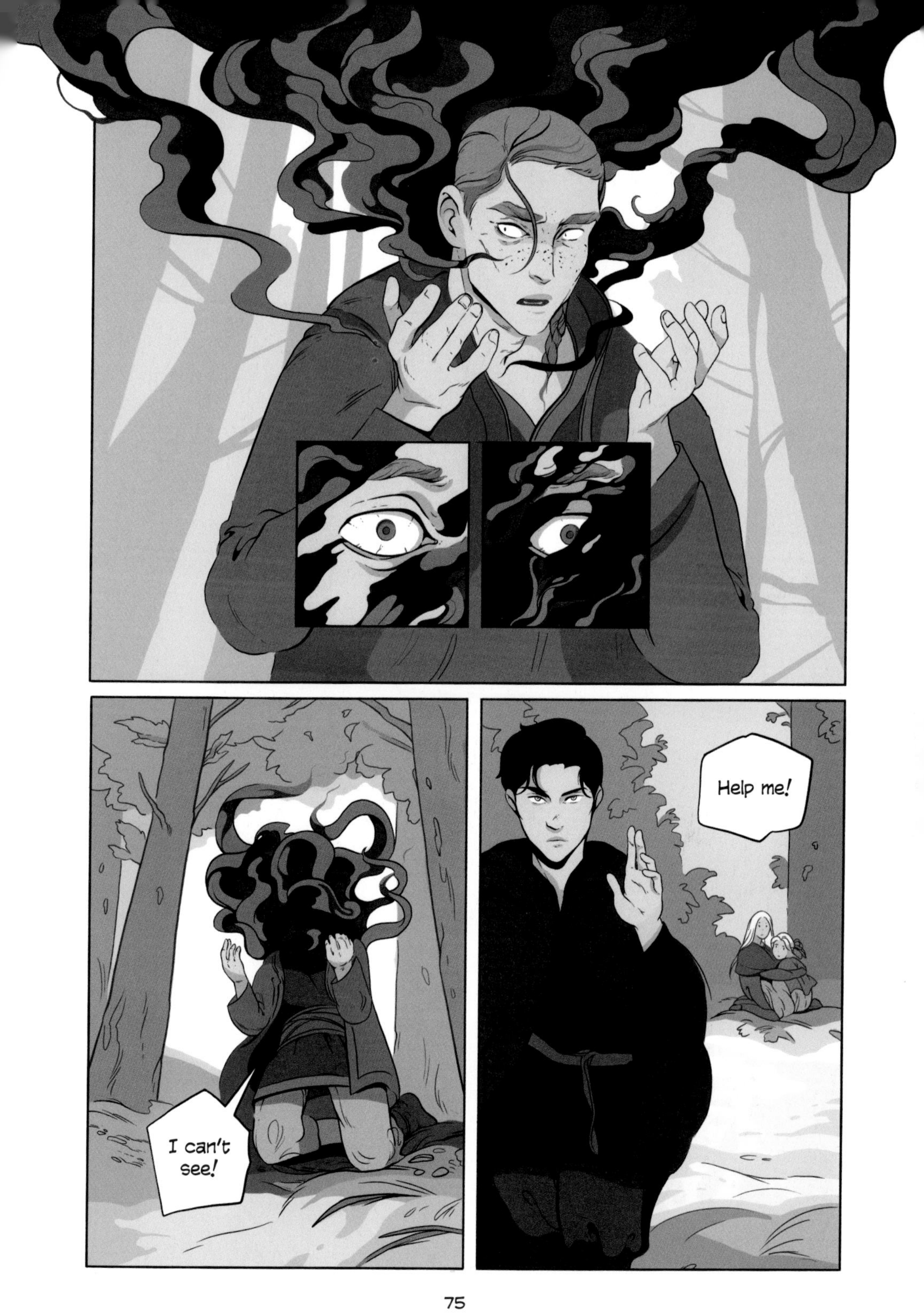
I can't see!
Help me!

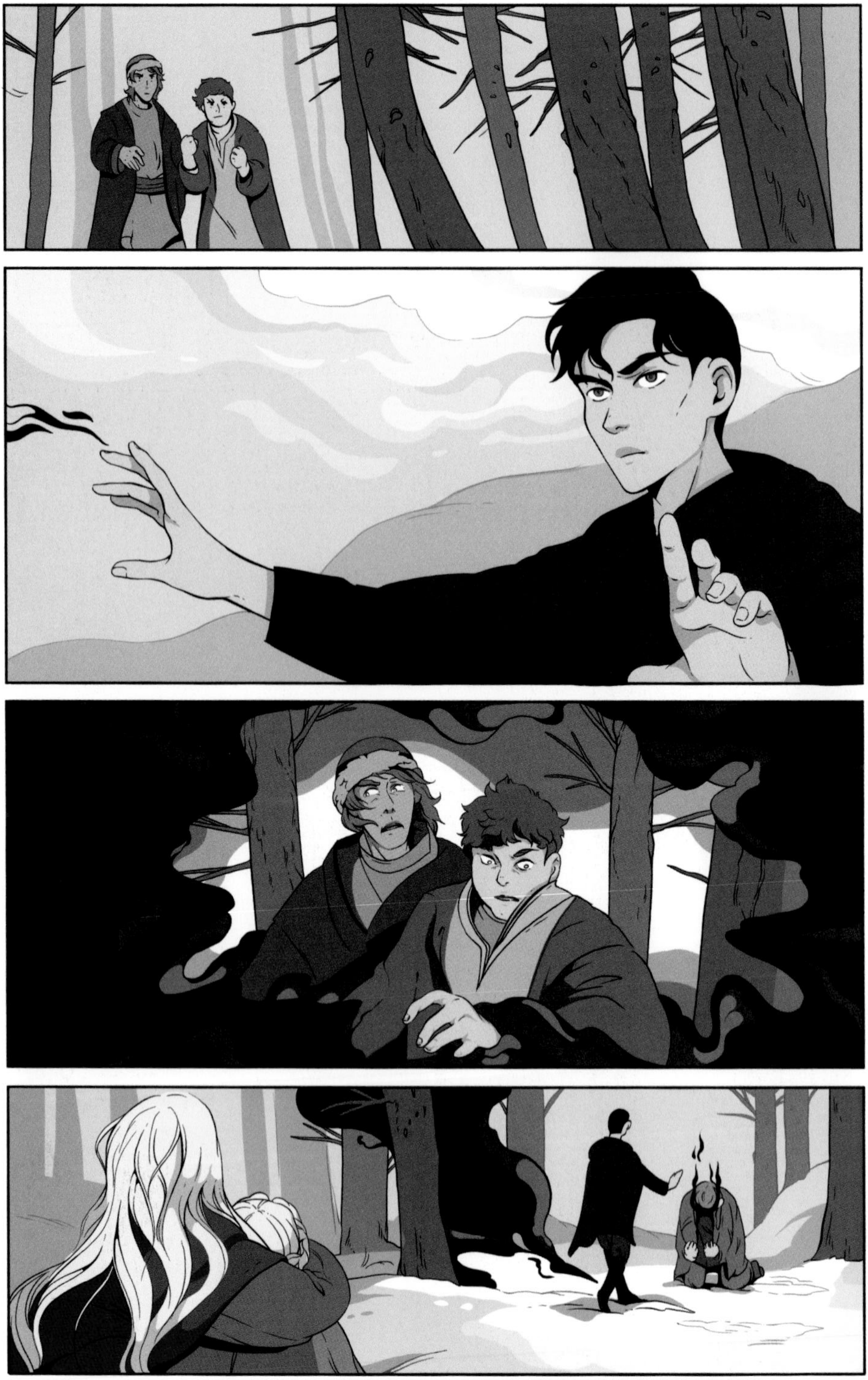

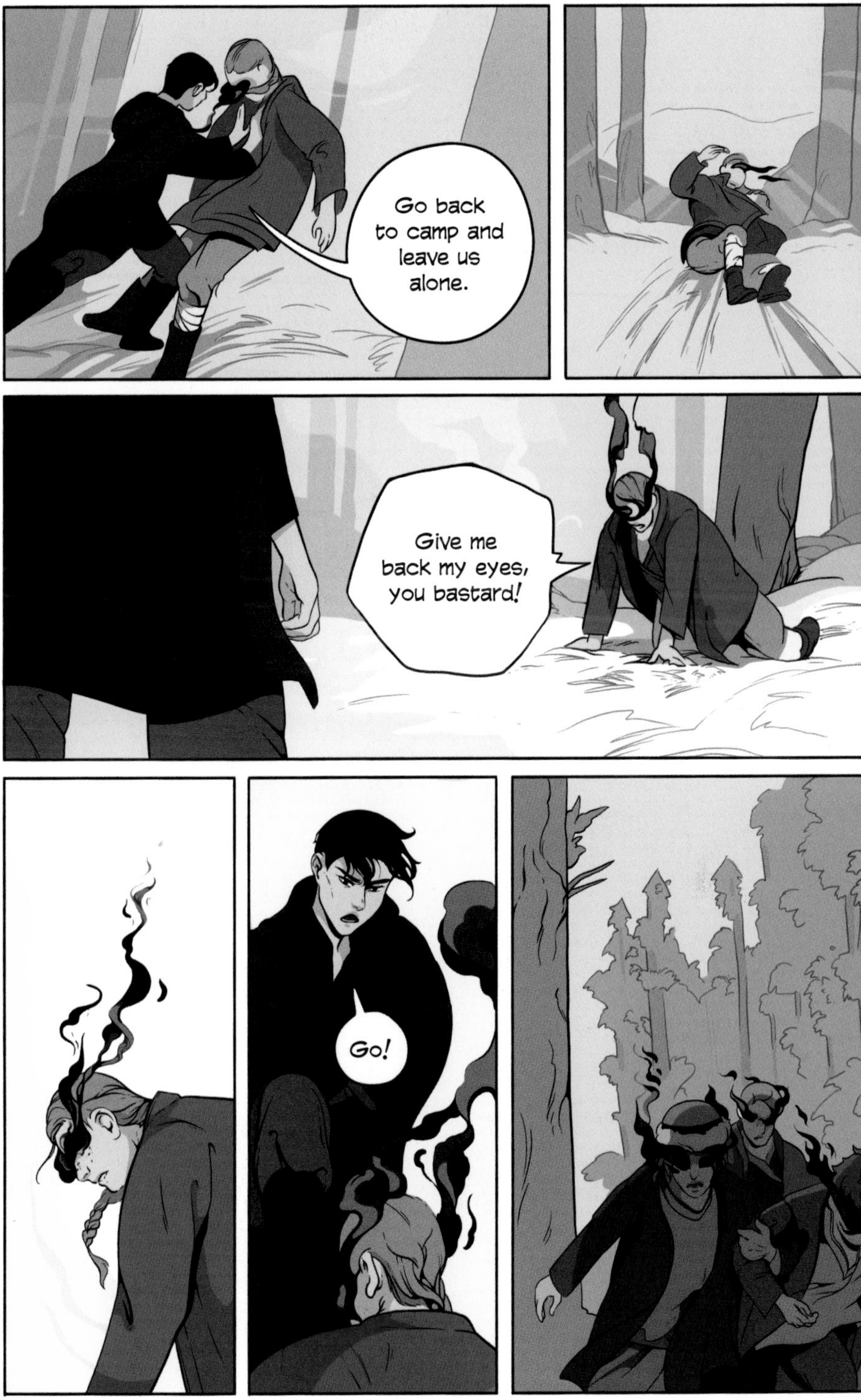
Go back to camp and leave us alone.
Give me back my eyes, you bastard!
Go!

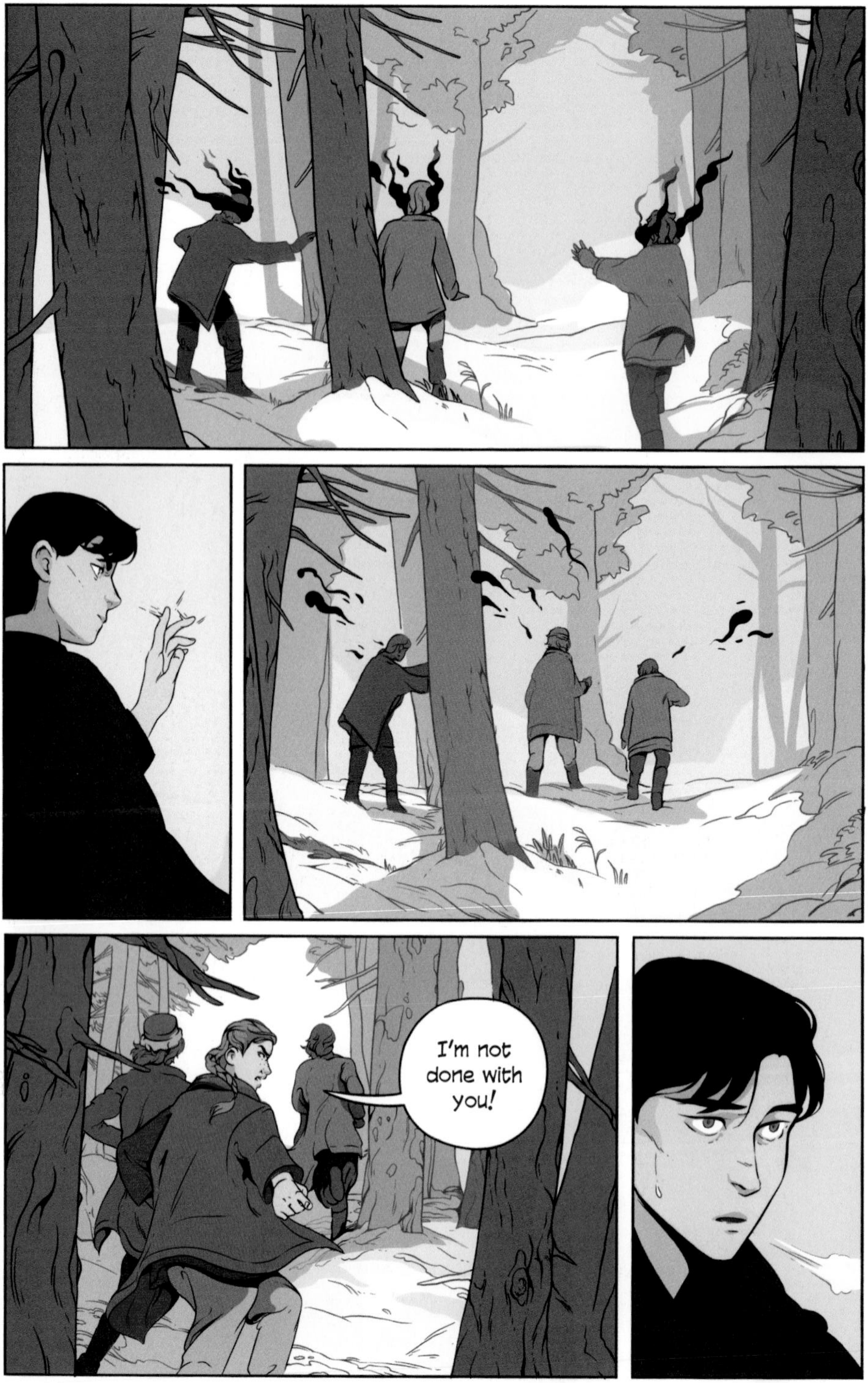
I'm not done with you!

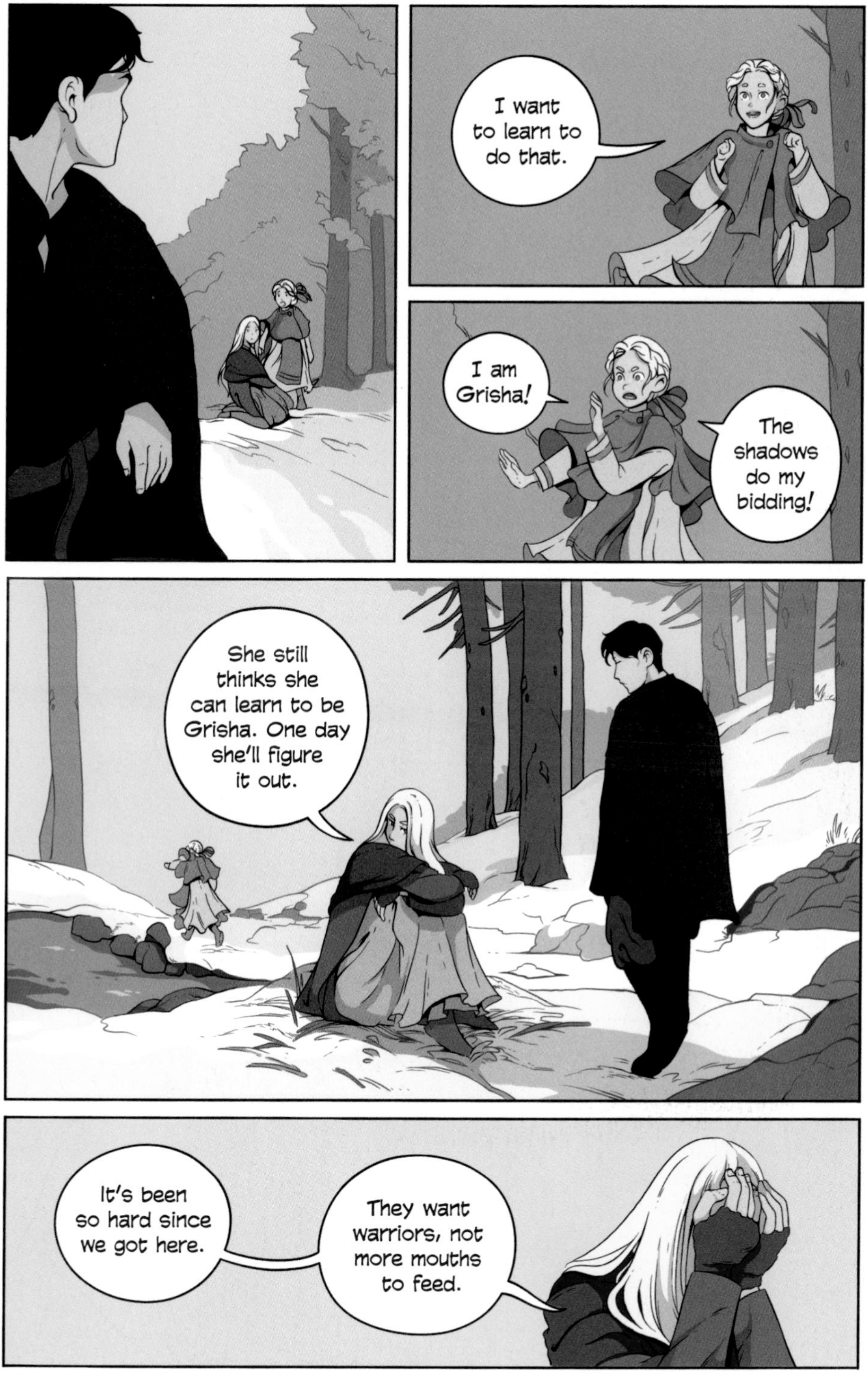

I want to learn to do that.
I am Grisha!
The shadows do my bidding!
She still thinks she can learn to be Grisha. One day she'll figure it out.
It's been so hard since we got here.
They want warriors, not more mouths to feed.

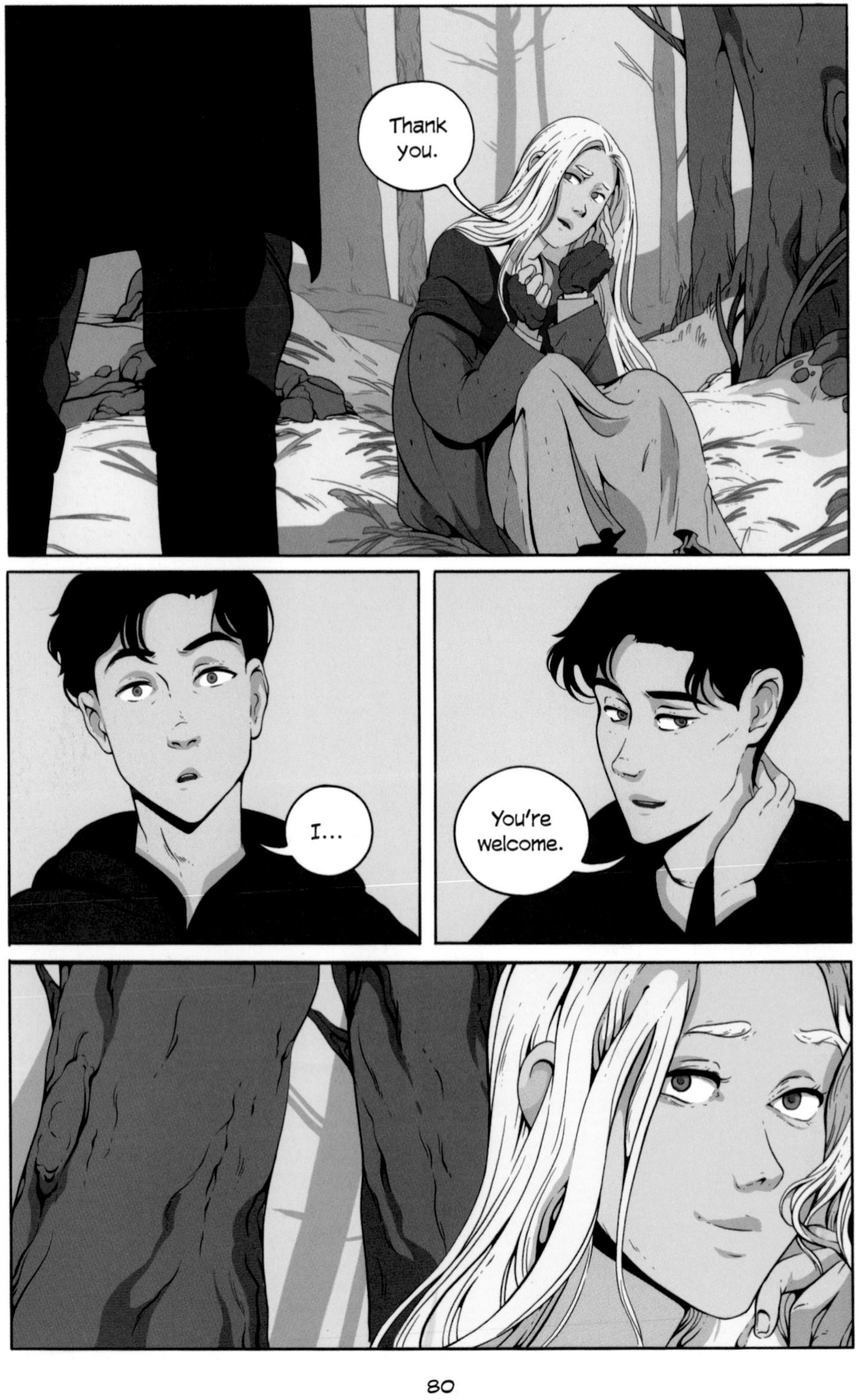
Thank you.
I...
You're welcome.

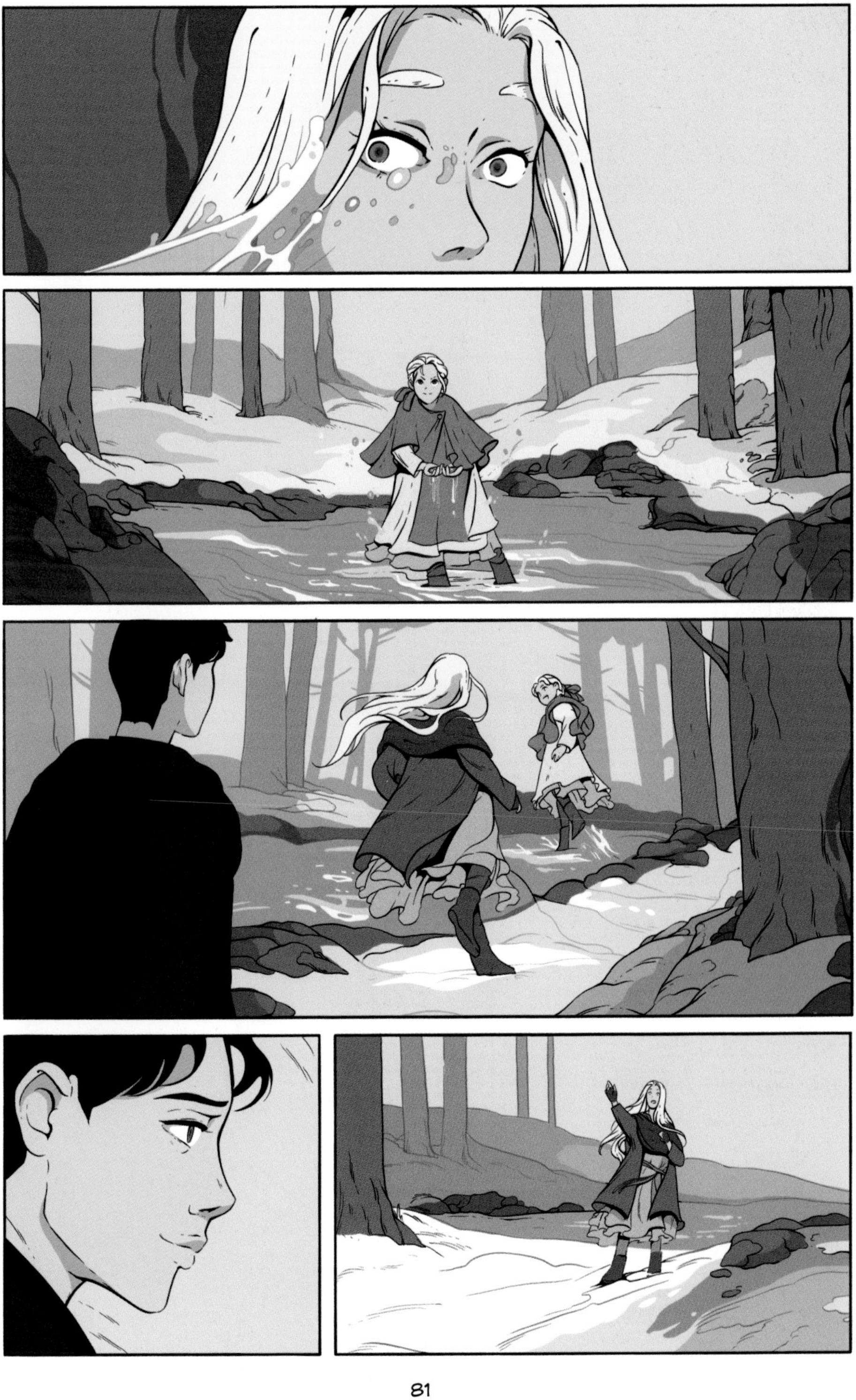

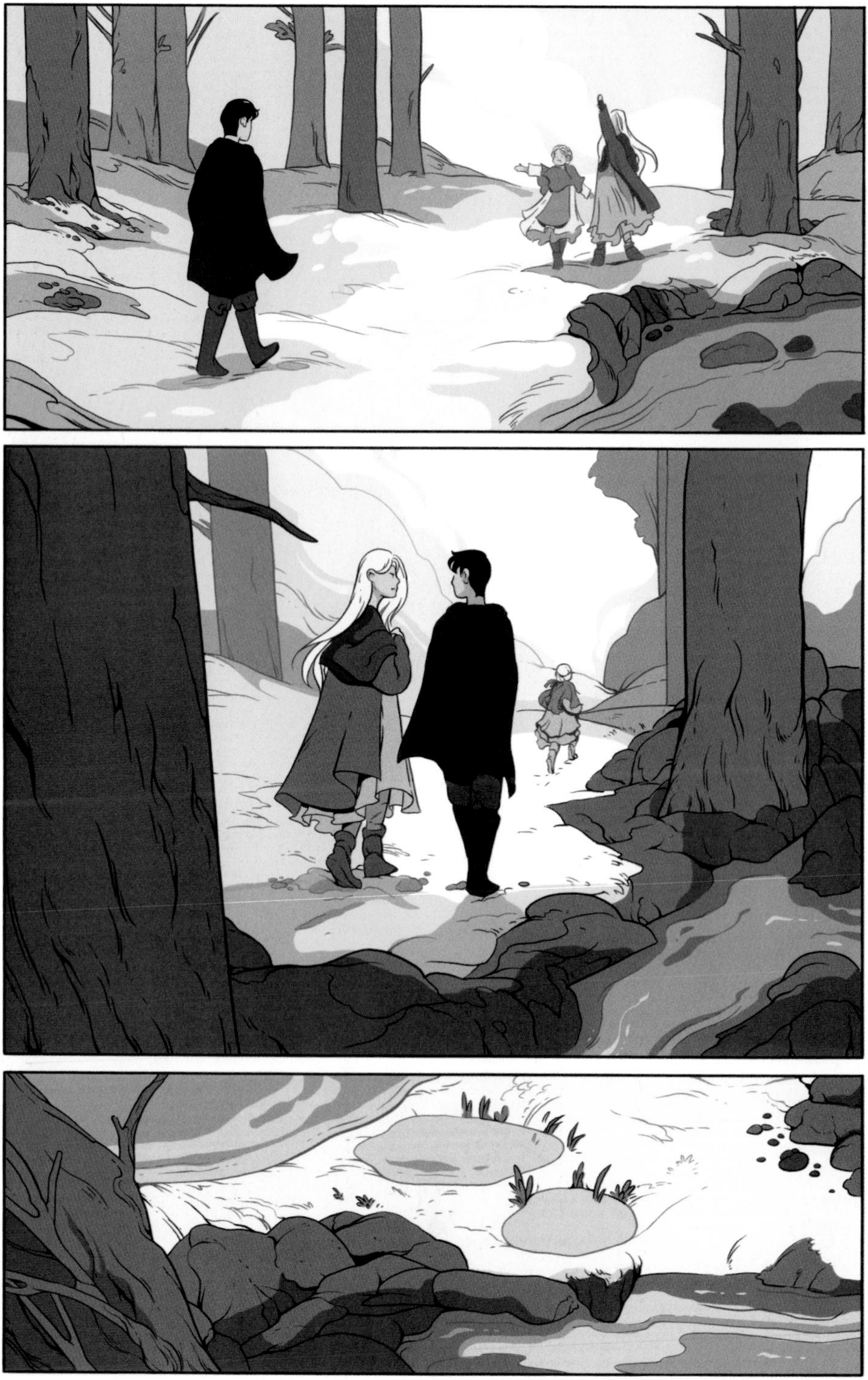

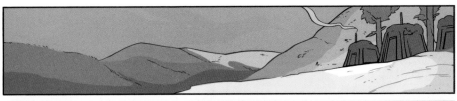

There you are.

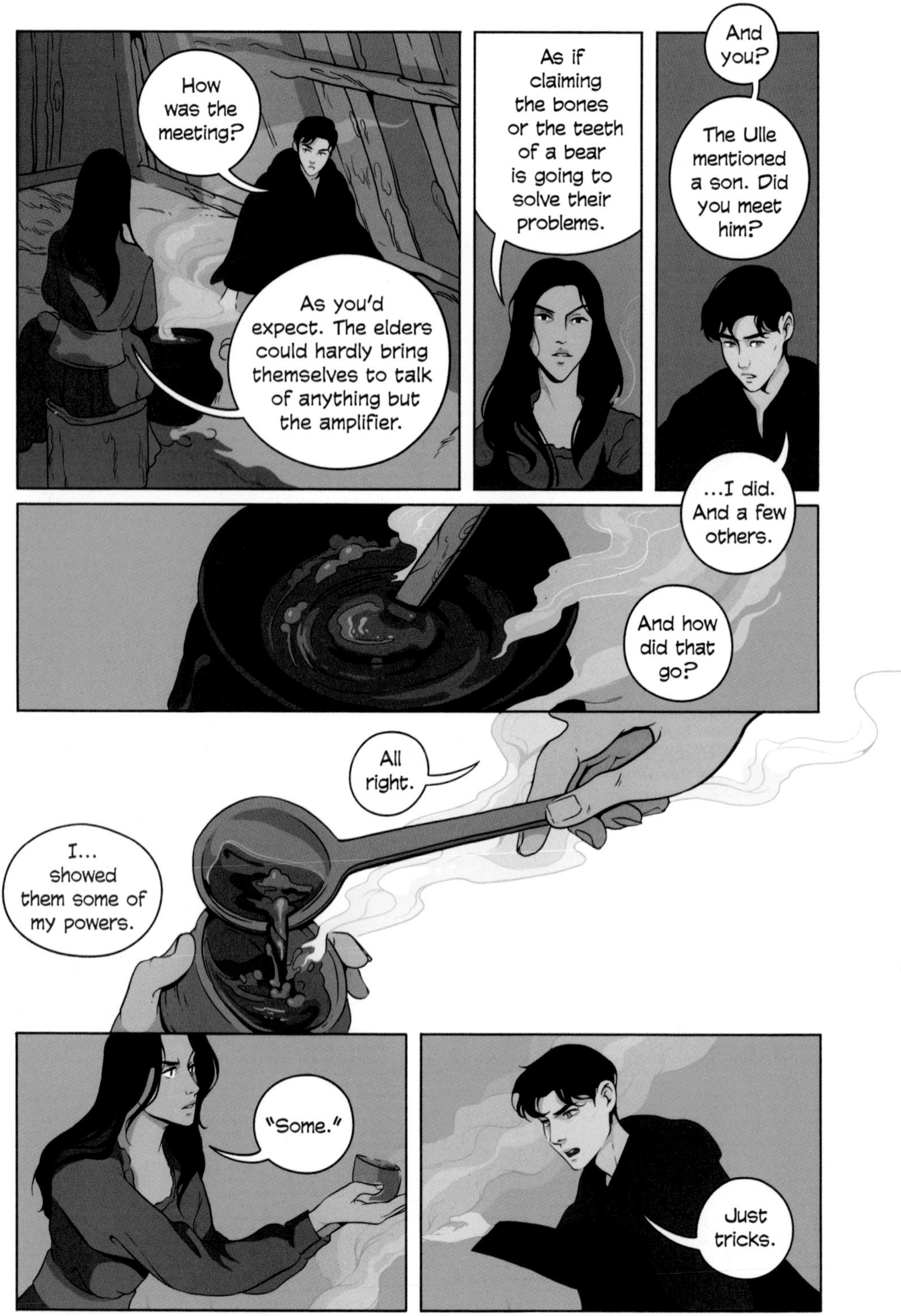
How was the meeting?
As you'd expect. The elders could hardly bring themselves to talk of anything but the amplifier.
As if claiming the bones or the teeth of a bear is going to solve their problems.
And you?
The Ulle mentioned a son. Did you meet him?
...I did. And a few others.
And how did that go?
All right.
I... showed them some of my powers.
"Some."
Just tricks.

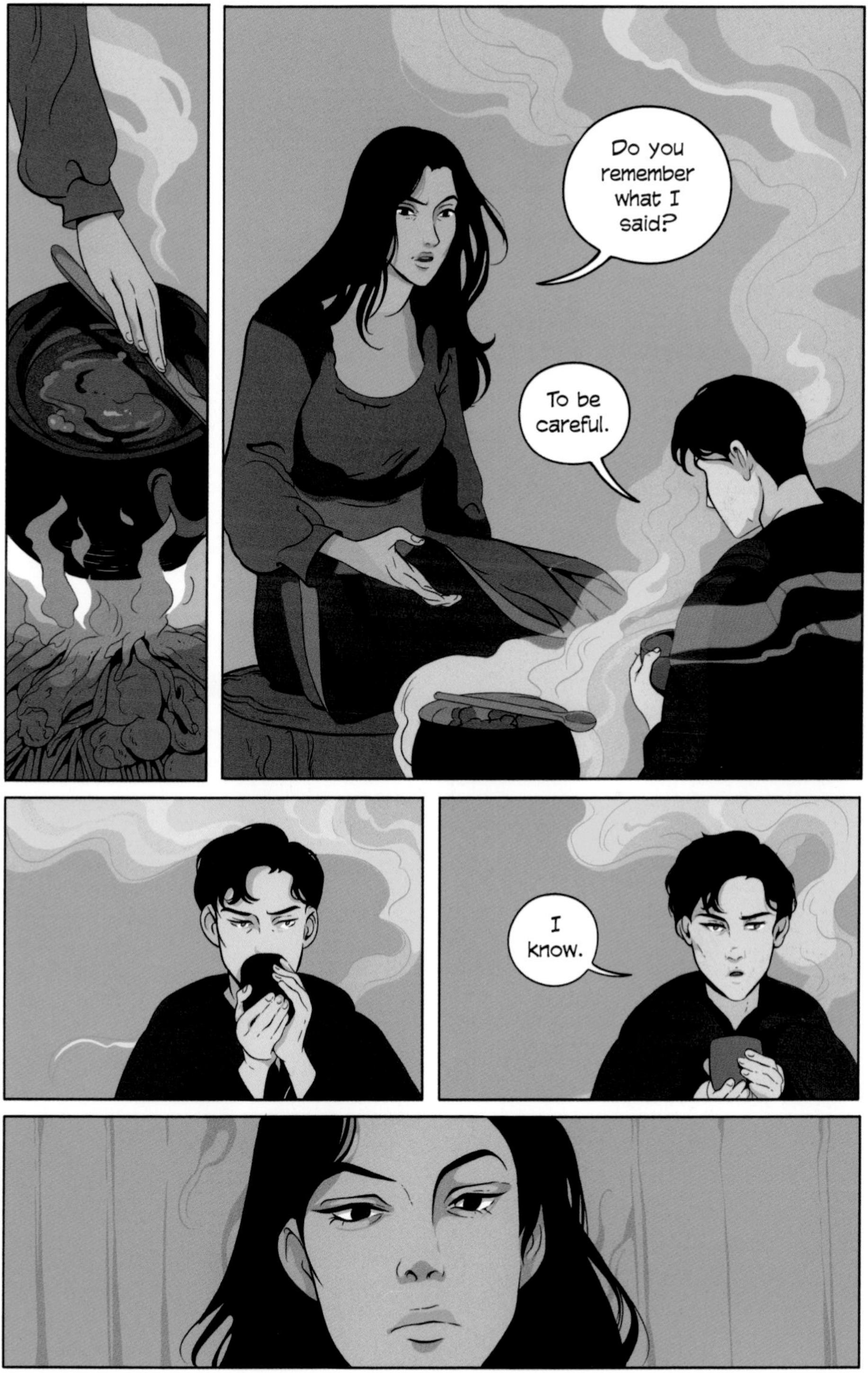

Do you remember what I said?
To be careful.
I know.

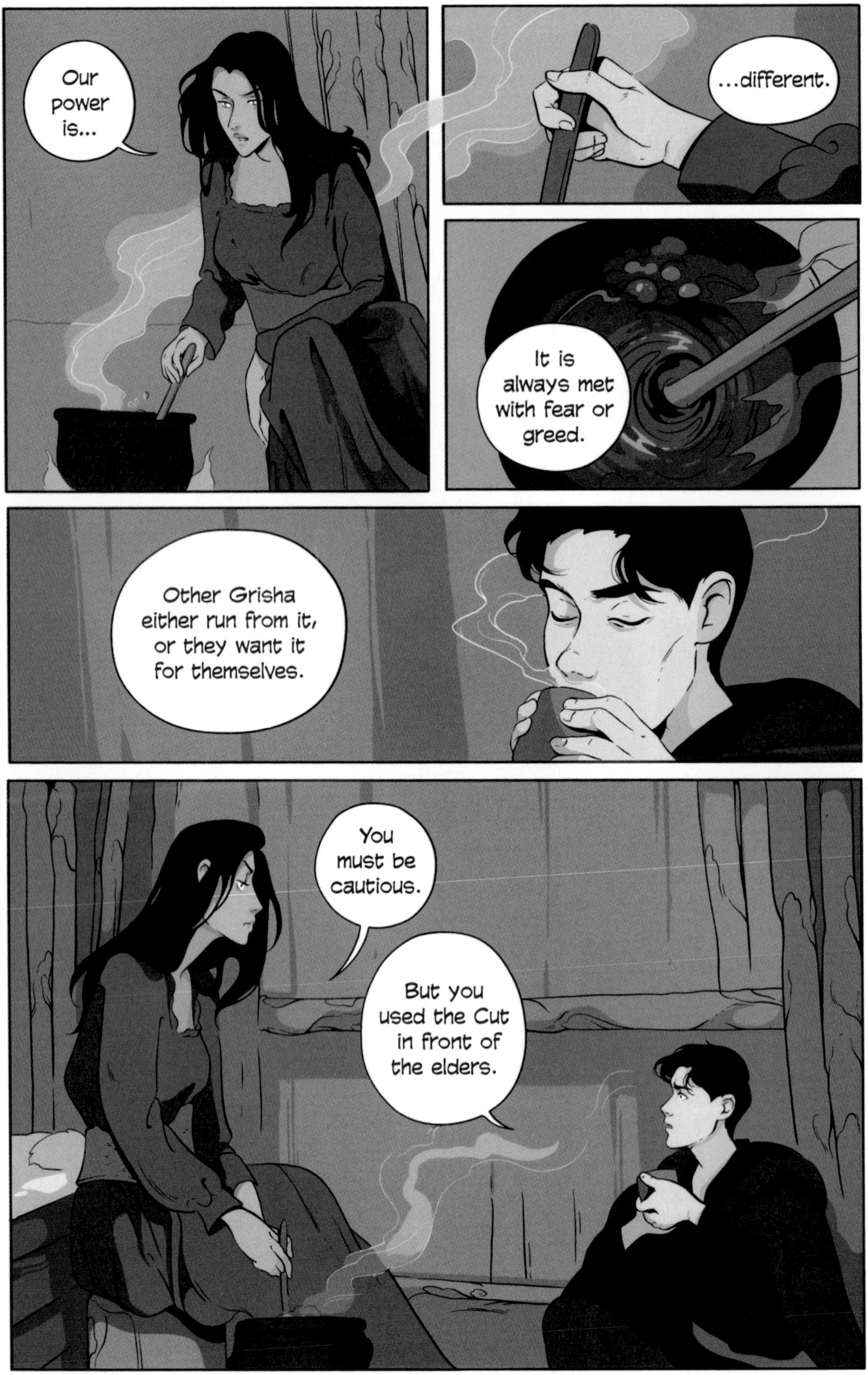
Our power is...
...different.
It is always met with fear or greed.
Other Grisha either run from it, or they want it for themselves.
You must be cautious.
But you used the Cut in front of the elders.

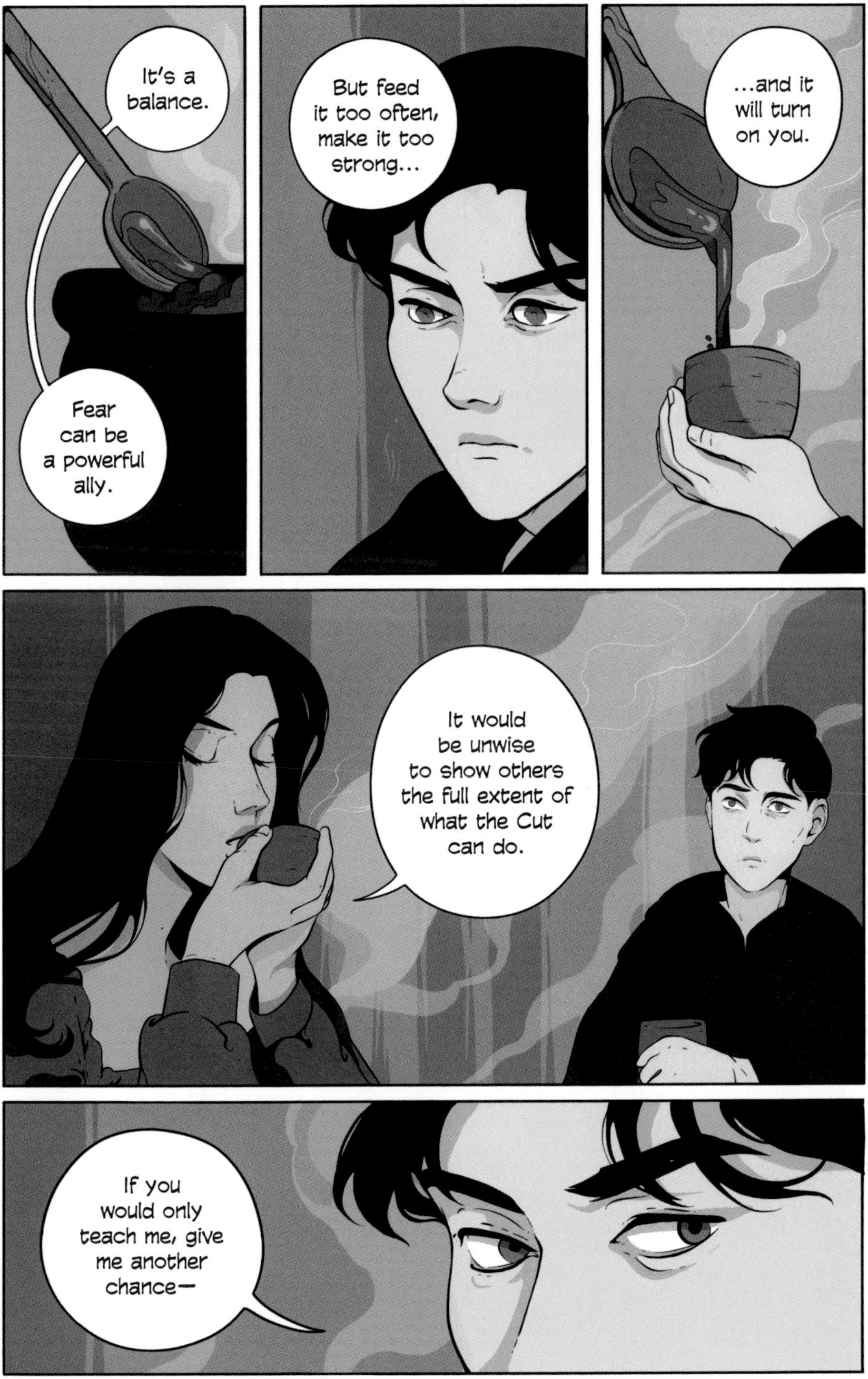
It's a balance.
Fear can be a powerful ally.
But feed it too often, make it too strong...
...and it will turn on you.
It would be unwise to show others the full extent of what the Cut can do.
If you would only teach me, give me another chance—

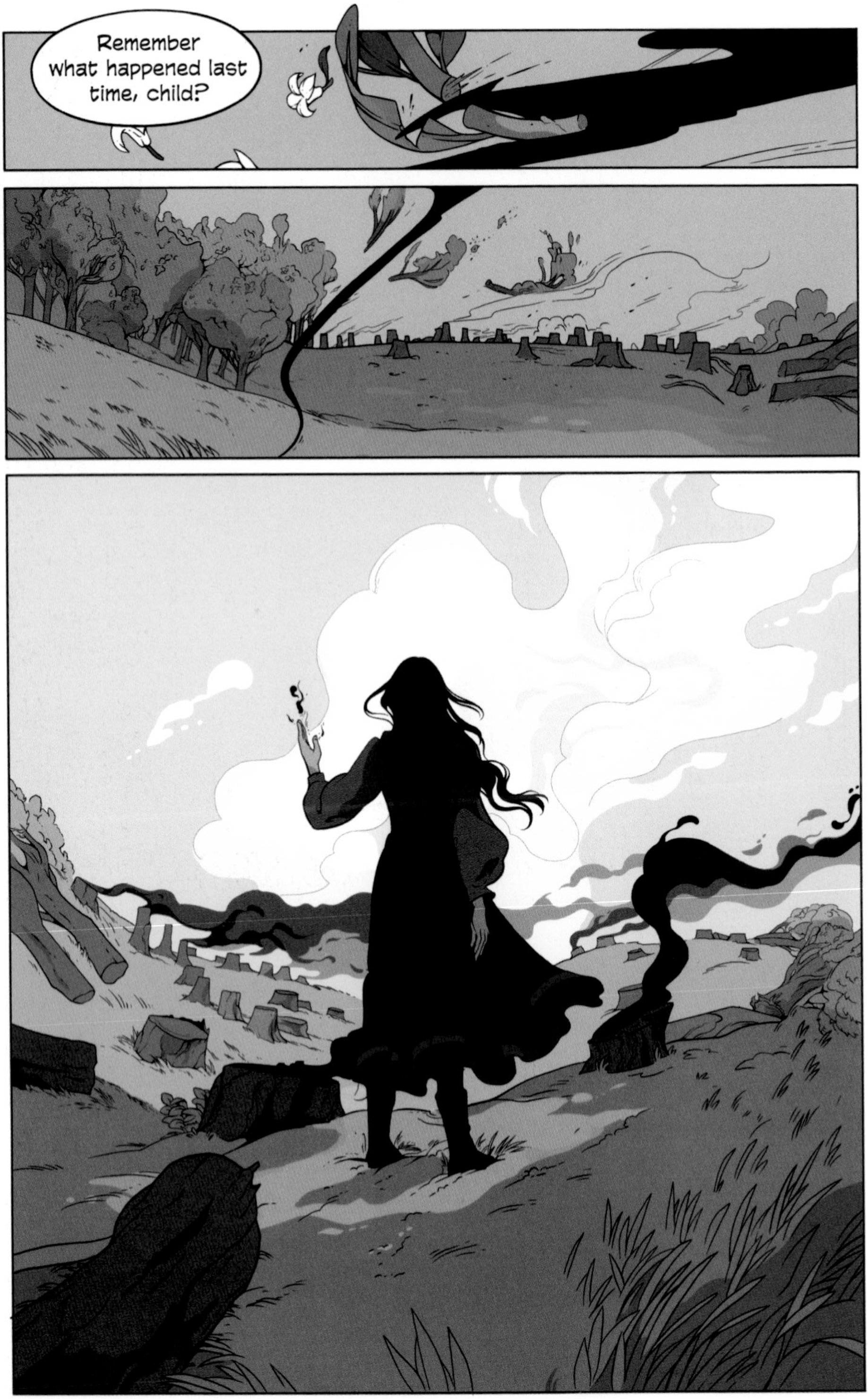
Remember what happened last time, child?

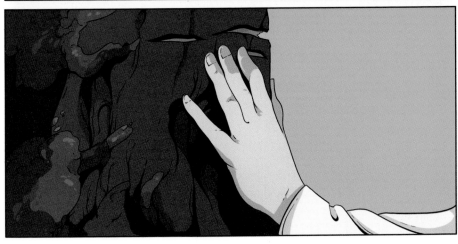

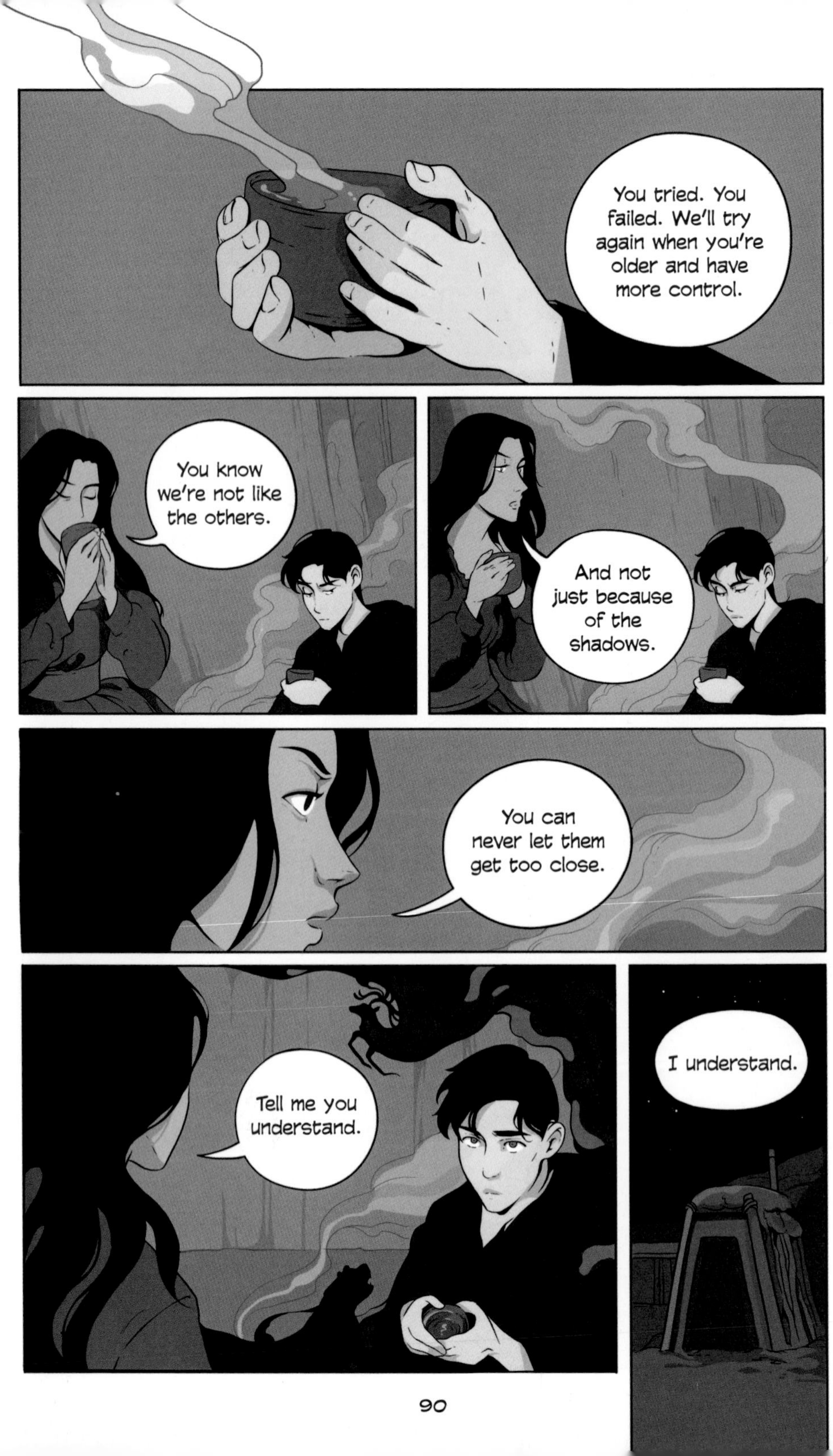
You tried. You failed. We'll try again when you're older and have more control.
You know we're not like the others.
And not just because of the shadows.
You can never let them get too close.
Tell me you understand.
I understand.

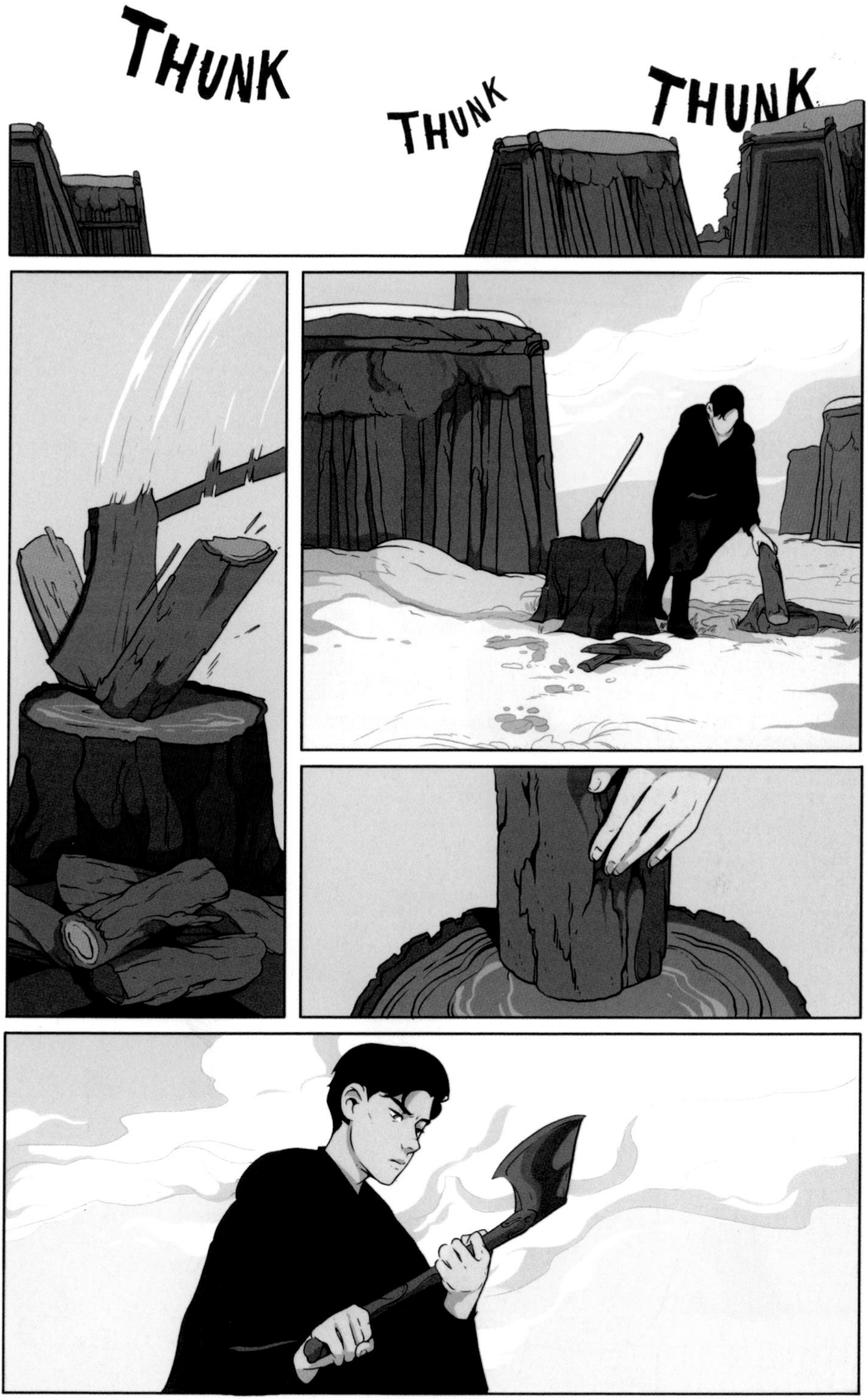
THUNK
THUNK
THUNK

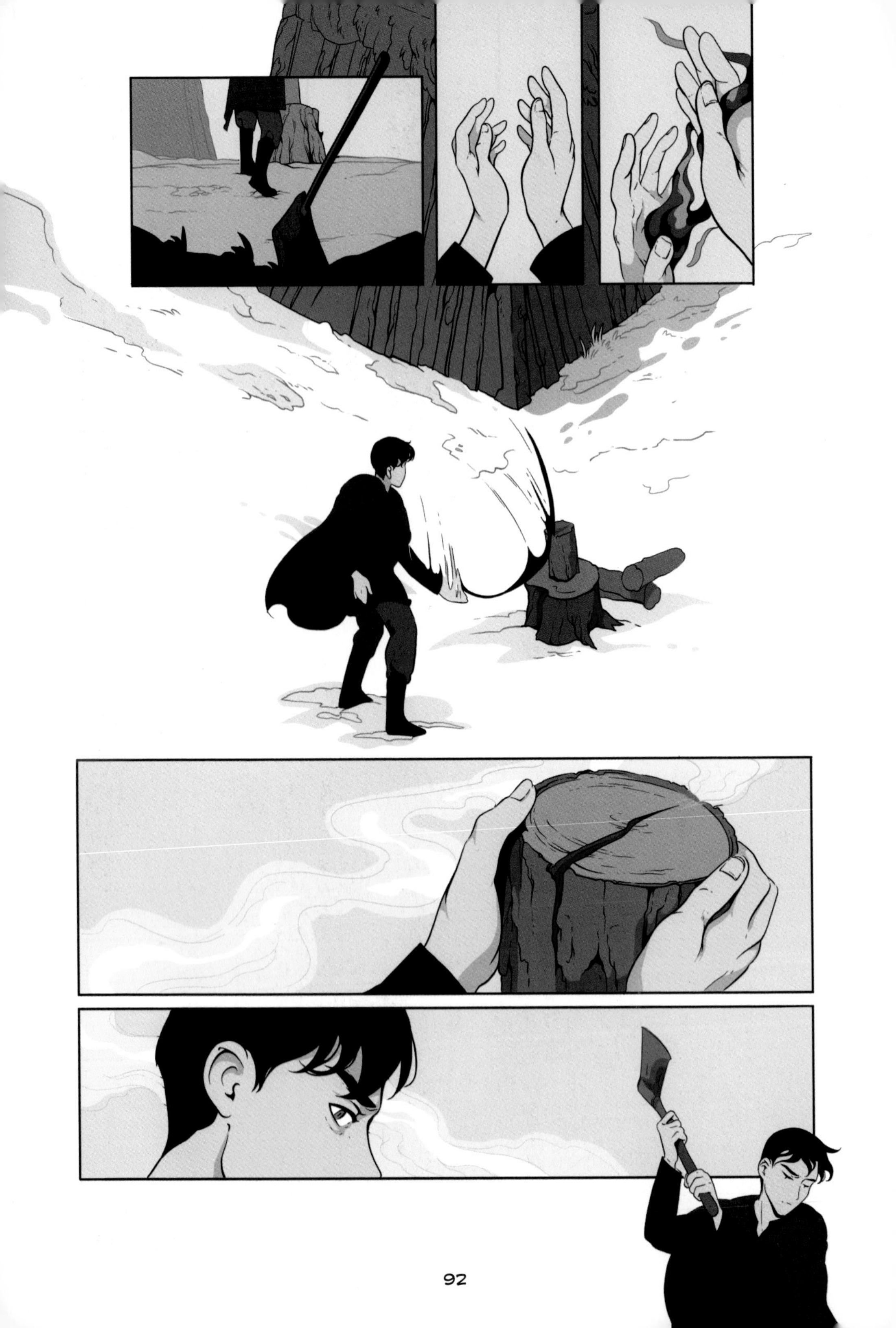

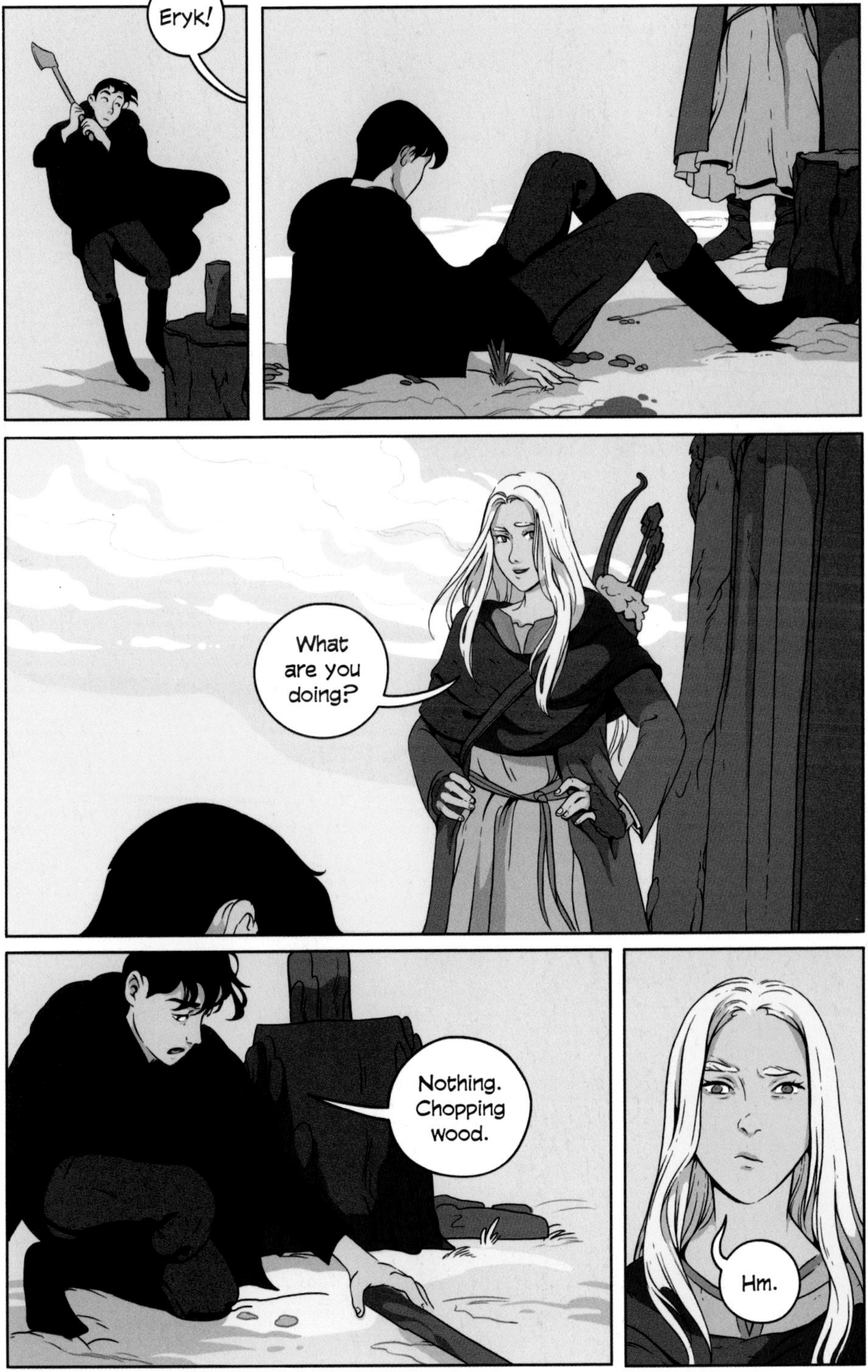

Eryk!
What are you doing?
Nothing. Chopping wood.
Hm.

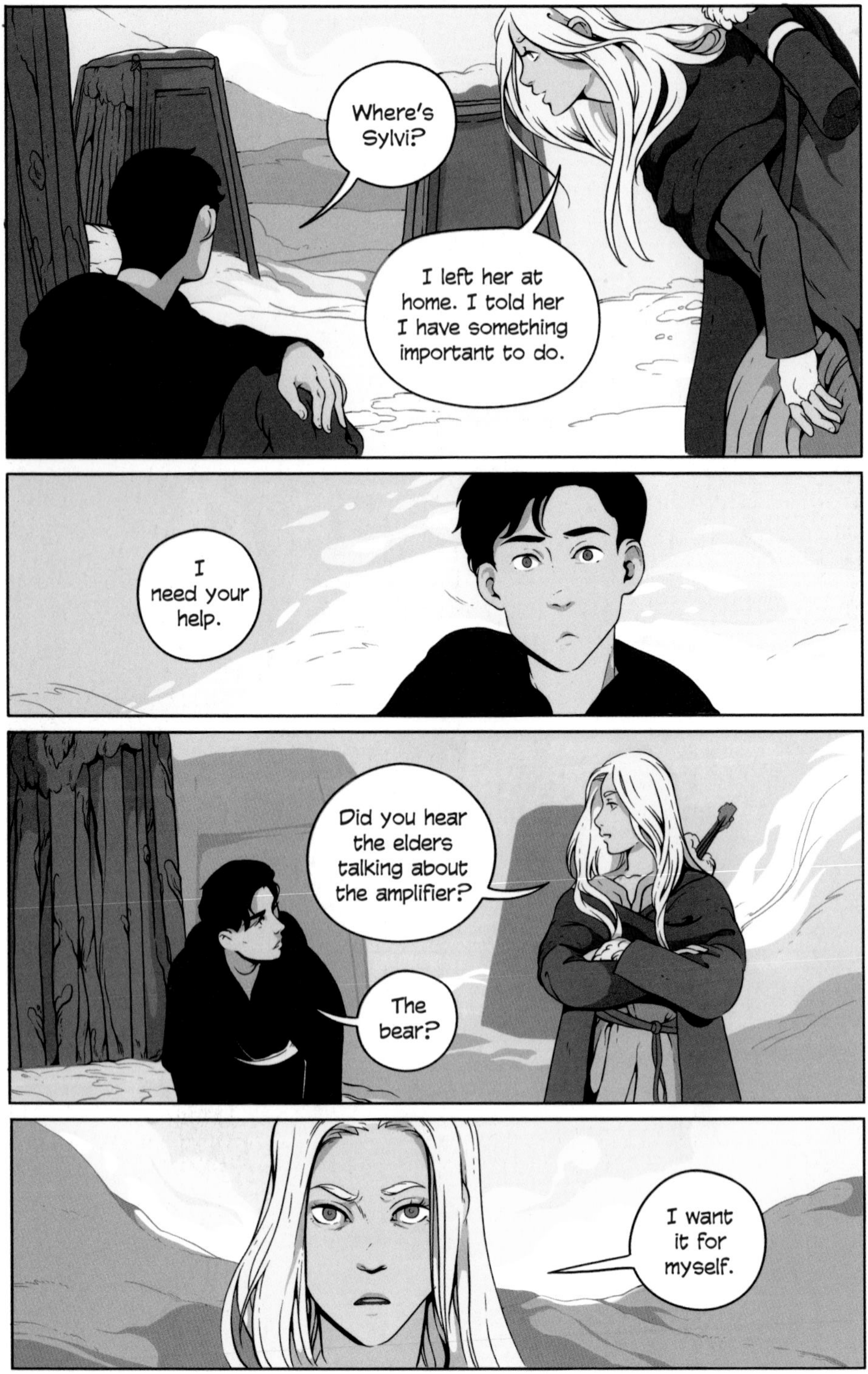
Where's Sylvi?
I left her at home. I told her I have something important to do.
I need your help.
Did you hear the elders talking about the amplifier?
The bear?
I want it for myself.

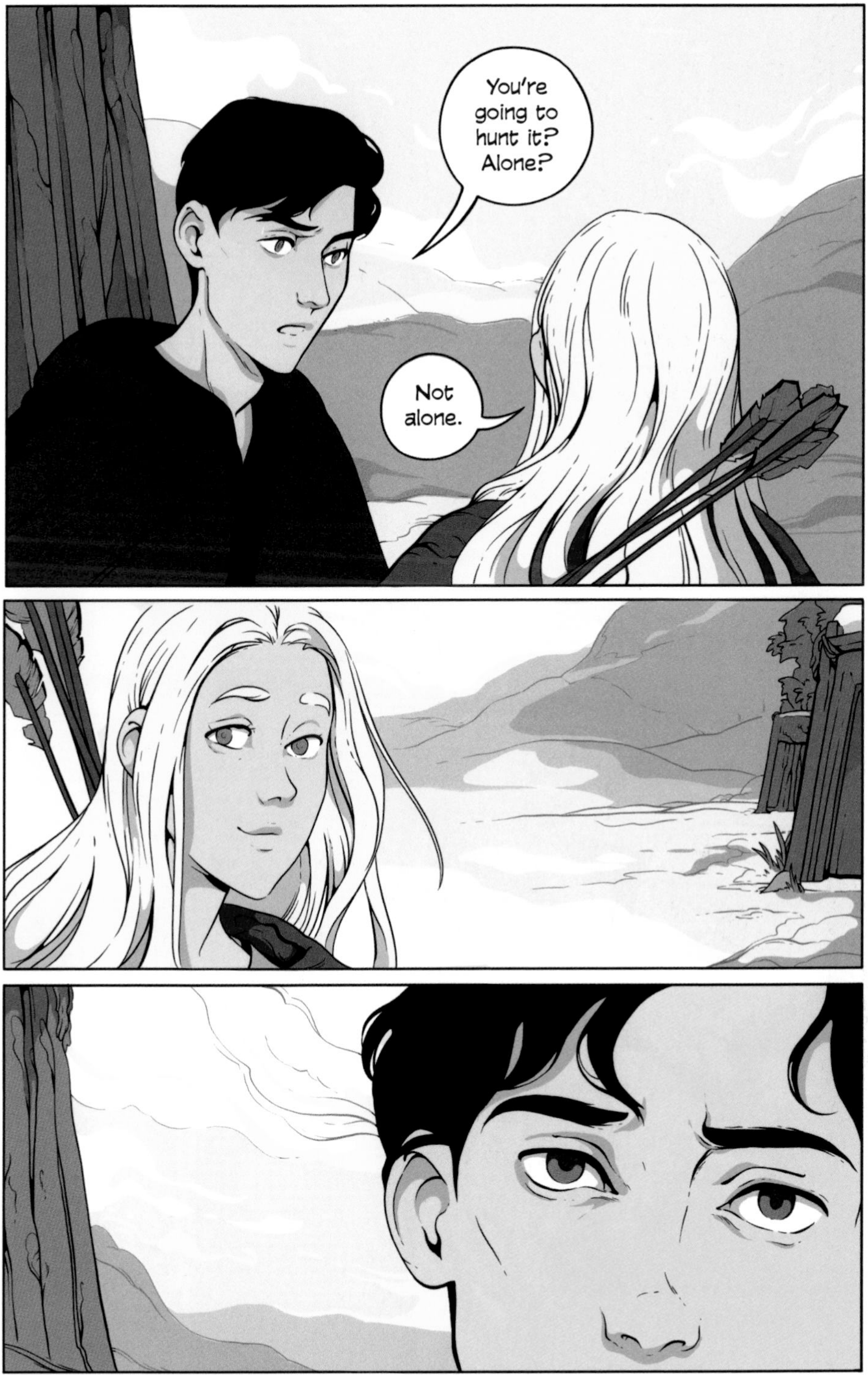
You're going to hunt it? Alone?
Not alone.

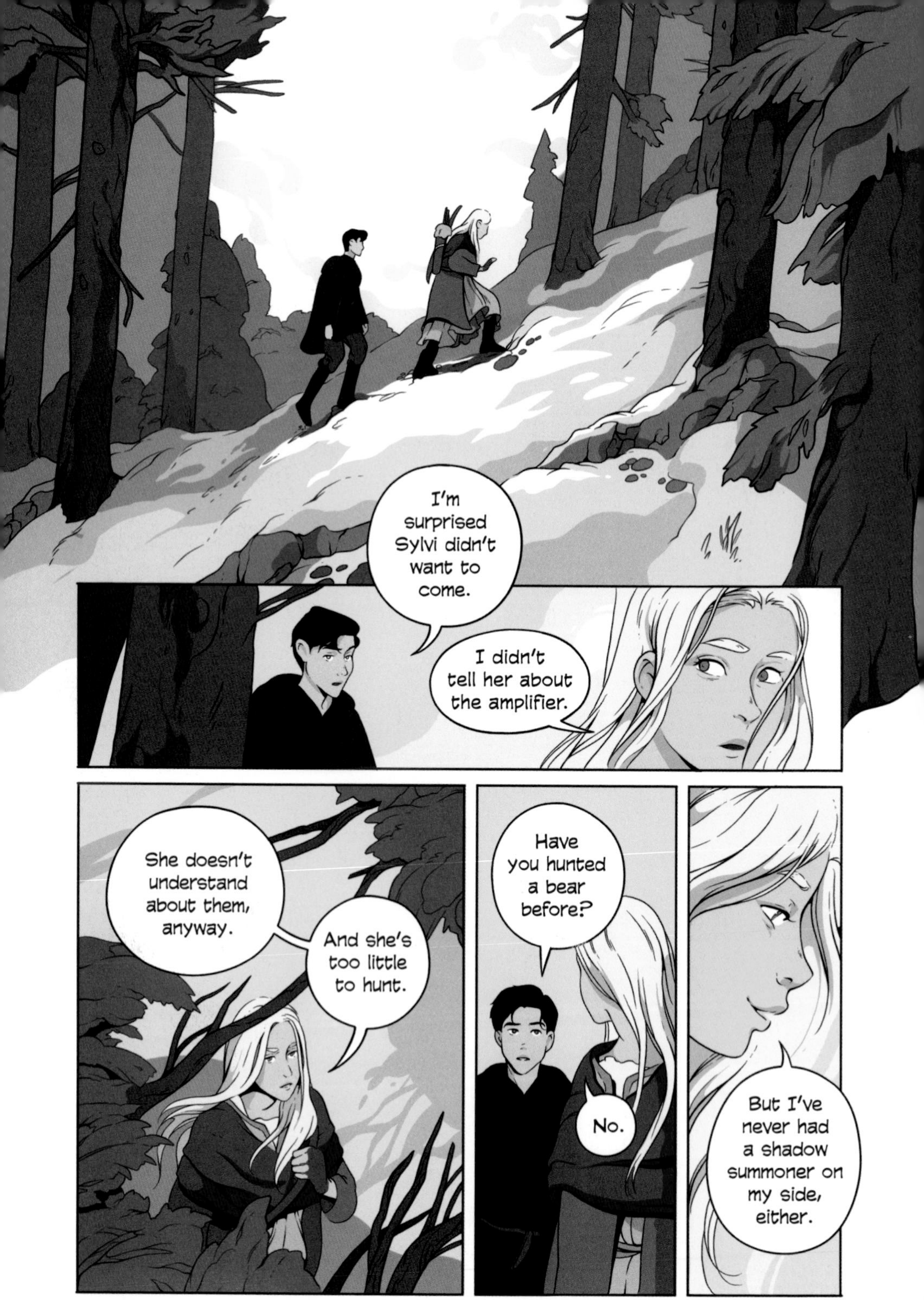
I'm surprised Sylvi didn't want to come.
I didn't tell her about the amplifier.
She doesn't understand about them, anyway.
And she's too little to hunt.
Have you hunted a bear before?
No.
But I've never had a shadow summoner on my side, either.

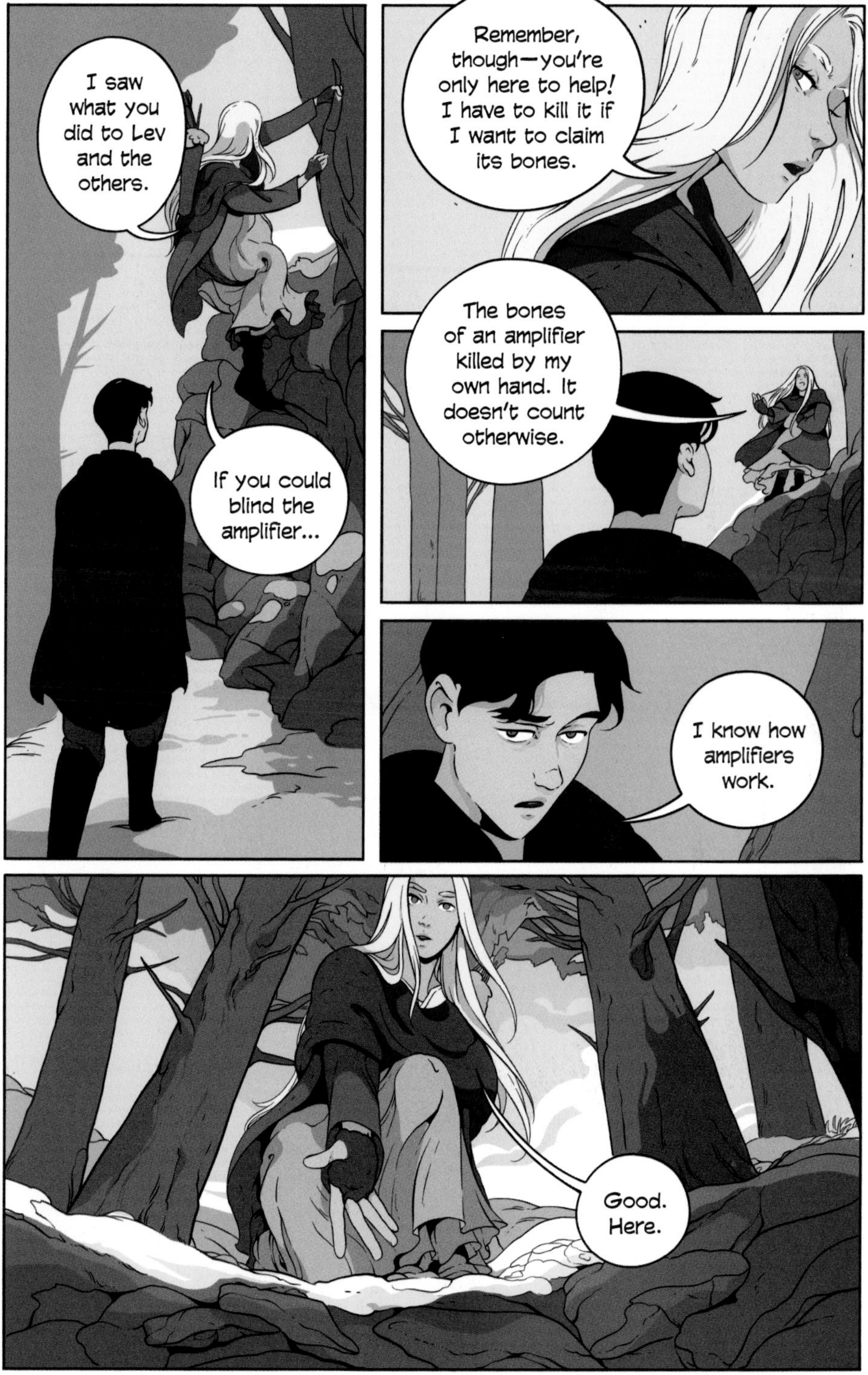
I saw what you did to Lev and the others.
If you could blind the amplifier...
Remember, though—you're only here to help! I have to kill it if I want to claim its bones.
The bones of an amplifier killed by my own hand. It doesn't count otherwise.
I know how amplifiers work.
Good. Here.

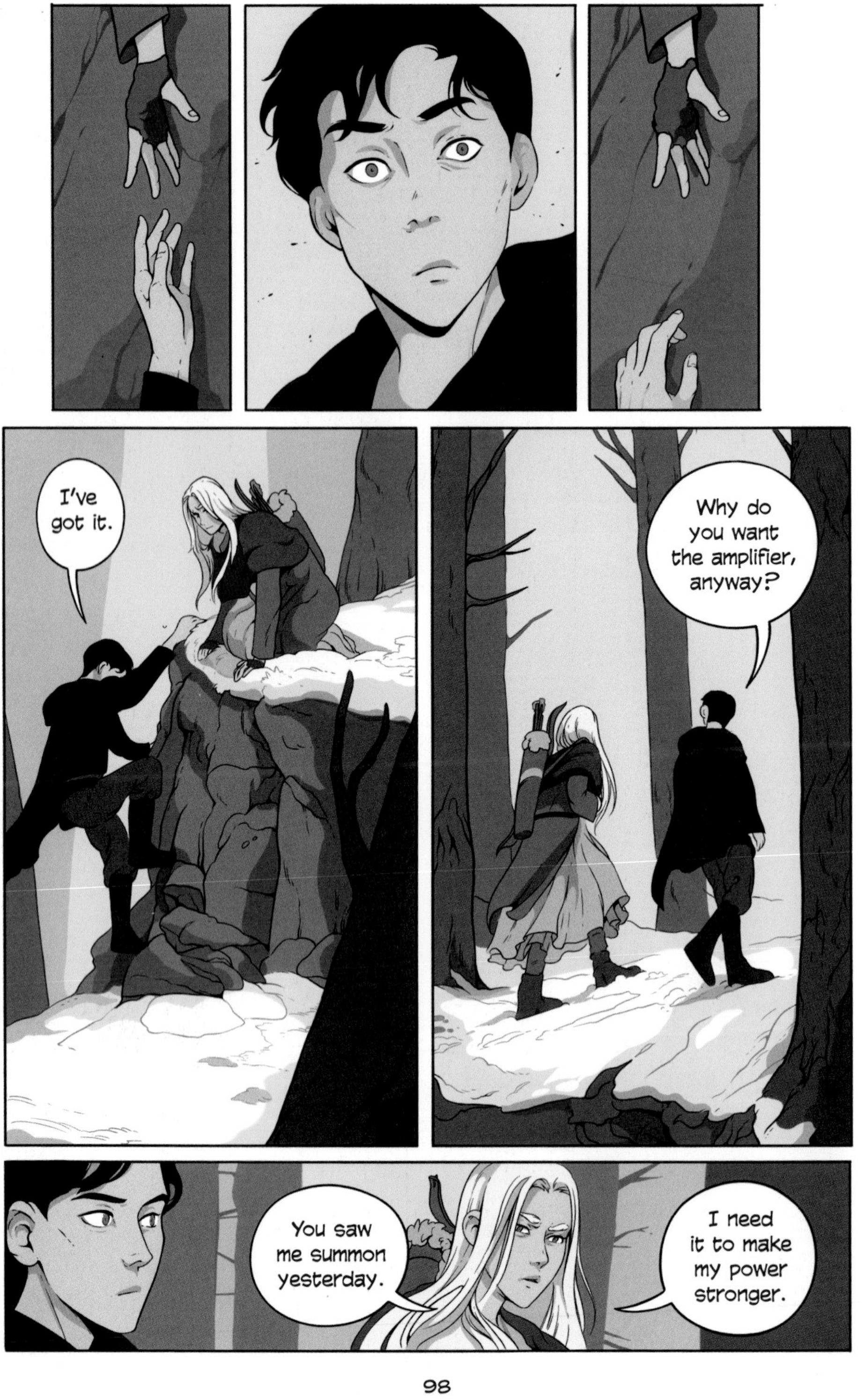
I've got it.
Why do you want the amplifier, anyway?
You saw me summon yesterday.
I need it to make my power stronger.

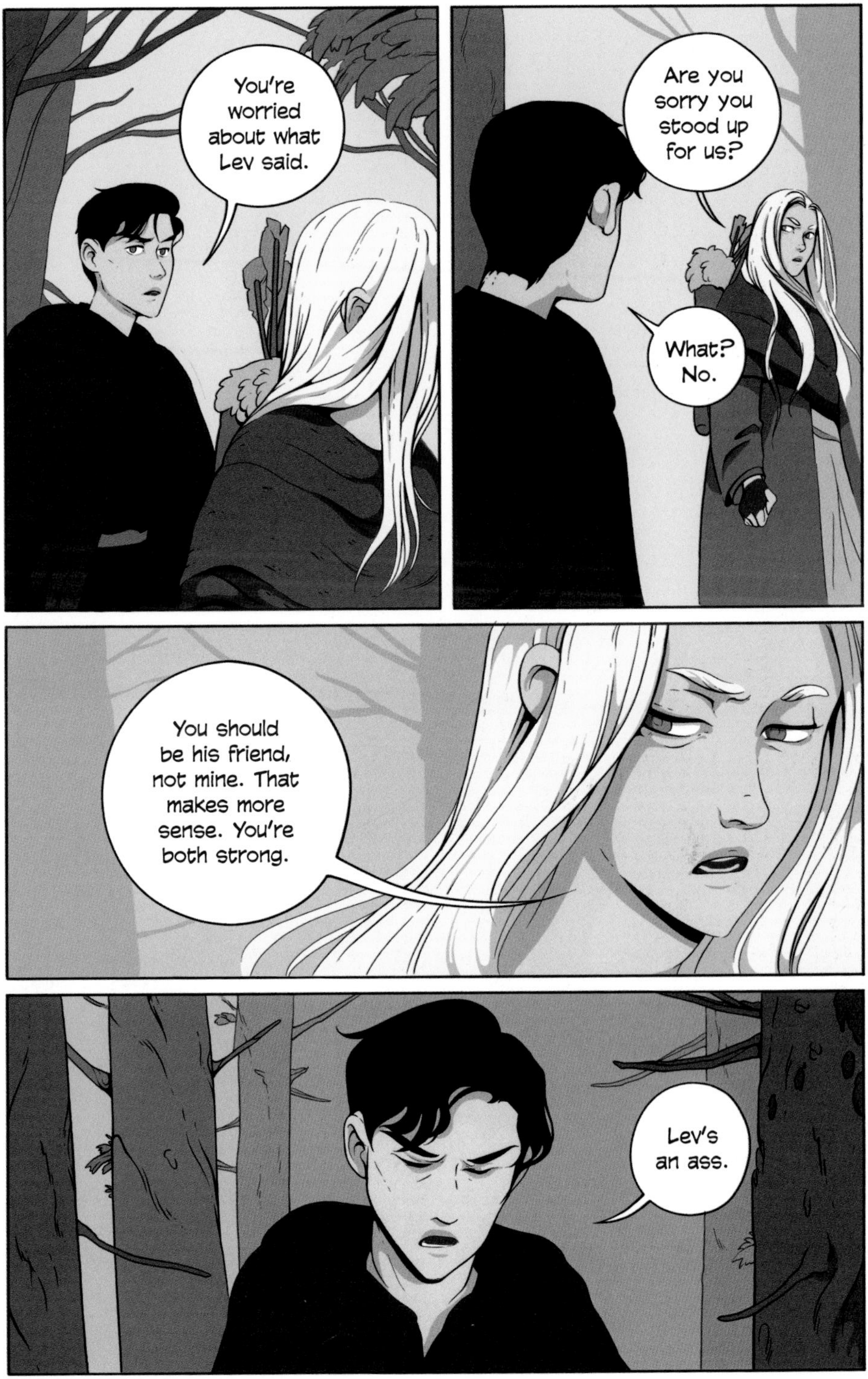
You're worried about what Lev said.
Are you sorry you stood up for us?
What? No.
You should be his friend, not mine. That makes more sense. You're both strong.
Lev's an ass.

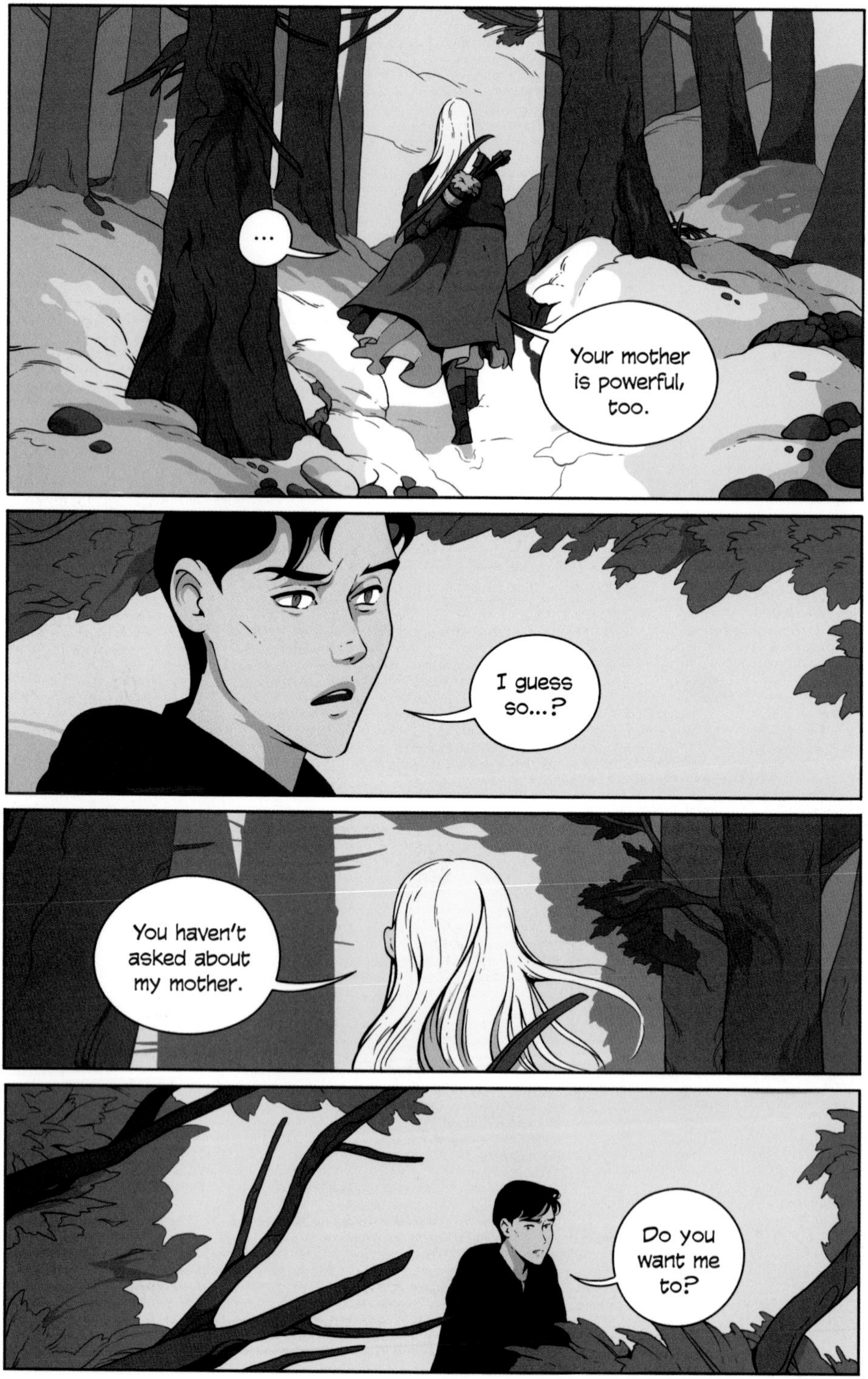
...
Your mother is powerful, too.
I guess so...?
You haven't asked about my mother.
Do you want me to?

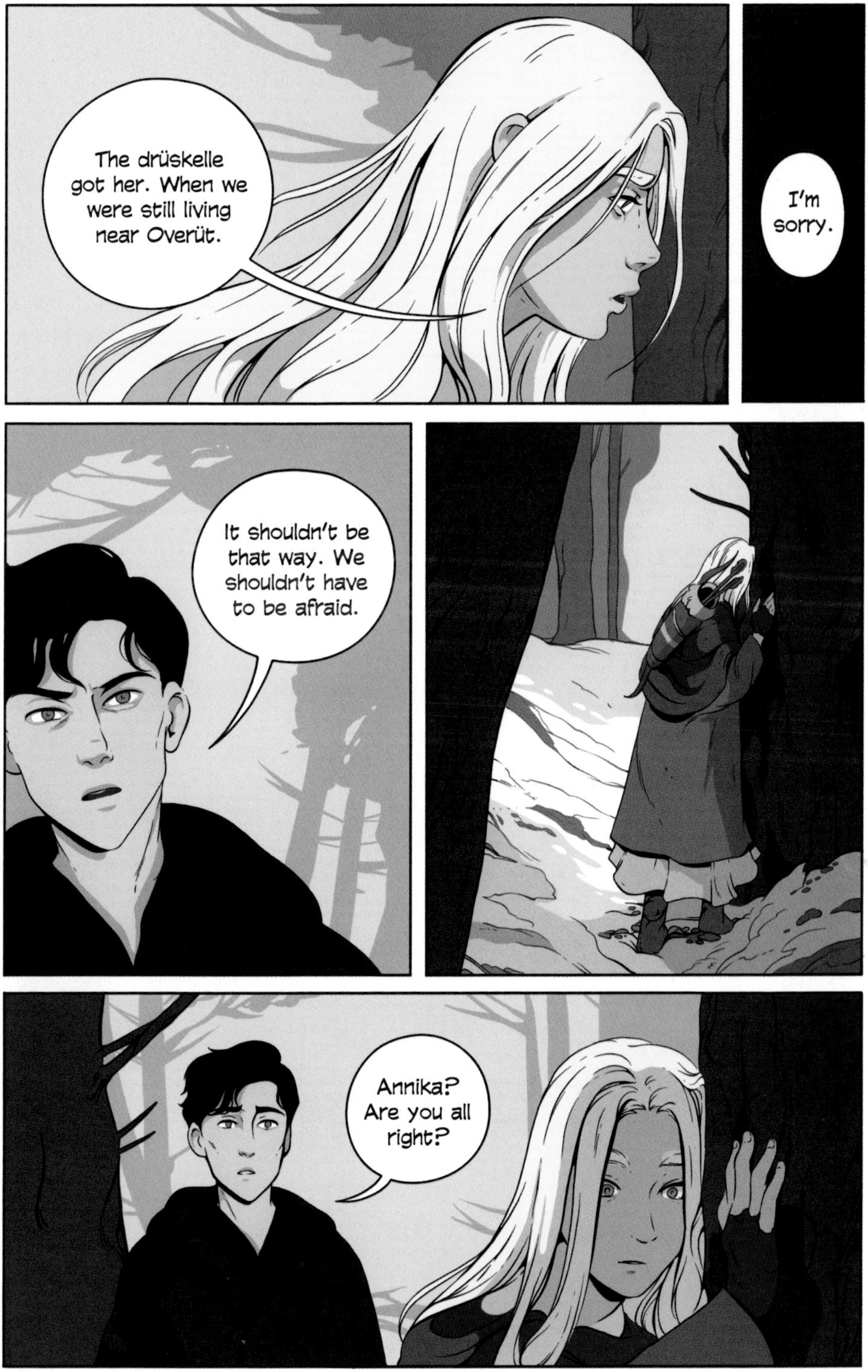
The drüskelle got her. When we were still living near Overüt.
I'm sorry.
It shouldn't be that way. We shouldn't have to be afraid.
Annika? Are you all right?

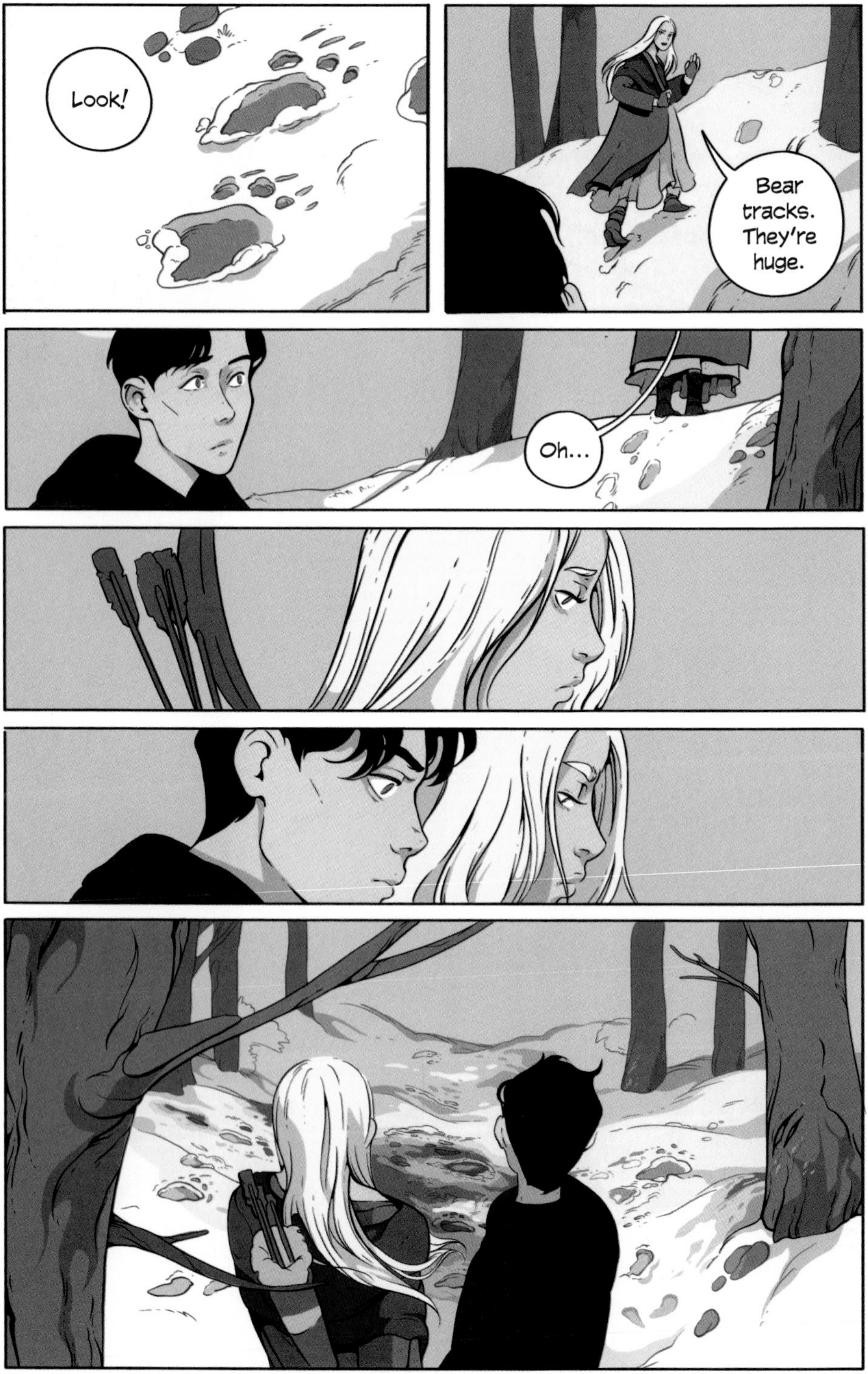
Look!
Bear tracks. They're huge.
Oh...

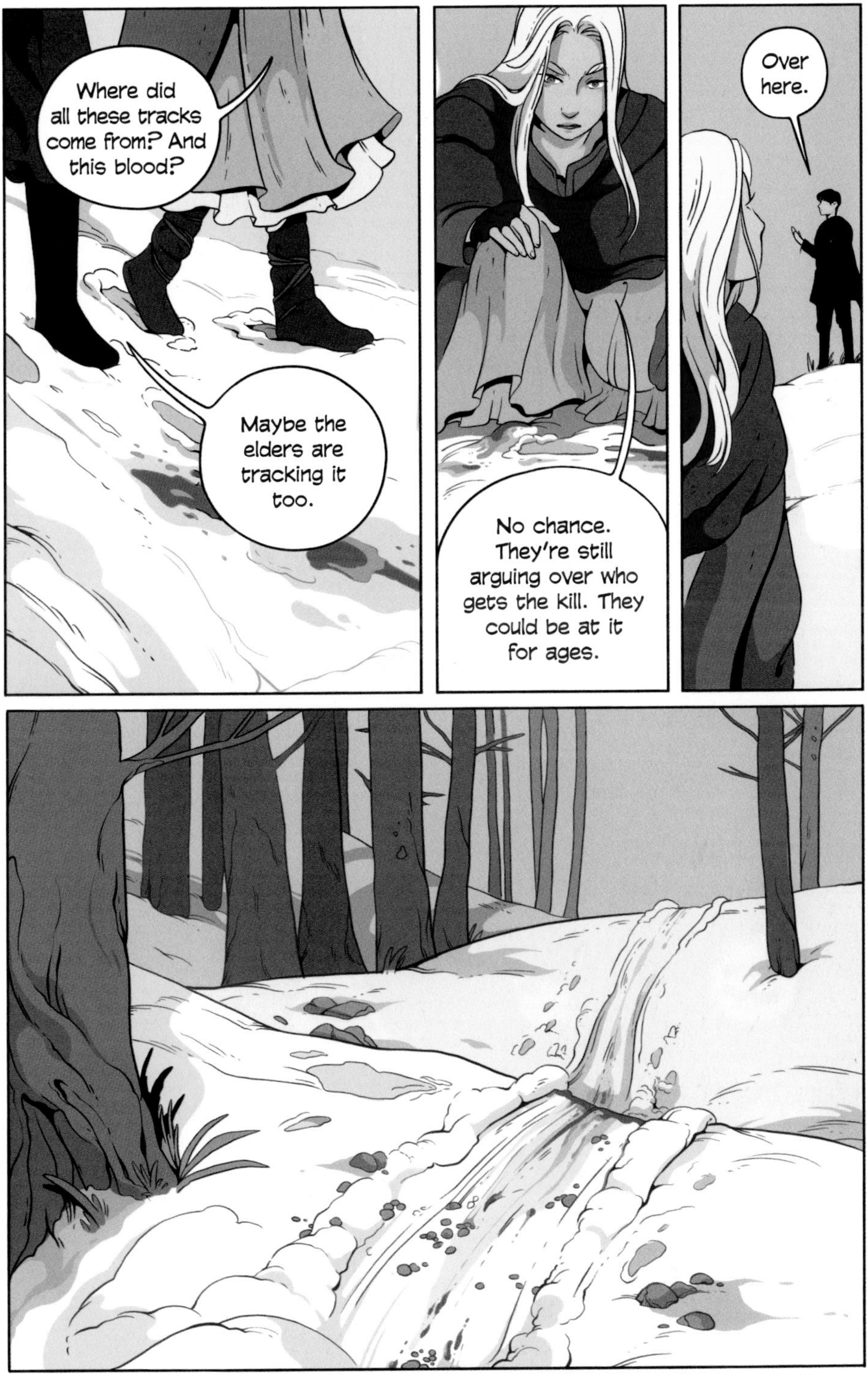
Where did all these tracks come from? And this blood?
Maybe the elders are tracking it too.
No chance. They're still arguing over who gets the kill. They could be at it for ages.
Over here.

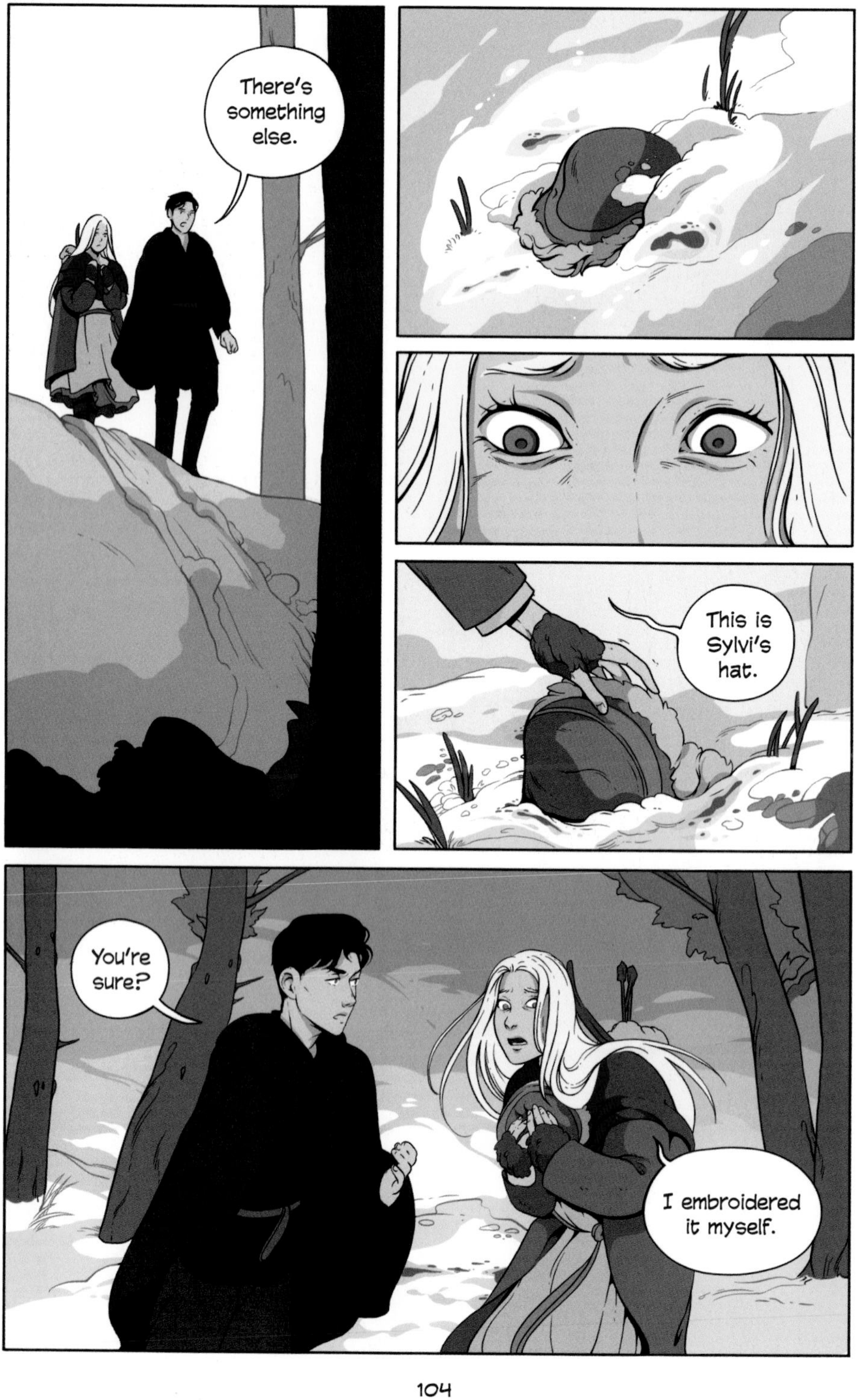
There's something else.
This is Sylvi's hat.
You're sure?
I embroidered it myself.

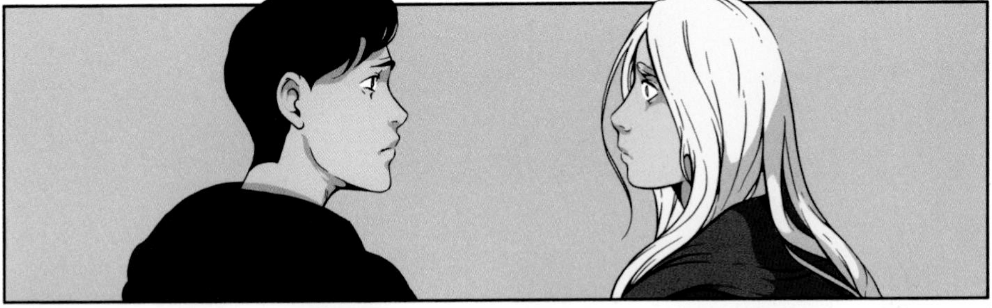

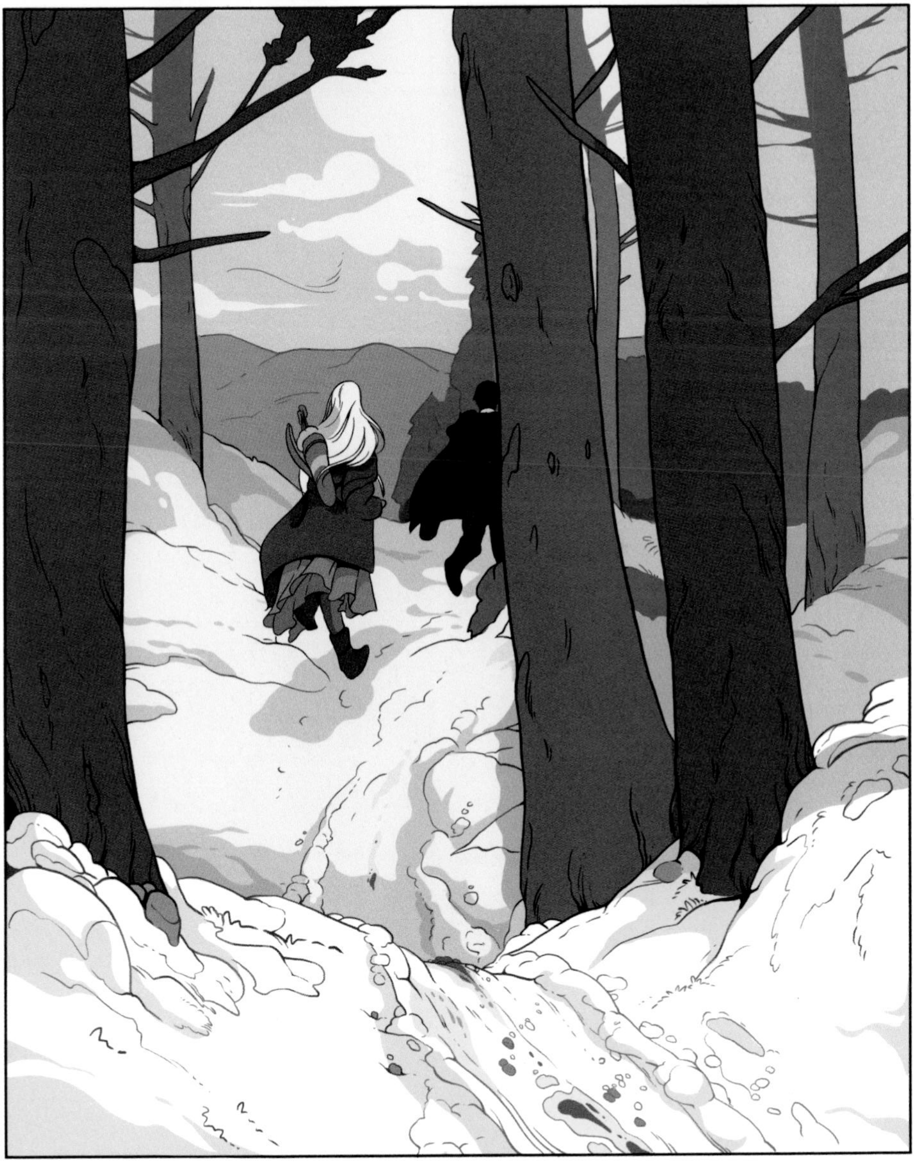

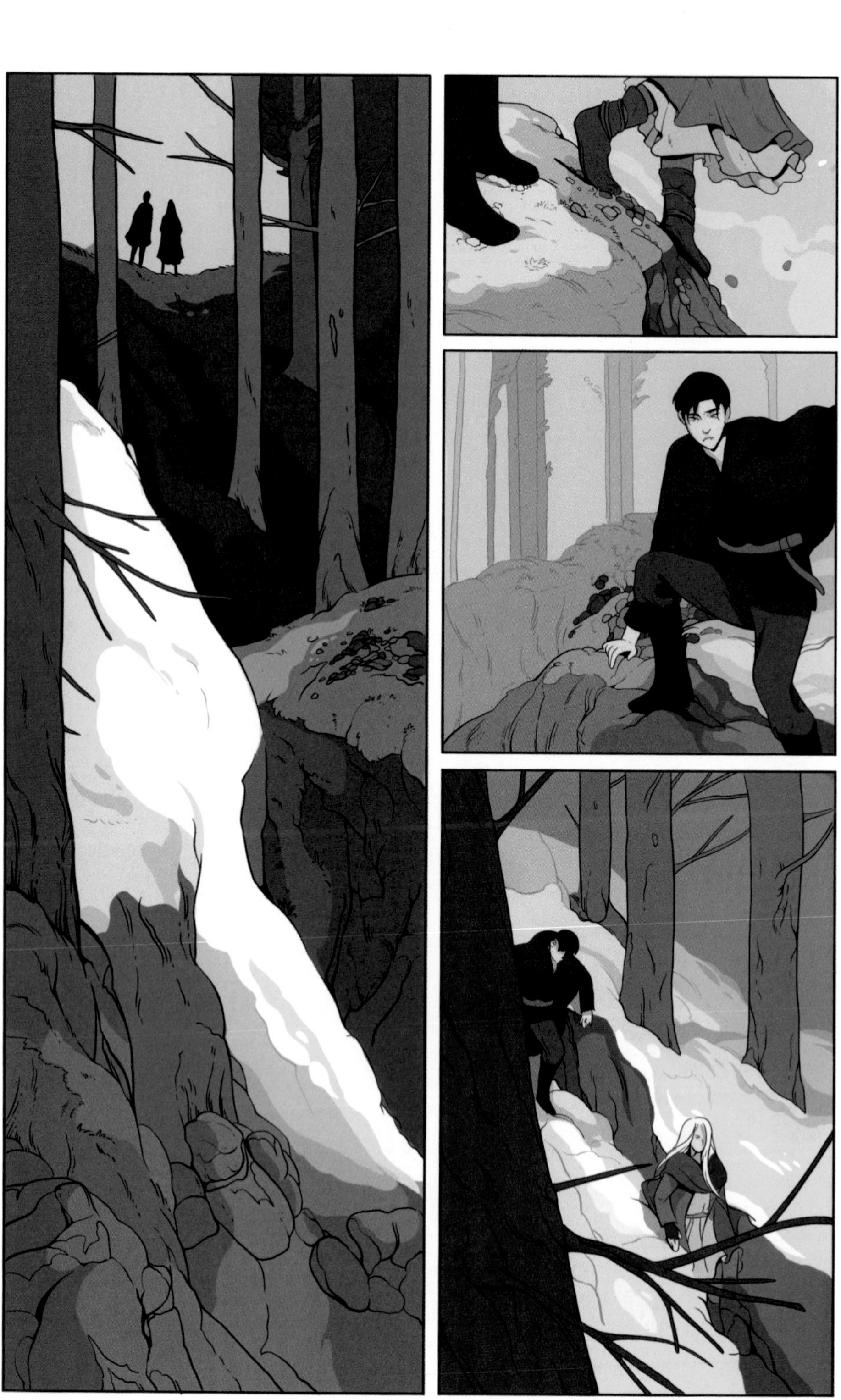

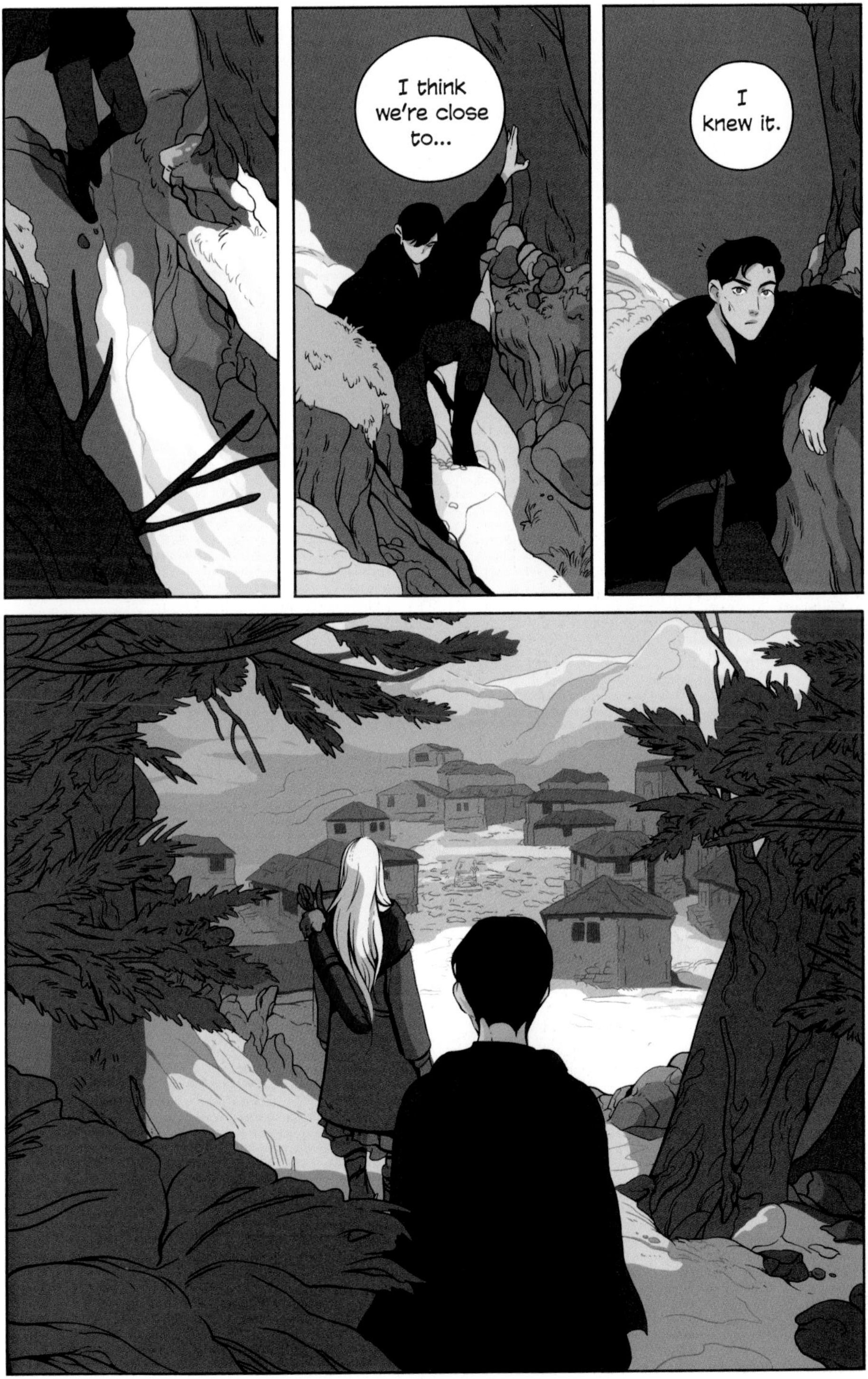
I think we're close to...
I knew it.

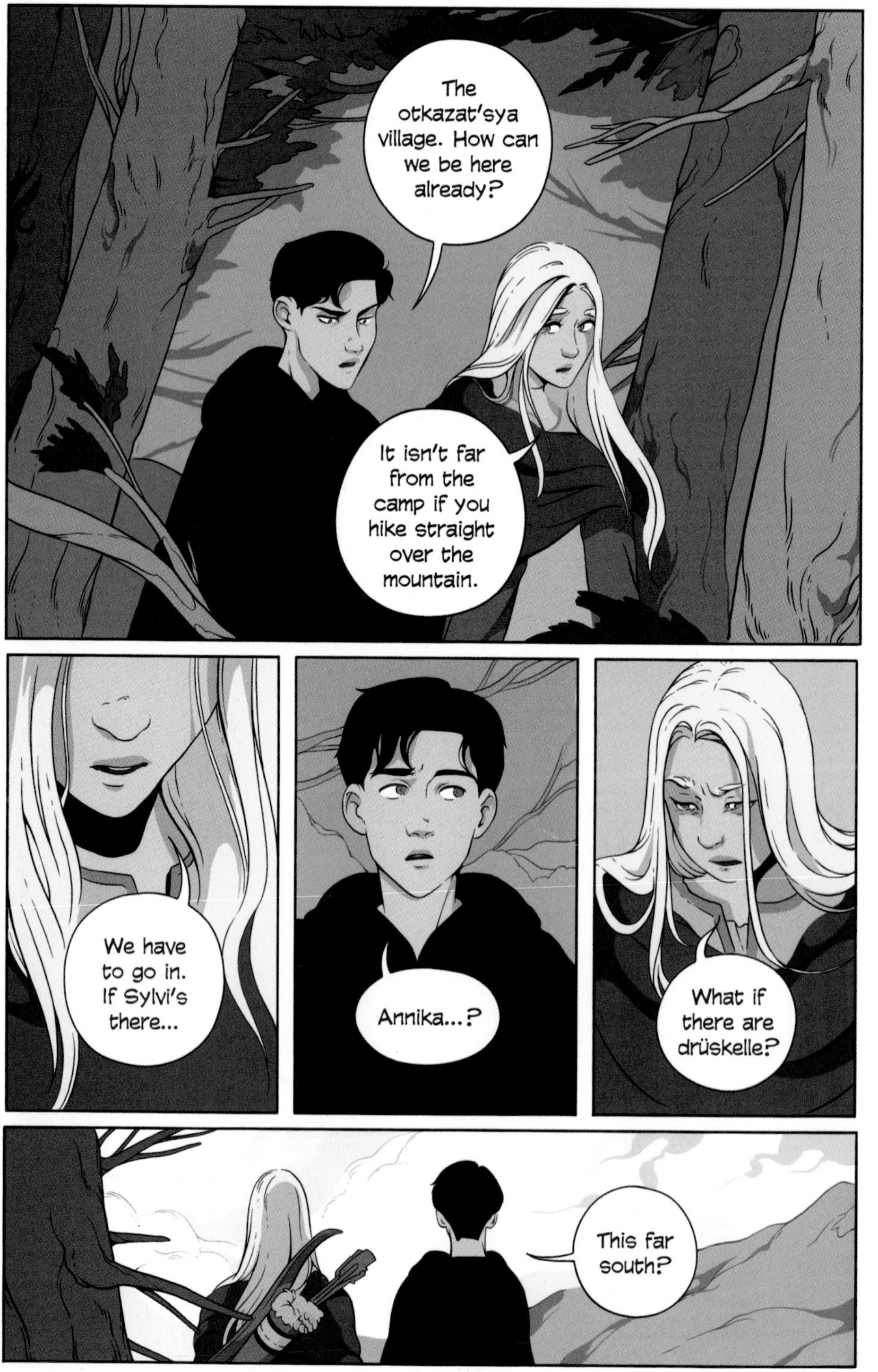
The otkazat'sya village. How can we be here already?
It isn't far from the camp if you hike straight over the mountain.
We have to go in. If Sylvi's there...
Annika...?
What if there are drüskelle?
This far south?

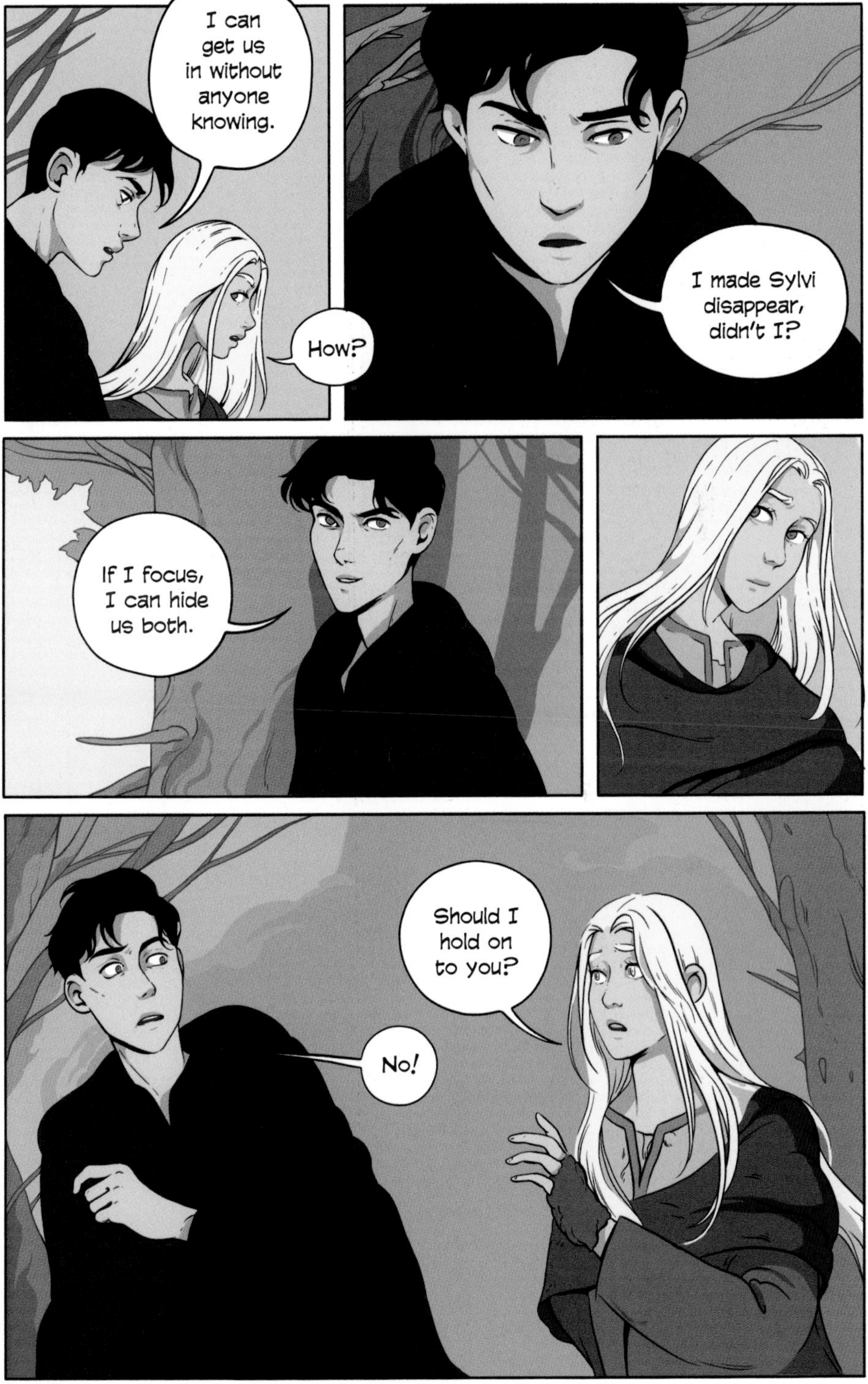
I can get us in without anyone knowing.
How?
I made Sylvi disappear, didn't I?
If I focus, I can hide us both.
Should I hold on to you?
No!

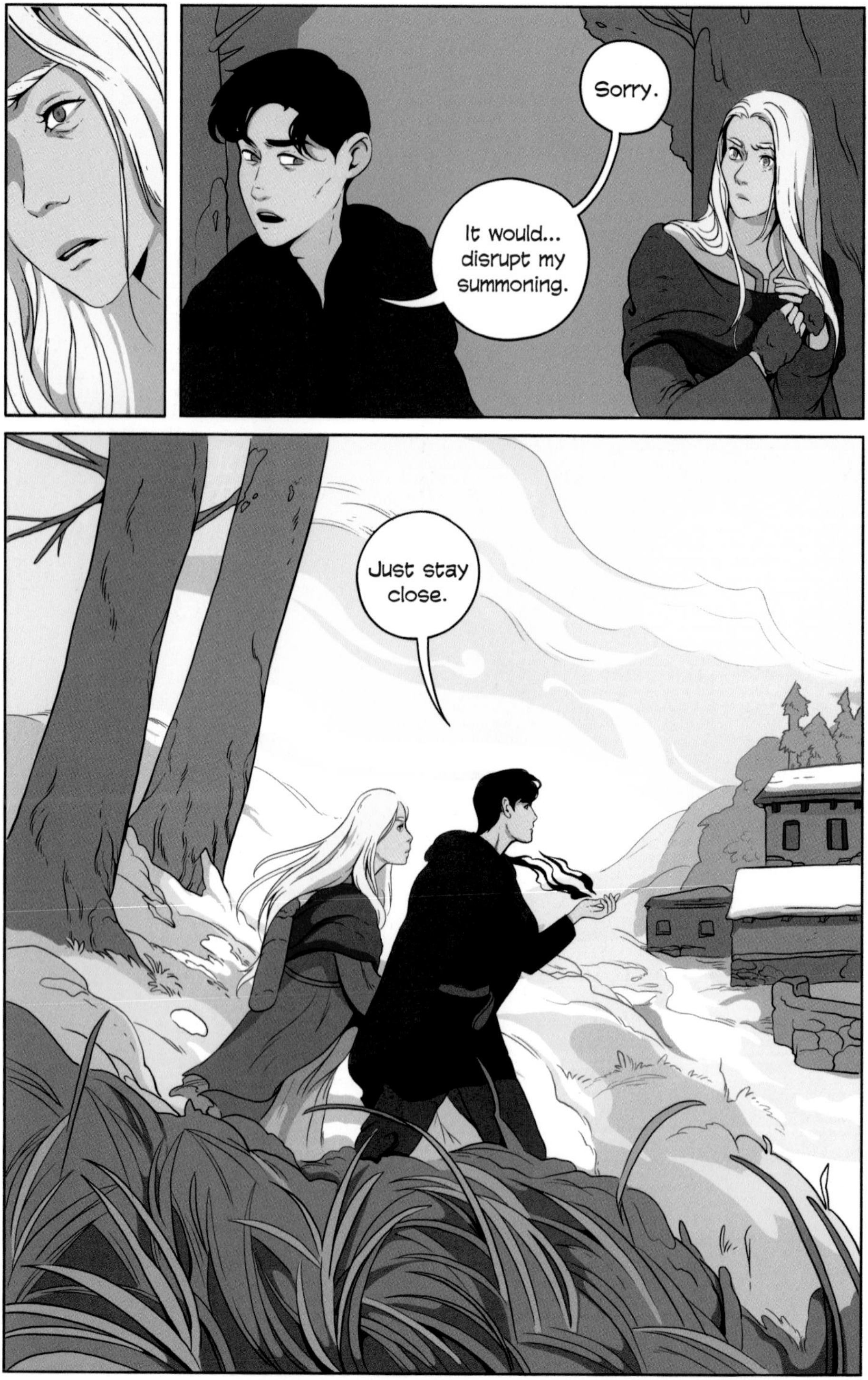
Sorry.
It would... disrupt my summoning.
Just stay close.

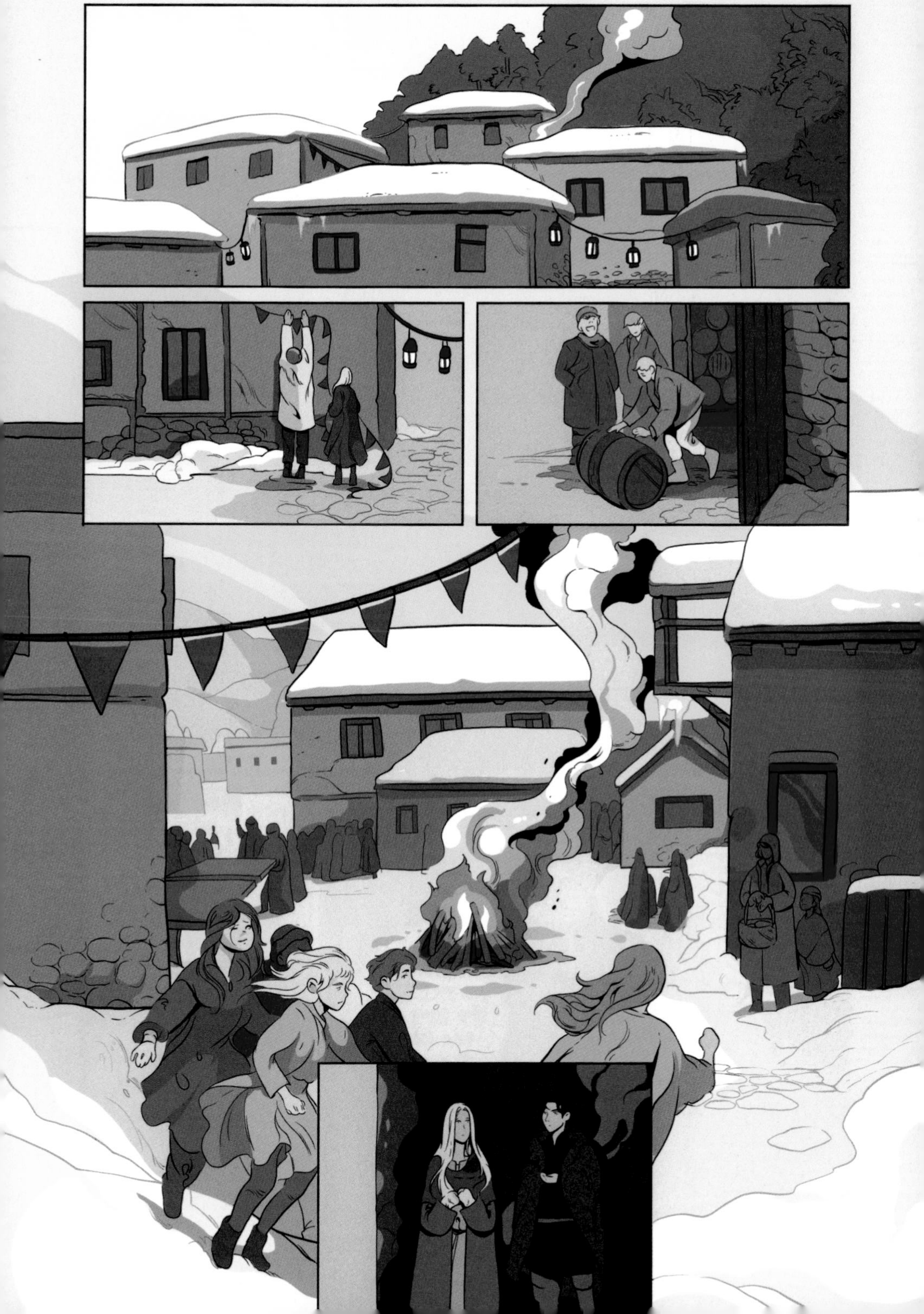

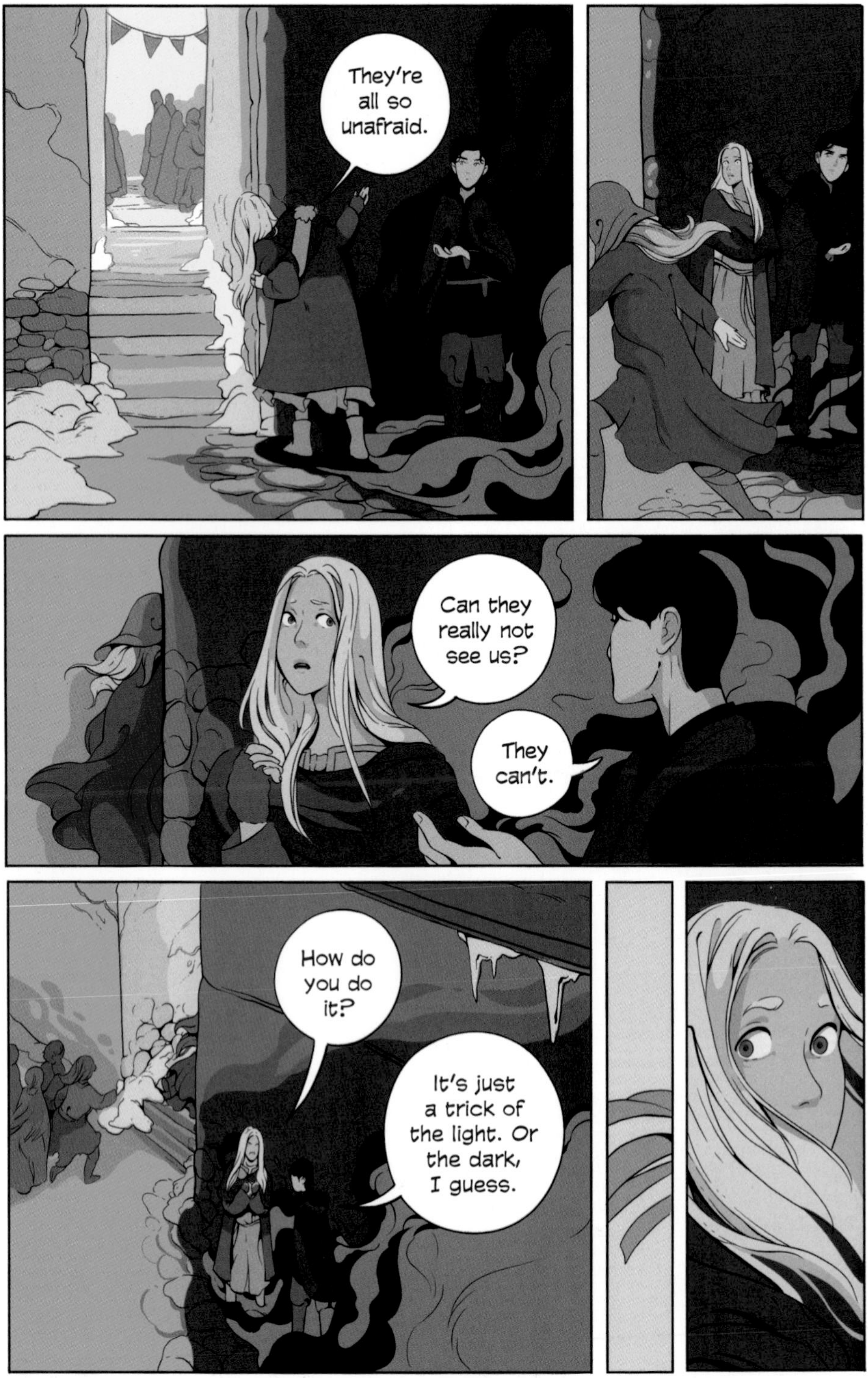
They're all so unafraid.
Can they really not see us?
They can't.
How do you do it?
It's just a trick of the light. Or the dark, I guess.

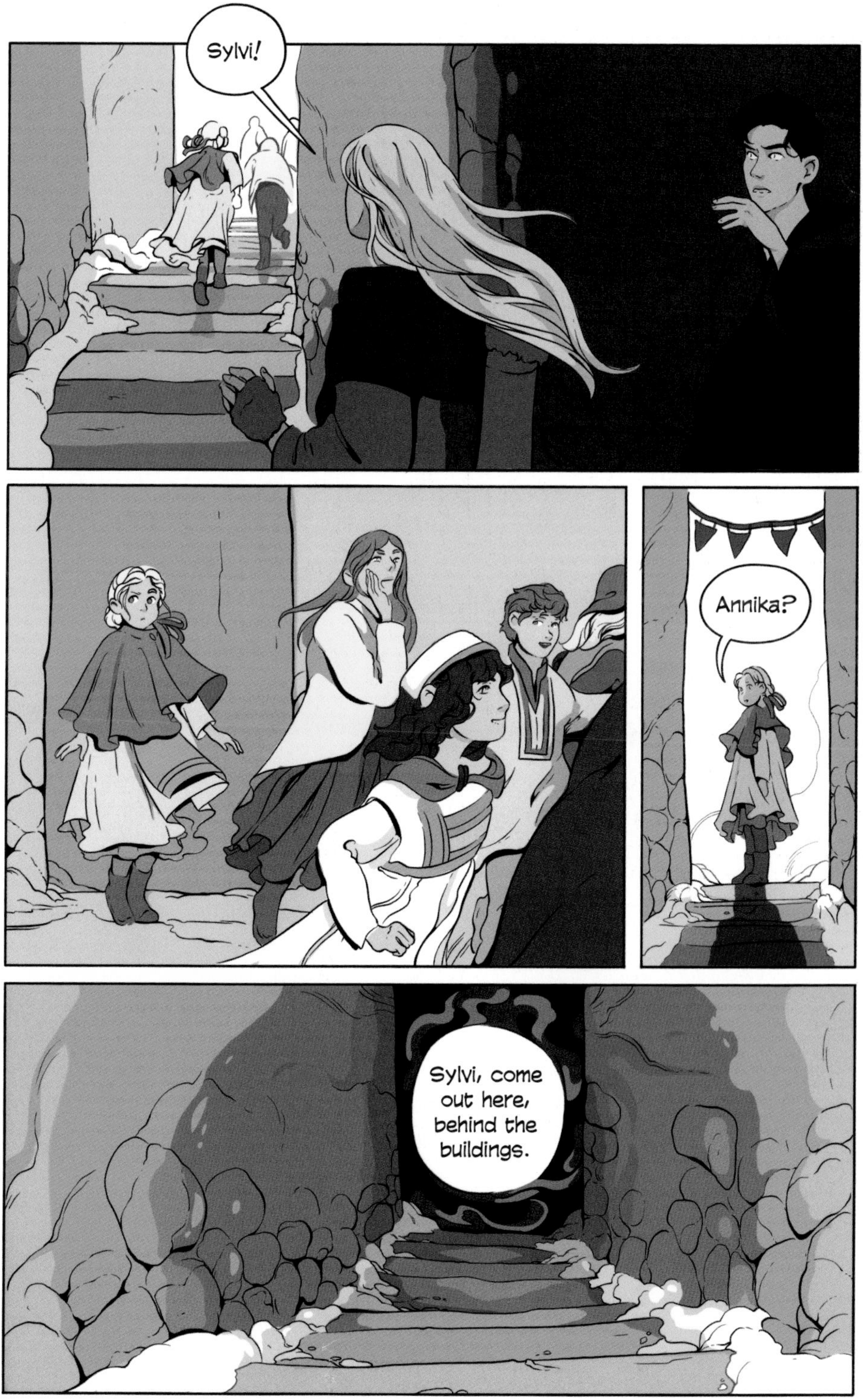
Sylvi!
Annika?
Sylvi, come out here, behind the buildings.

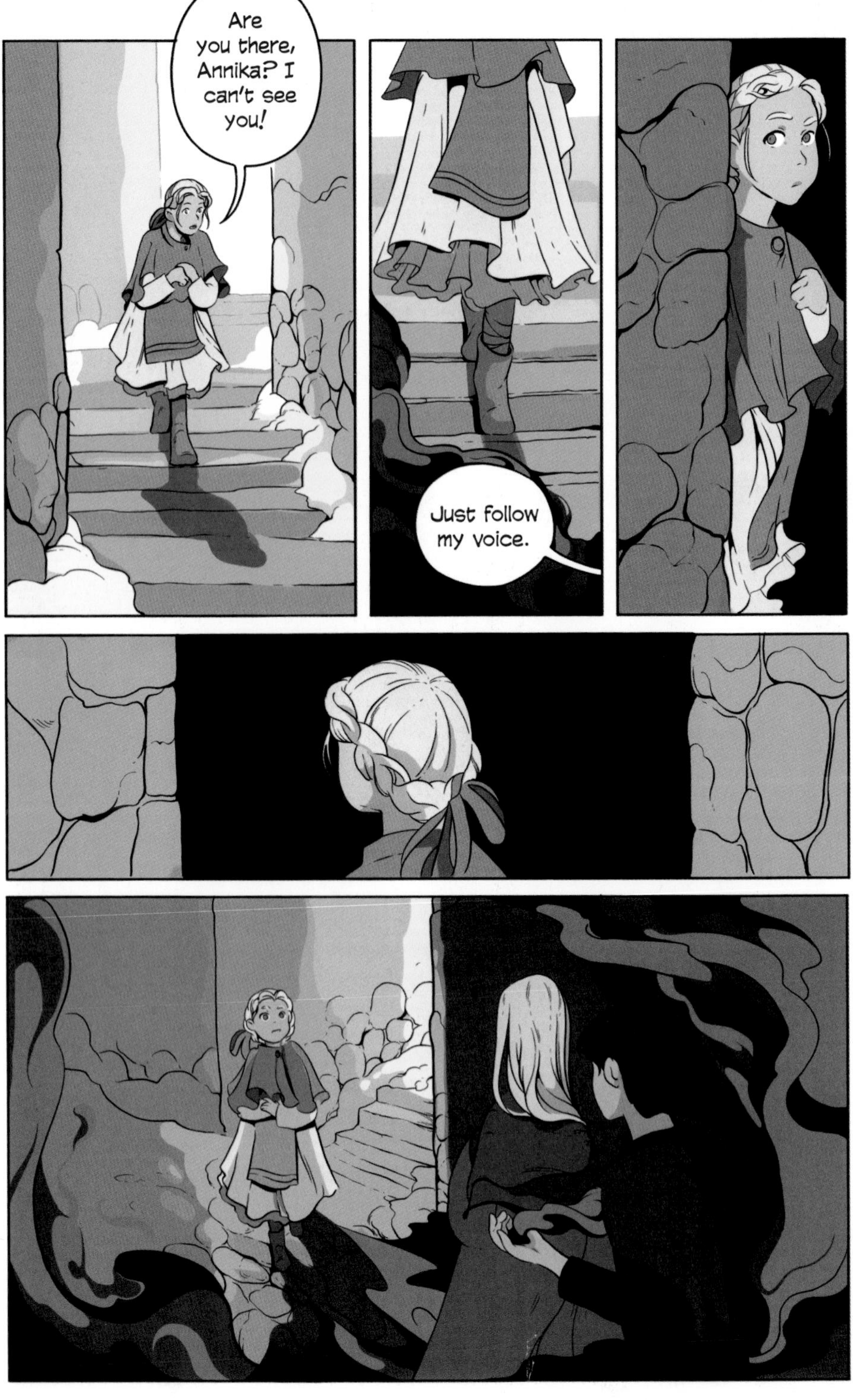
Are you there, Annika? I can't see you!
Just follow my voice.

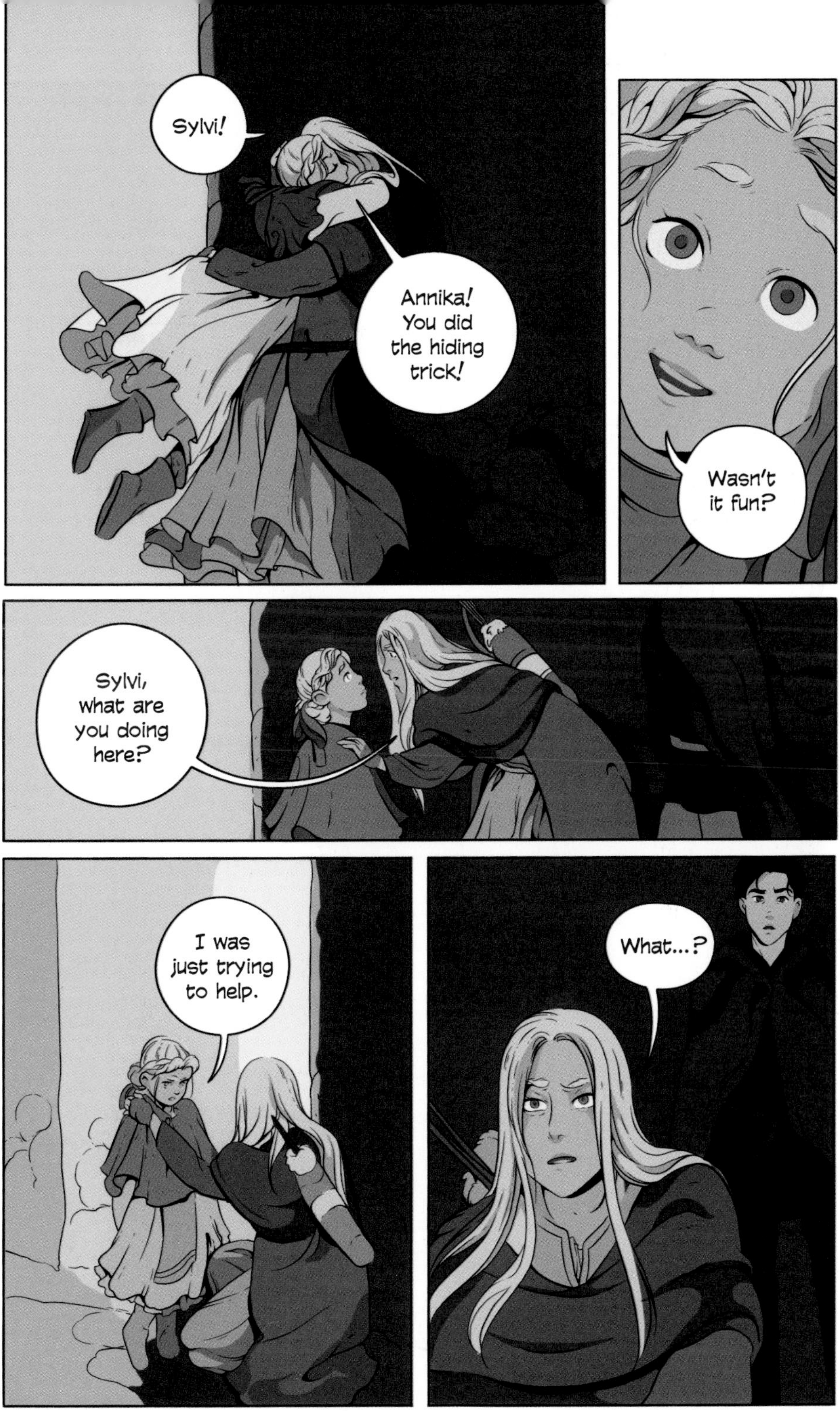
Sylvi!
Annika! You did the hiding trick!
Wasn't it fun?
Sylvi, what are you doing here?
I was just trying to help.
What...?

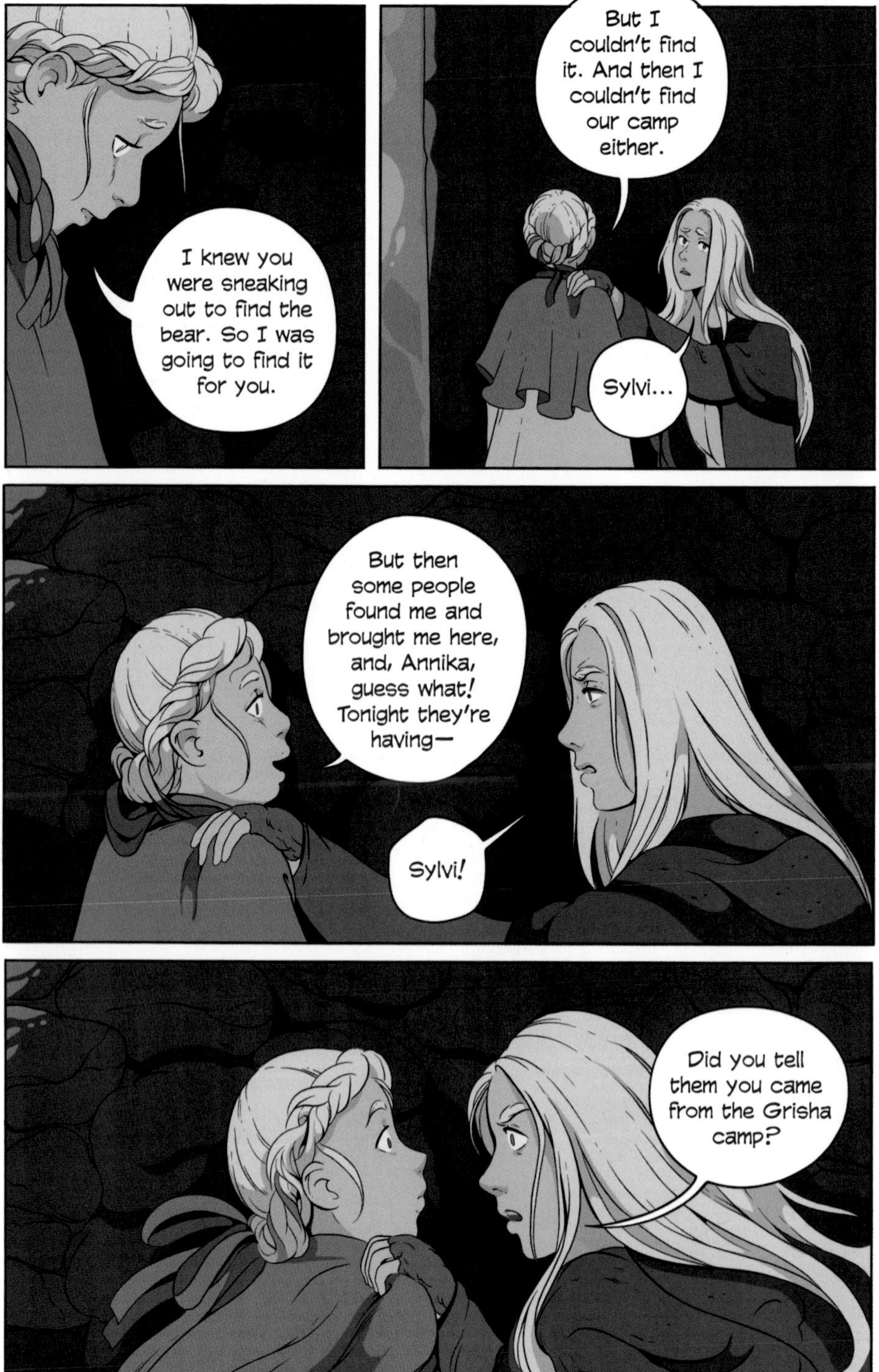
I knew you were sneaking out to find the bear. So I was going to find it for you.
But I couldn't find it. And then I couldn't find our camp either.
Sylvi...
But then some people found me and brought me here, and, Annika, guess what! Tonight they're having—
Sylvi!
Did you tell them you came from the Grisha camp?

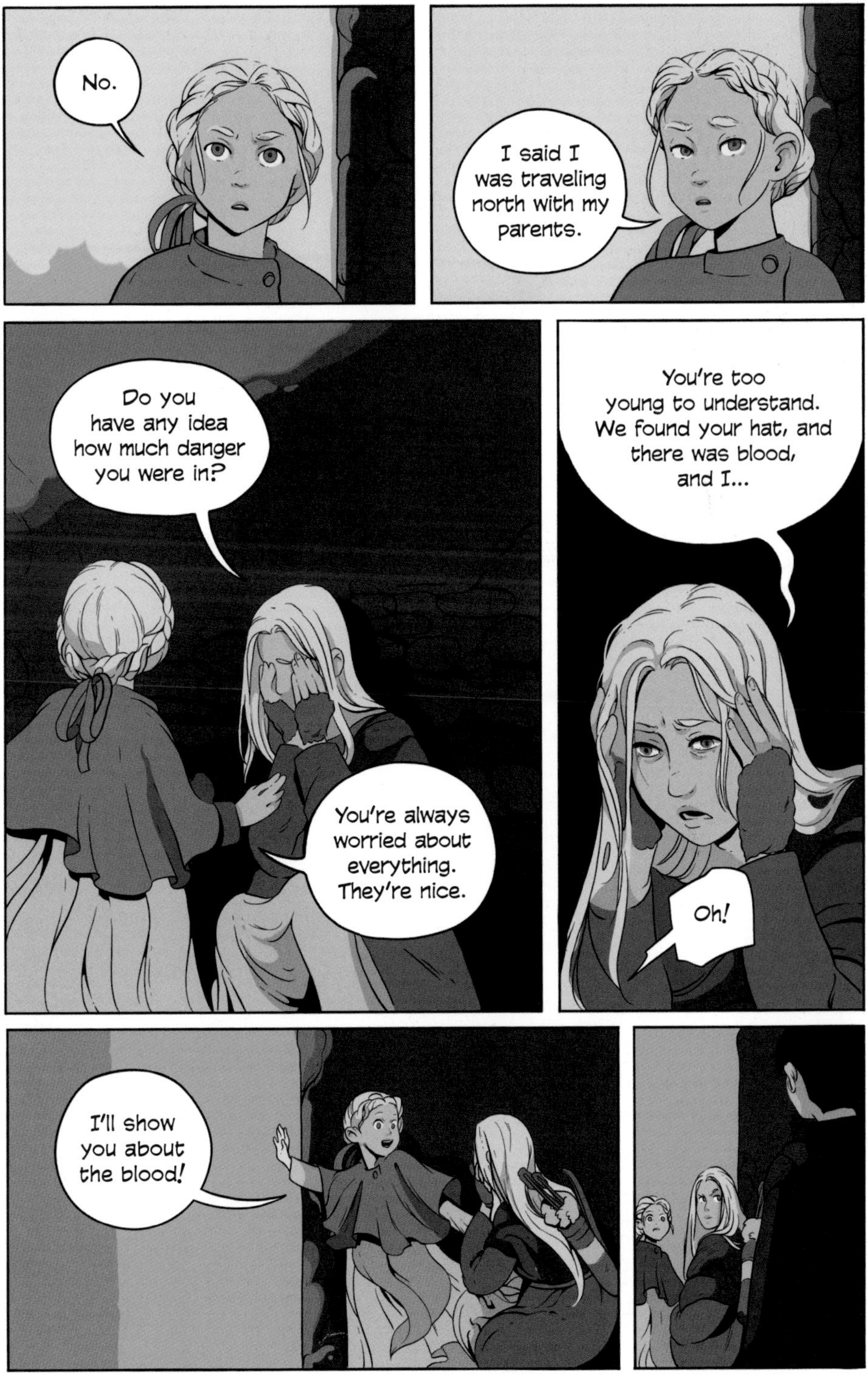
No.
I said I was traveling north with my parents.
Do you have any idea how much danger you were in?
You're always worried about everything. They're nice.
You're too young to understand. We found your hat, and there was blood, and I...
Oh!
I'll show you about the blood!

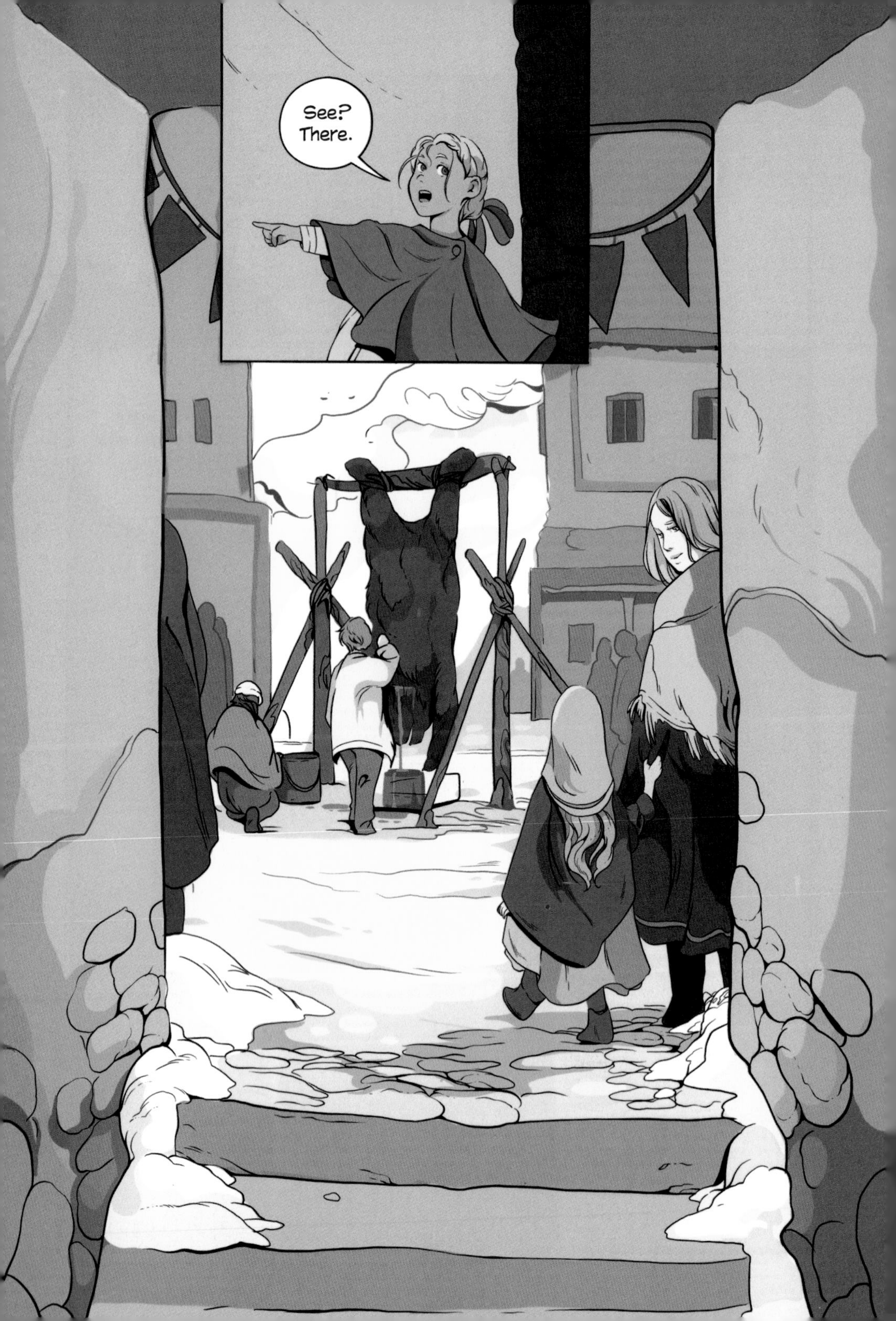
See? There.

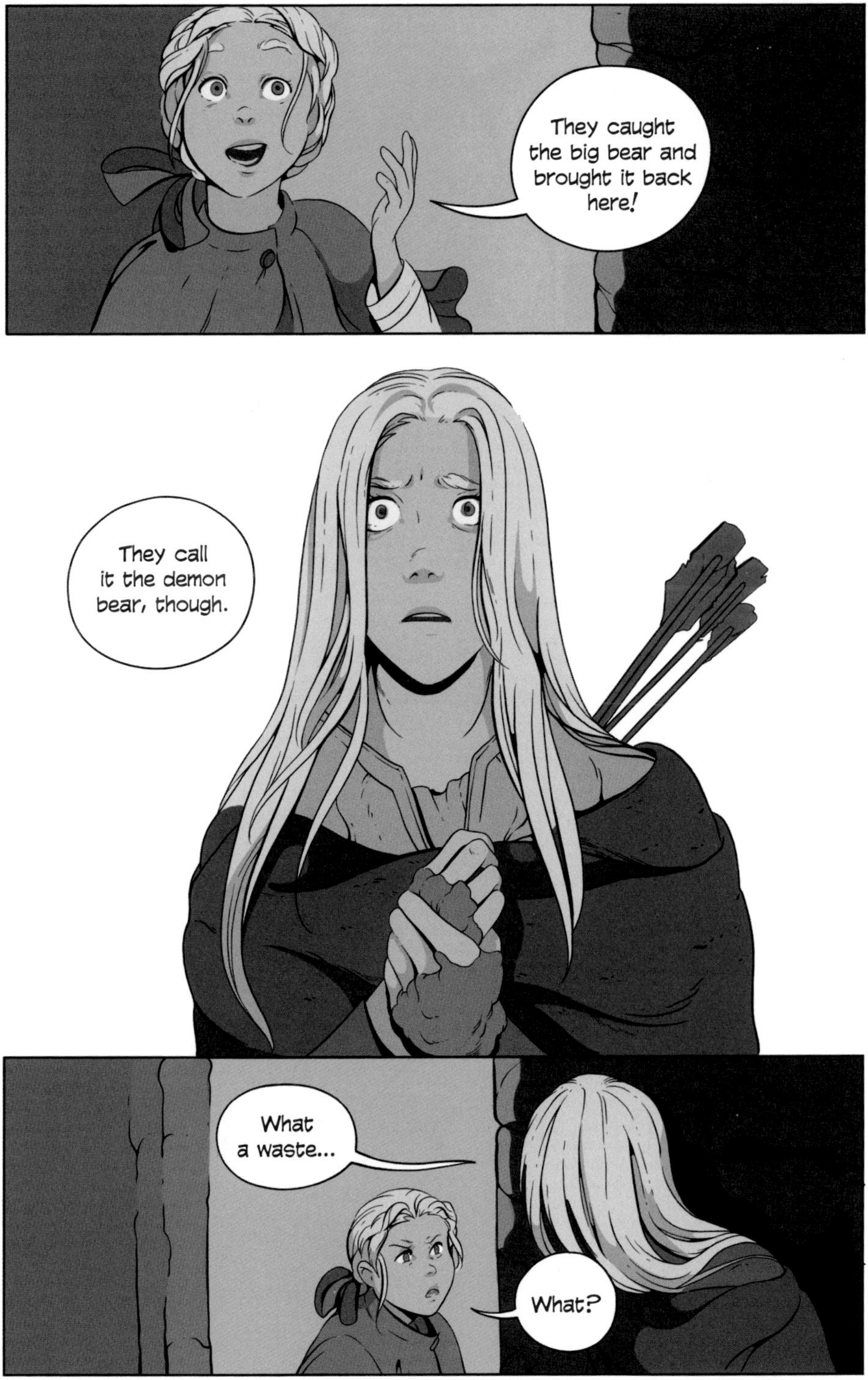
They caught the big bear and brought it back here!
They call it the demon bear, though.
What a waste...
What?

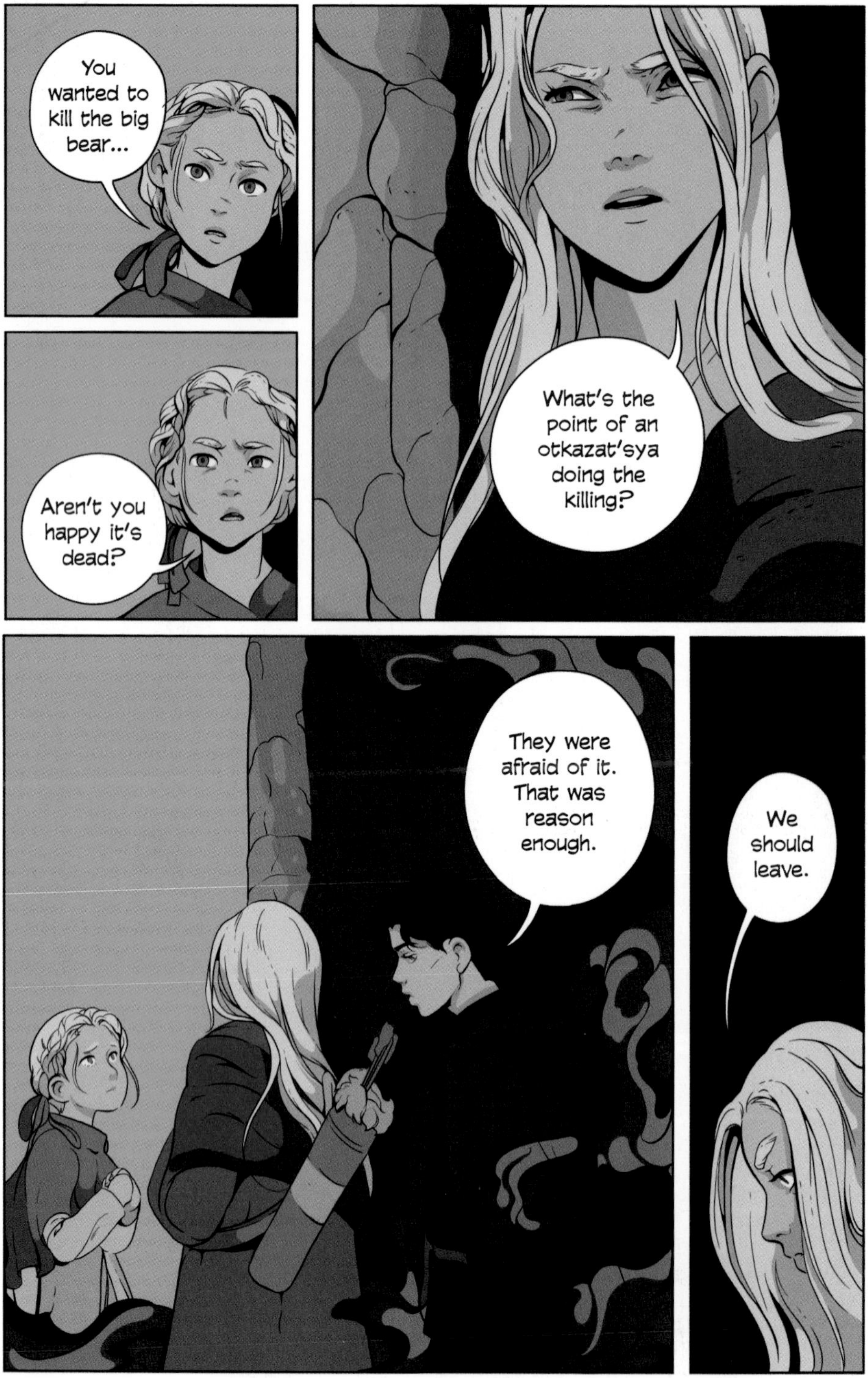

You wanted to kill the big bear...
Aren't you happy it's dead?
What's the point of an otkazat'sya doing the killing?
They were afraid of it. That was reason enough.
We should leave.

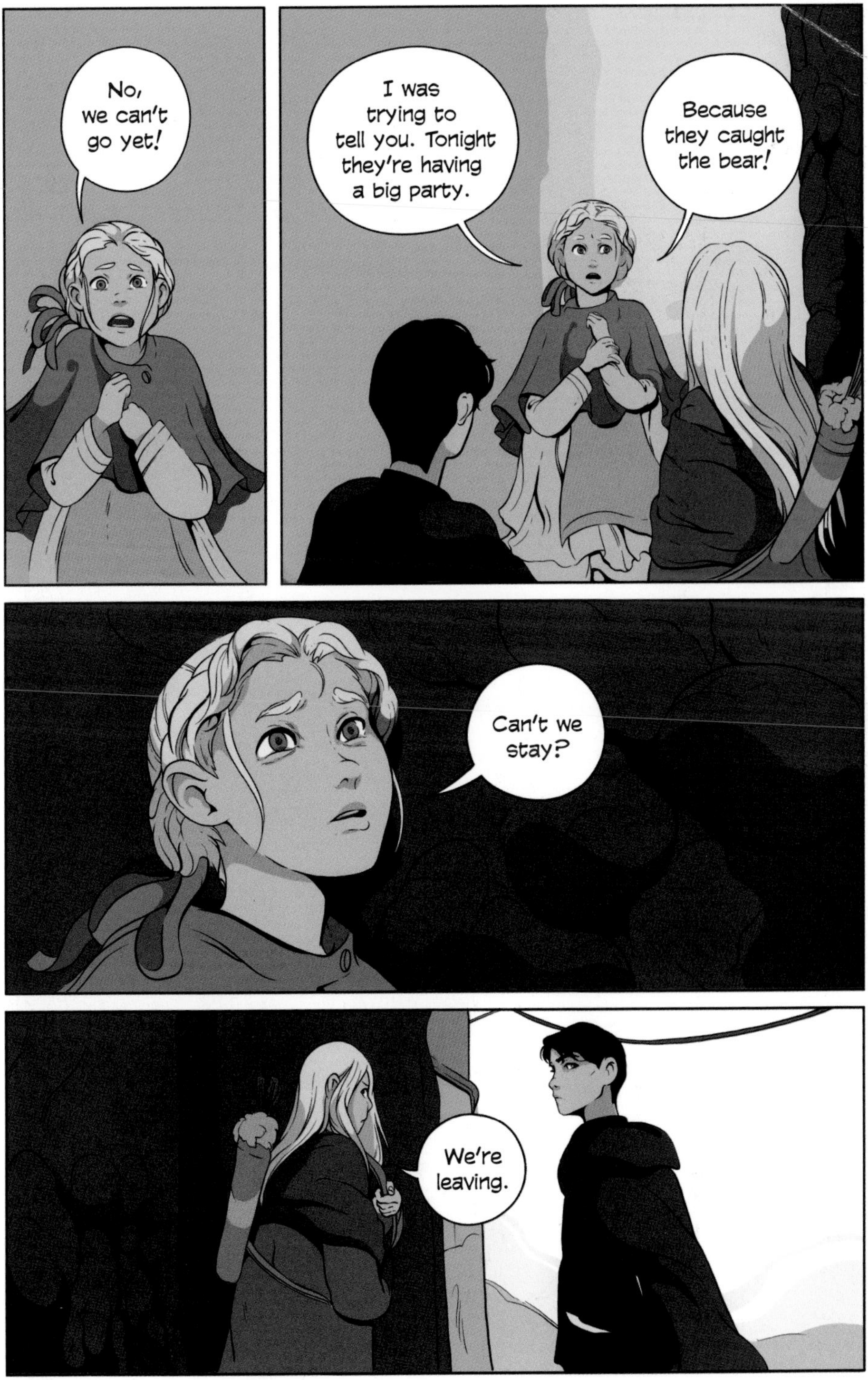
No, we can't go yet!
I was trying to tell you. Tonight they're having a big party.
Because they caught the bear!
Can't we stay?
We're leaving.

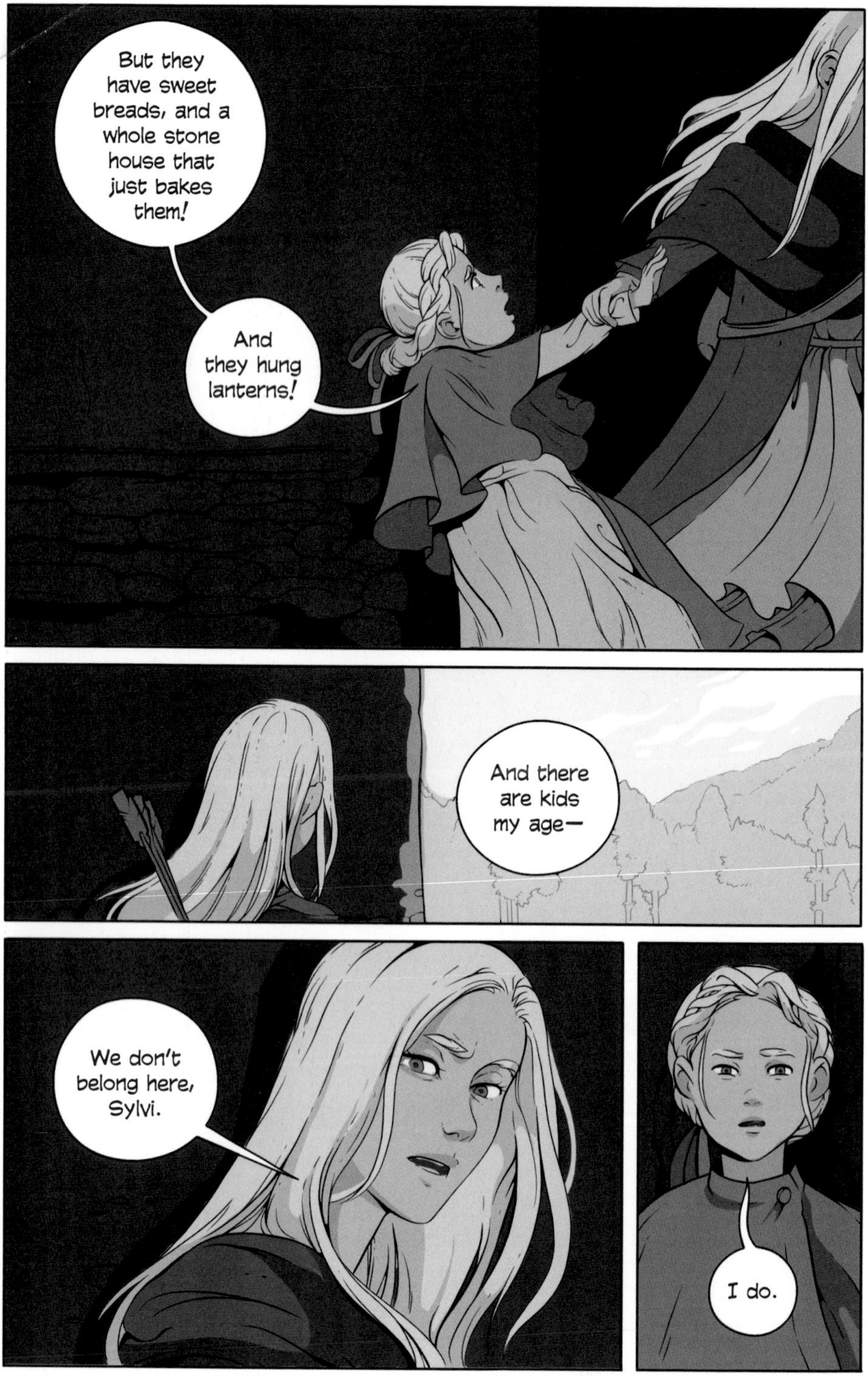
But they have sweet breads, and a whole stone house that just bakes them!
And they hung lanterns!
And there are kids my age—
We don't belong here, Sylvi.
I do.

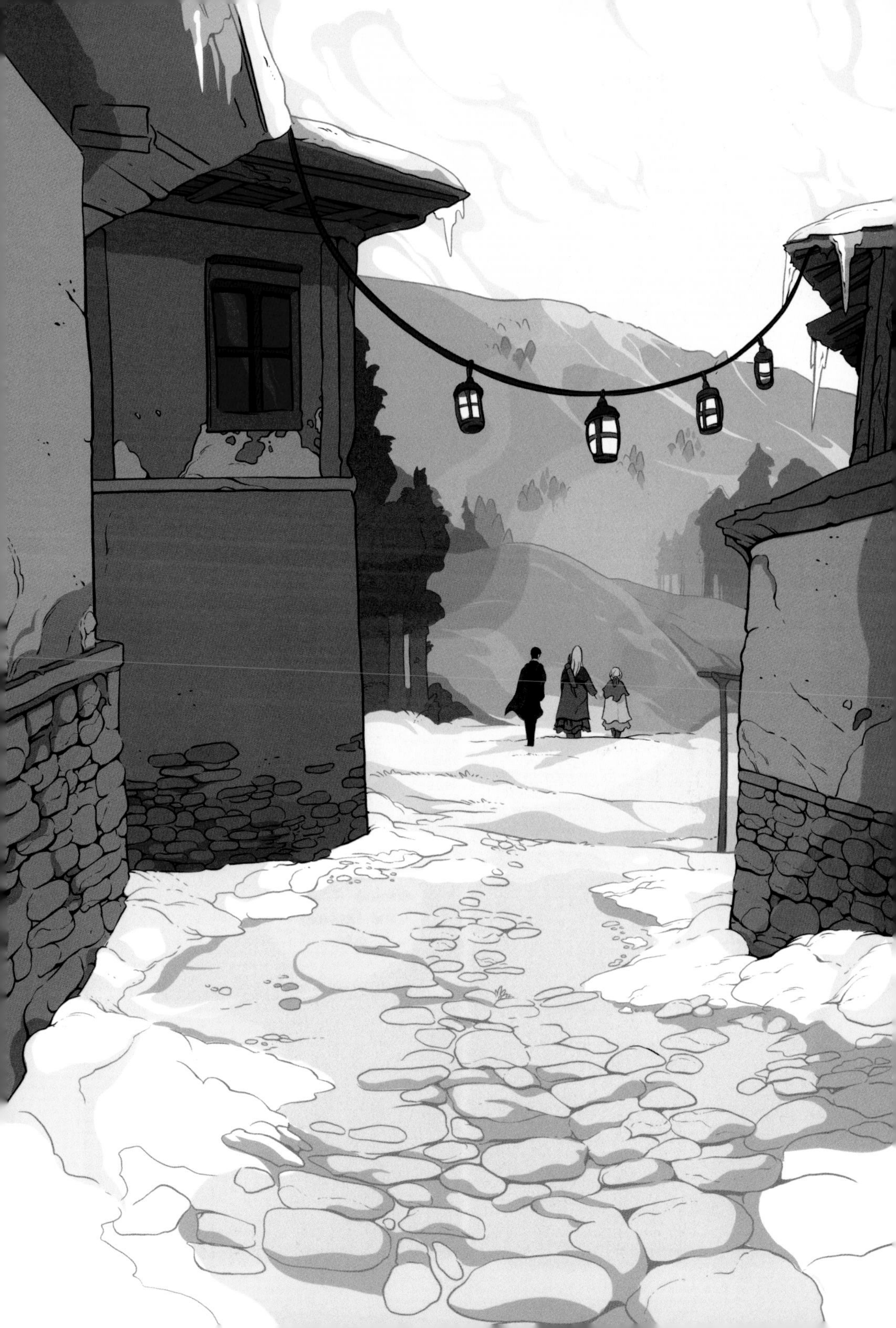

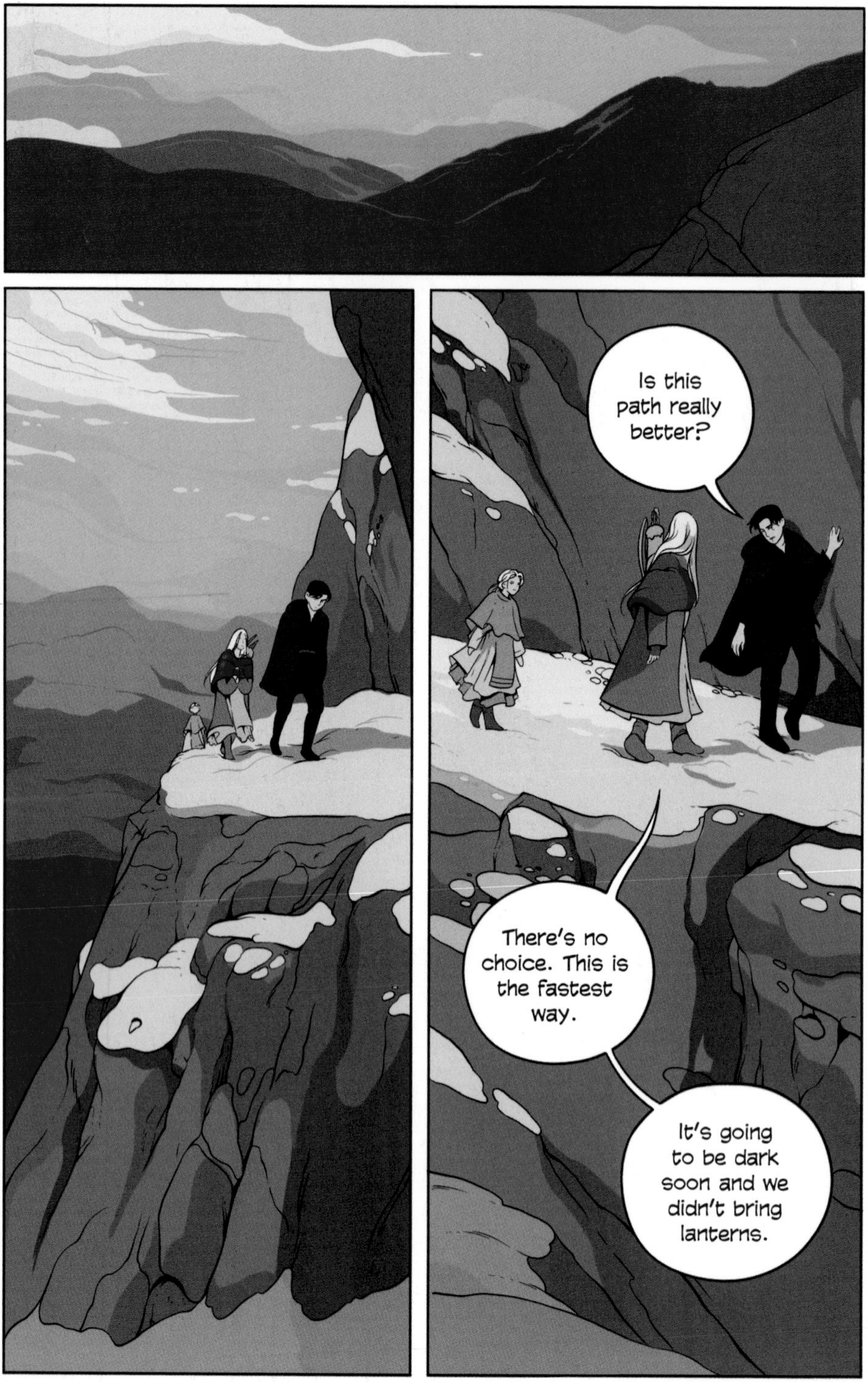

Is this path really better?
There's no choice. This is the fastest way.
It's going to be dark soon and we didn't bring lanterns.

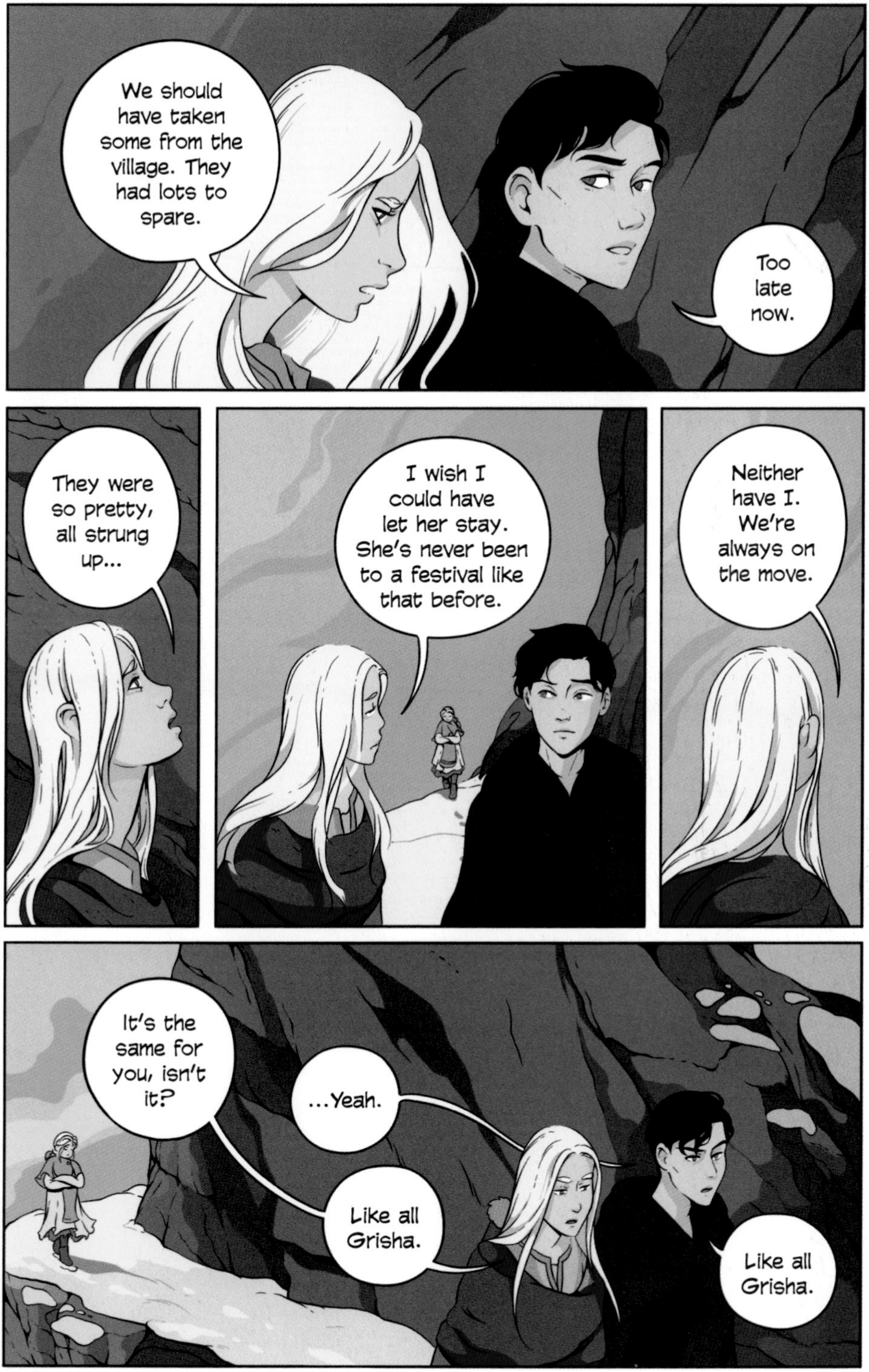
We should have taken some from the village. They had lots to spare.
Too late now.
They were so pretty, all strung up...
I wish I could have let her stay. She's never been to a festival like that before.
Neither have I. We're always on the move.
It's the same for you, isn't it?
...Yeah.
Like all Grisha.
Like all Grisha.

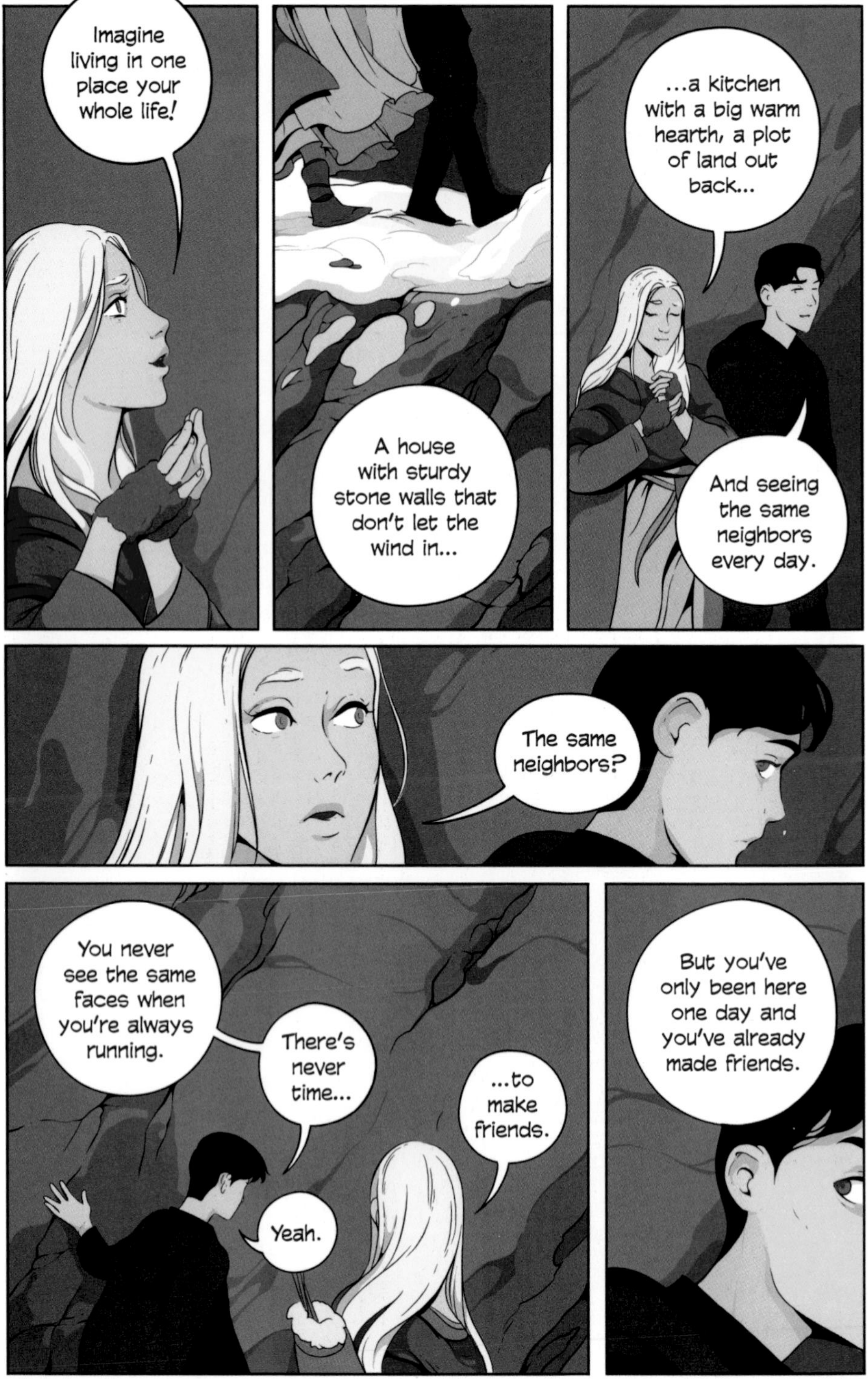
Imagine living in one place your whole life!
A house with sturdy stone walls that don't let the wind in...
...a kitchen with a big warm hearth, a plot of land out back...
And seeing the same neighbors every day.
The same neighbors?
You never see the same faces when you're always running.
There's never time...
...to make friends.
Yeah.
But you've only been here one day and you've already made friends.

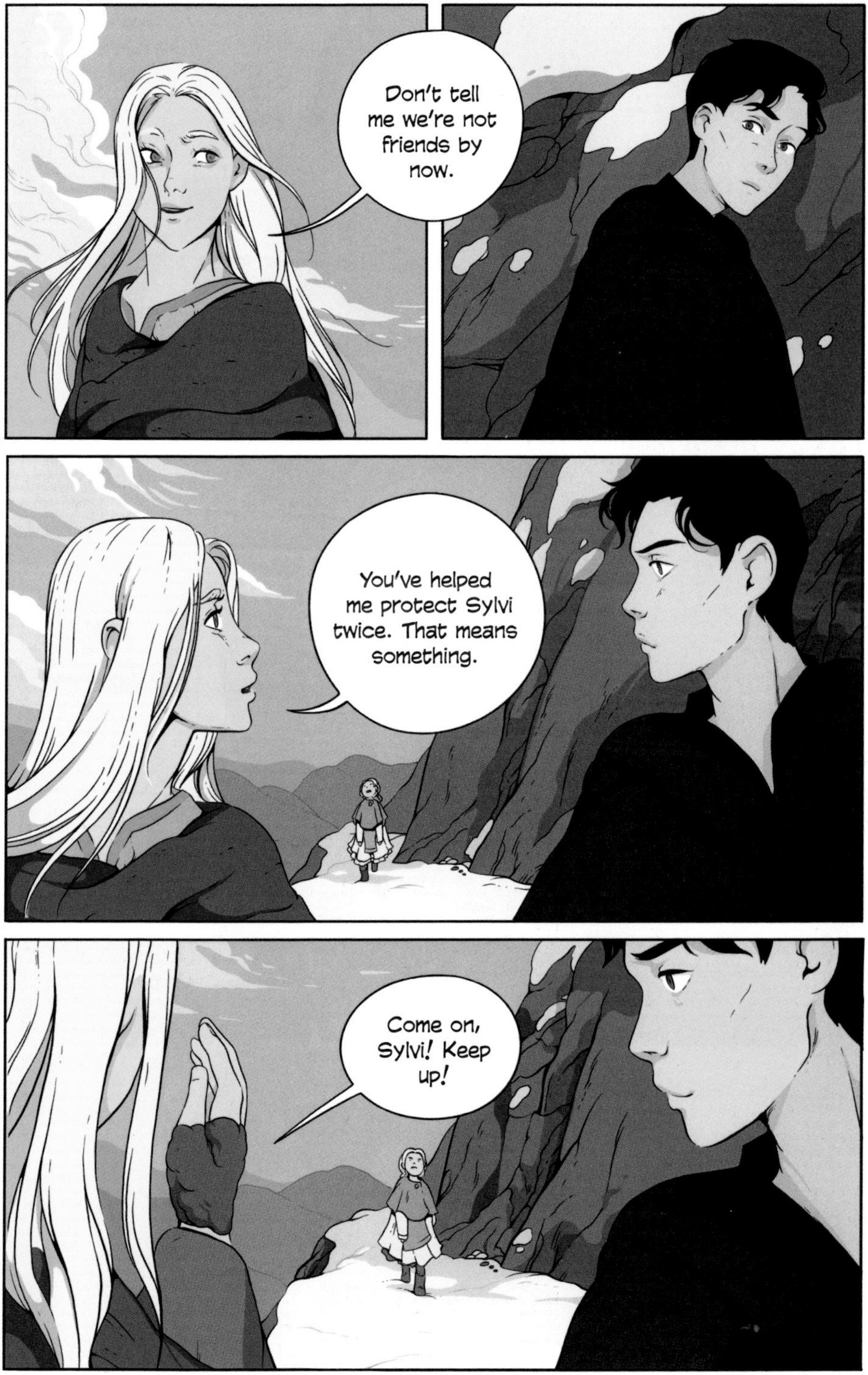
Don't tell me we're not friends by now.
You've helped me protect Sylvi twice. That means something.
Come on, Sylvi! Keep up!

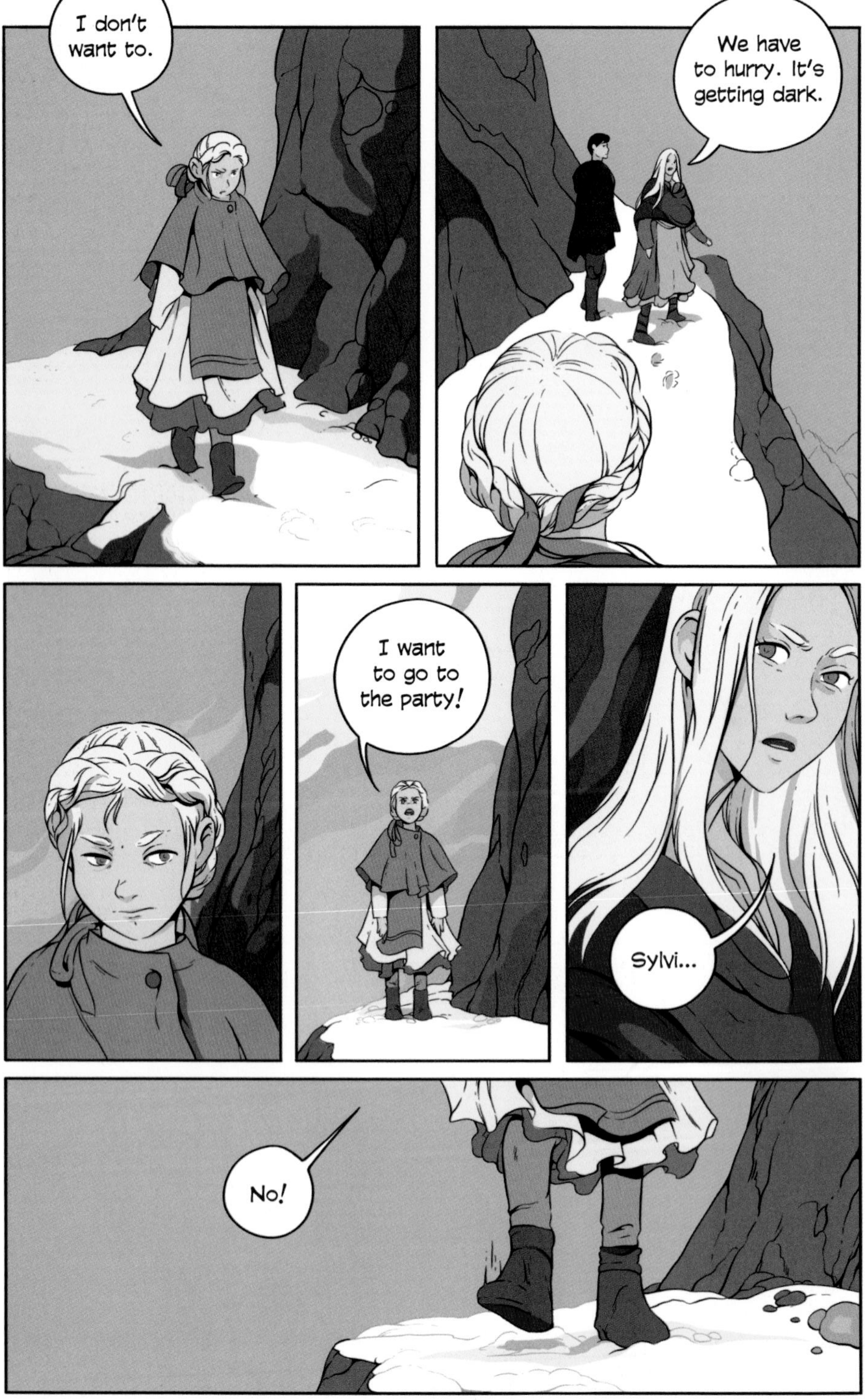
I don't want to.
We have to hurry. It's getting dark.
I want to go to the party!
Sylvi...
No!

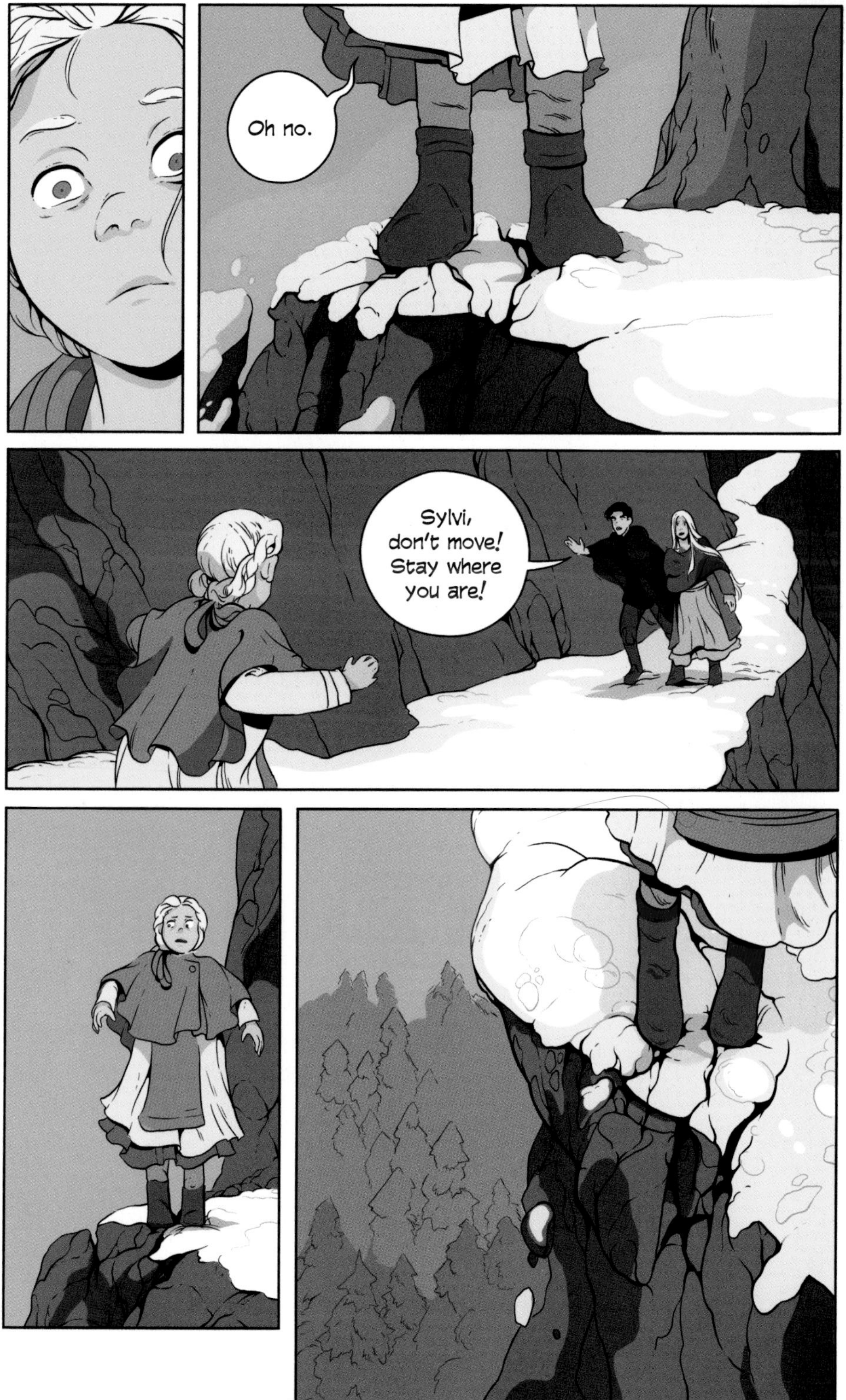
Oh no.
Sylvi, don't move! Stay where you are!

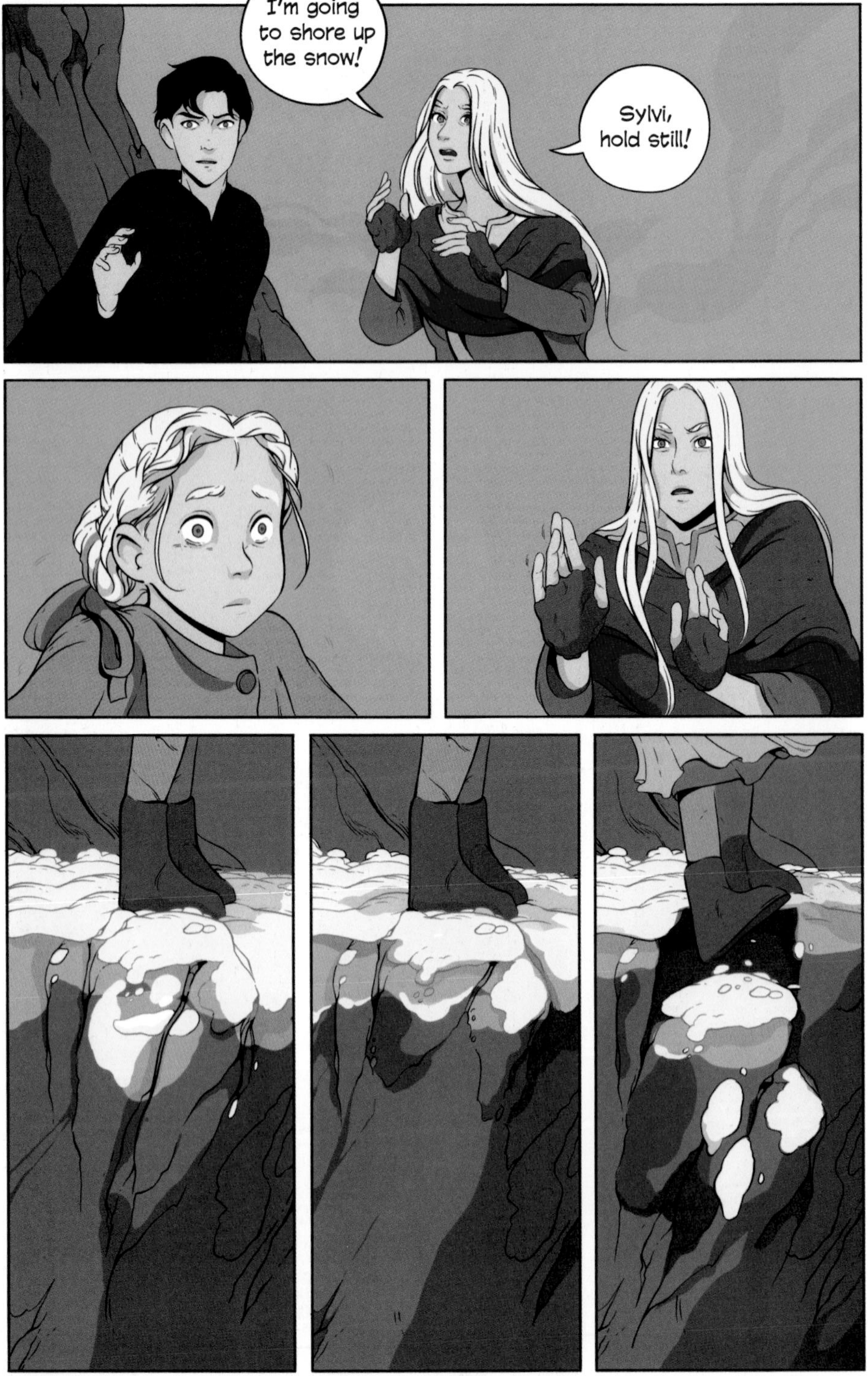
I'm going to shore up the snow!
Sylvi, hold still!

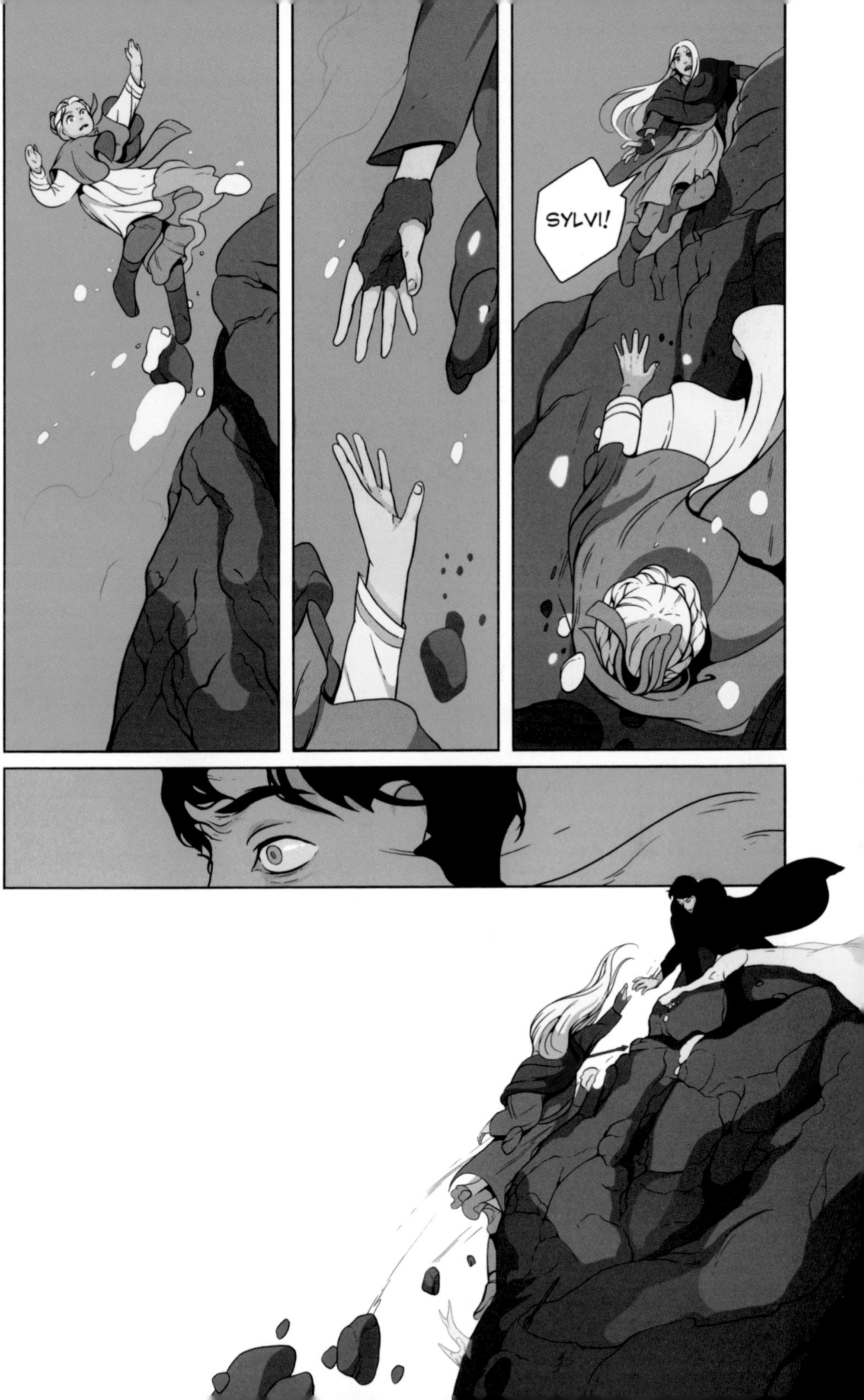
SYLVI!

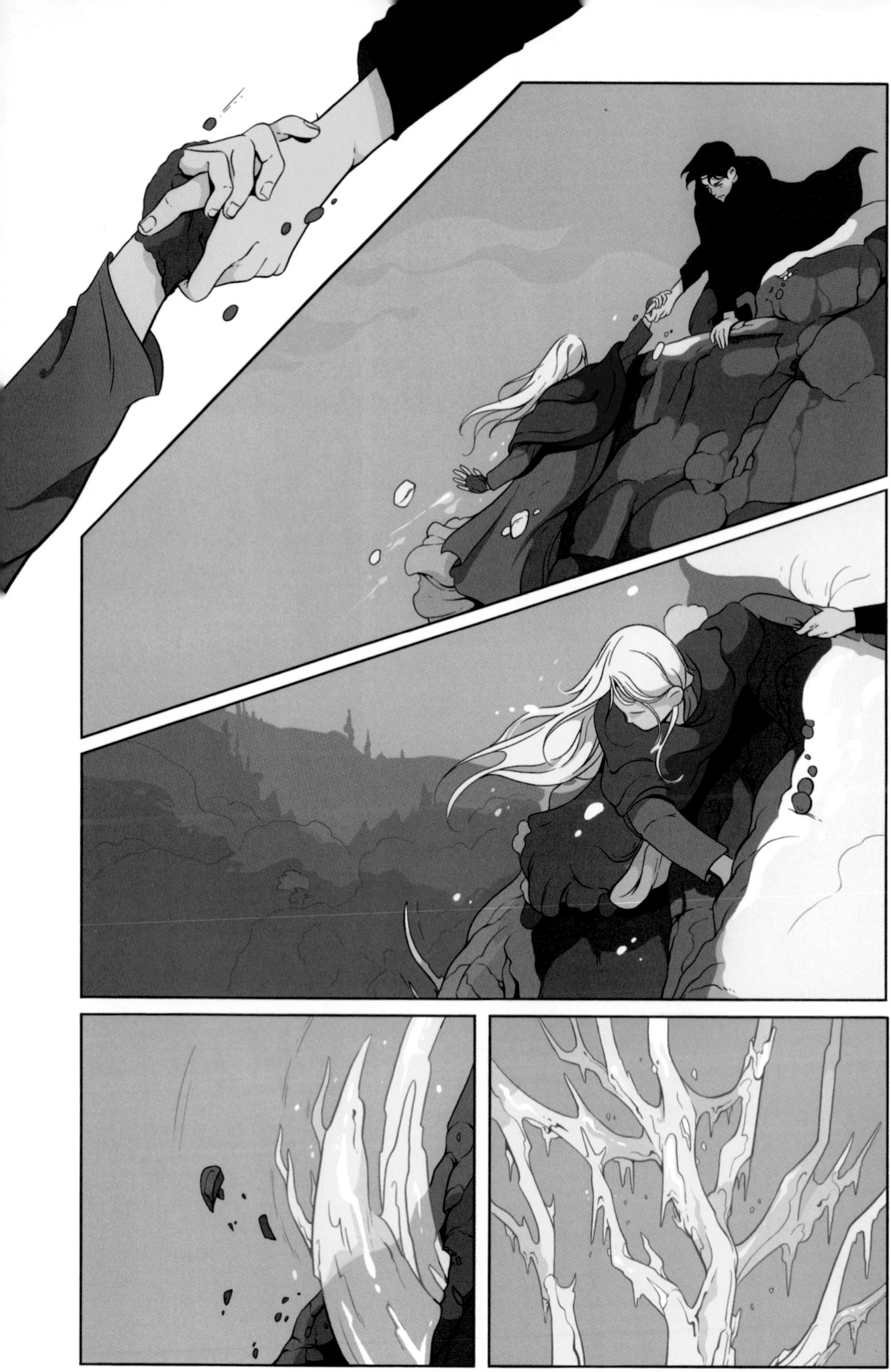

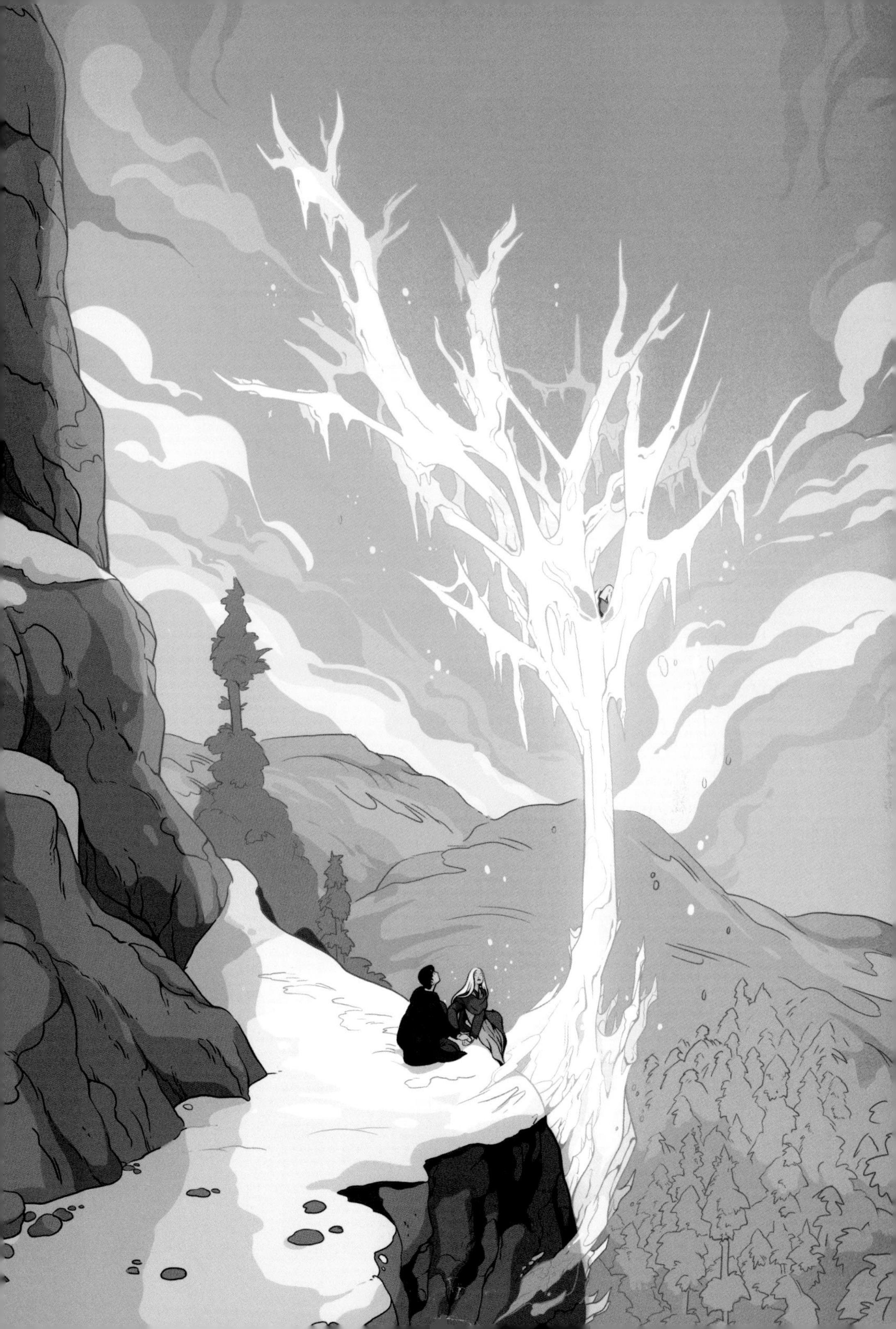

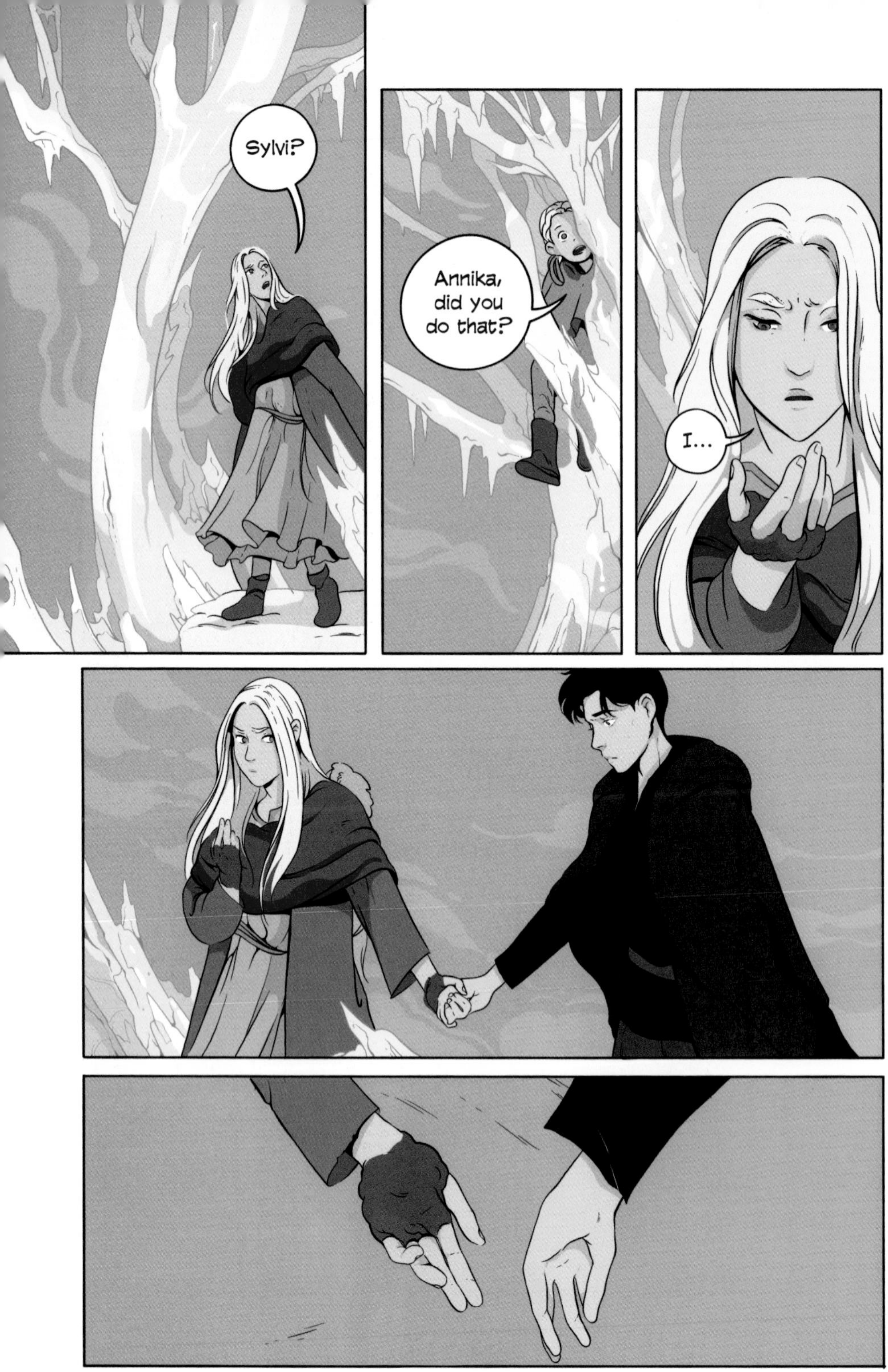
Sylvi?
Annika, did you do that?
I...

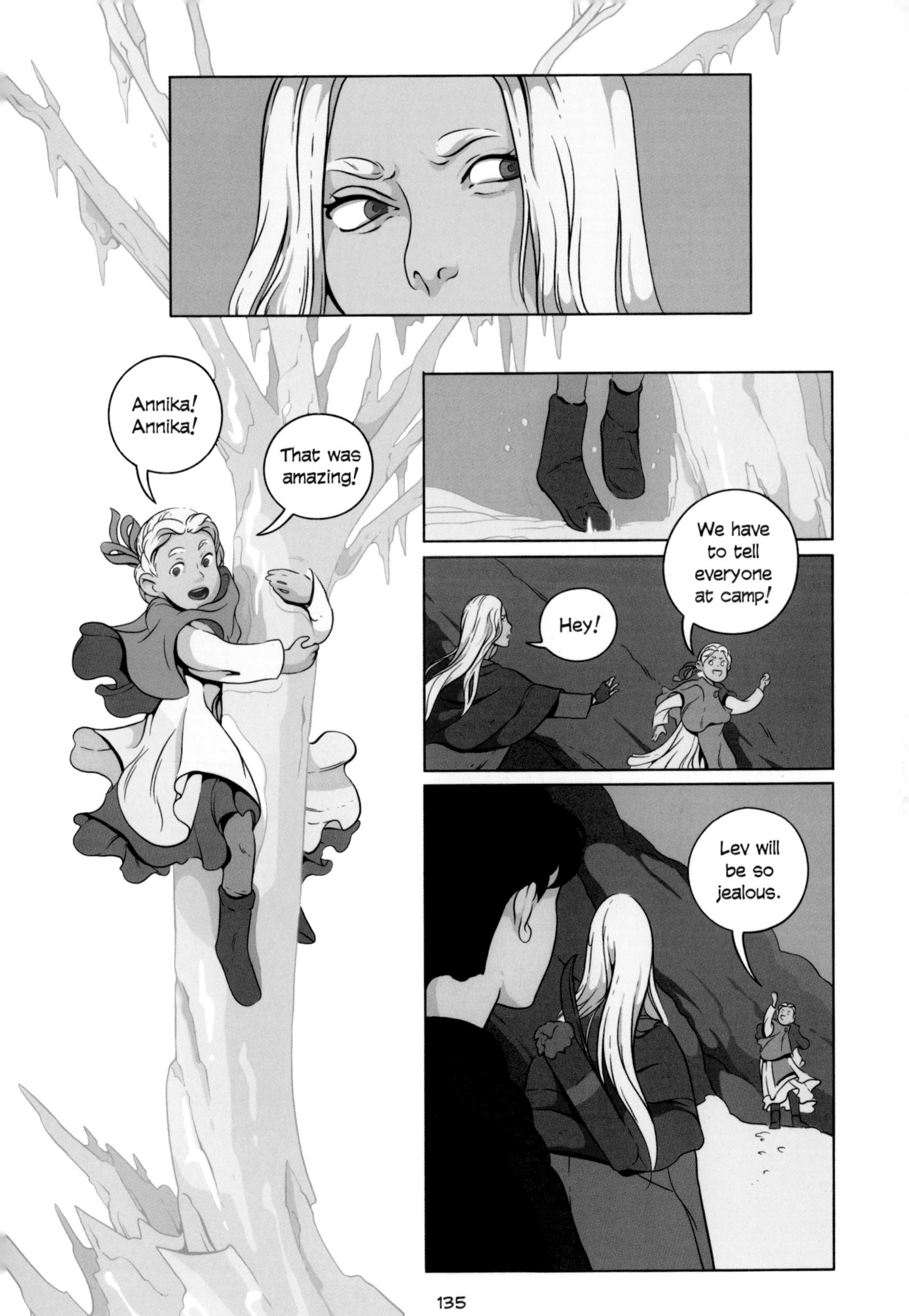
Annika! Annika!
That was amazing!
We have to tell everyone at camp!
Hey!
Lev will be so jealous.

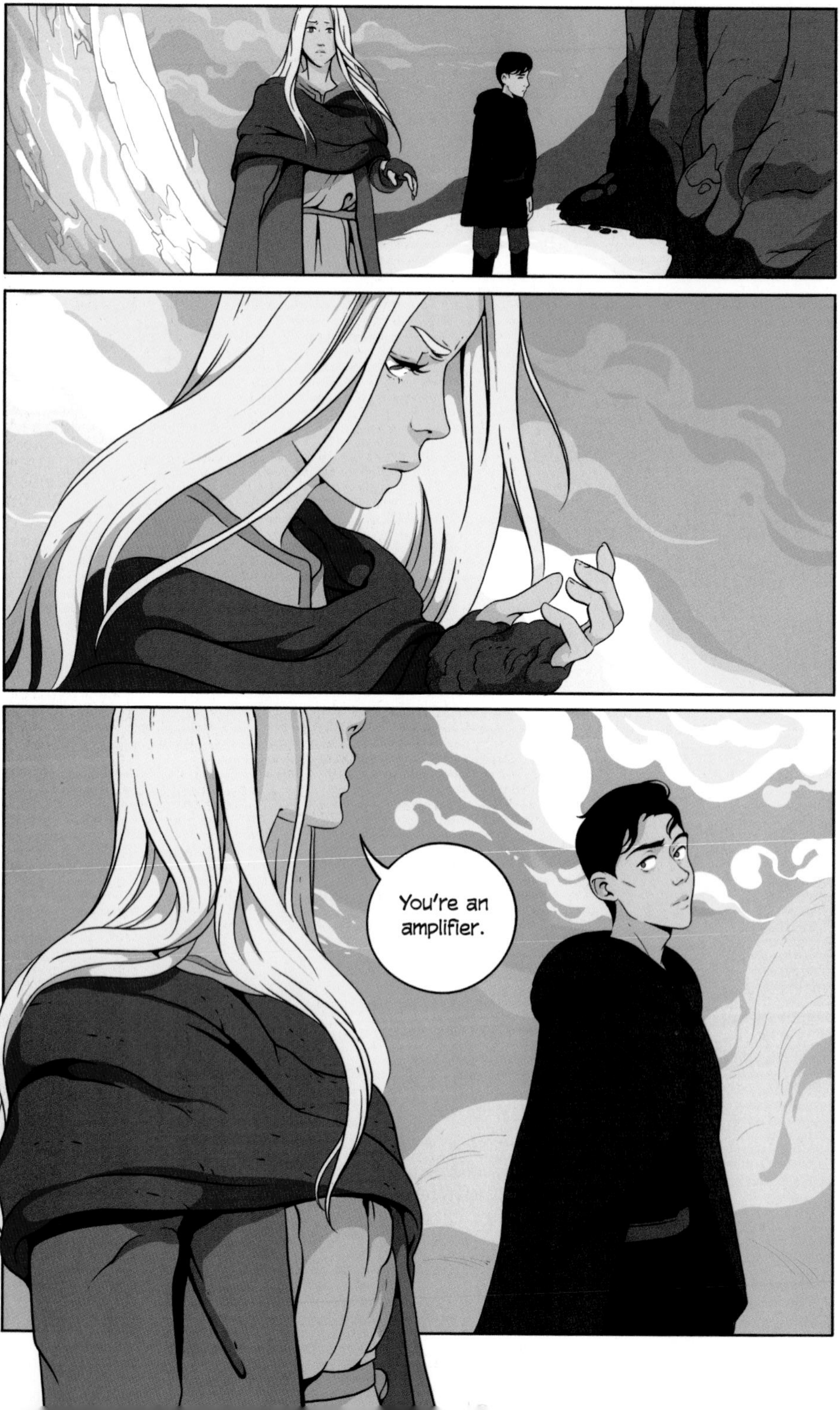
You're an amplifier.

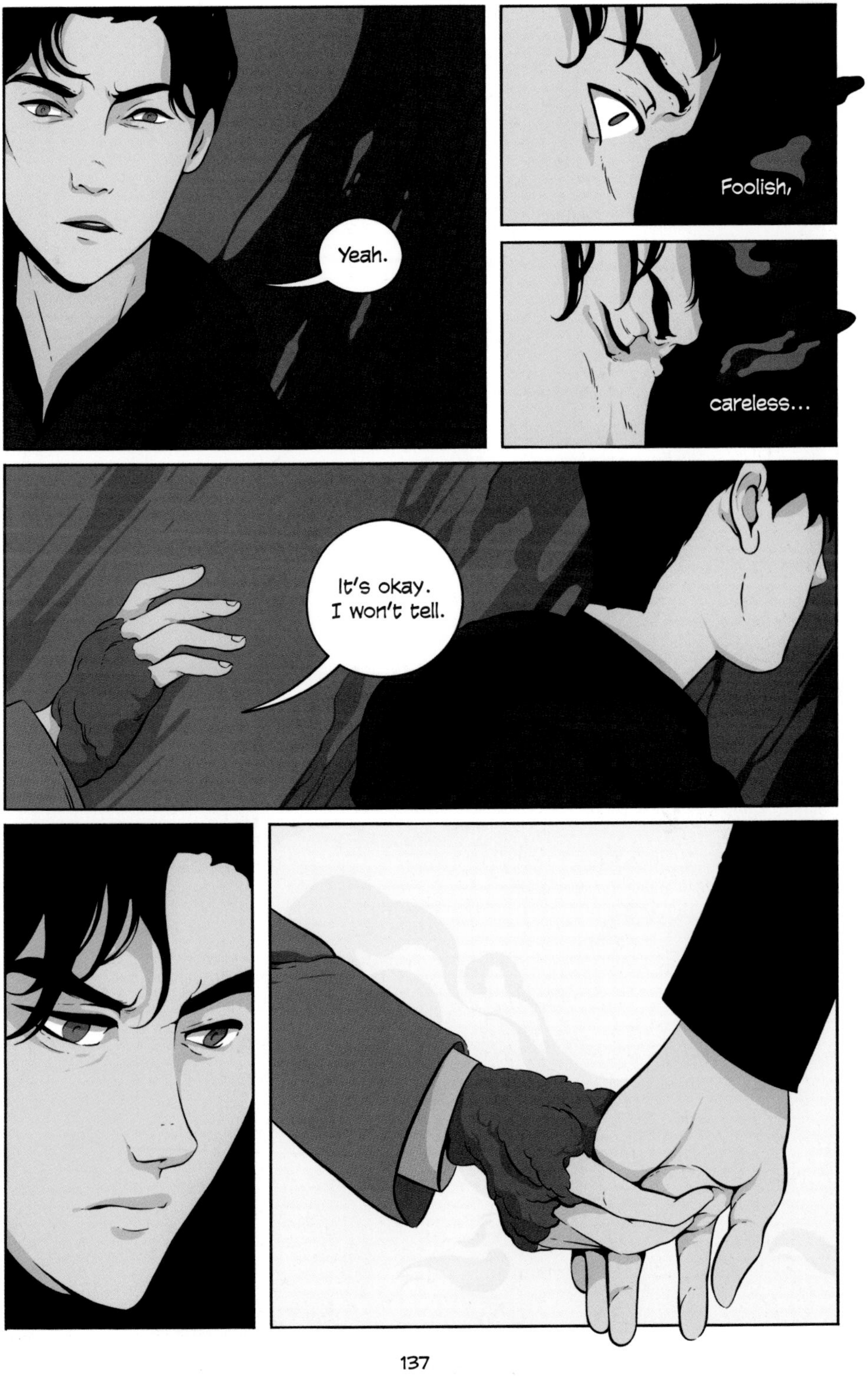
Yeah.
Foolish,
careless...
It's okay. I won't tell.

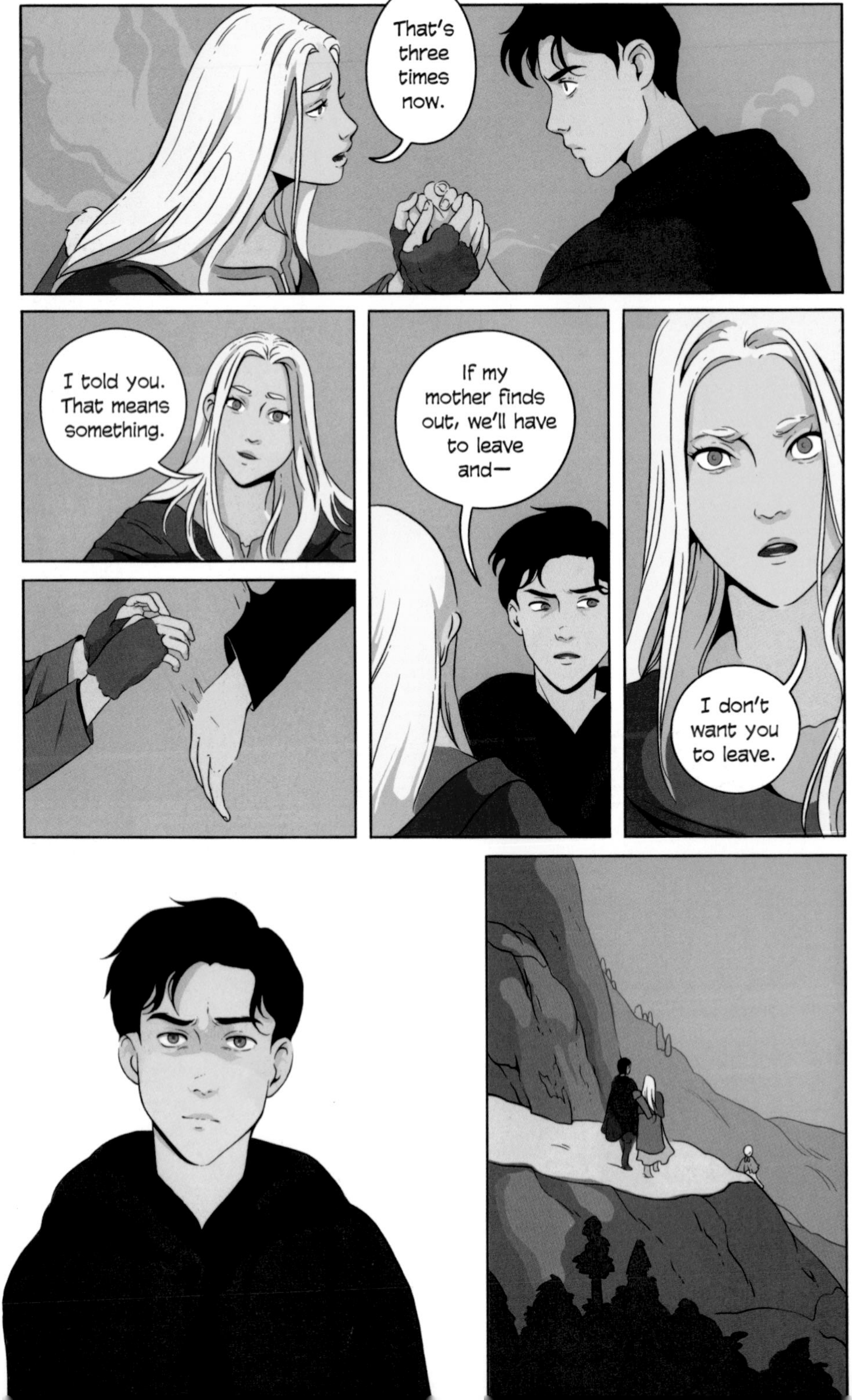
That's three times now.
I told you. That means something.
If my mother finds out, we'll have to leave and—
I don't want you to leave.

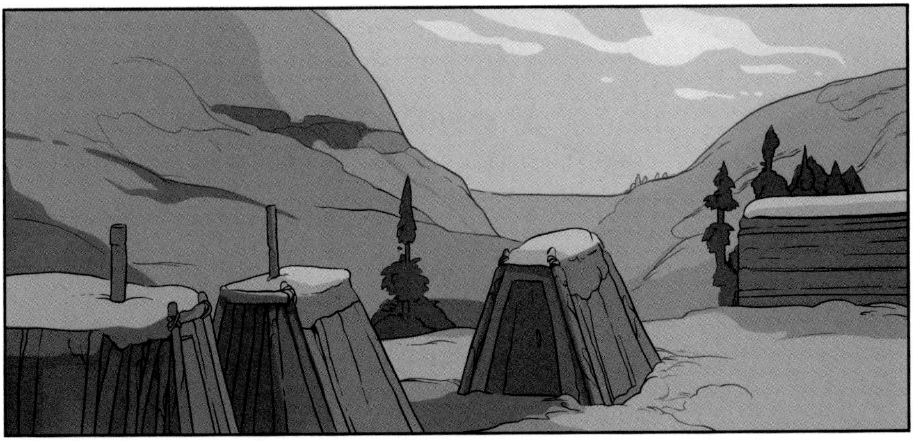

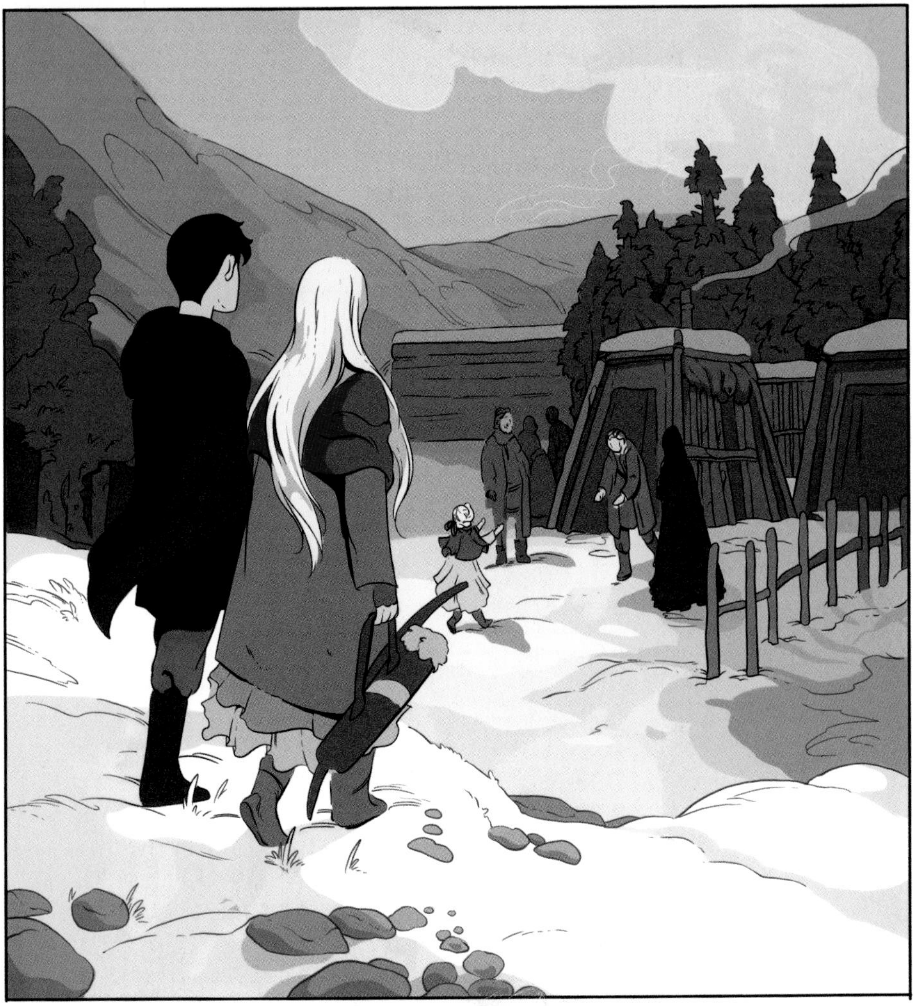

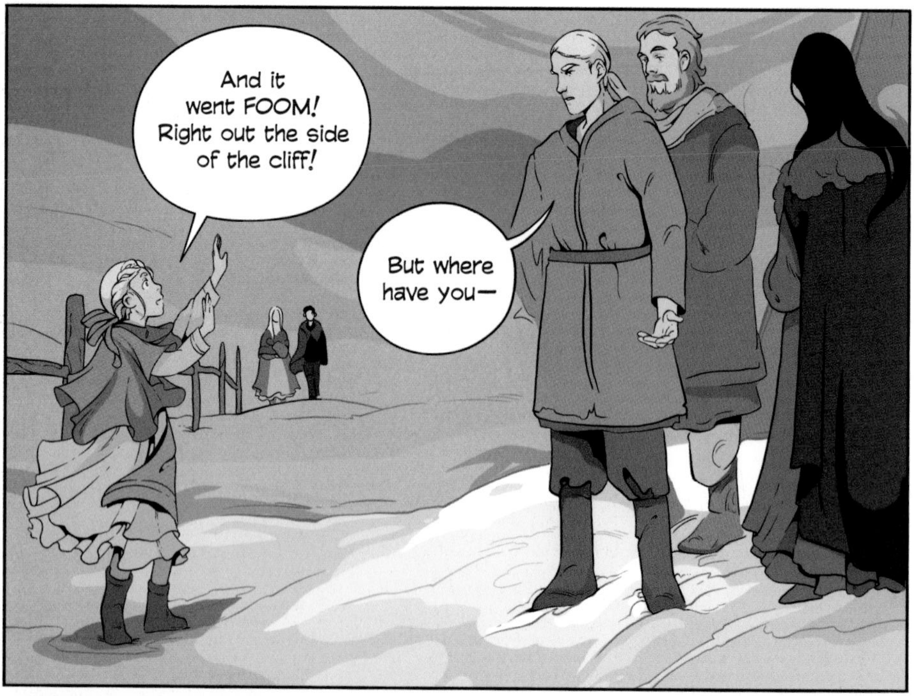
And it went FOOM! Right out the side of the cliff!
But where have you—

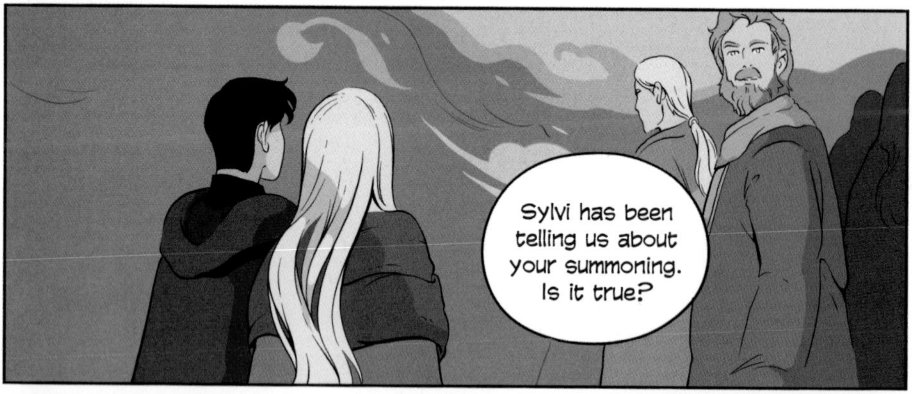
Sylvi has been telling us about your summoning. Is it true?

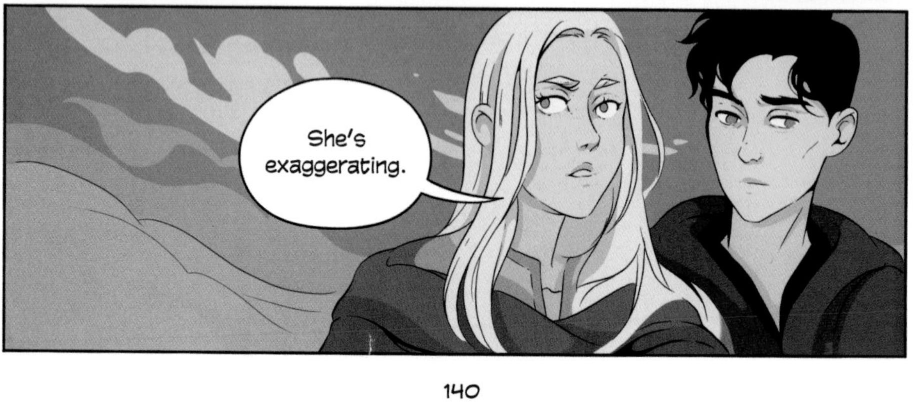
She's exaggerating.

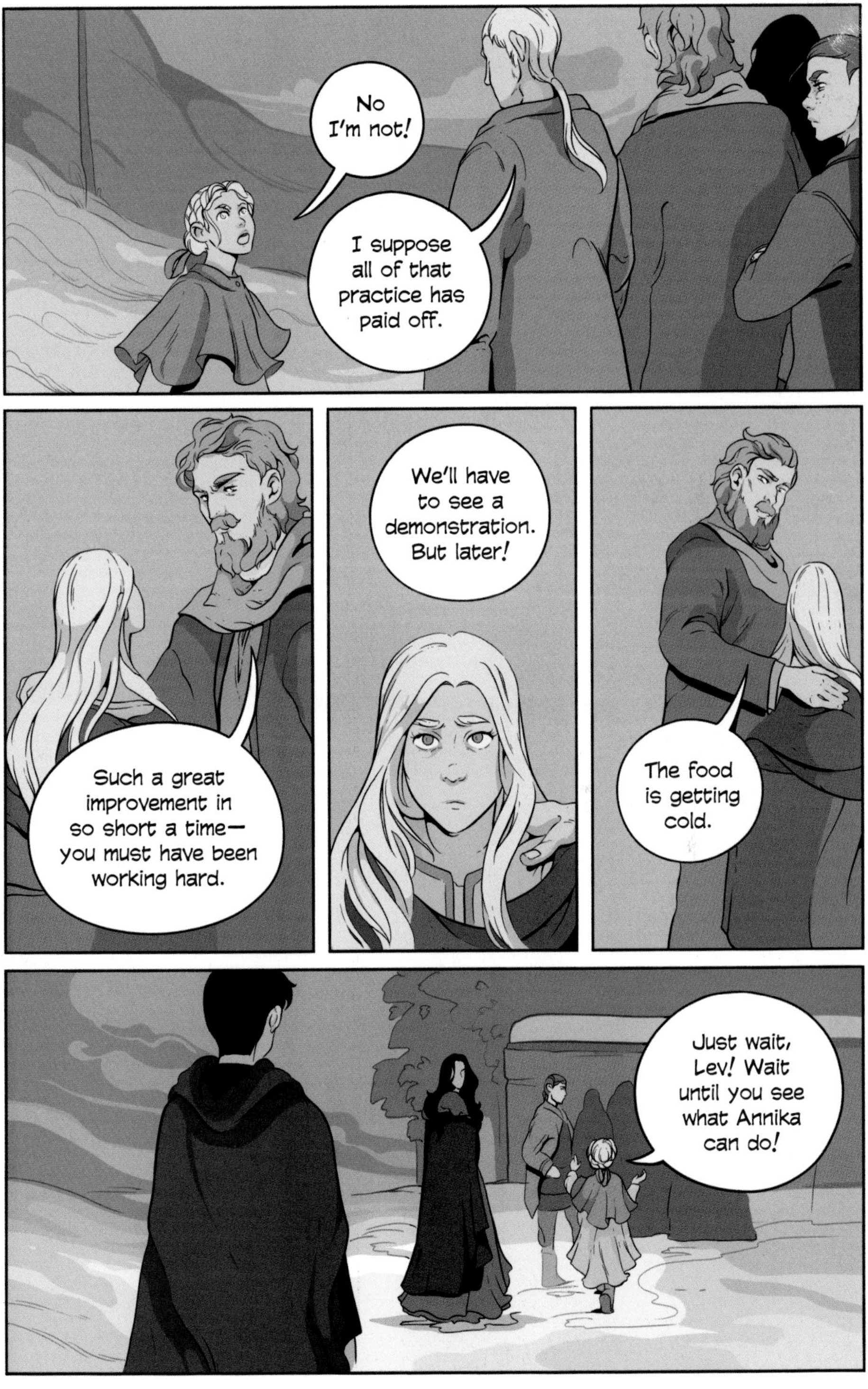
No I'm not!
I suppose all of that practice has paid off.
Such a great improvement in so short a time—you must have been working hard.
We'll have to see a demonstration. But later!
The food is getting cold.
Just wait, Lev! Wait until you see what Annika can do!

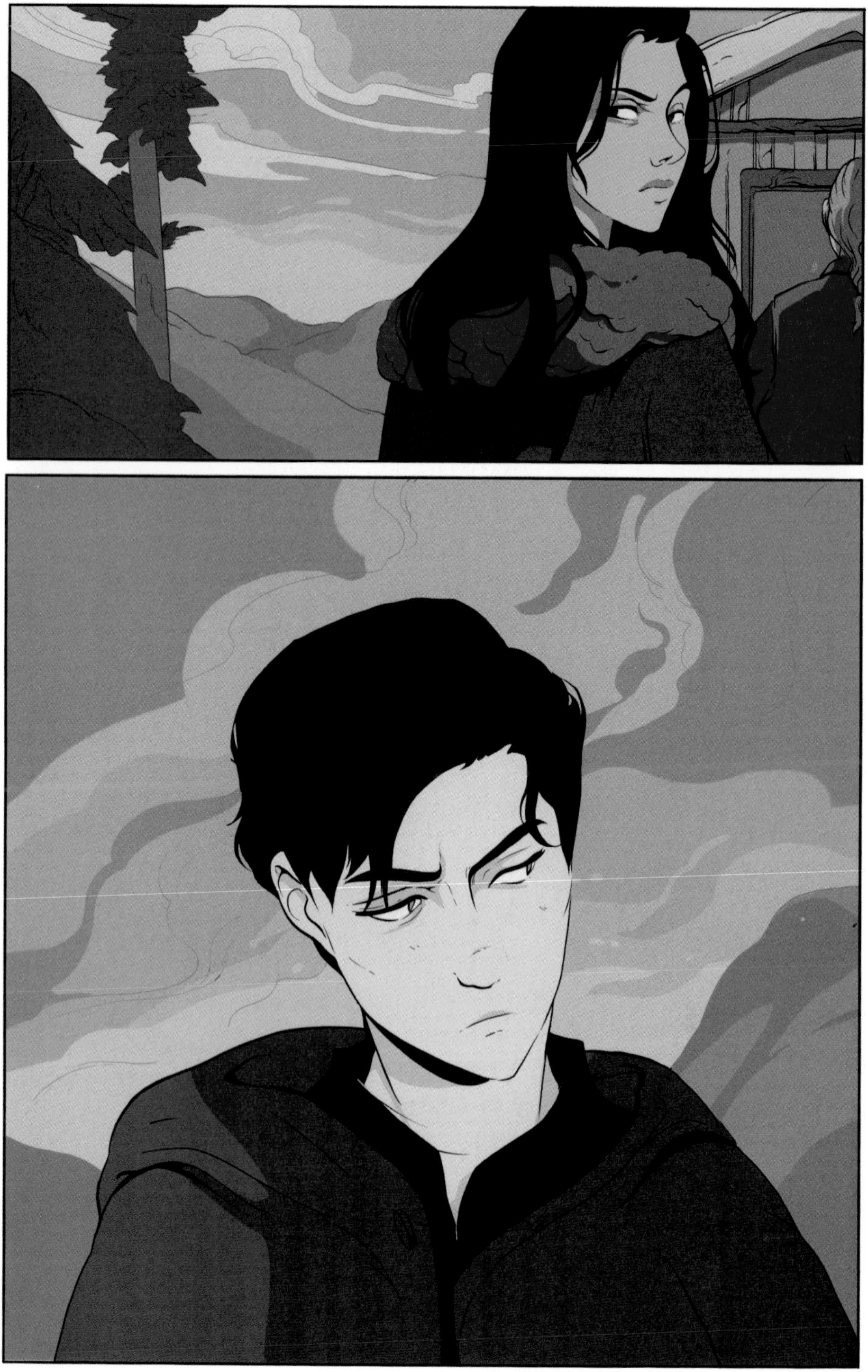

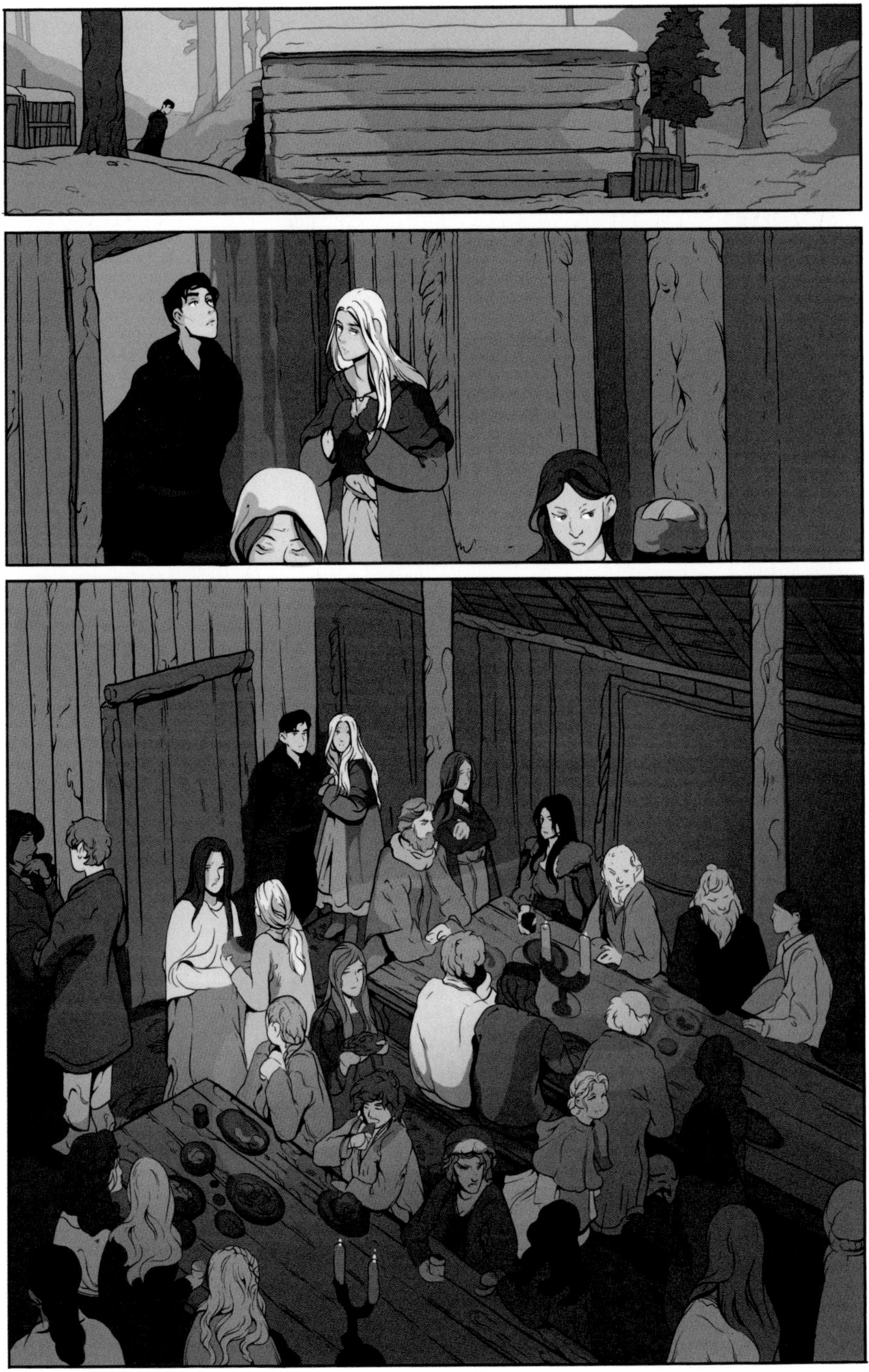

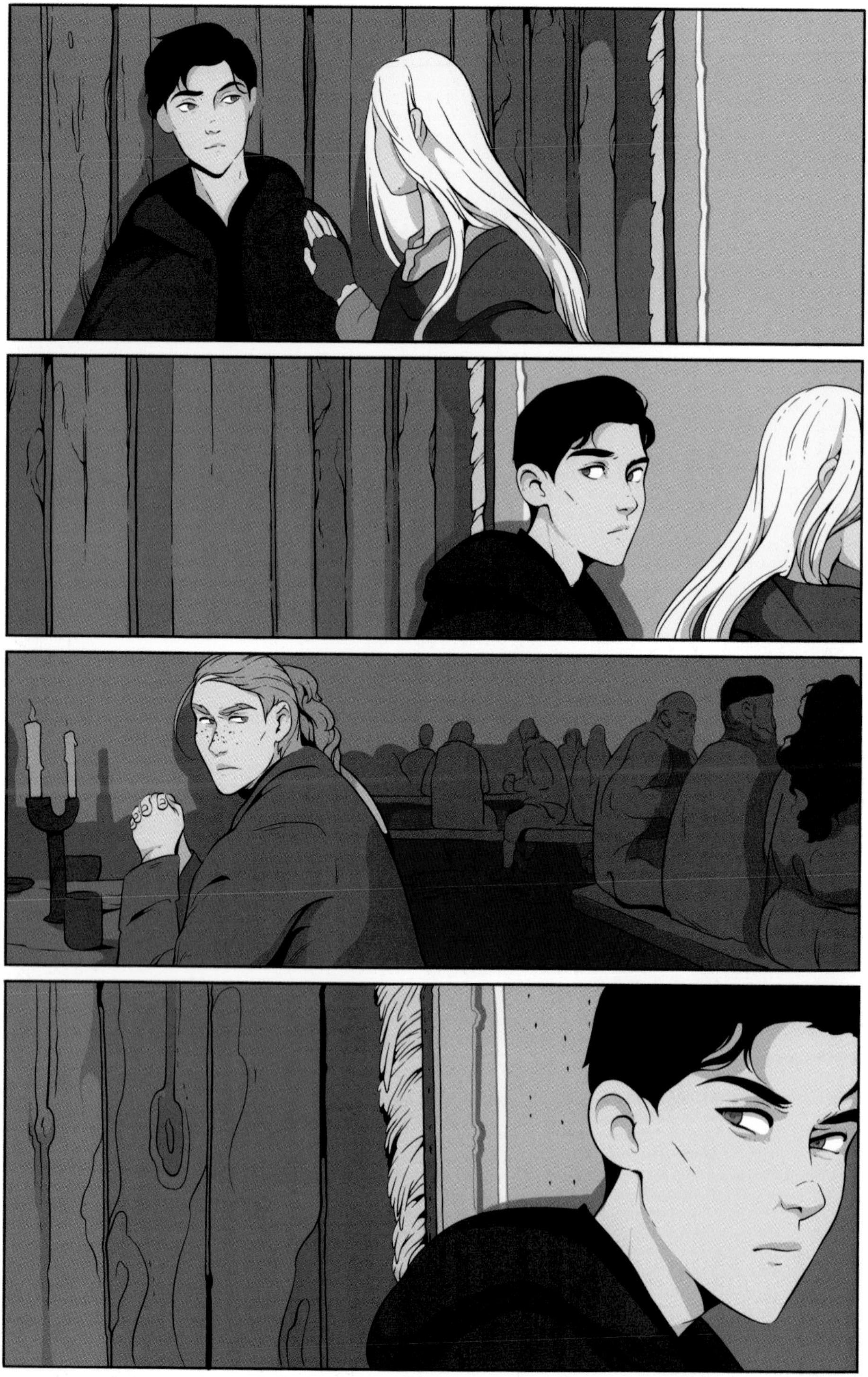

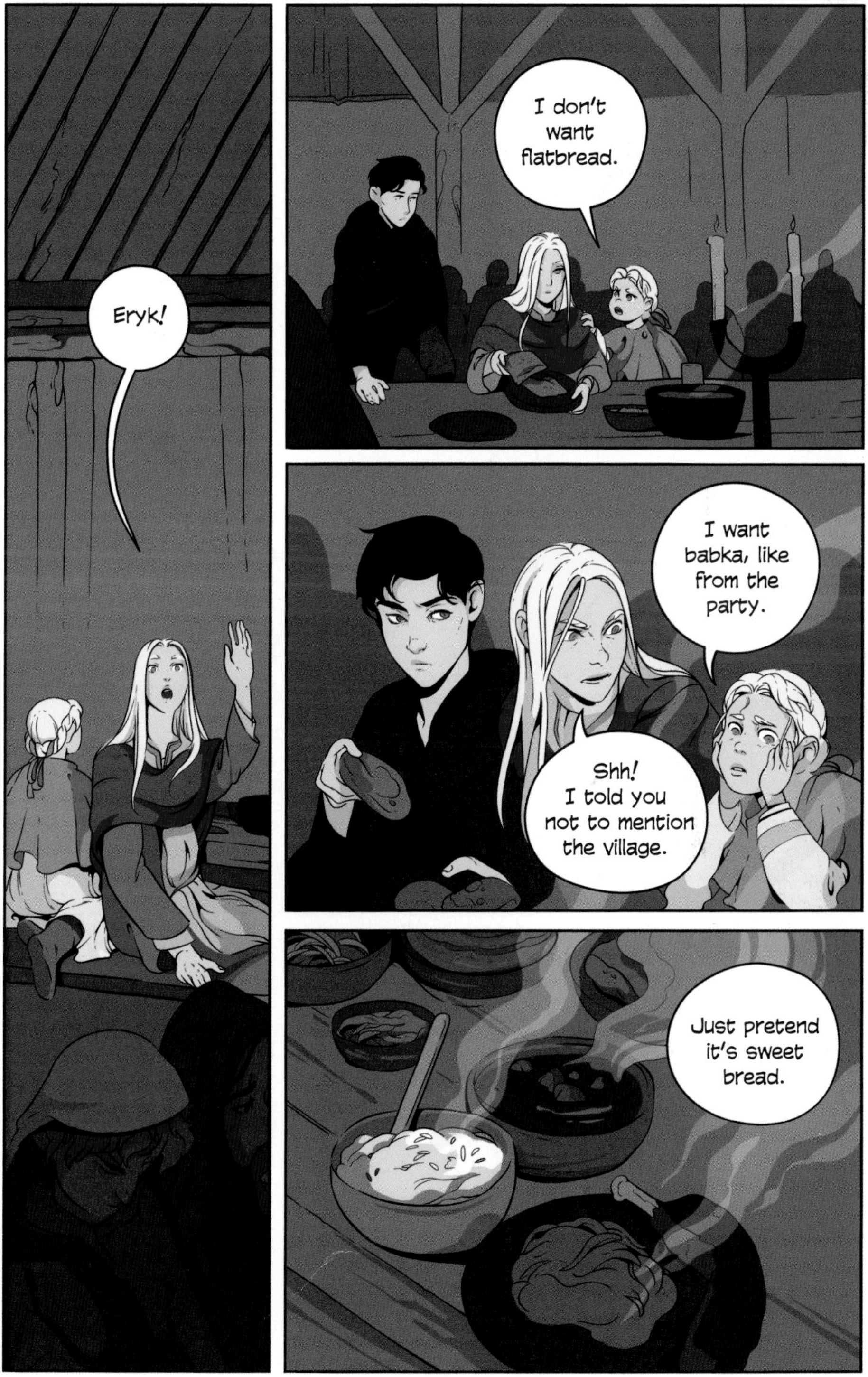

Eryk!
I don't want flatbread.
I want babka, like from the party.
Shh! I told you not to mention the village.
Just pretend it's sweet bread.

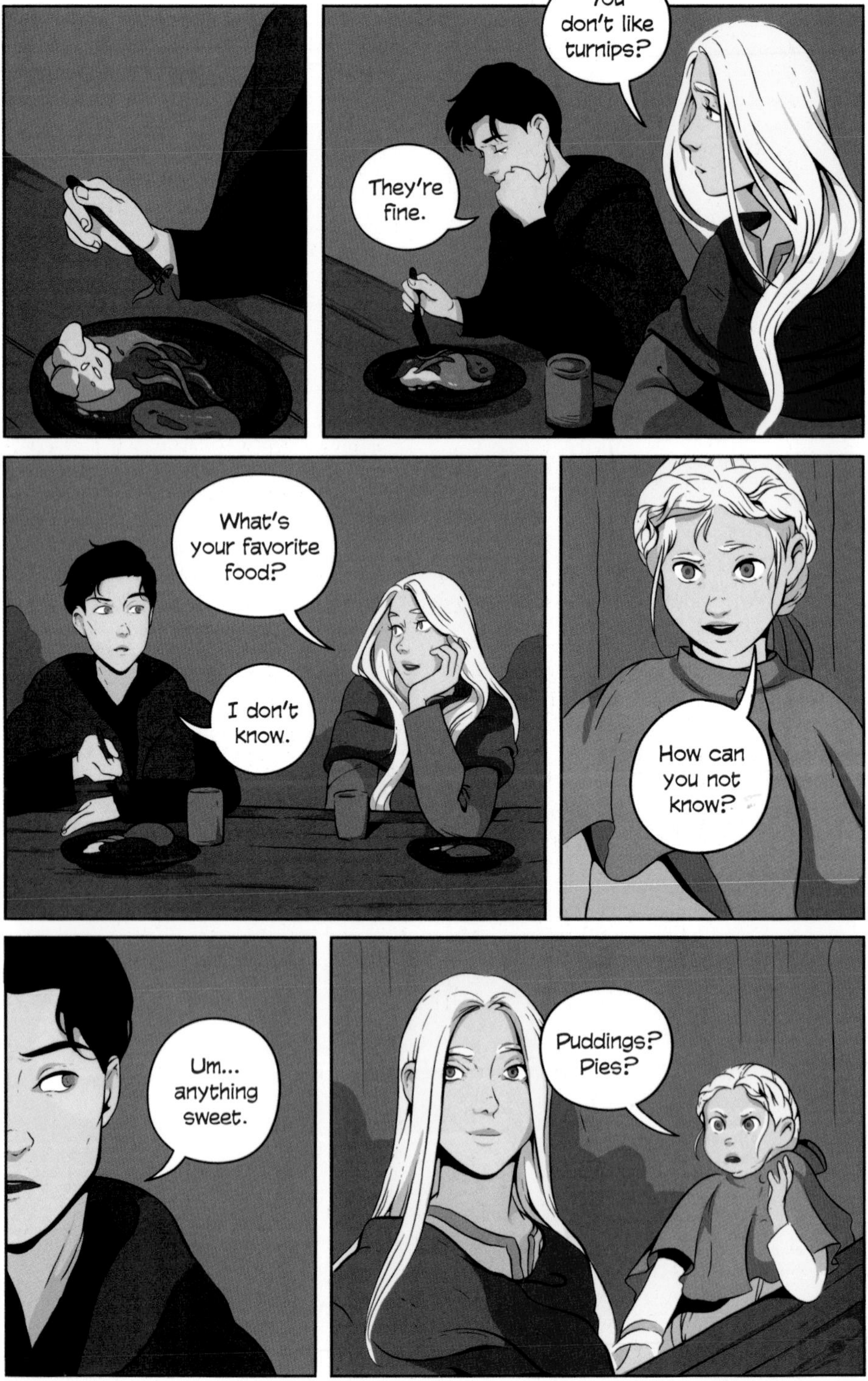
You don't like turnips?
They're fine.
What's your favorite food?
I don't know.
How can you not know?
Um... anything sweet.
Puddings? Pies?

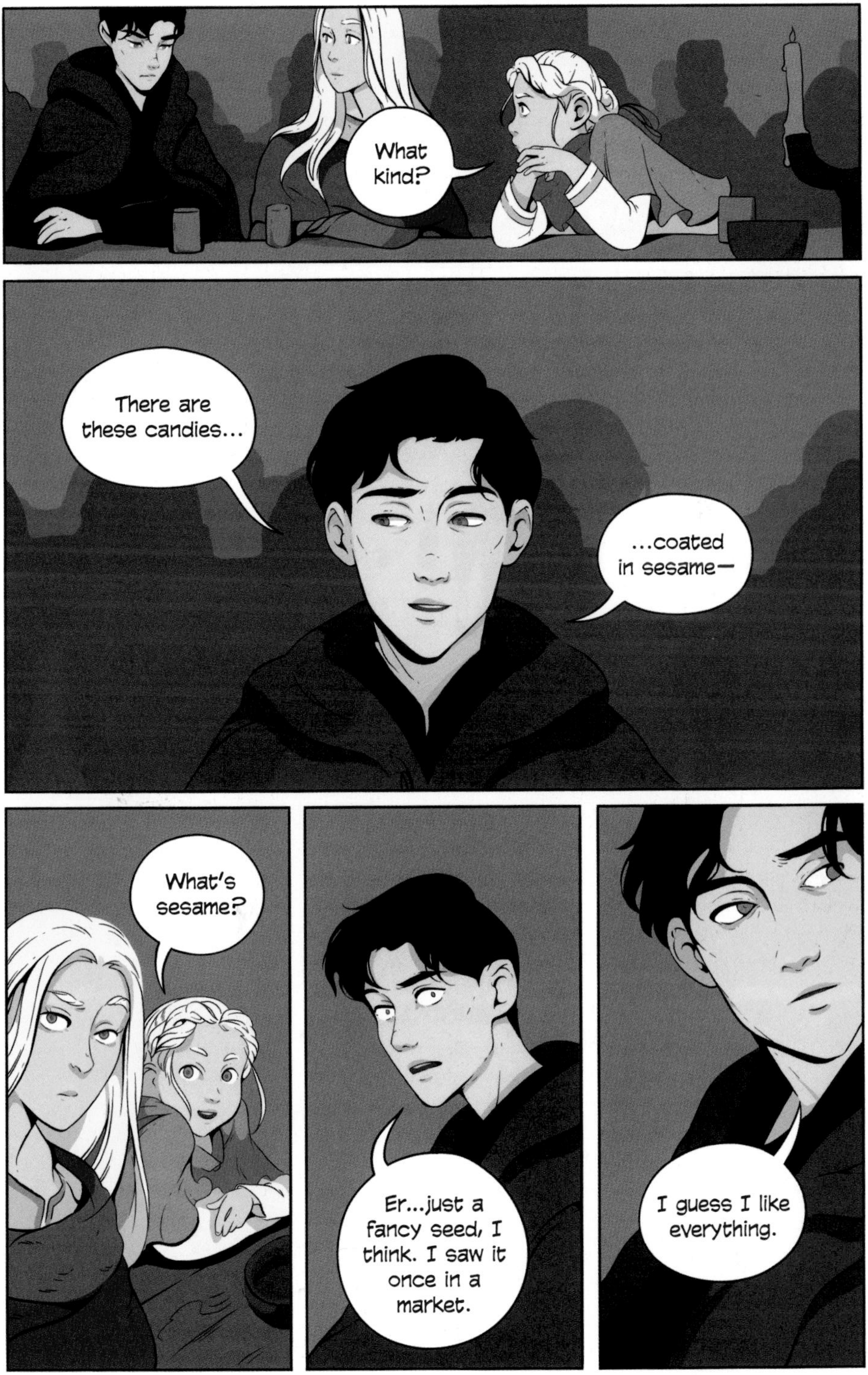
What kind?
There are these candies...
...coated in sesame—
What's sesame?
Er...just a fancy seed, I think. I saw it once in a market.
I guess I like everything.

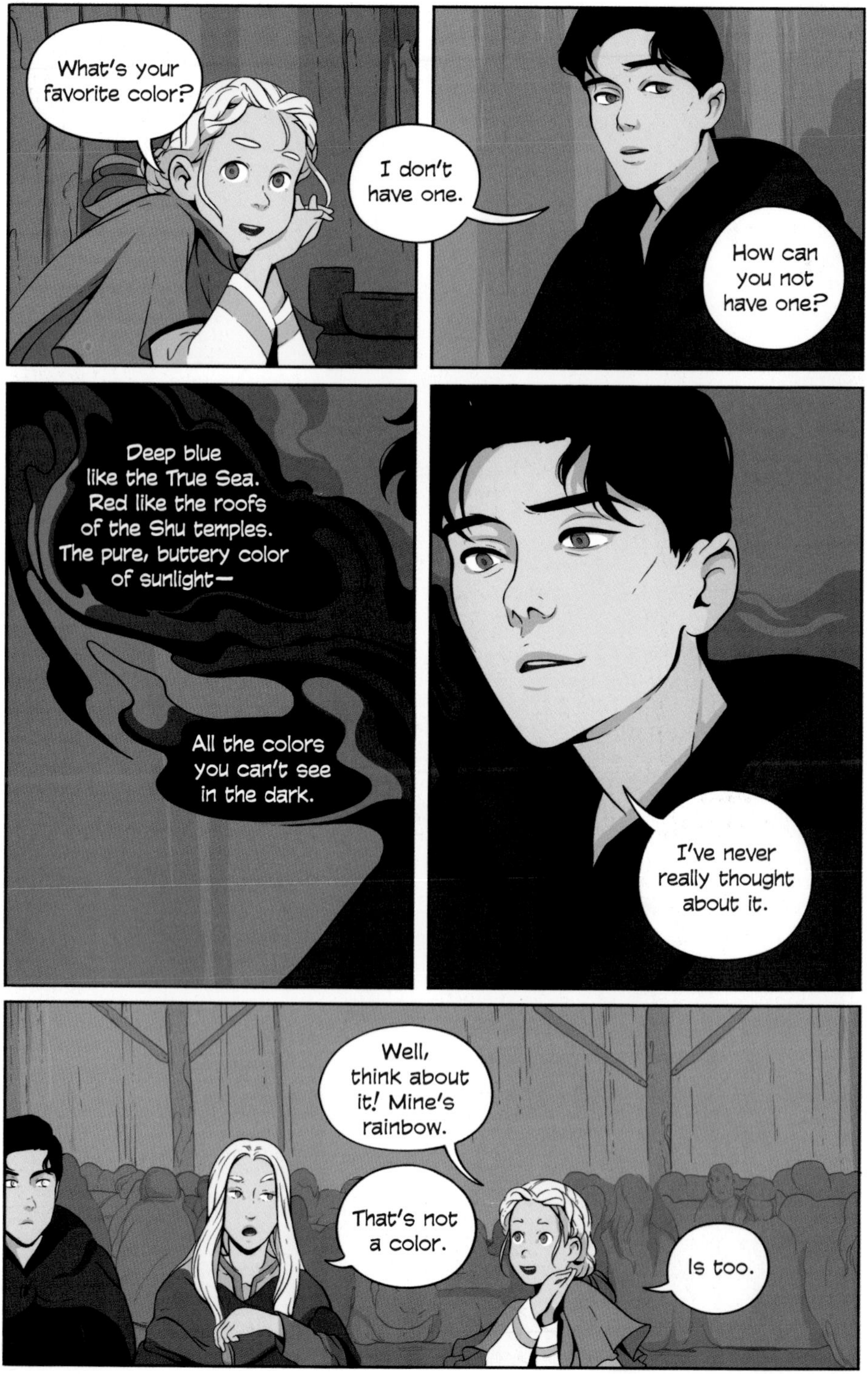
What's your favorite color?
I don't have one.
How can you not have one?
Deep blue like the True Sea. Red like the roofs of the Shu temples. The pure, buttery color of sunlight—
All the colors you can't see in the dark.
I've never really thought about it.
Well, think about it! Mine's rainbow.
That's not a color.
Is too.

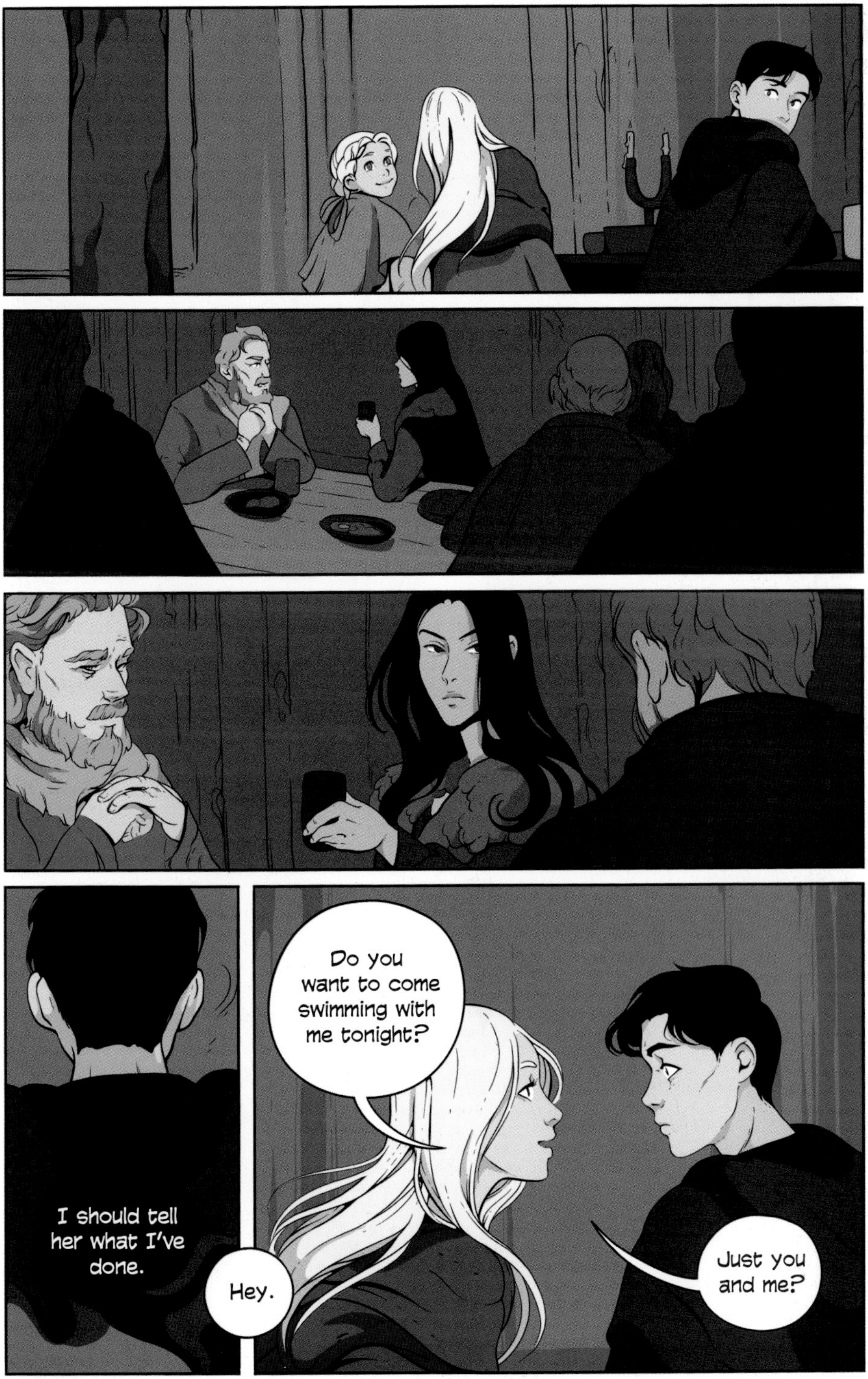
I should tell her what I've done.
Hey.
Do you want to come swimming with me tonight?
Just you and me?

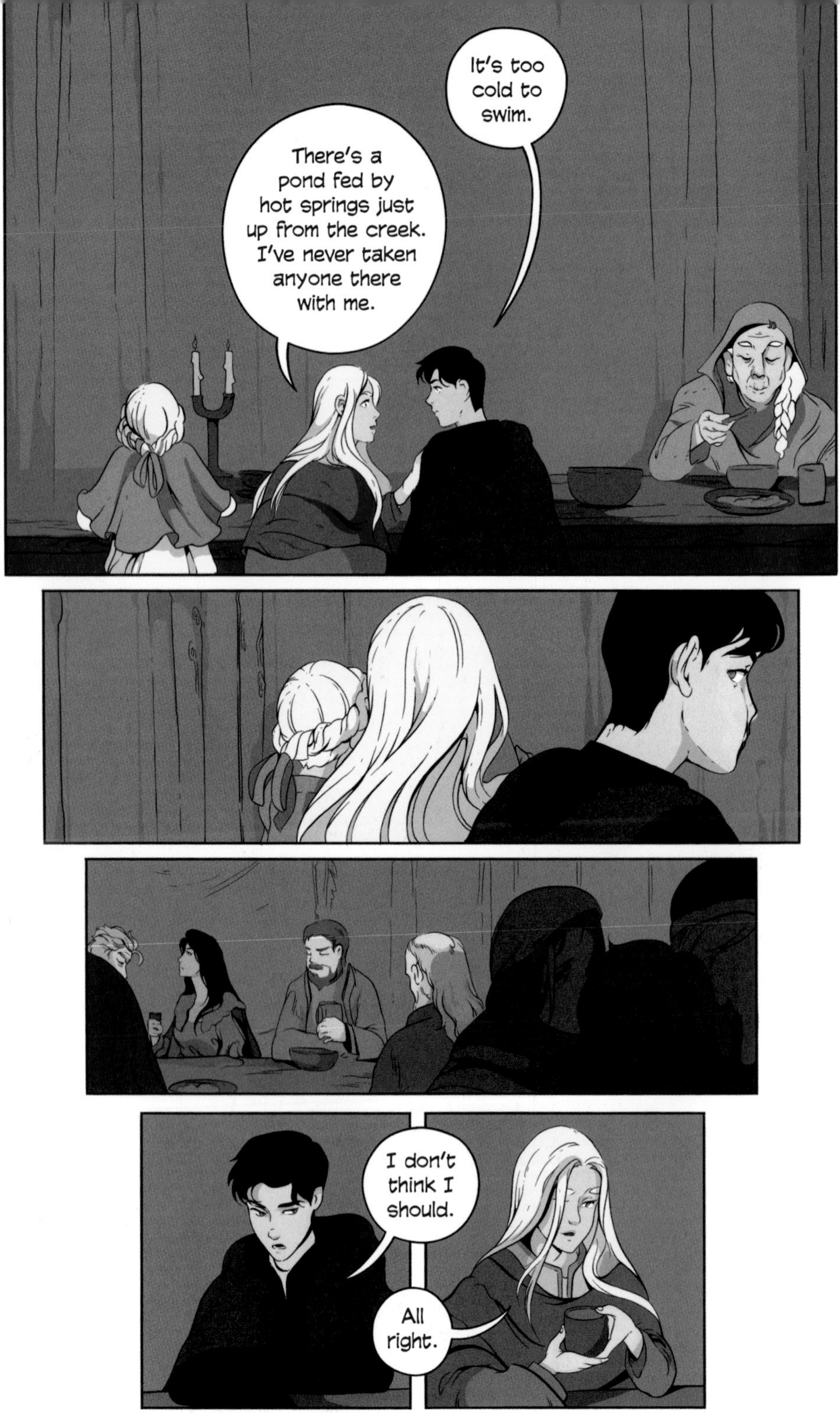
There's a pond fed by hot springs just up from the creek. I've never taken anyone there with me.
It's too cold to swim.
I don't think I should.
All right.

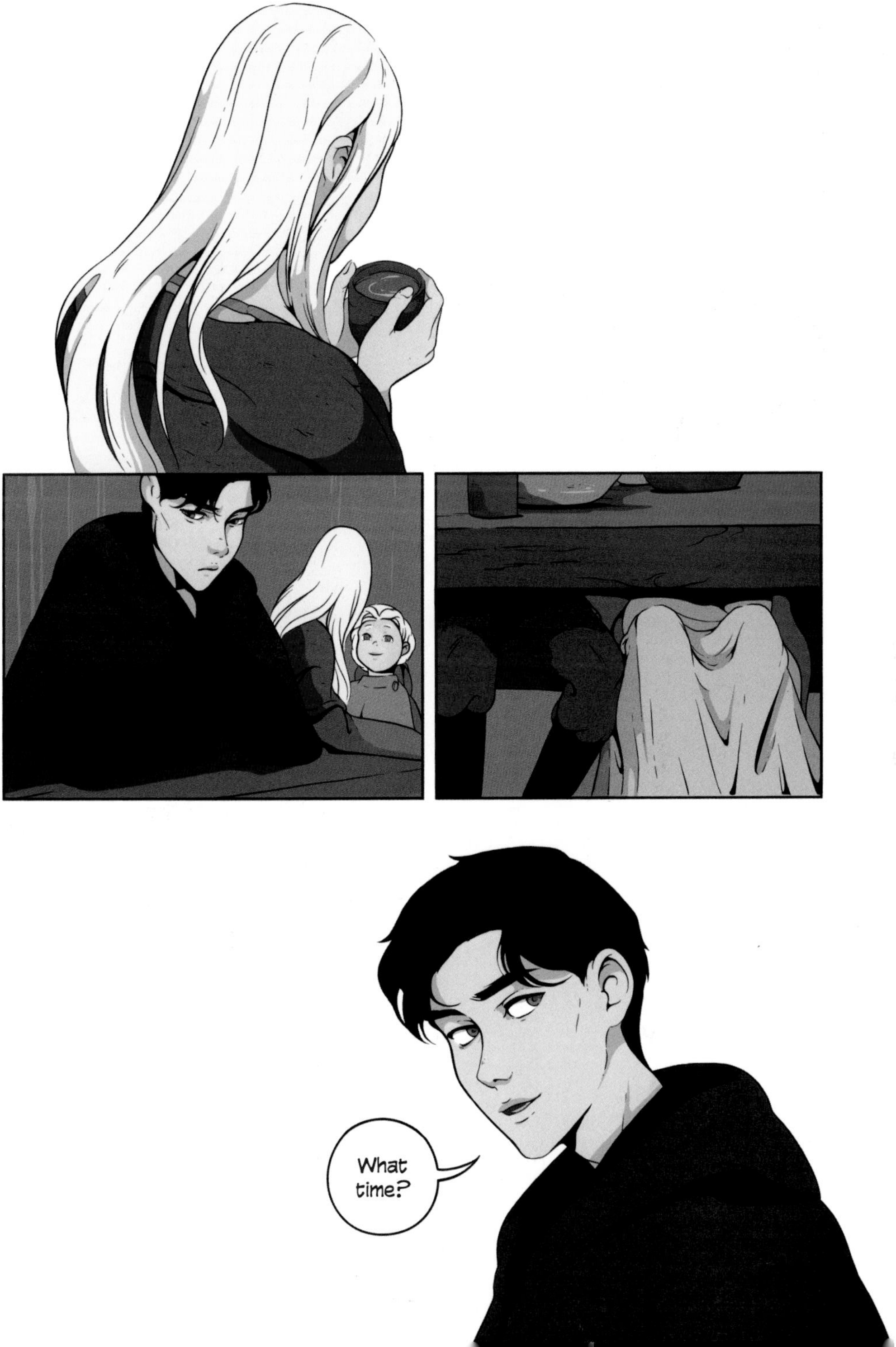
What time?

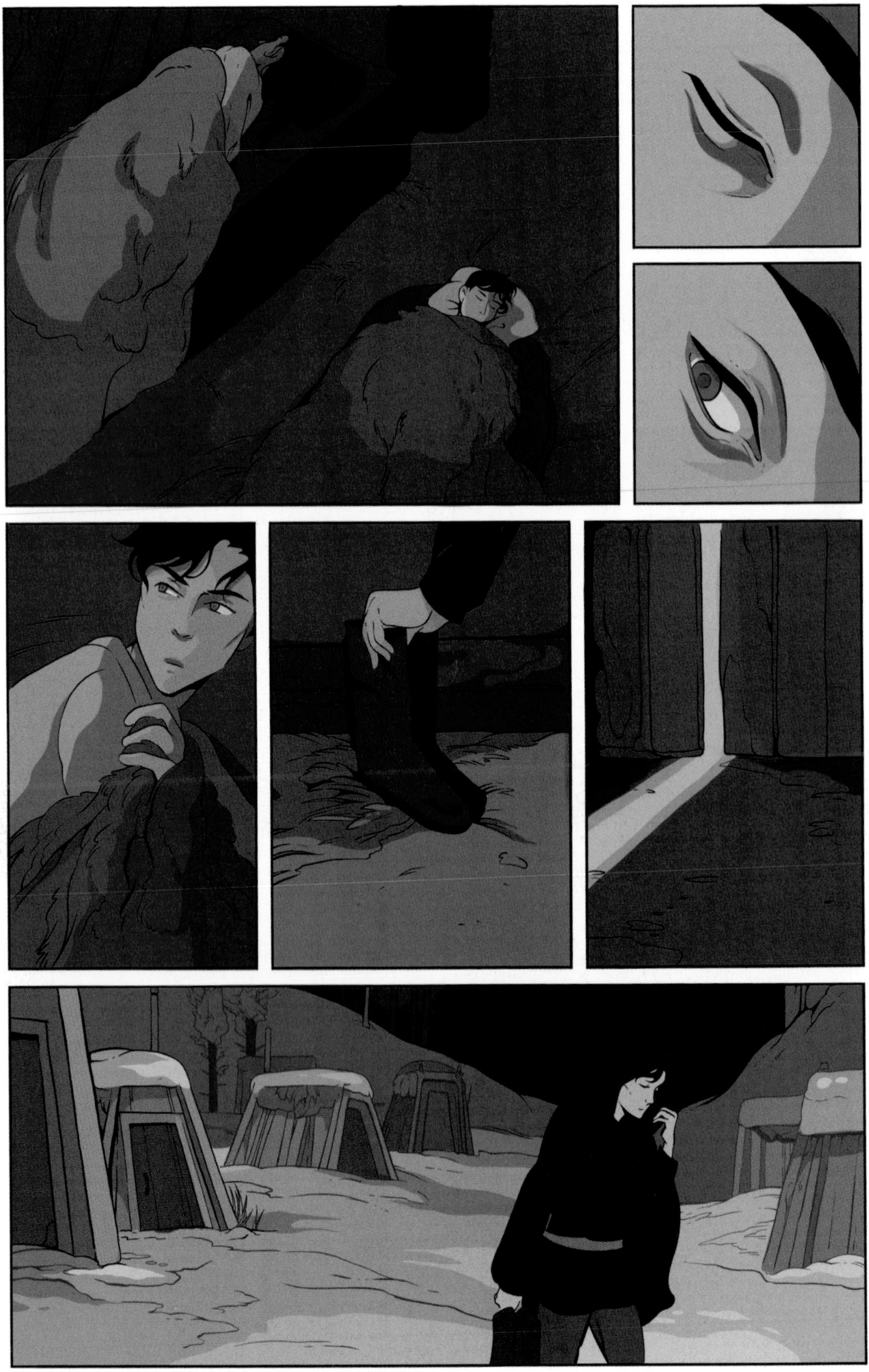

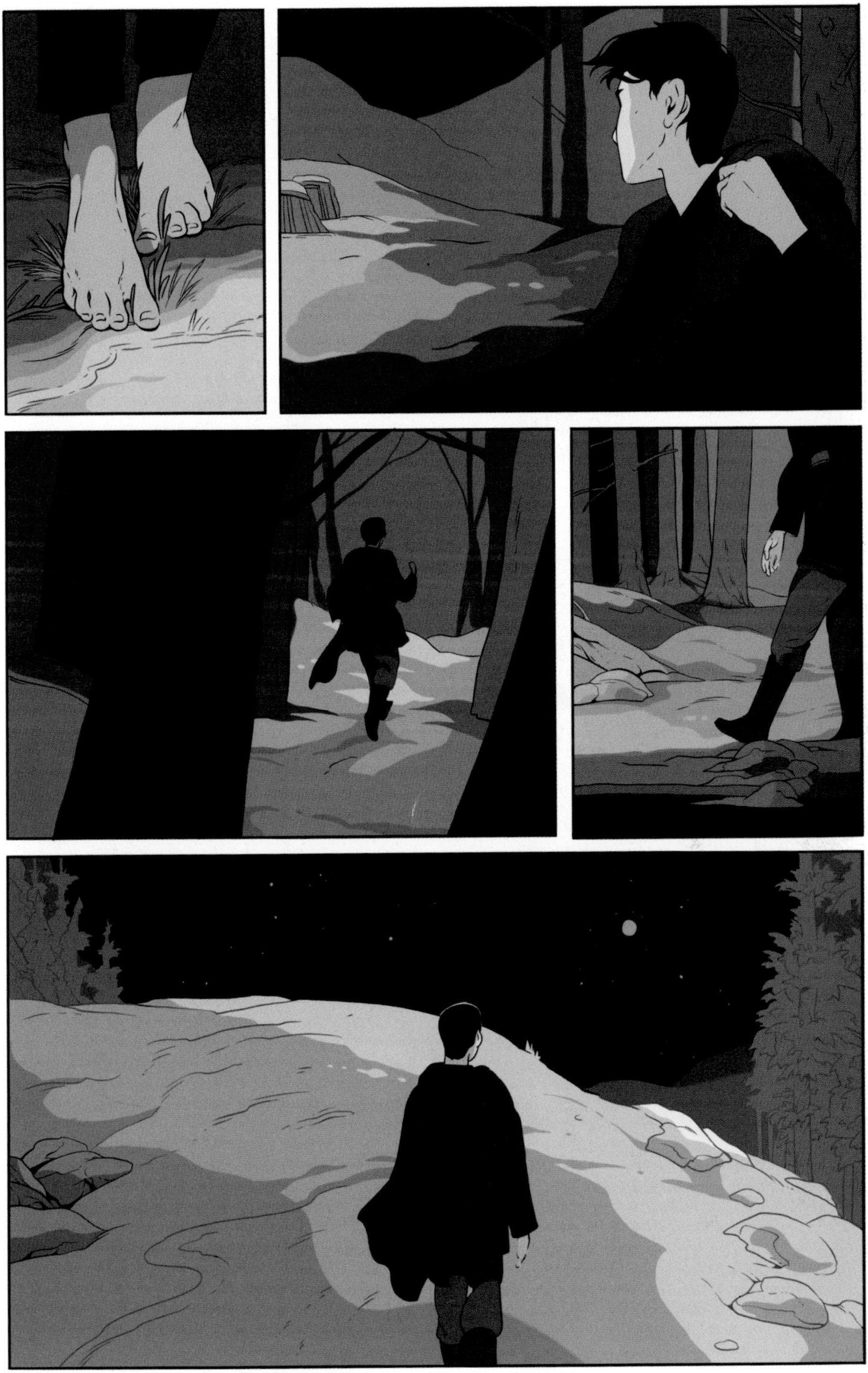

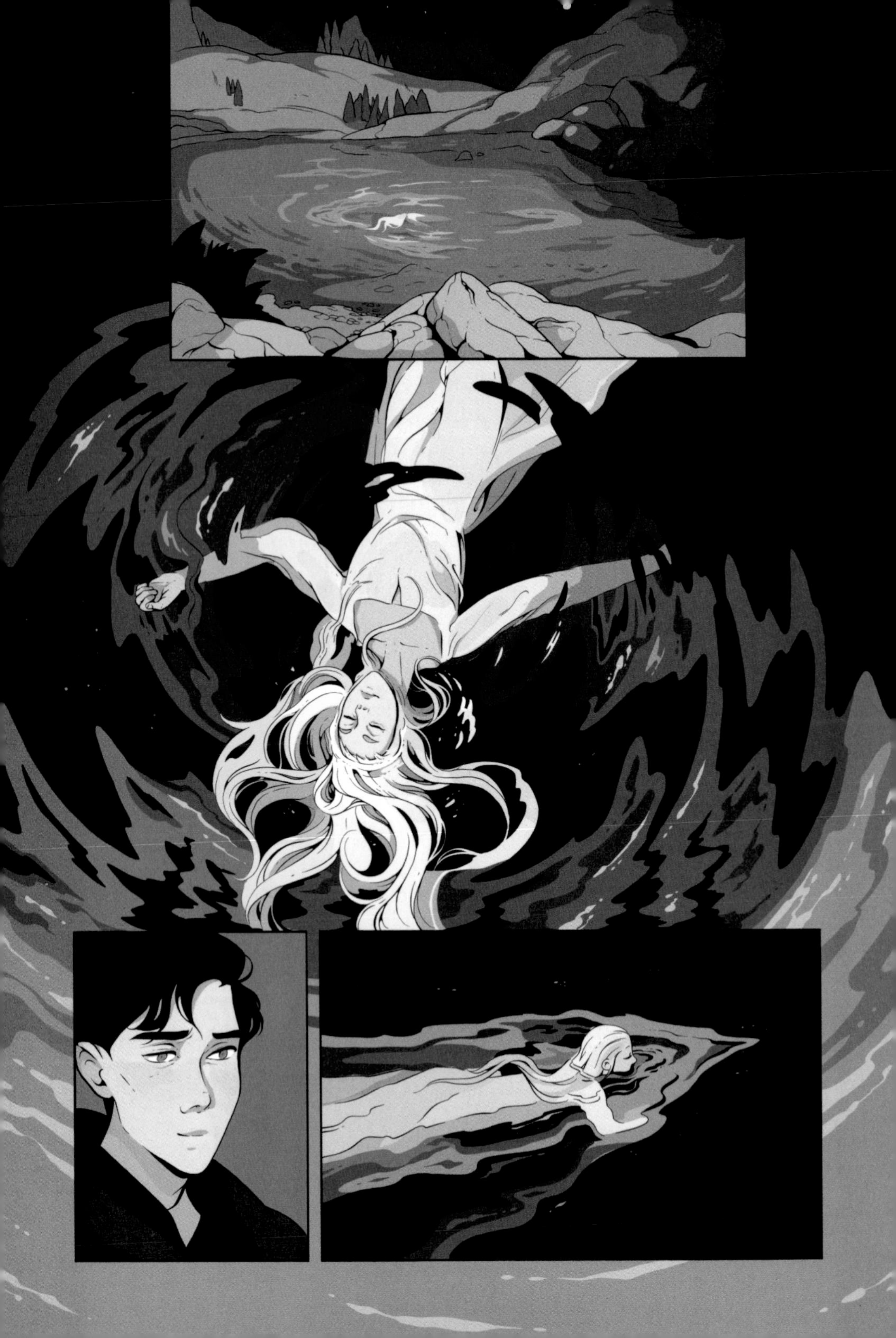

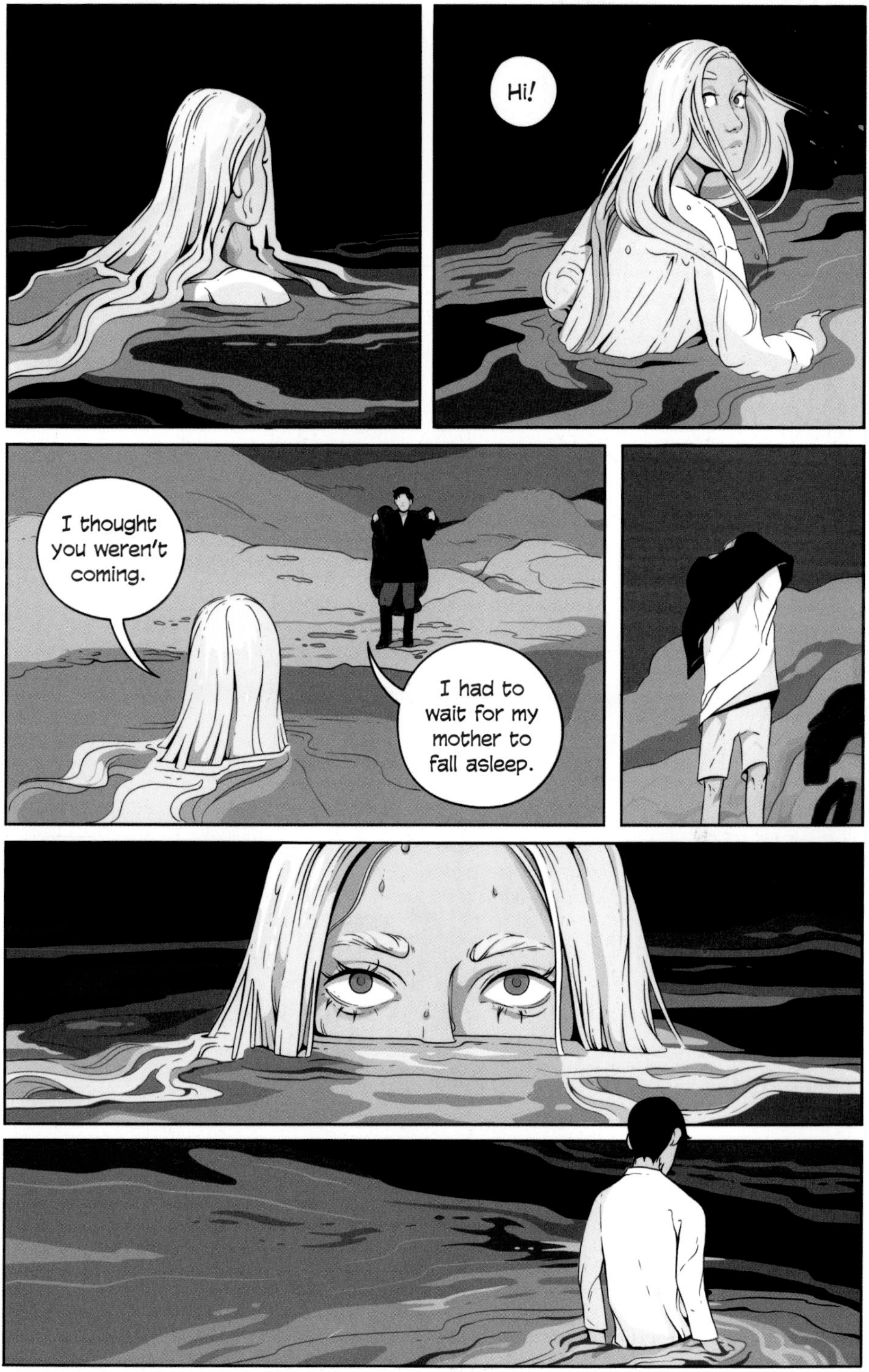
Hi!
I thought you weren't coming.
I had to wait for my mother to fall asleep.

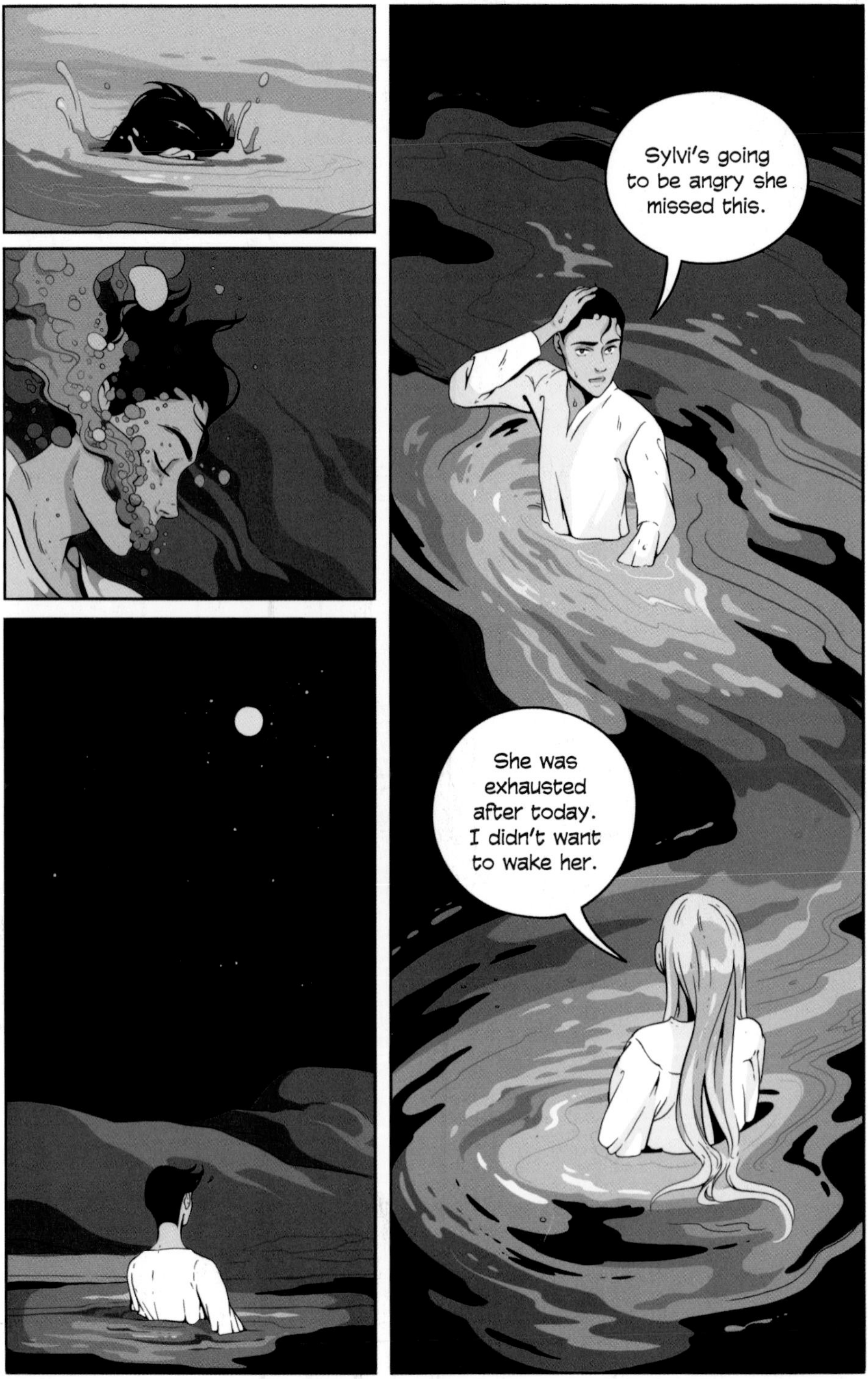
Sylvi's going to be angry she missed this.
She was exhausted after today. I didn't want to wake her.

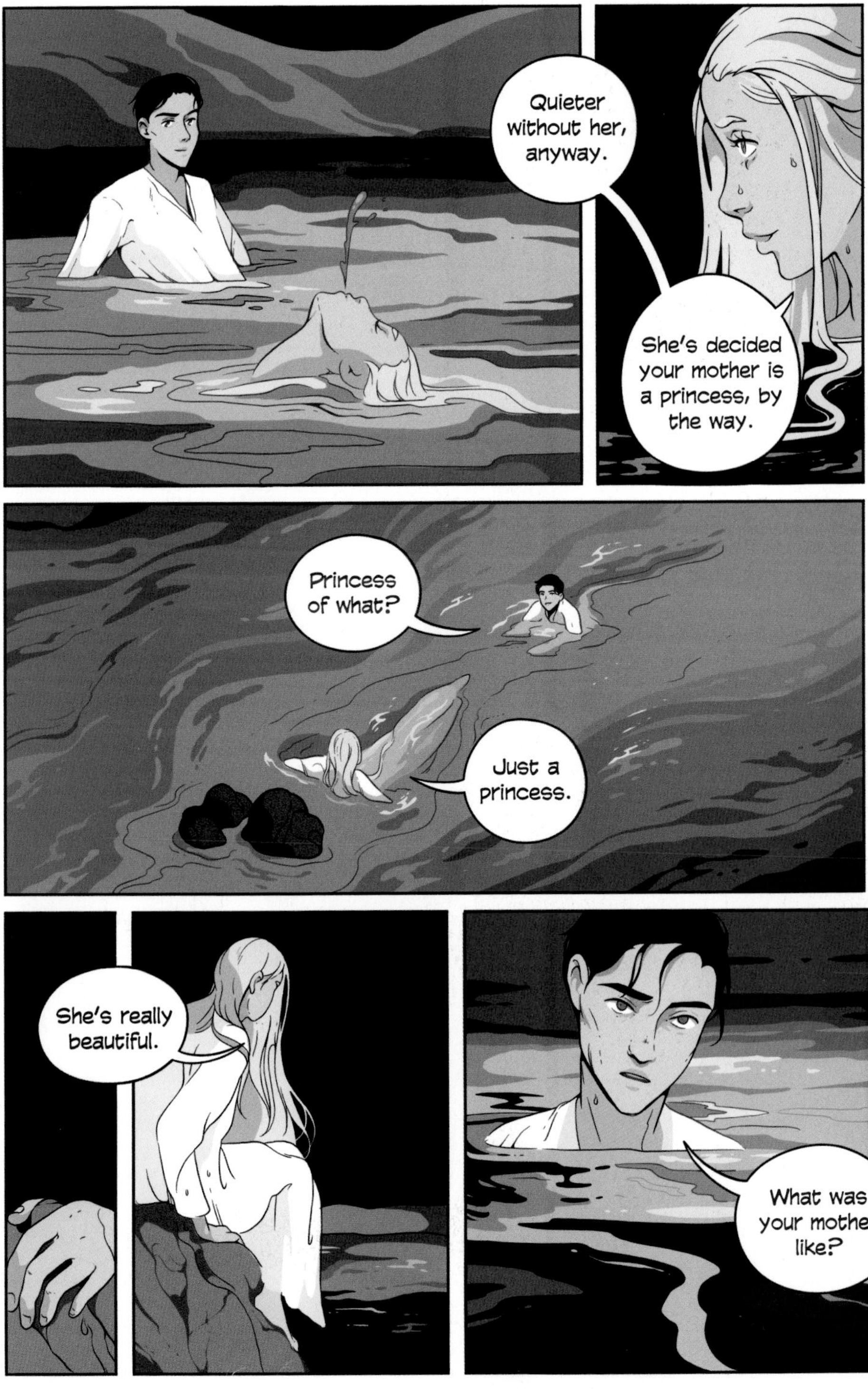
Quieter without her, anyway.
She's decided your mother is a princess, by the way.
Princess of what?
Just a princess.
She's really beautiful.
What was your mother like?

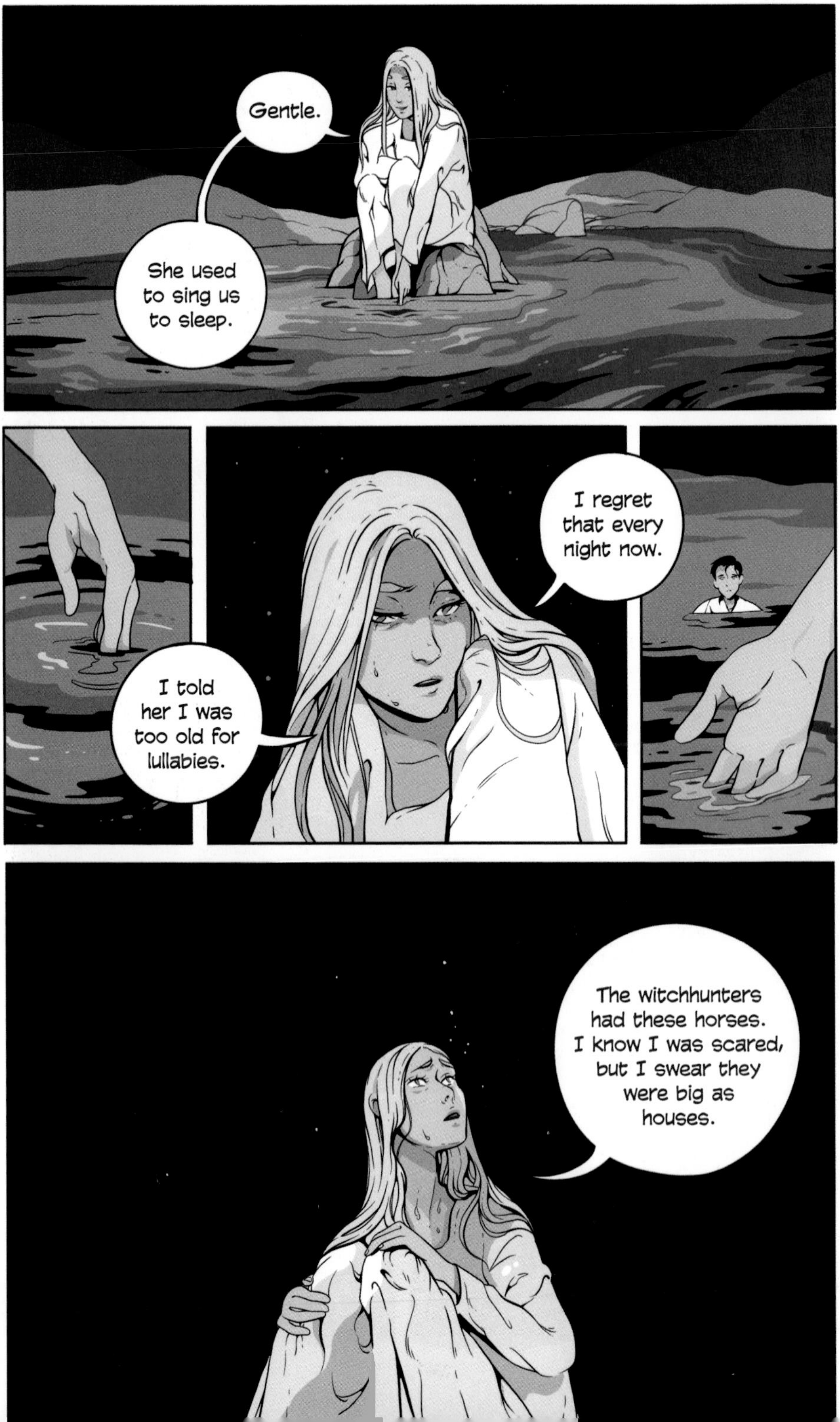
Gentle.
She used to sing us to sleep.
I told her I was too old for lullabies.
I regret that every night now.
The witchhunters had these horses. I know I was scared, but I swear they were big as houses.

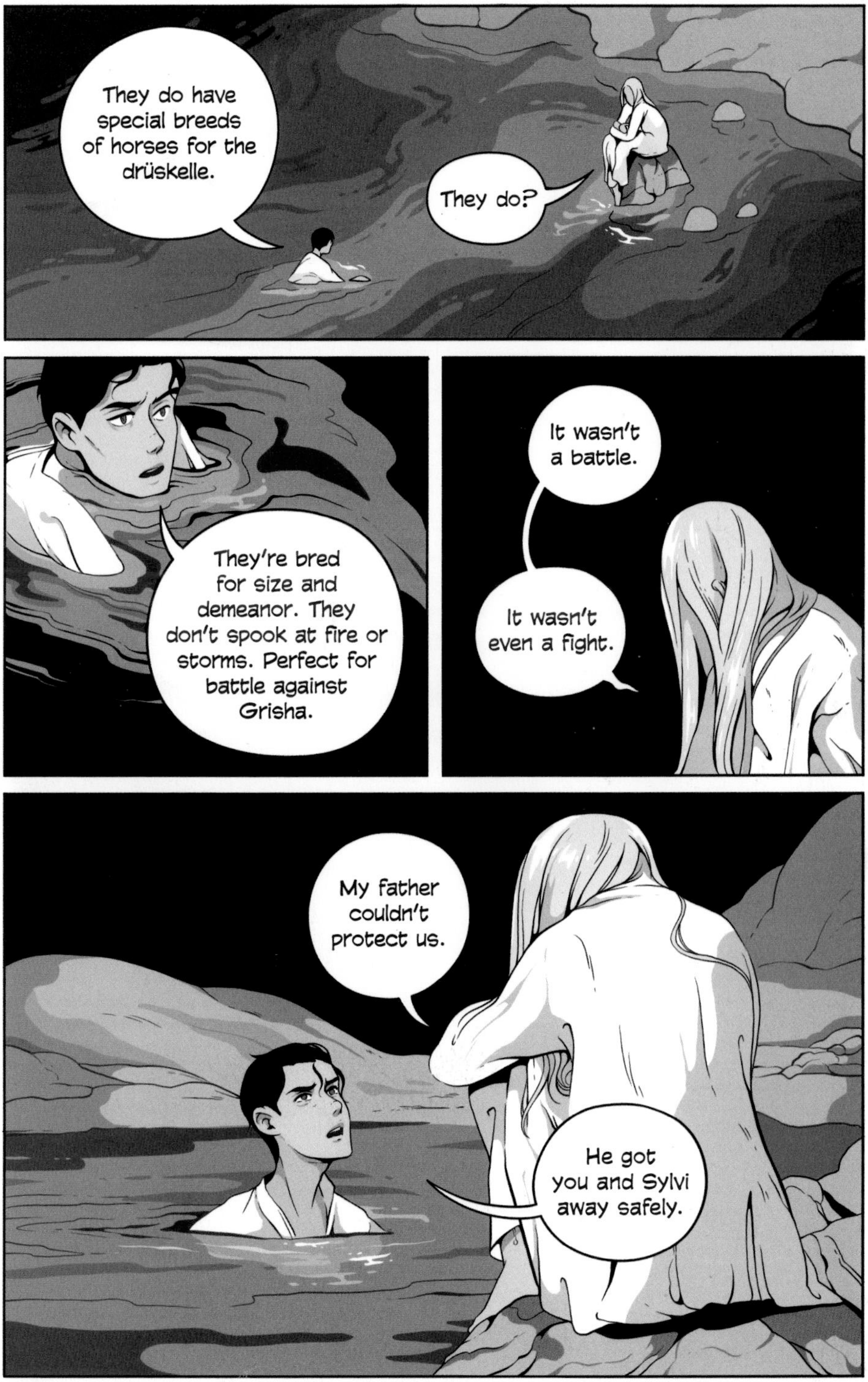
They do have special breeds of horses for the drüskelle.
They do?
They're bred for size and demeanor. They don't spook at fire or storms. Perfect for battle against Grisha.
It wasn't a battle.
It wasn't even a fight.
My father couldn't protect us.
He got you and Sylvi away safely.

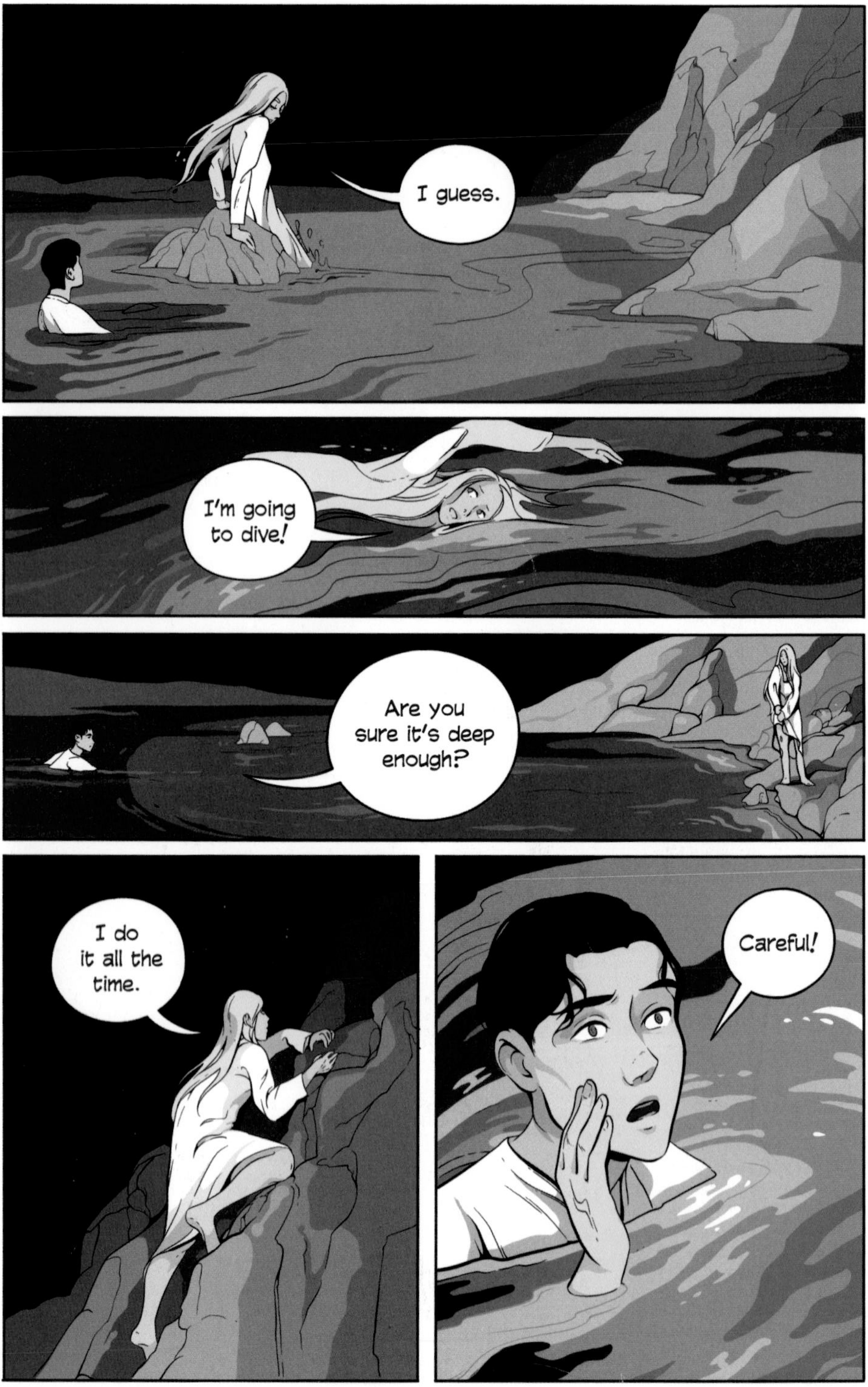
I guess.
I'm going to dive!
Are you sure it's deep enough?
I do it all the time.
Careful!

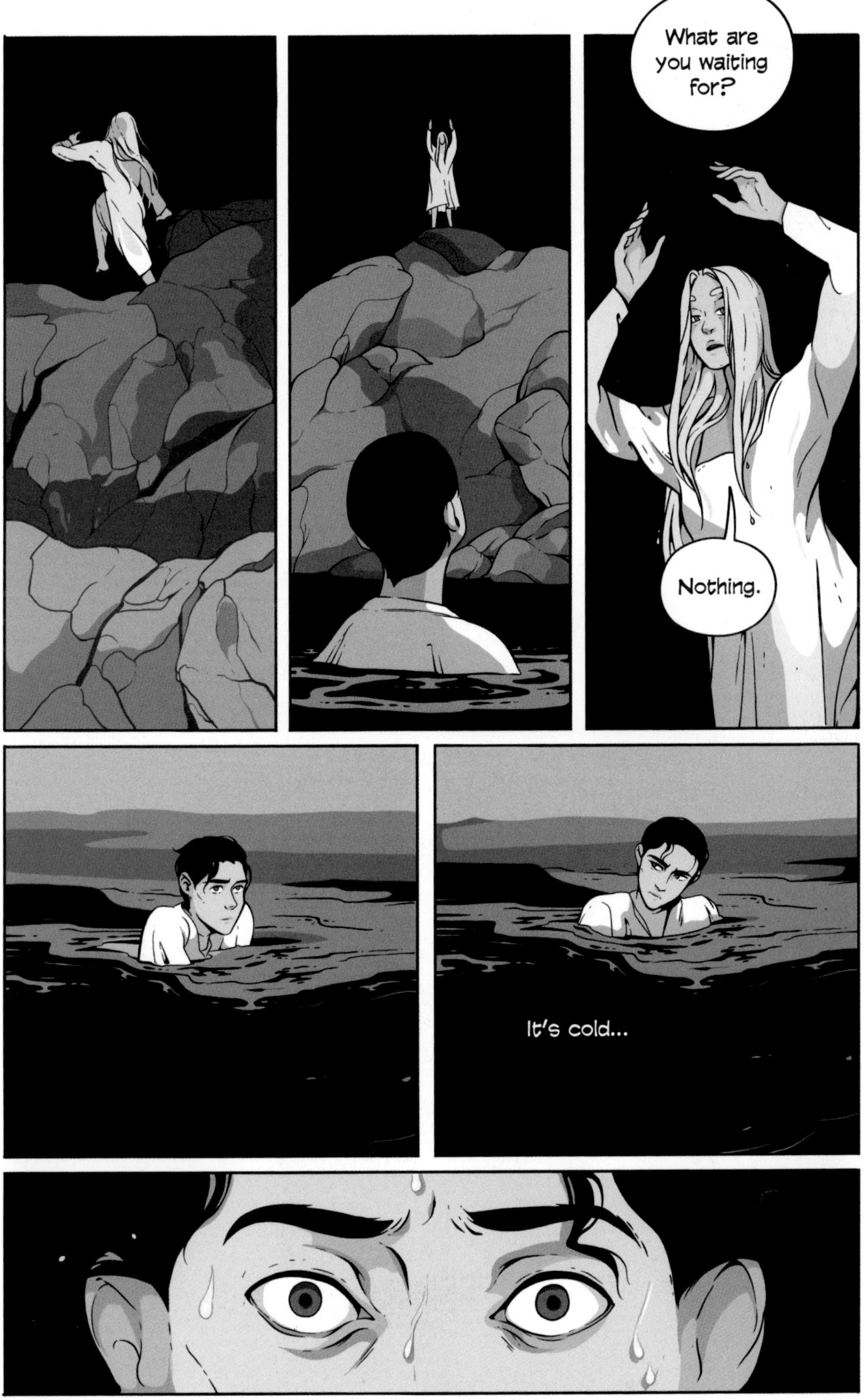
What are you waiting for?
Nothing.
It's cold...

What are you doing?

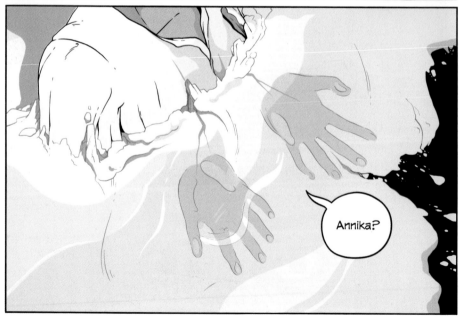

Annika?

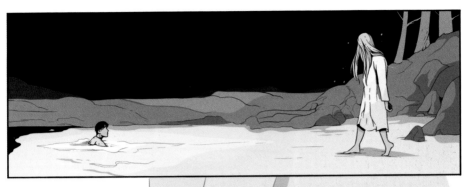

I'm sorry.

I need an amplifier.

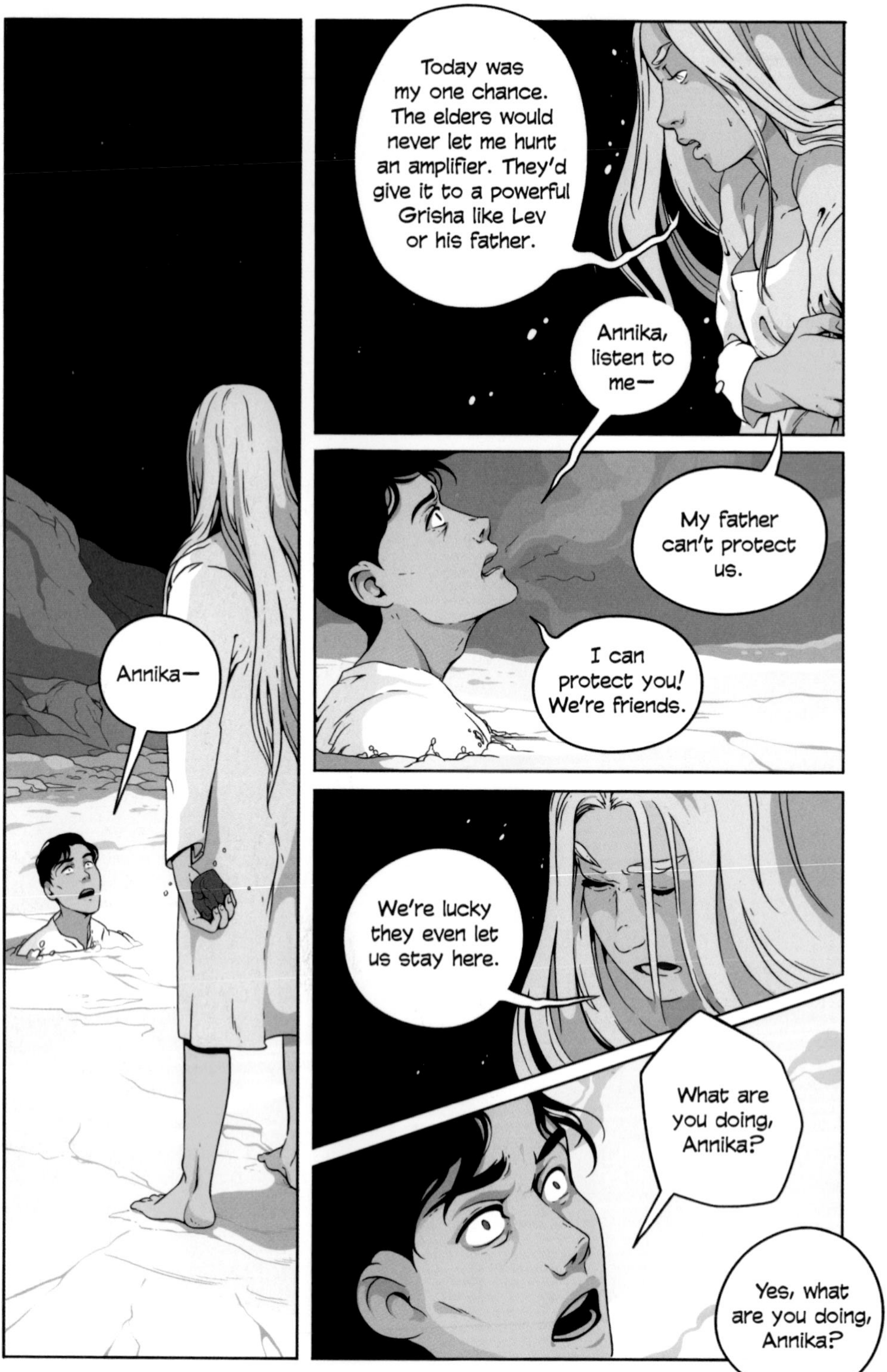
Annika—
Today was my one chance. The elders would never let me hunt an amplifier. They'd give it to a powerful Grisha like Lev or his father.
Annika, listen to me—
My father can't protect us.
I can protect you! We're friends.
We're lucky they even let us stay here.
What are you doing, Annika?
Yes, what are you doing, Annika?

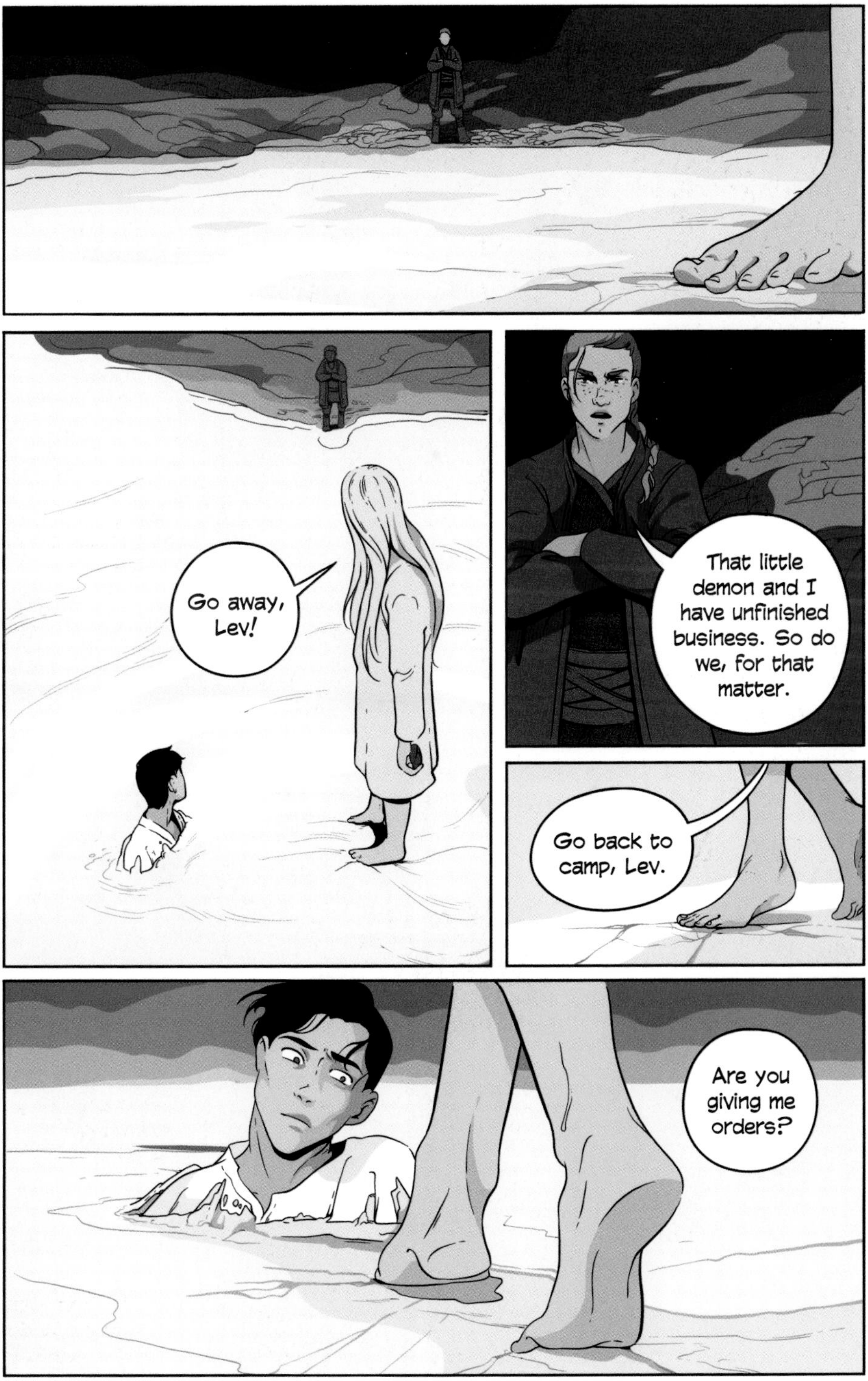
Go away, Lev!
That little demon and I have unfinished business. So do we, for that matter.
Go back to camp, Lev.
Are you giving me orders?

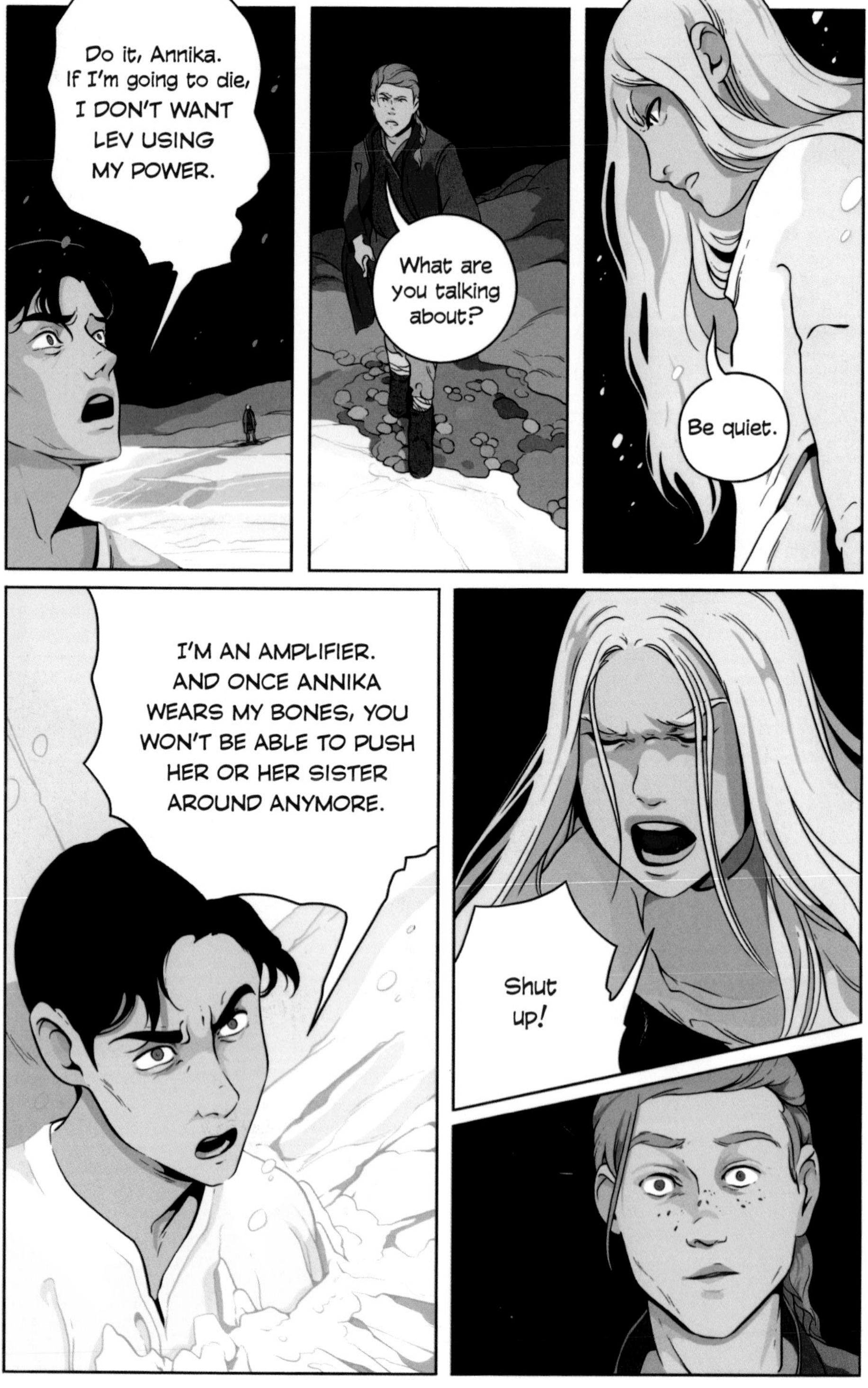
Do it, Annika. If I'm going to die, I DON'T WANT LEV USING MY POWER.
What are you talking about?
Be quiet.
I'M AN AMPLIFIER. AND ONCE ANNIKA WEARS MY BONES, YOU WON'T BE ABLE TO PUSH HER OR HER SISTER AROUND ANYMORE.
Shut up!

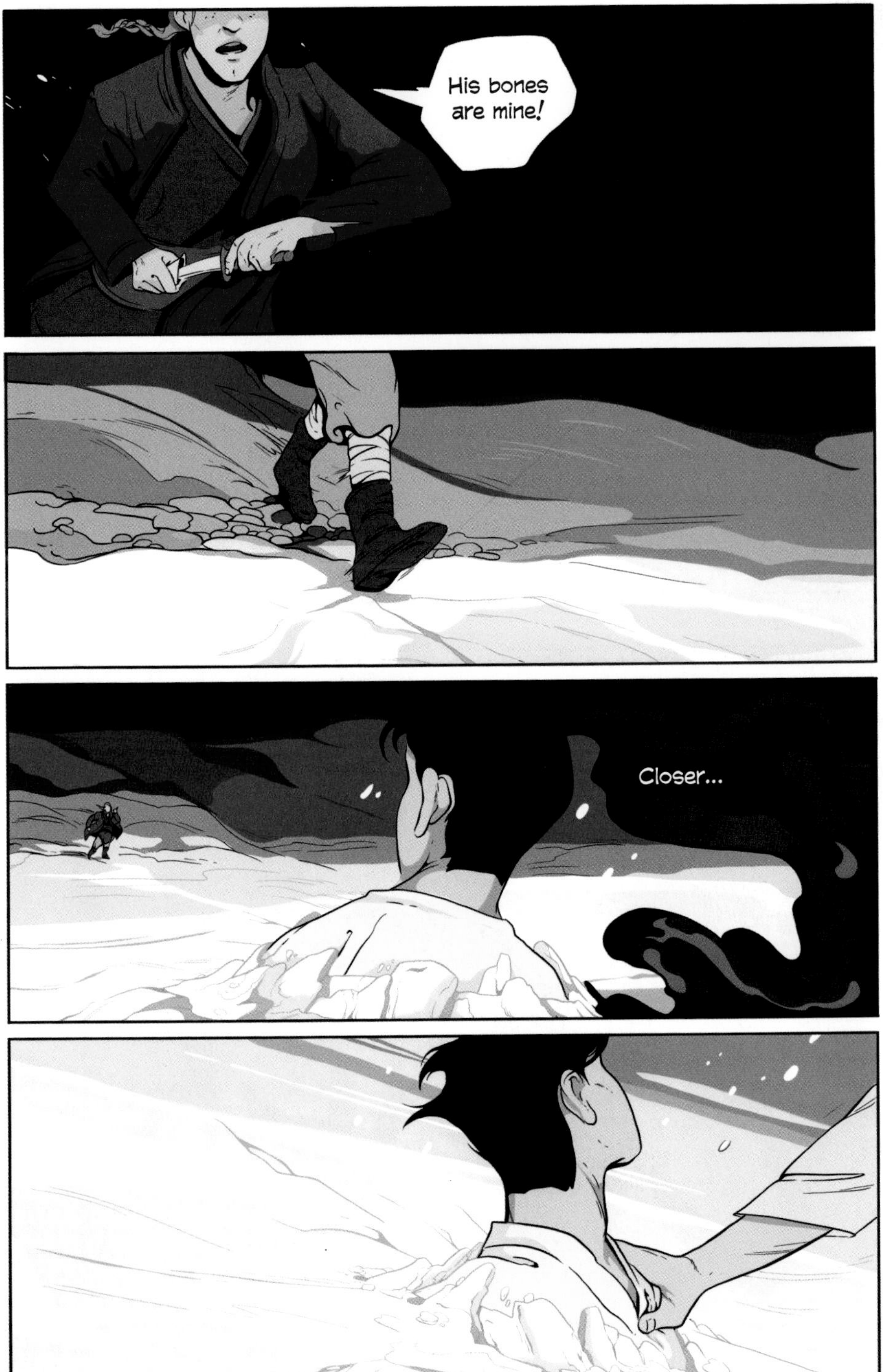
His bones are mine!
Closer...

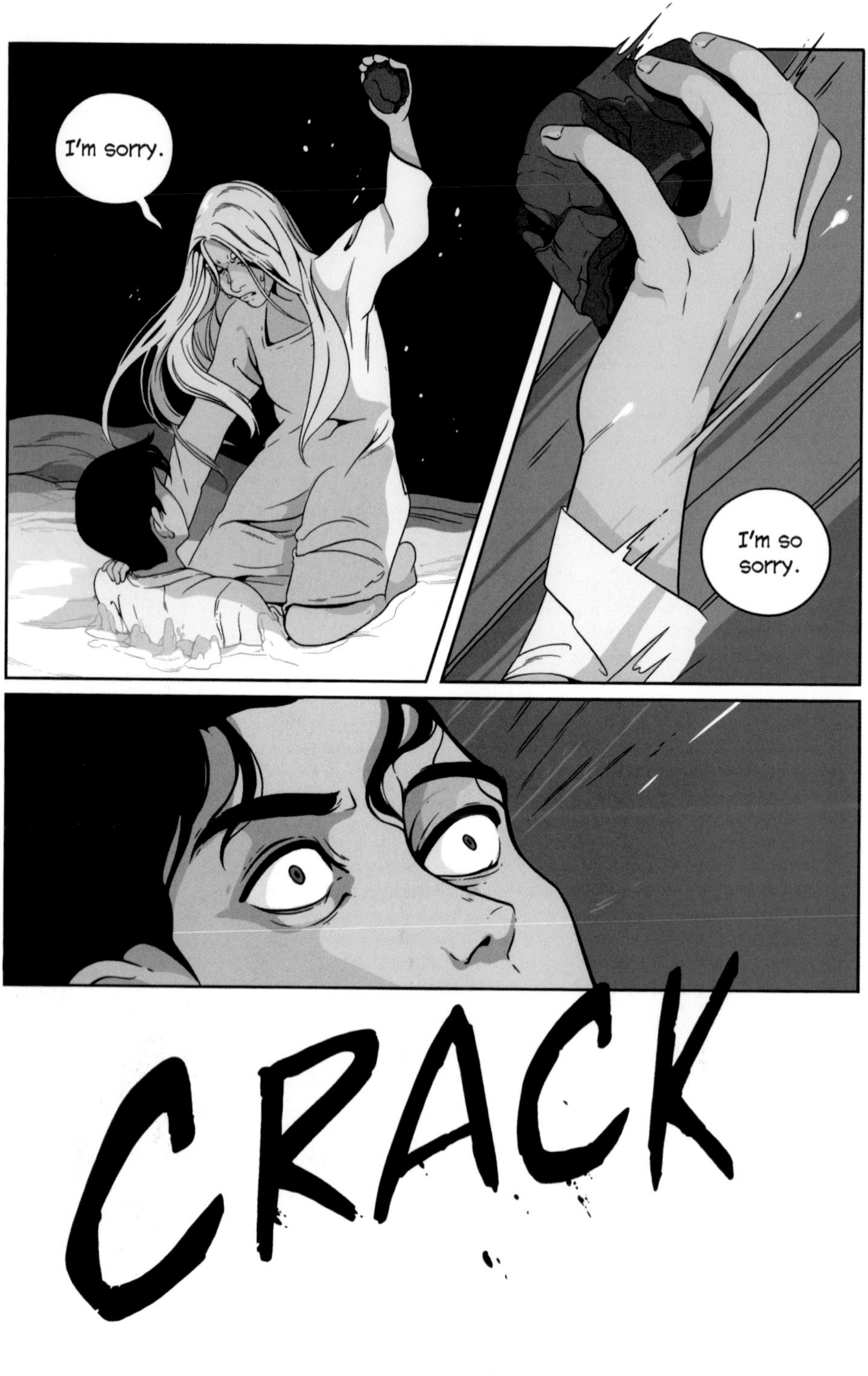
I'm sorry.
I'm so sorry.
CRACK

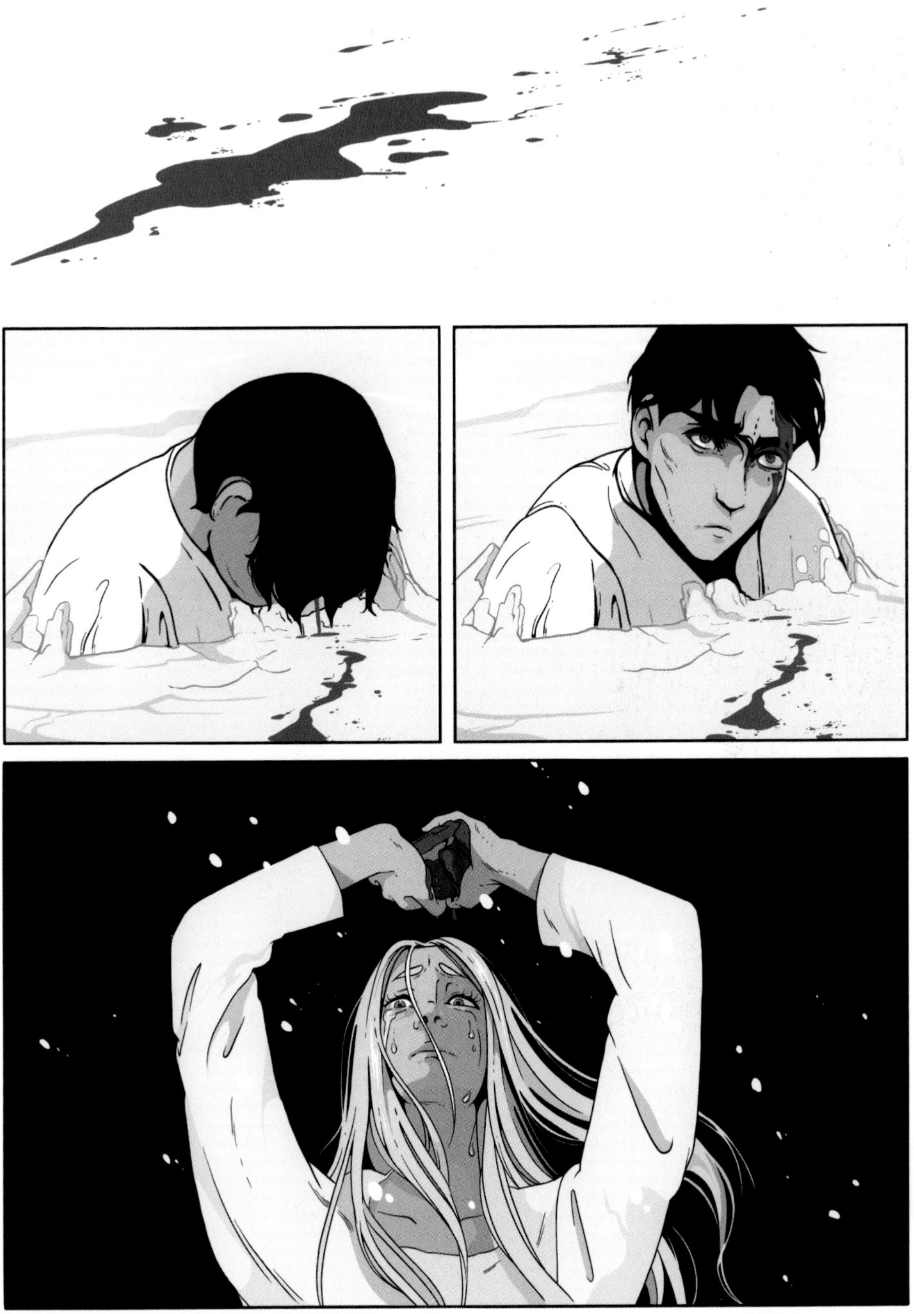

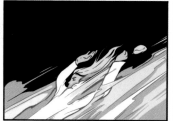

No! He's mine!

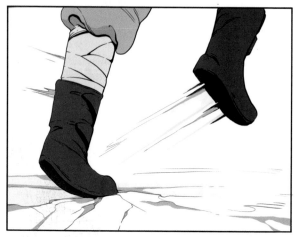

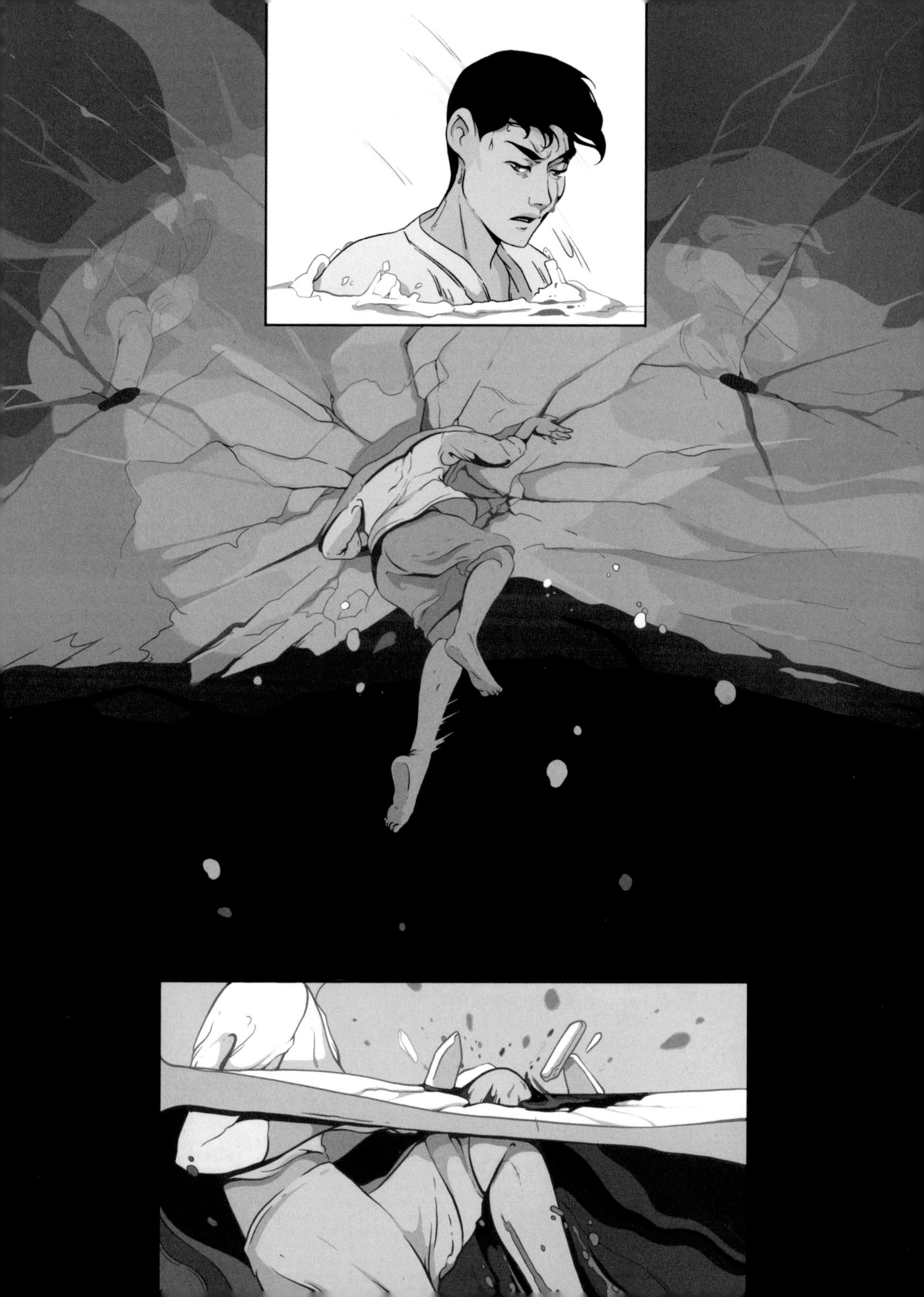

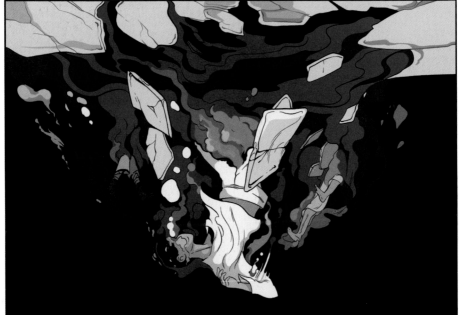

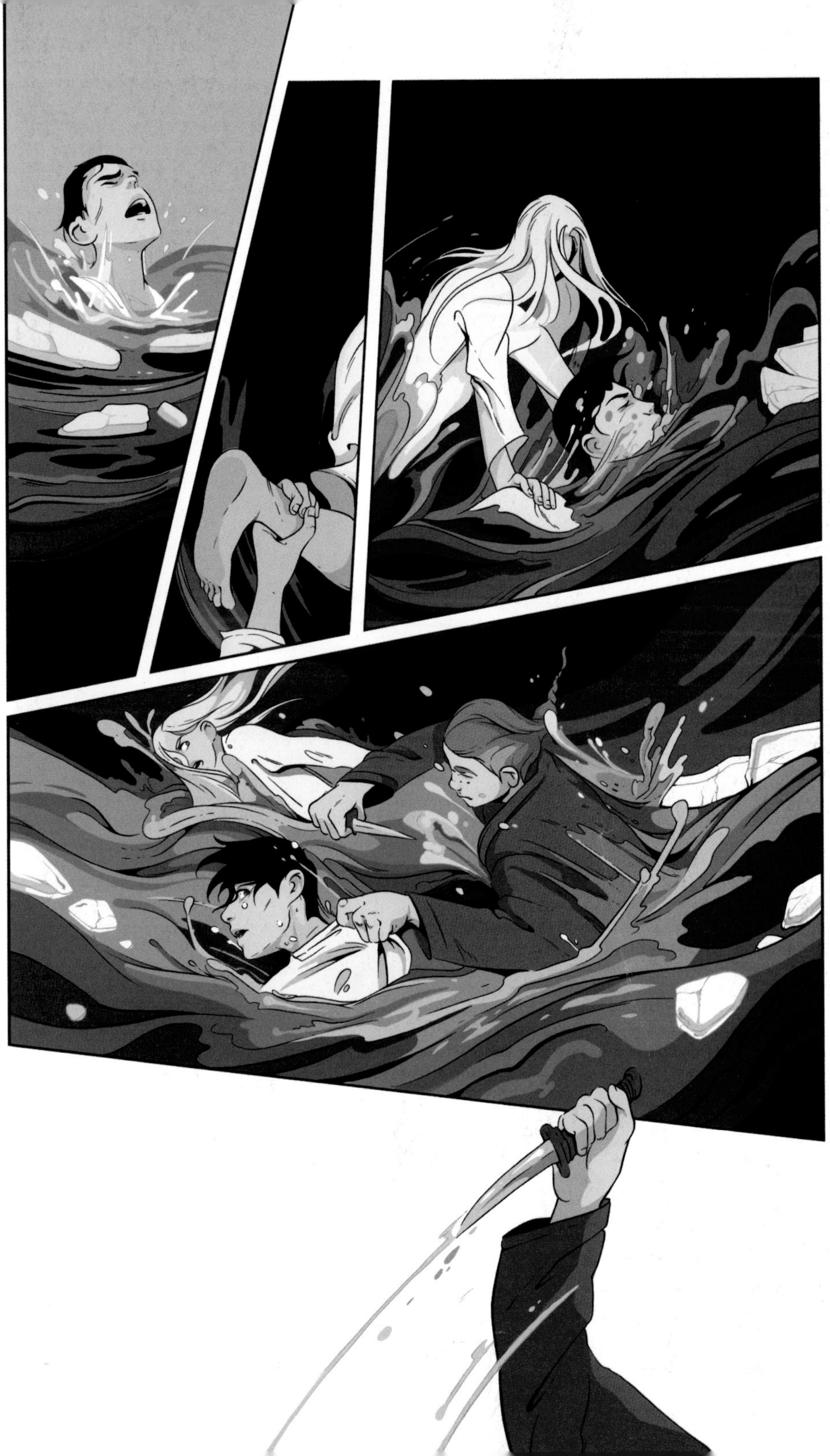

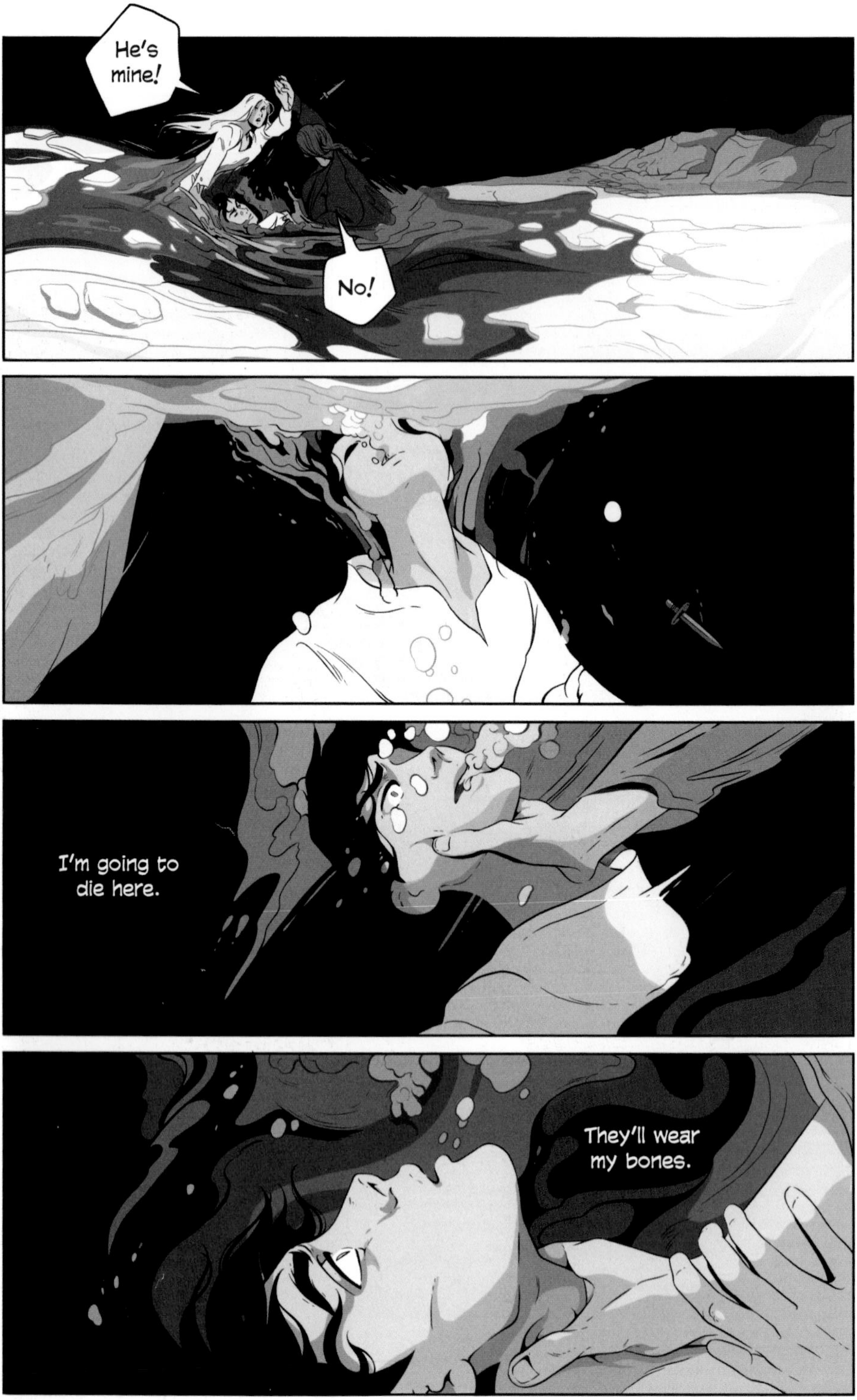
He's mine!
No!
I'm going to die here.
They'll wear my bones.

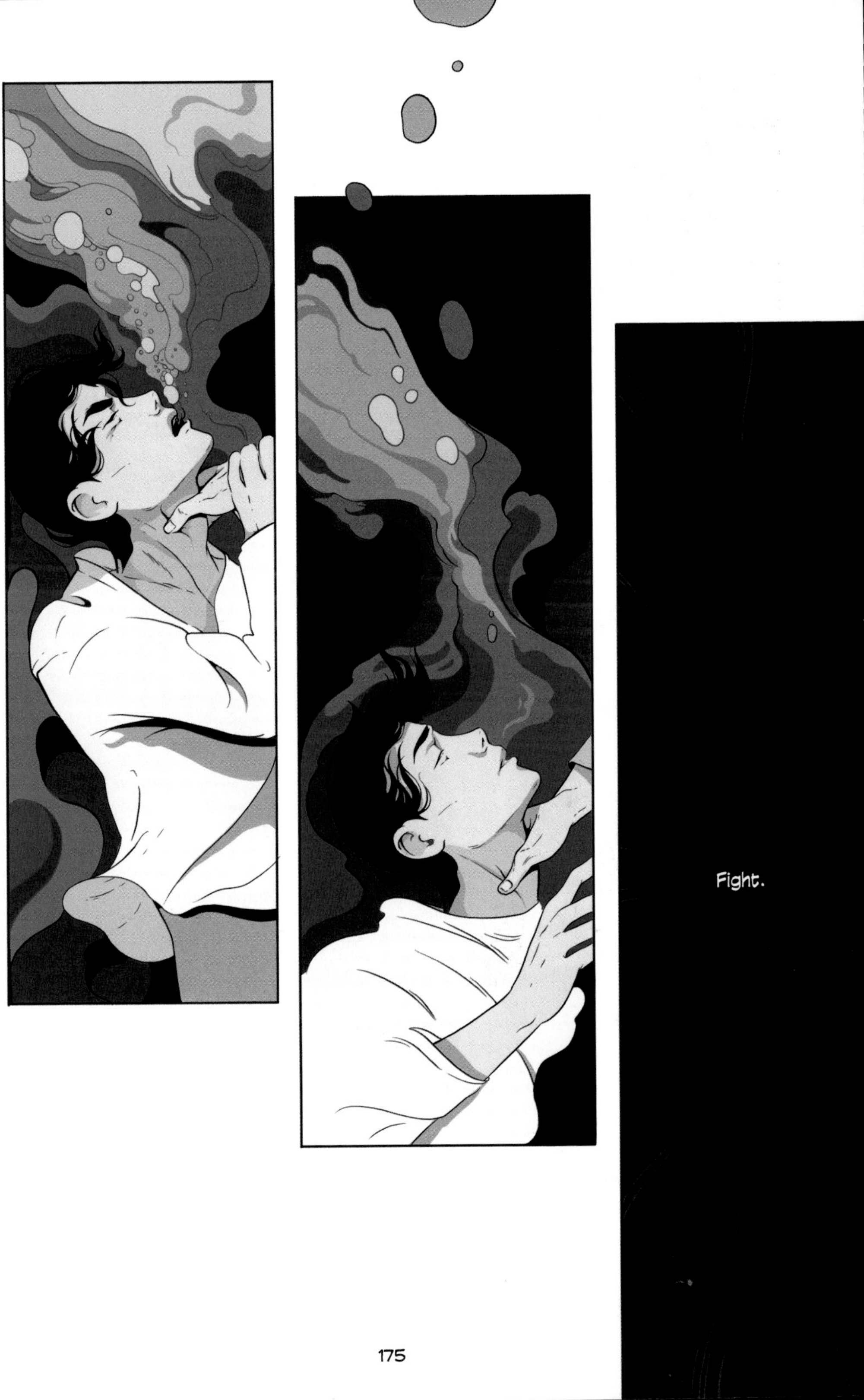
Fight.

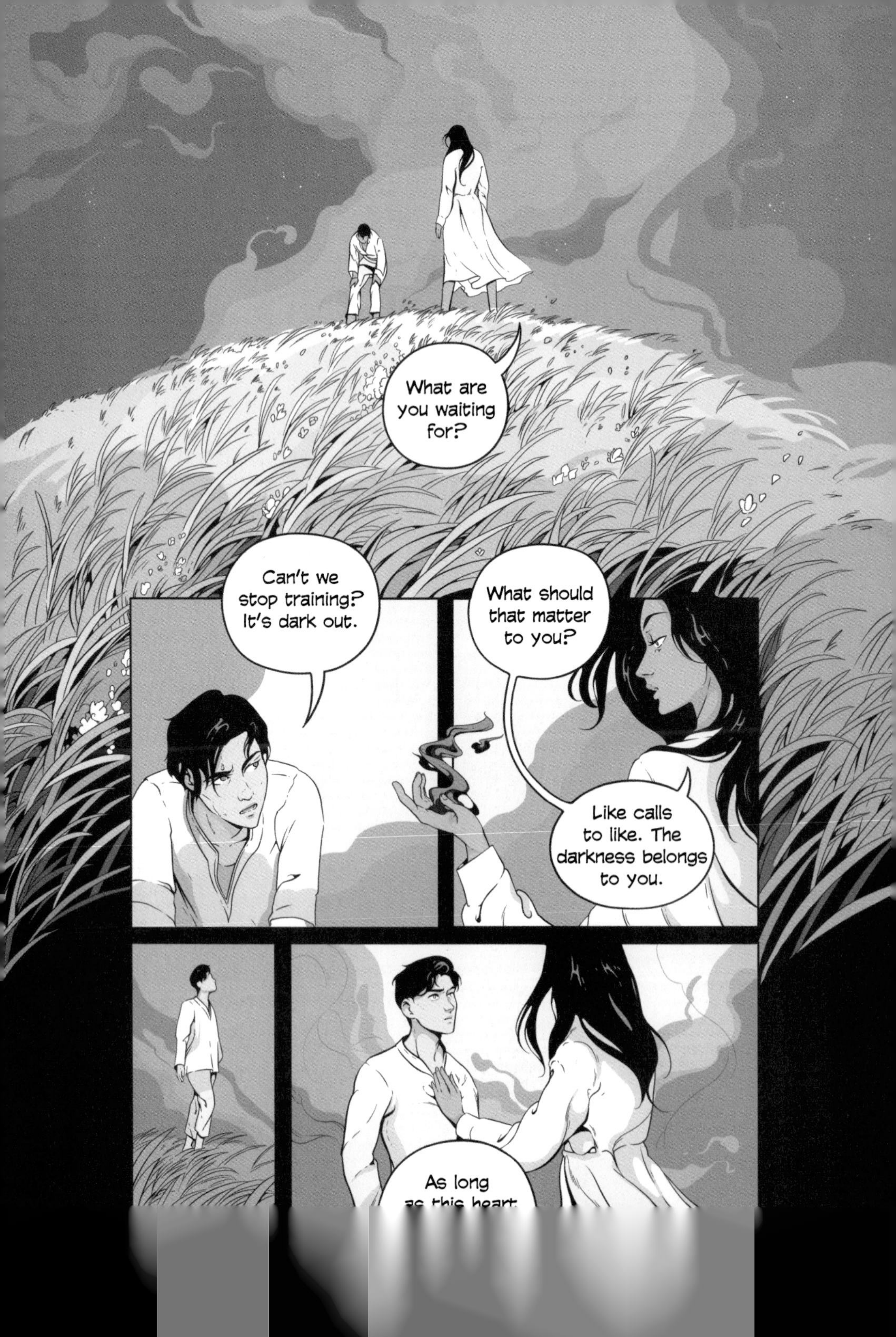
What are you waiting for?
Can't we stop training? It's dark out.
What should that matter to you?
Like calls to like. The darkness belongs to you.
As long

Aleksander.

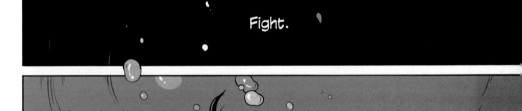

Fight.

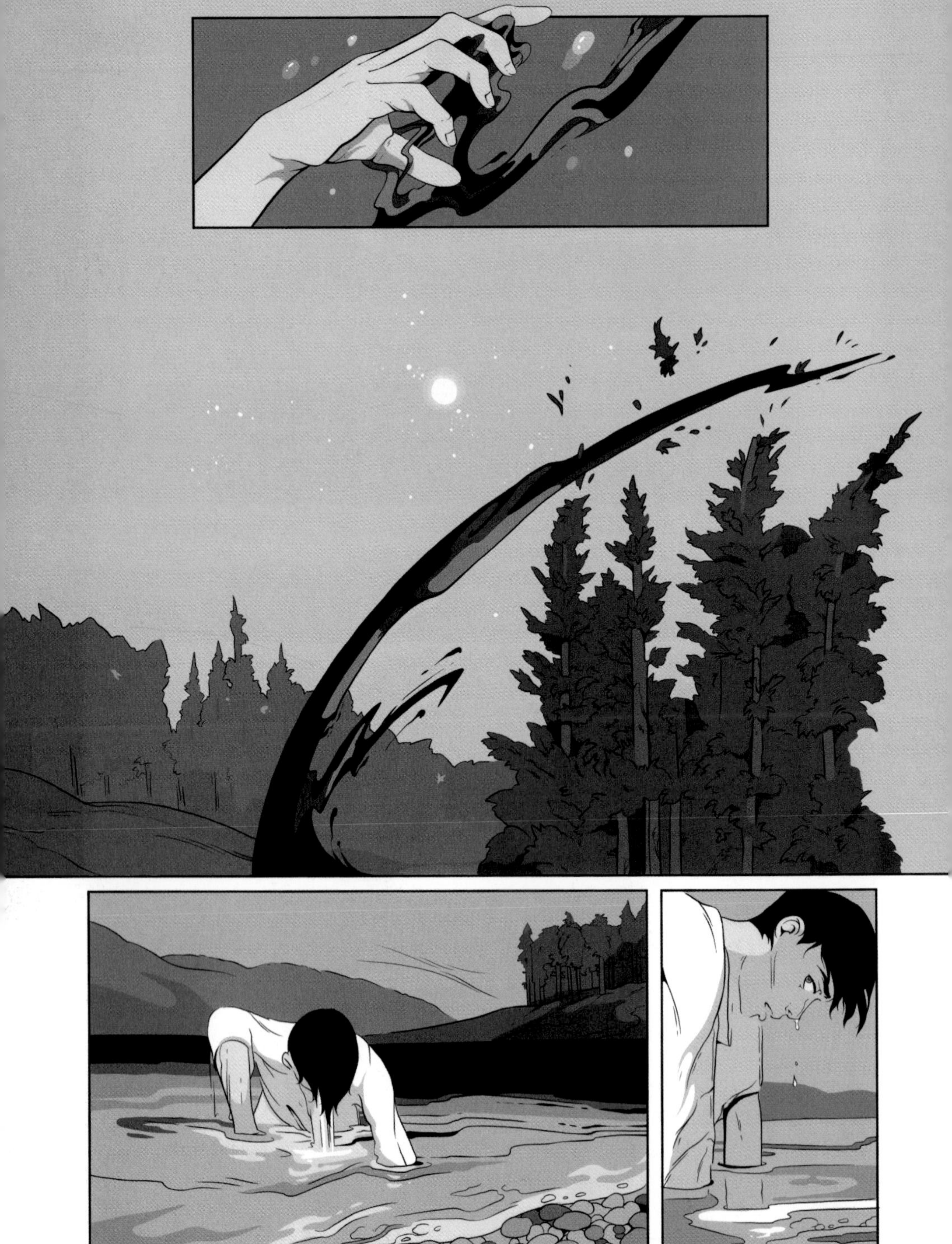

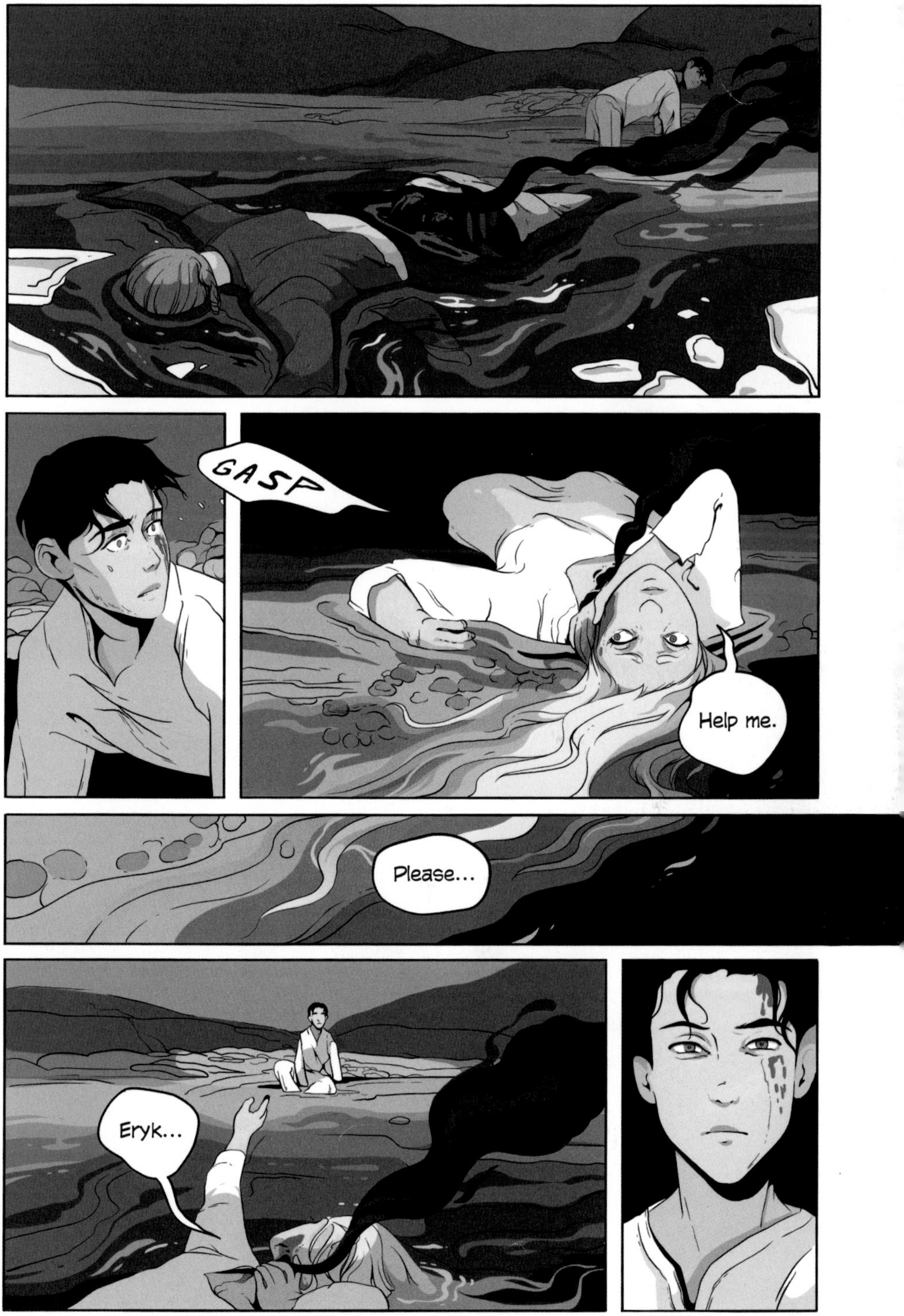
GASP
Help me.
Please...
Eryk...

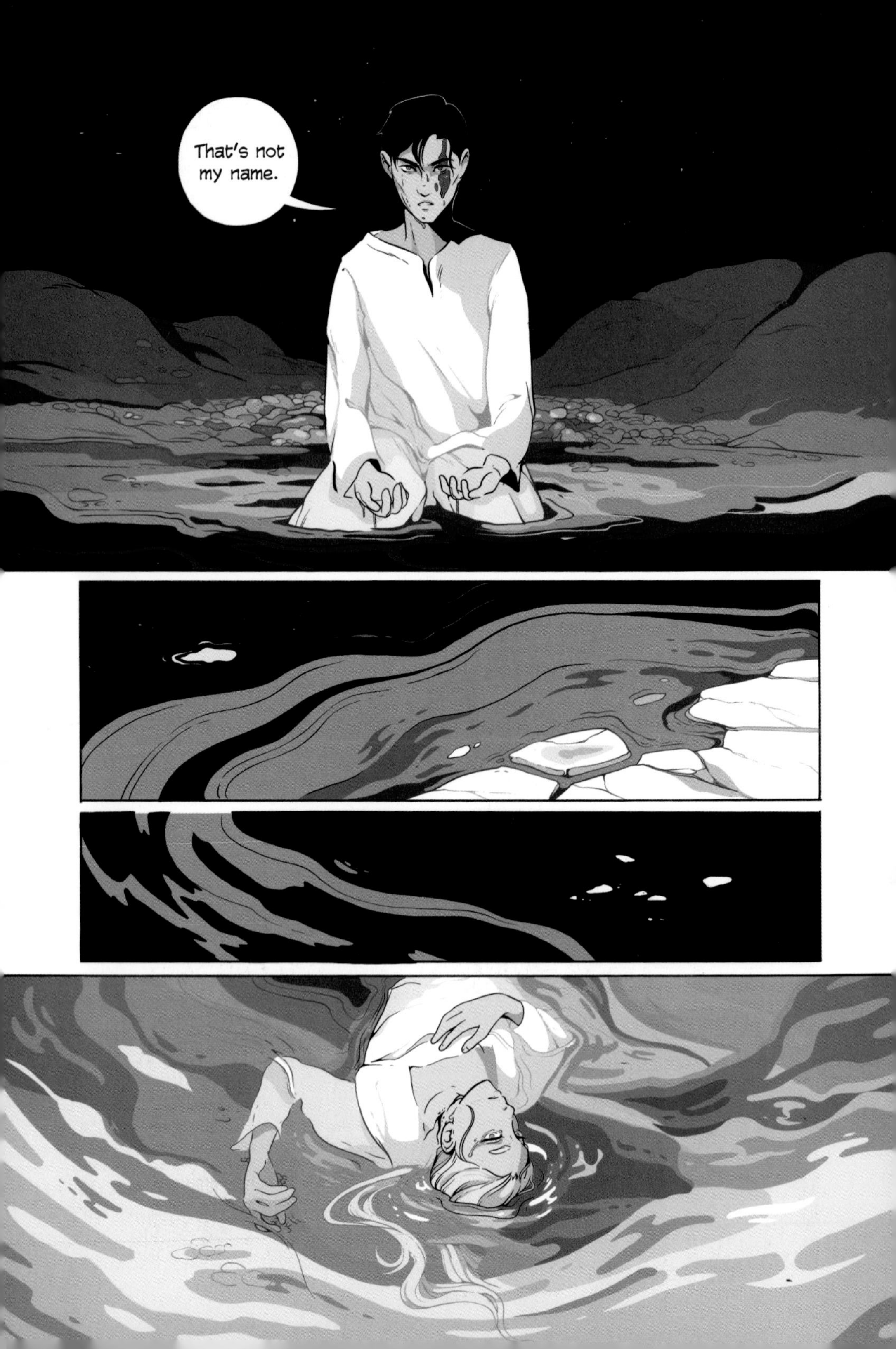
That's not my name.

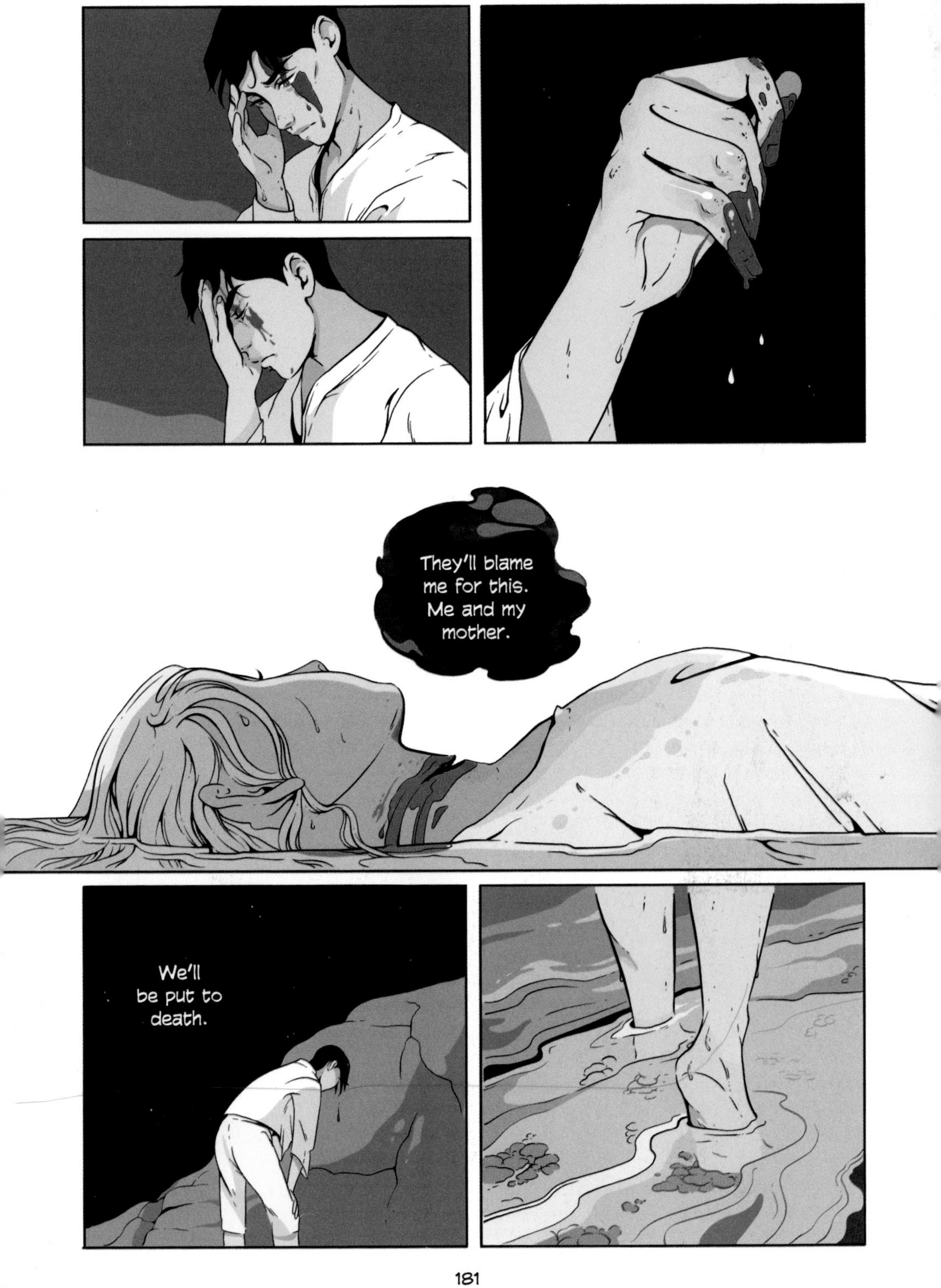
They'll blame me for this. Me and my mother.
We'll be put to death.

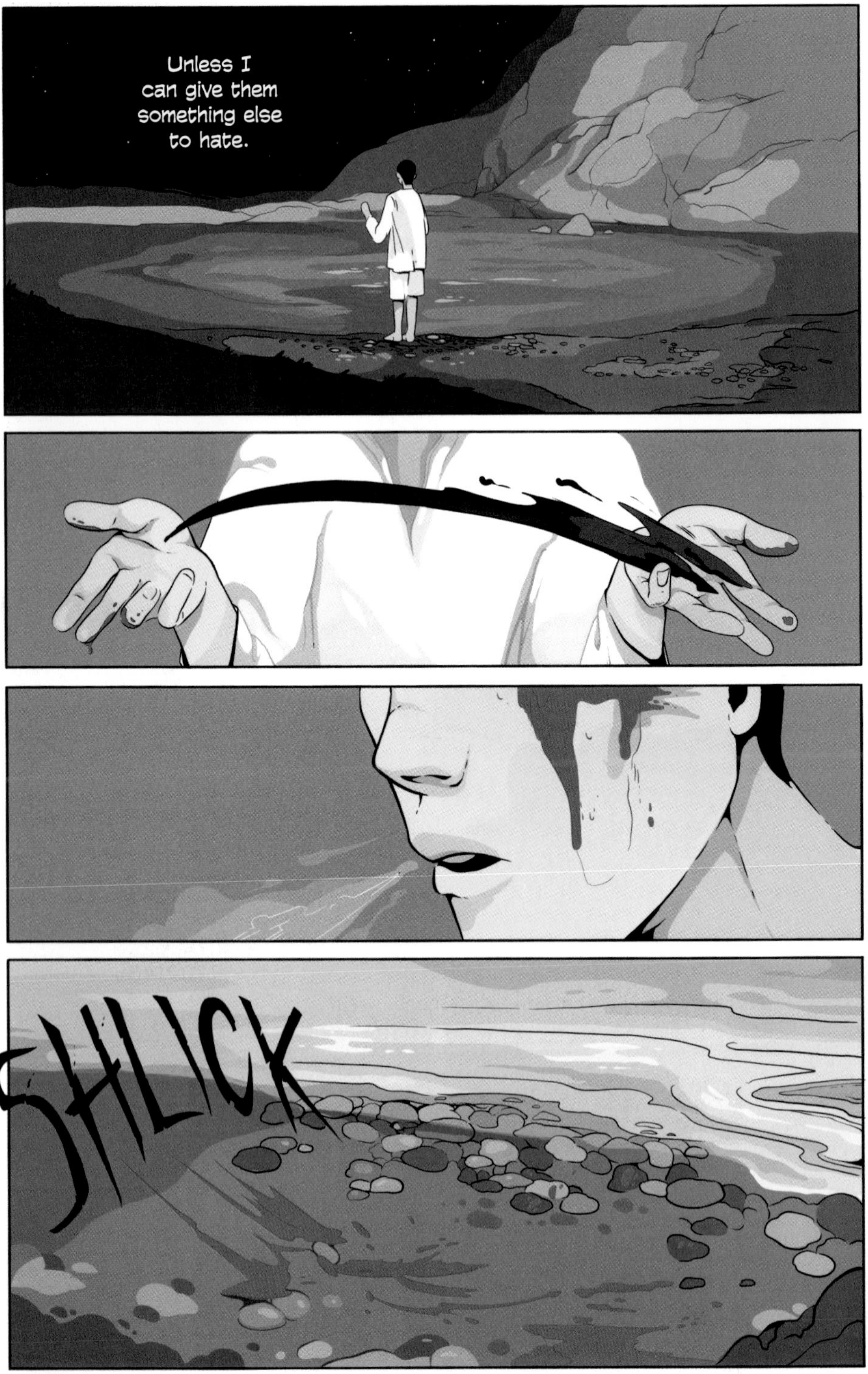
Unless I can give them something else to hate.
SHLICK

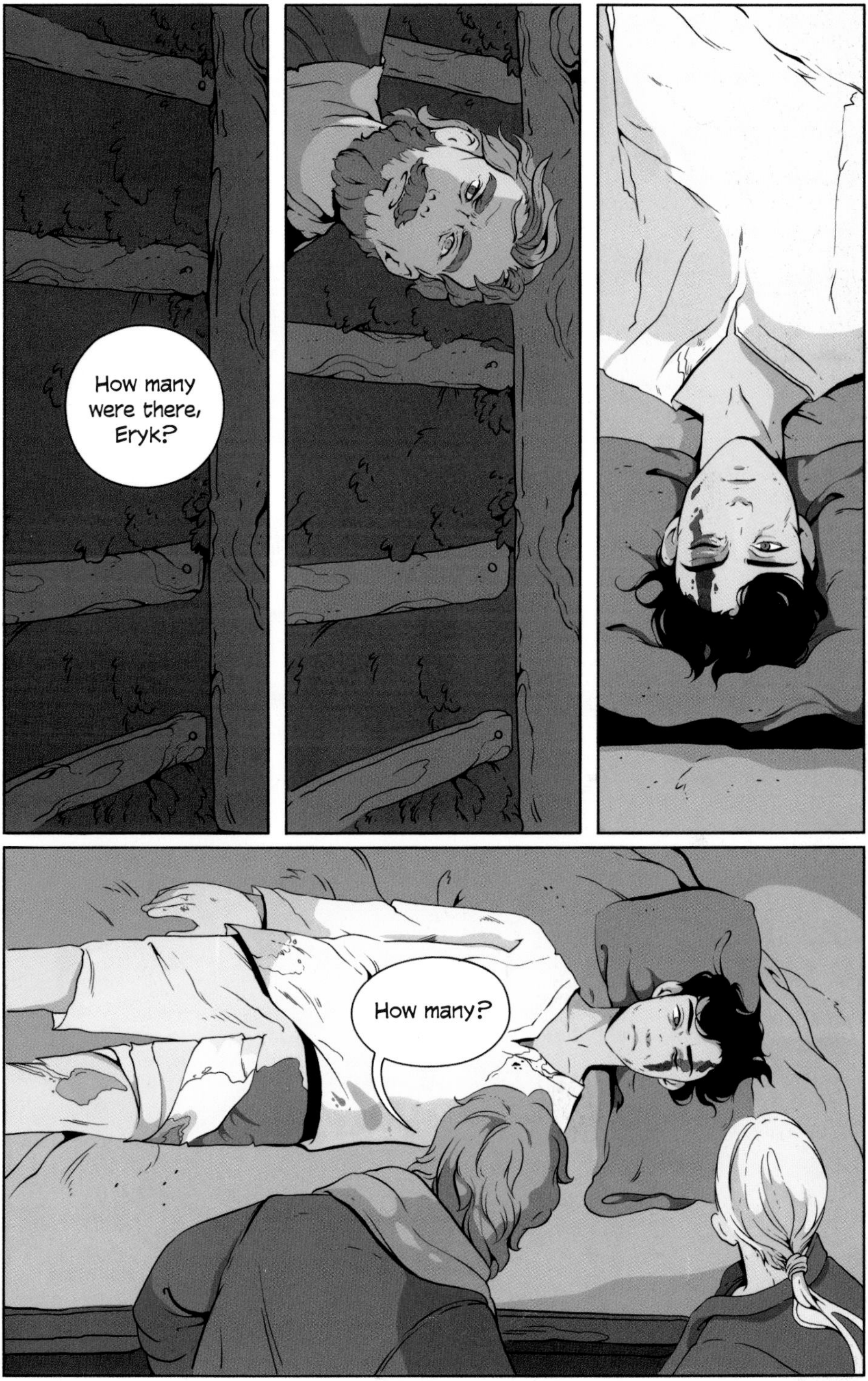
How many were there, Eryk?
How many?

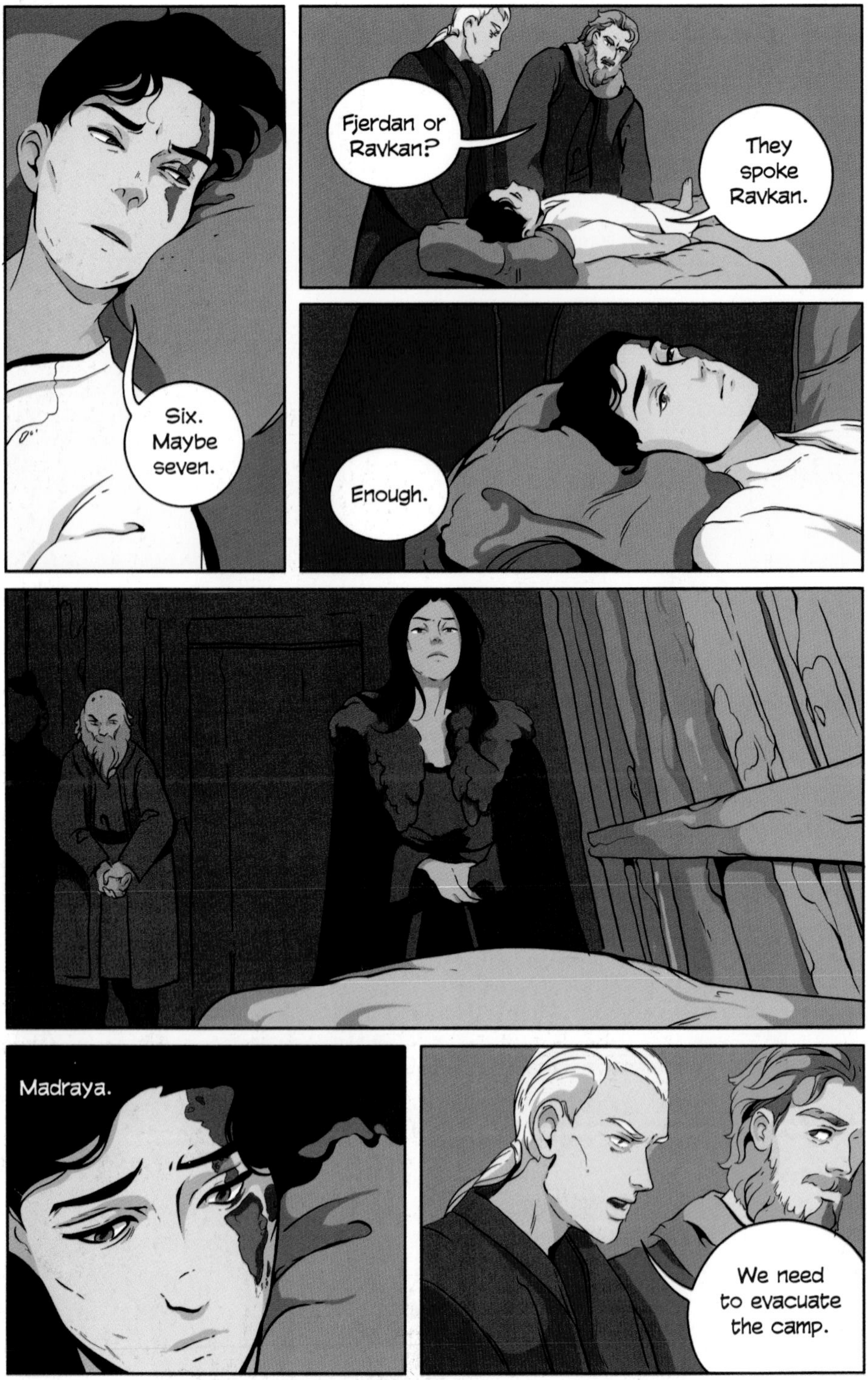
Fjerdan or Ravkan?
They spoke Ravkan.
Six. Maybe seven.
Enough.
Madraya.
We need to evacuate the camp.

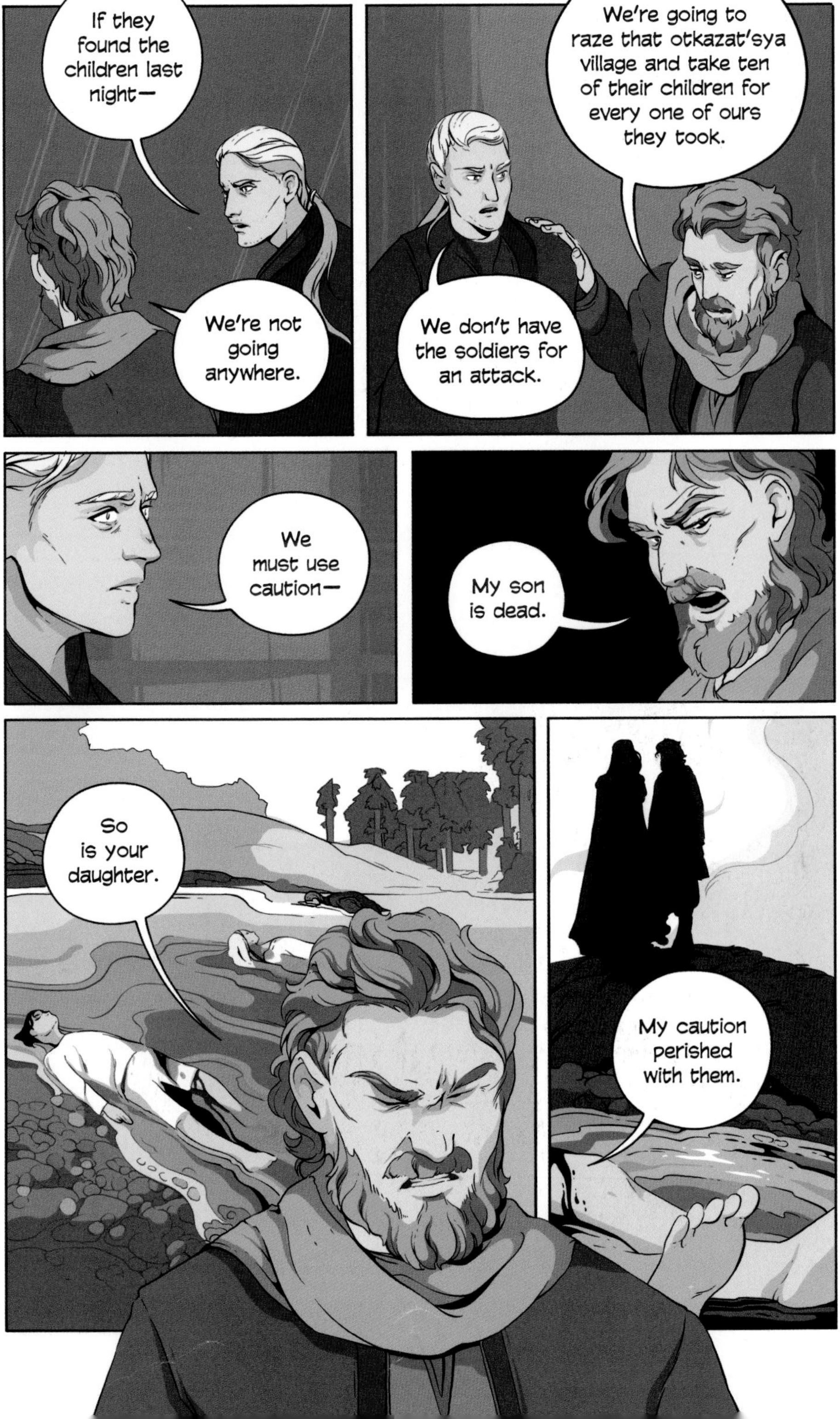
If they found the children last night—
We're not going anywhere.
We're going to raze that otkazat'sya village and take ten of their children for every one of ours they took.
We don't have the soldiers for an attack.
We must use caution—
My son is dead.
So is your daughter.
My caution perished with them.

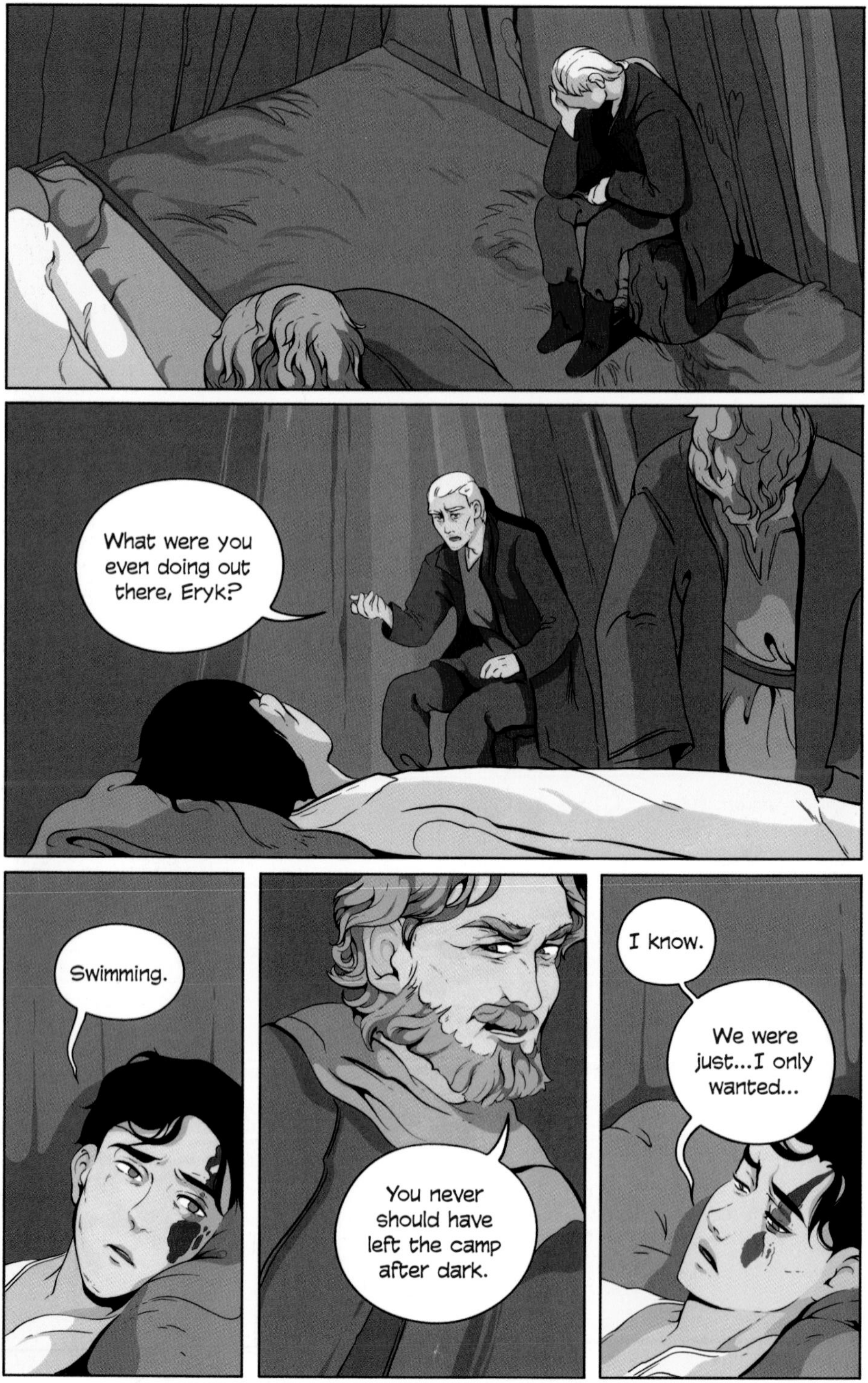
What were you even doing out there, Eryk?
Swimming.
You never should have left the camp after dark.
I know.
We were just...I only wanted...

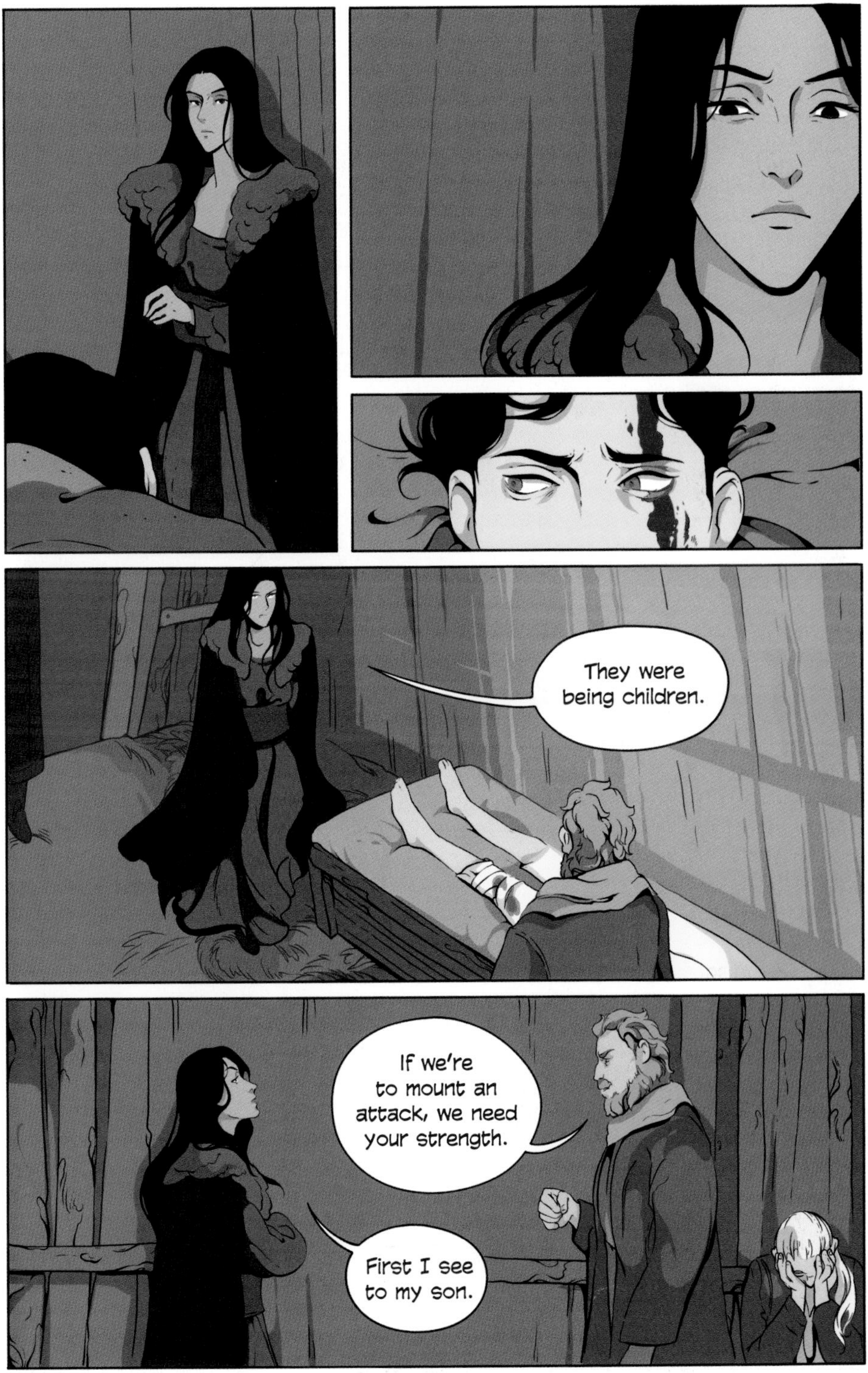
They were being children.
If we're to mount an attack, we need your strength.
First I see to my son.

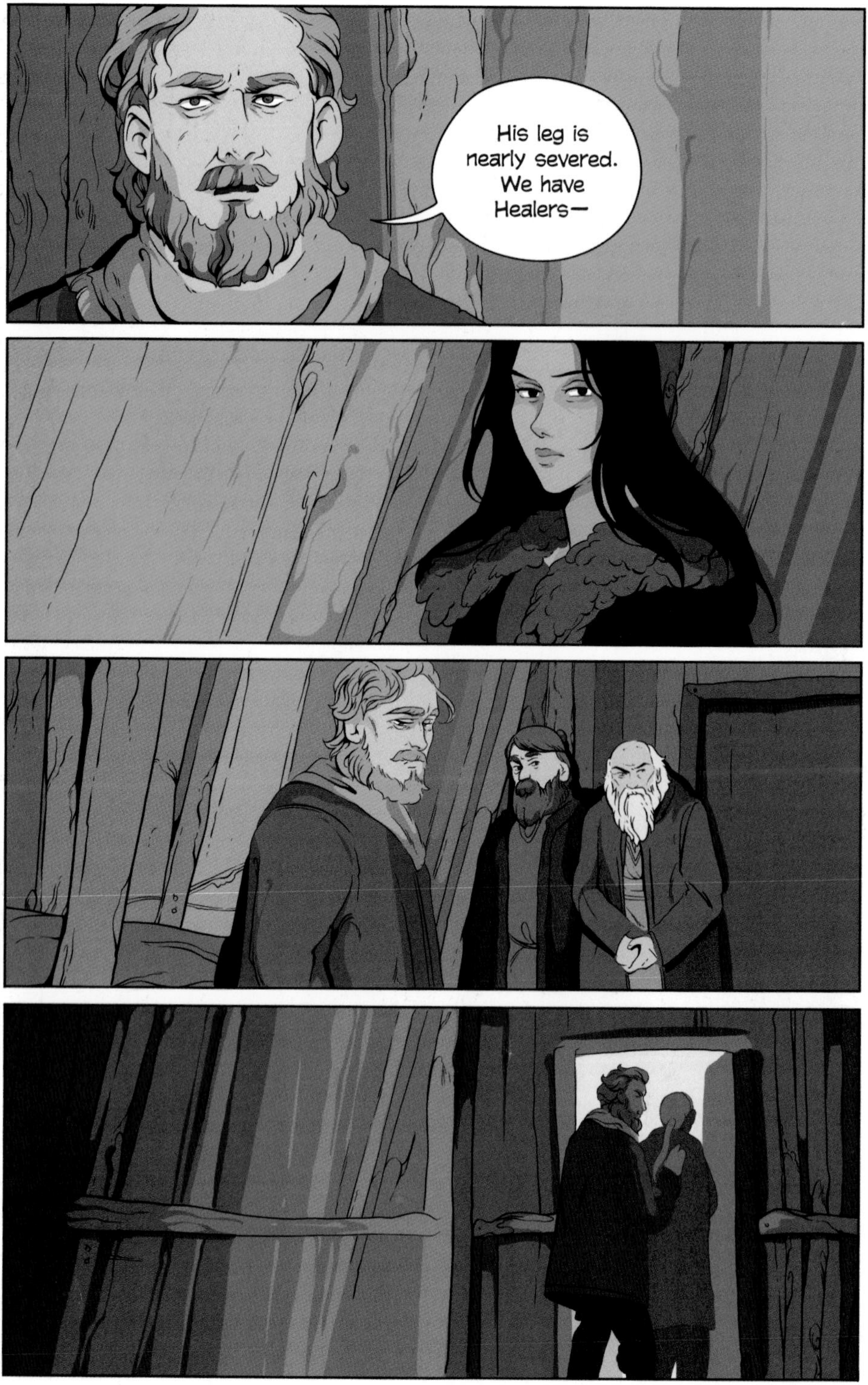
His leg is nearly severed. We have Healers—

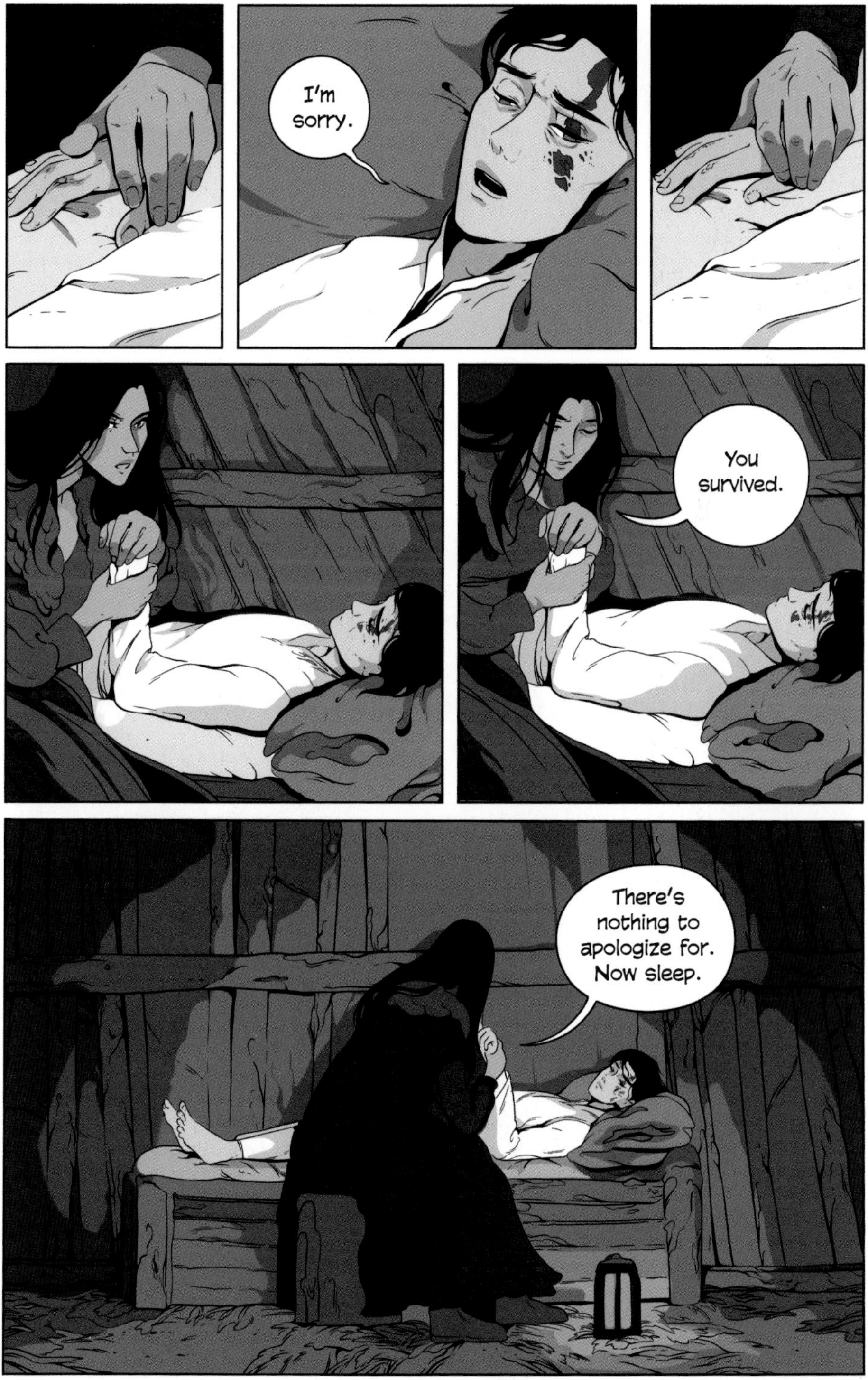
I'm sorry.
You survived.
There's nothing to apologize for. Now sleep.

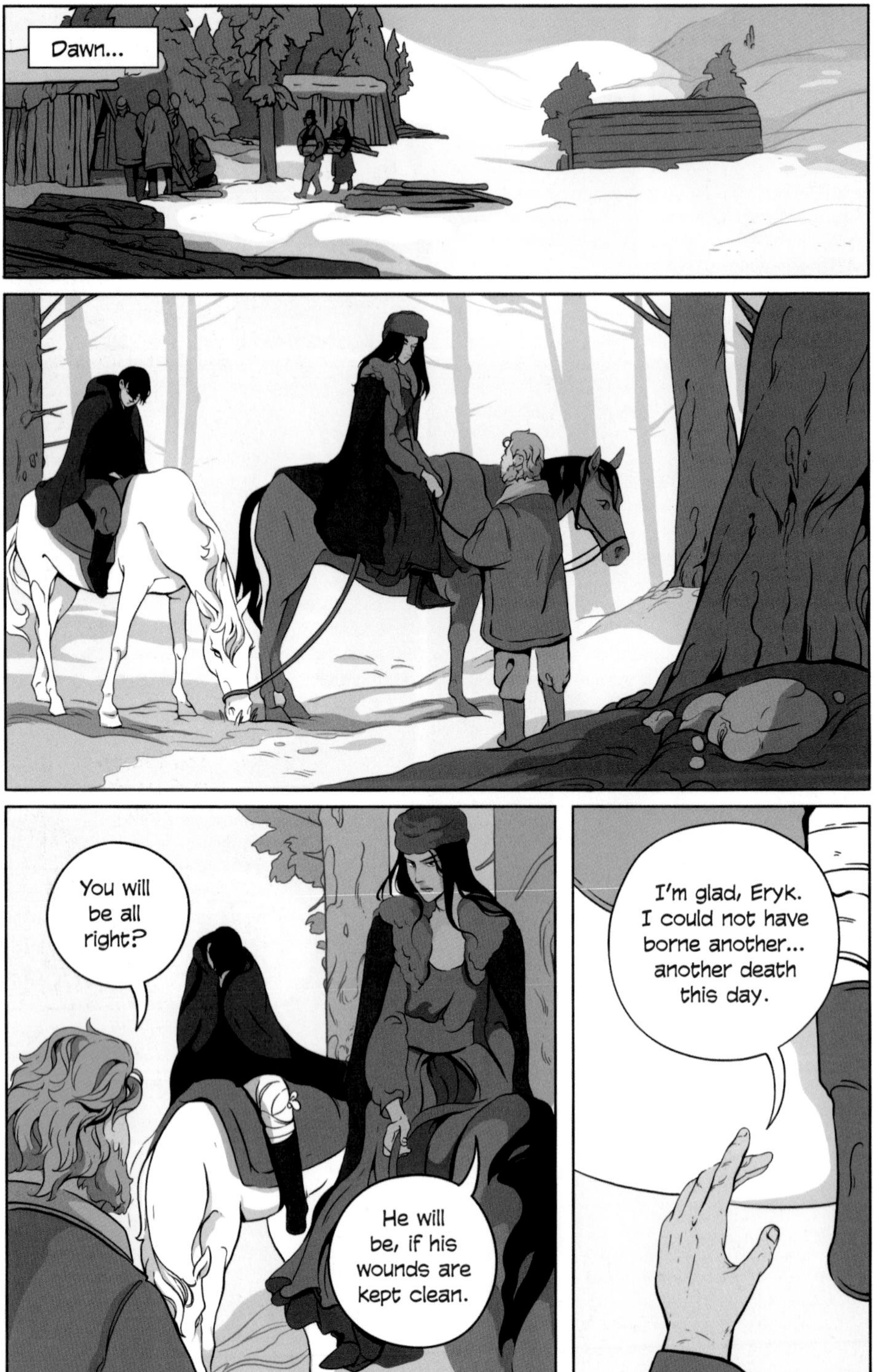
Dawn...
You will be all right?
He will be, if his wounds are kept clean.
I'm glad, Eryk. I could not have borne another... another death this day.

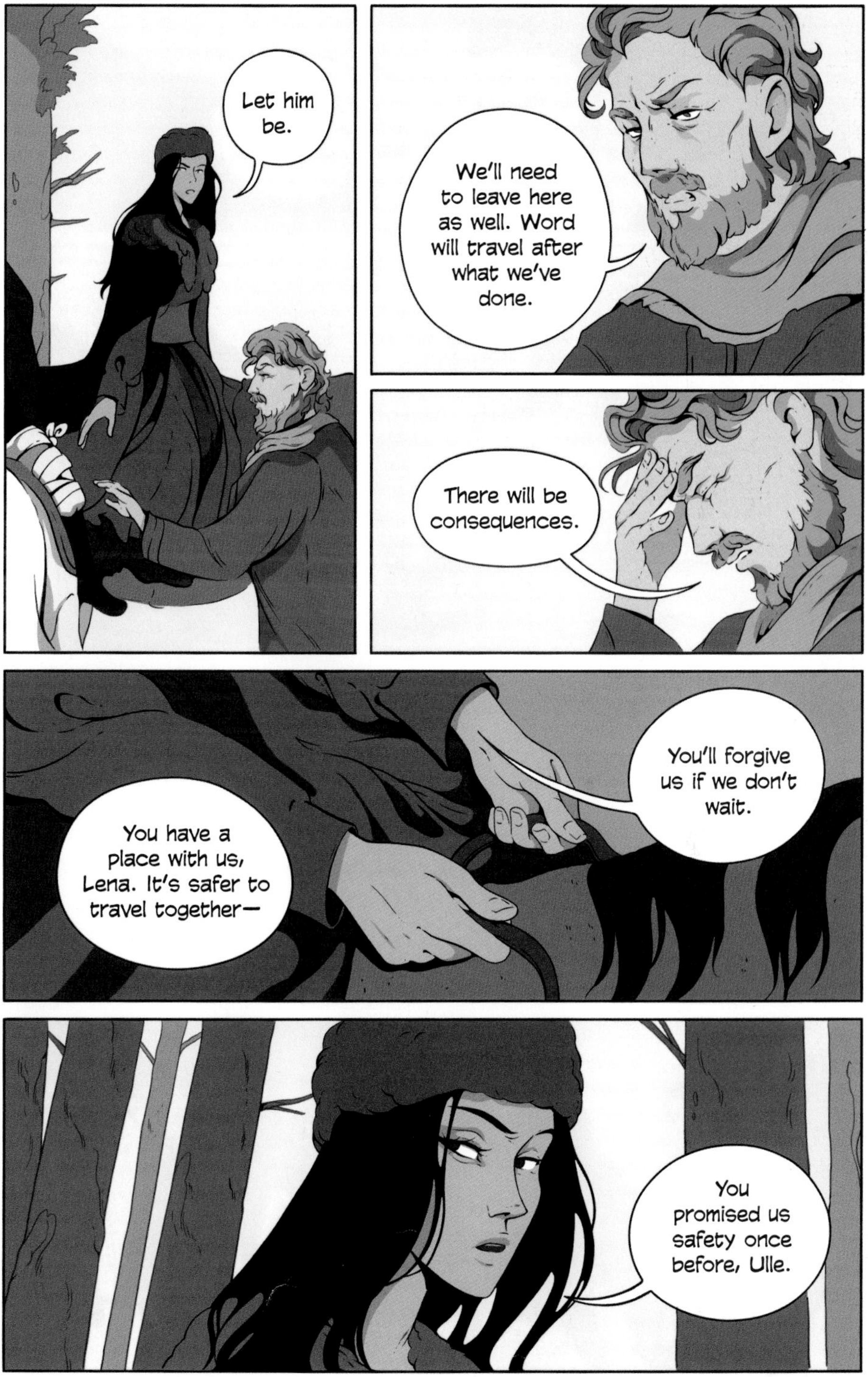
Let him be.
We'll need to leave here as well. Word will travel after what we've done.
There will be consequences.
You'll forgive us if we don't wait.
You have a place with us, Lena. It's safer to travel together—
You promised us safety once before, Ulle.

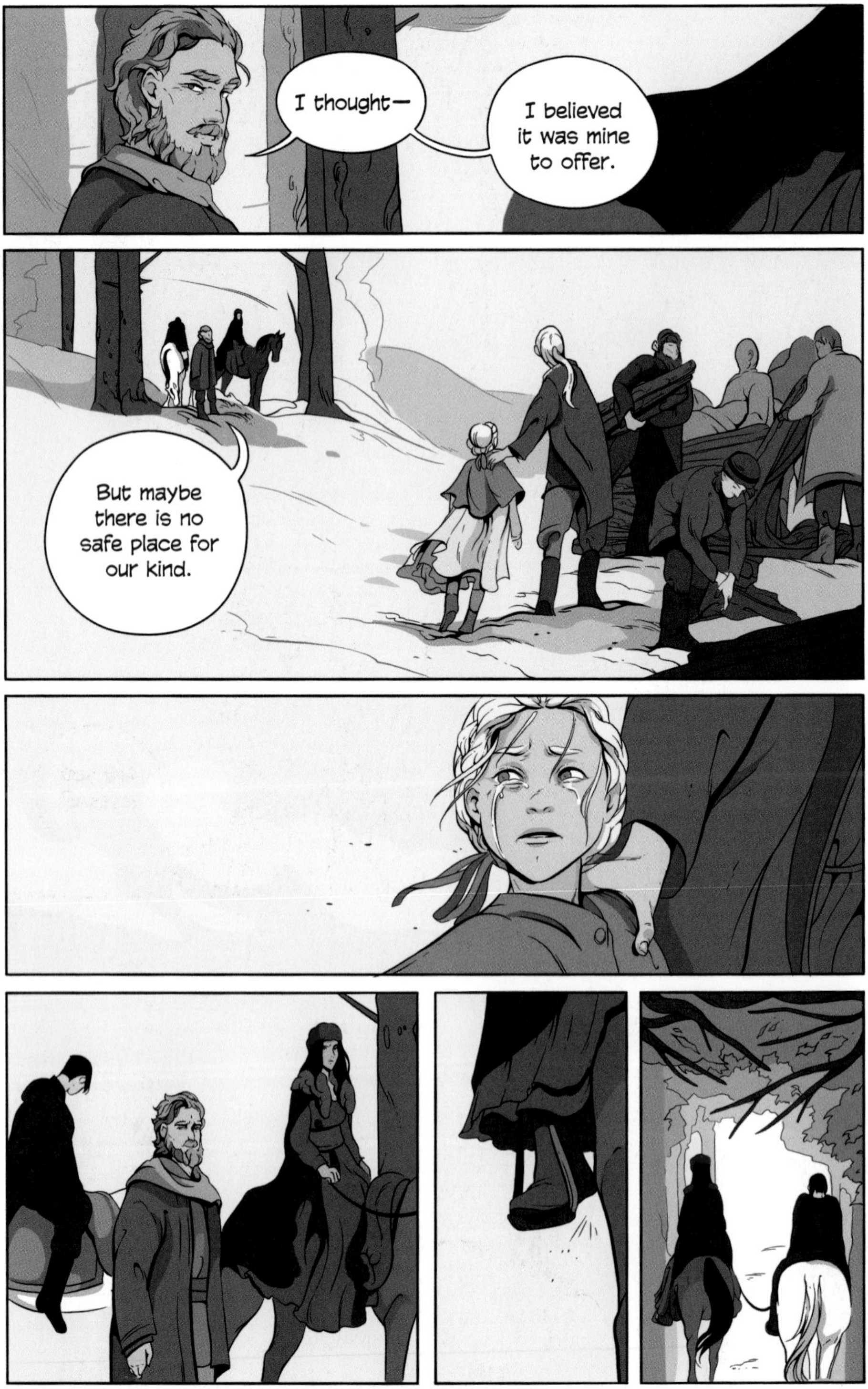
I thought—
I believed it was mine to offer.
But maybe there is no safe place for our kind.

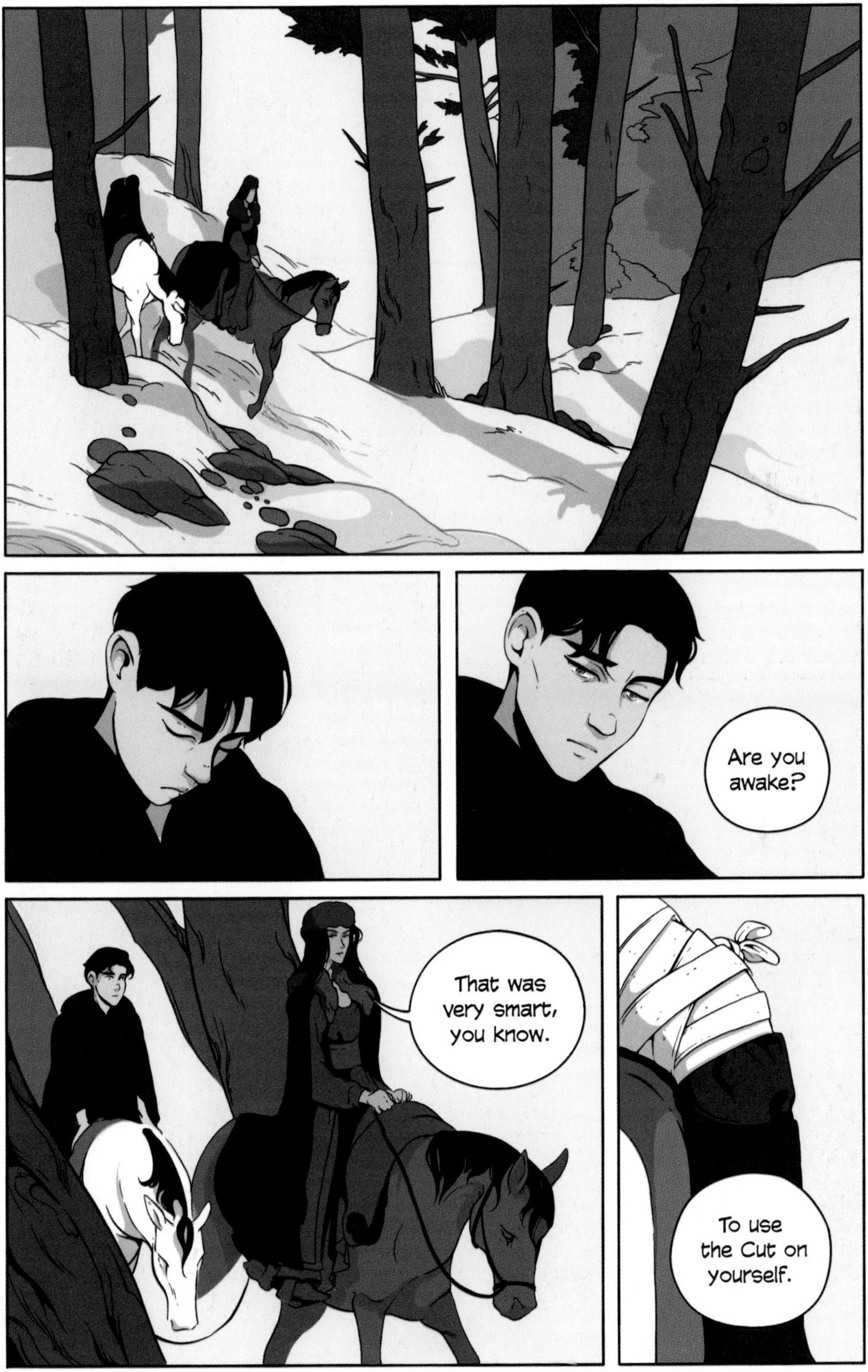
Are you awake?
That was very smart, you know.
To use the Cut on yourself.

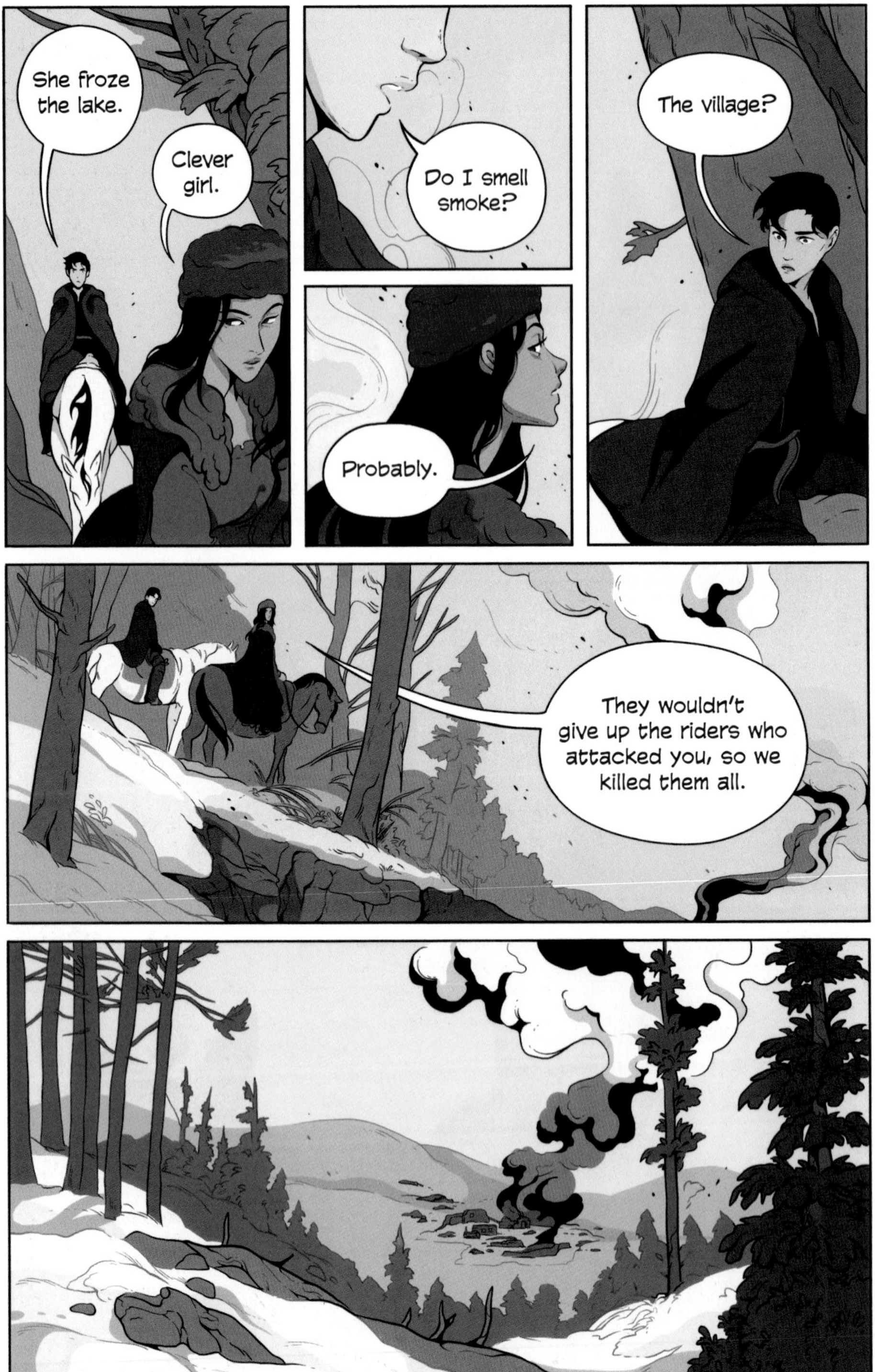
She froze the lake.
Clever girl.
Do I smell smoke?
Probably.
The village?
They wouldn't give up the riders who attacked you, so we killed them all.

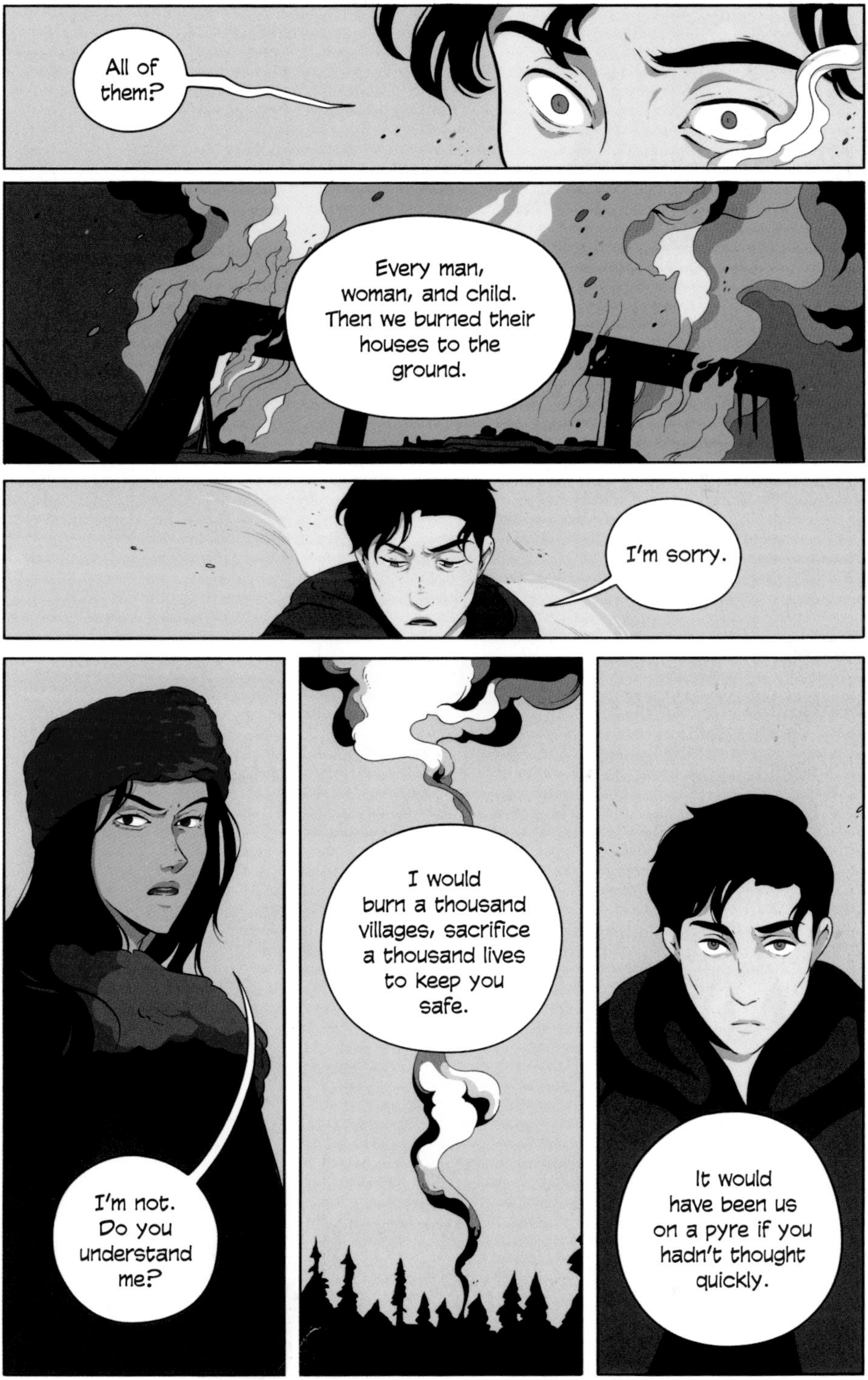
All of them?
Every man, woman, and child. Then we burned their houses to the ground.
I'm sorry.
I'm not. Do you understand me?
I would burn a thousand villages, sacrifice a thousand lives to keep you safe.
It would have been us on a pyre if you hadn't thought quickly.

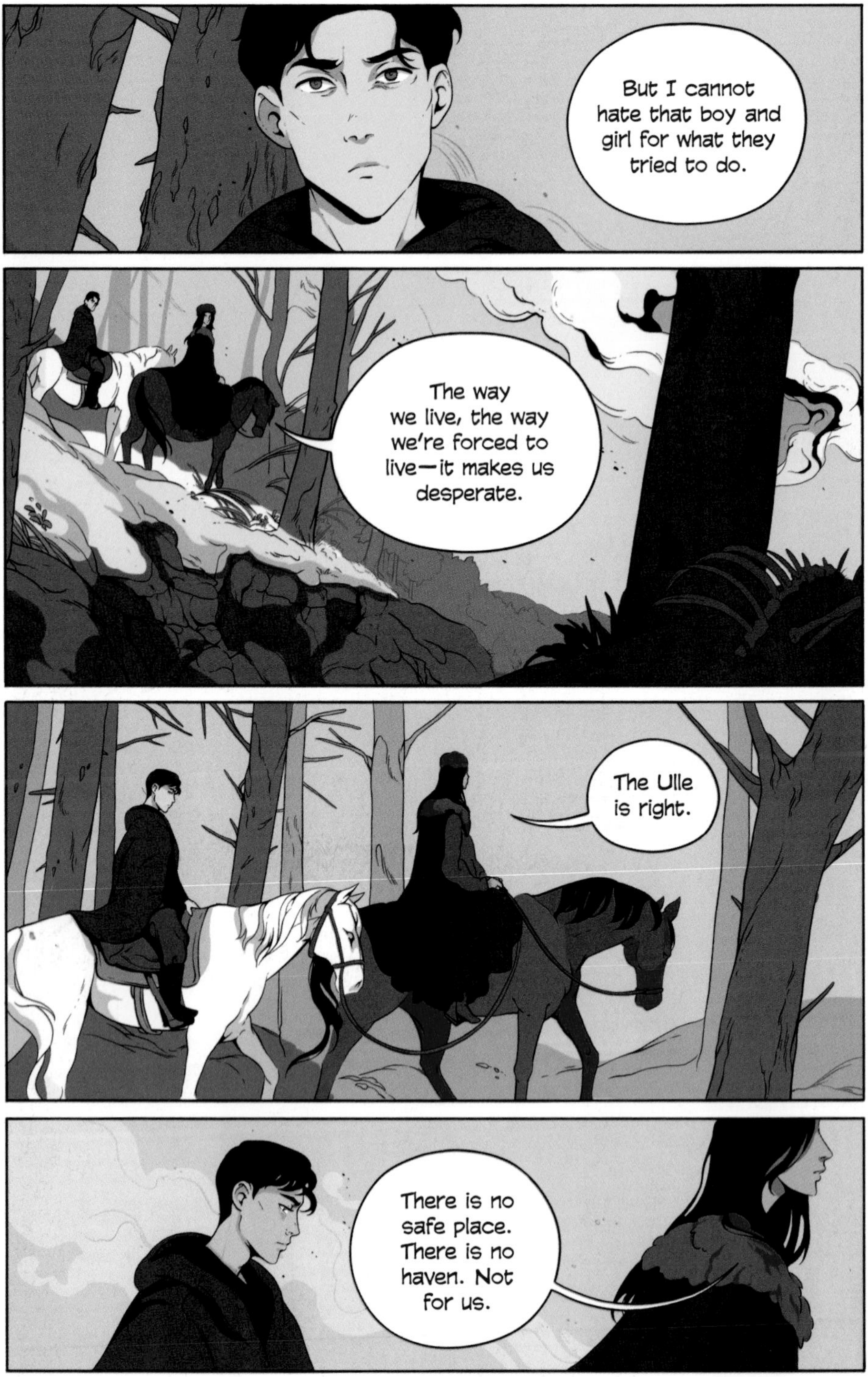
But I cannot hate that boy and girl for what they tried to do.
The way we live, the way we're forced to live—it makes us desperate.
The Ulle is right.
There is no safe place. There is no haven. Not for us.

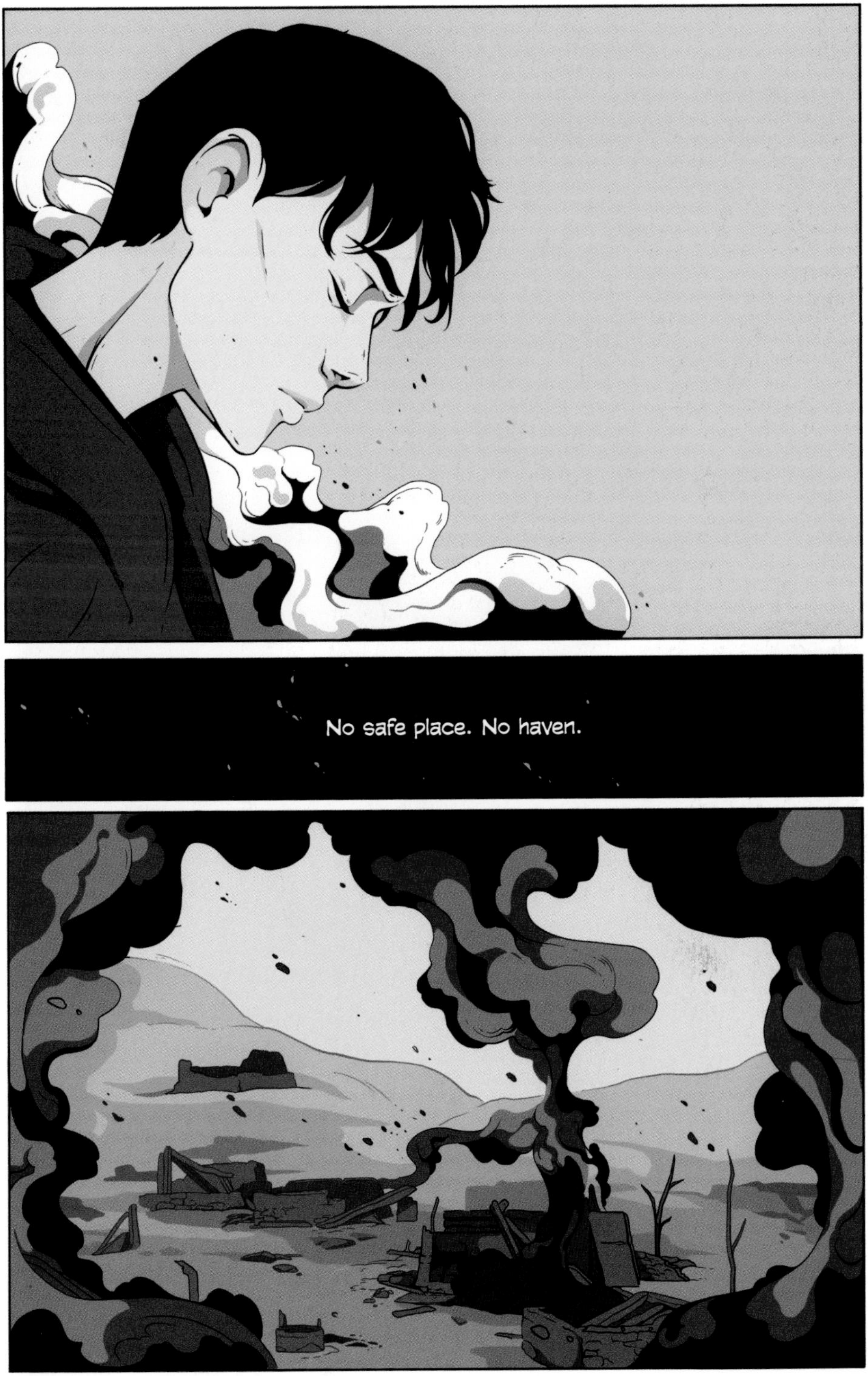
No safe place. No haven.

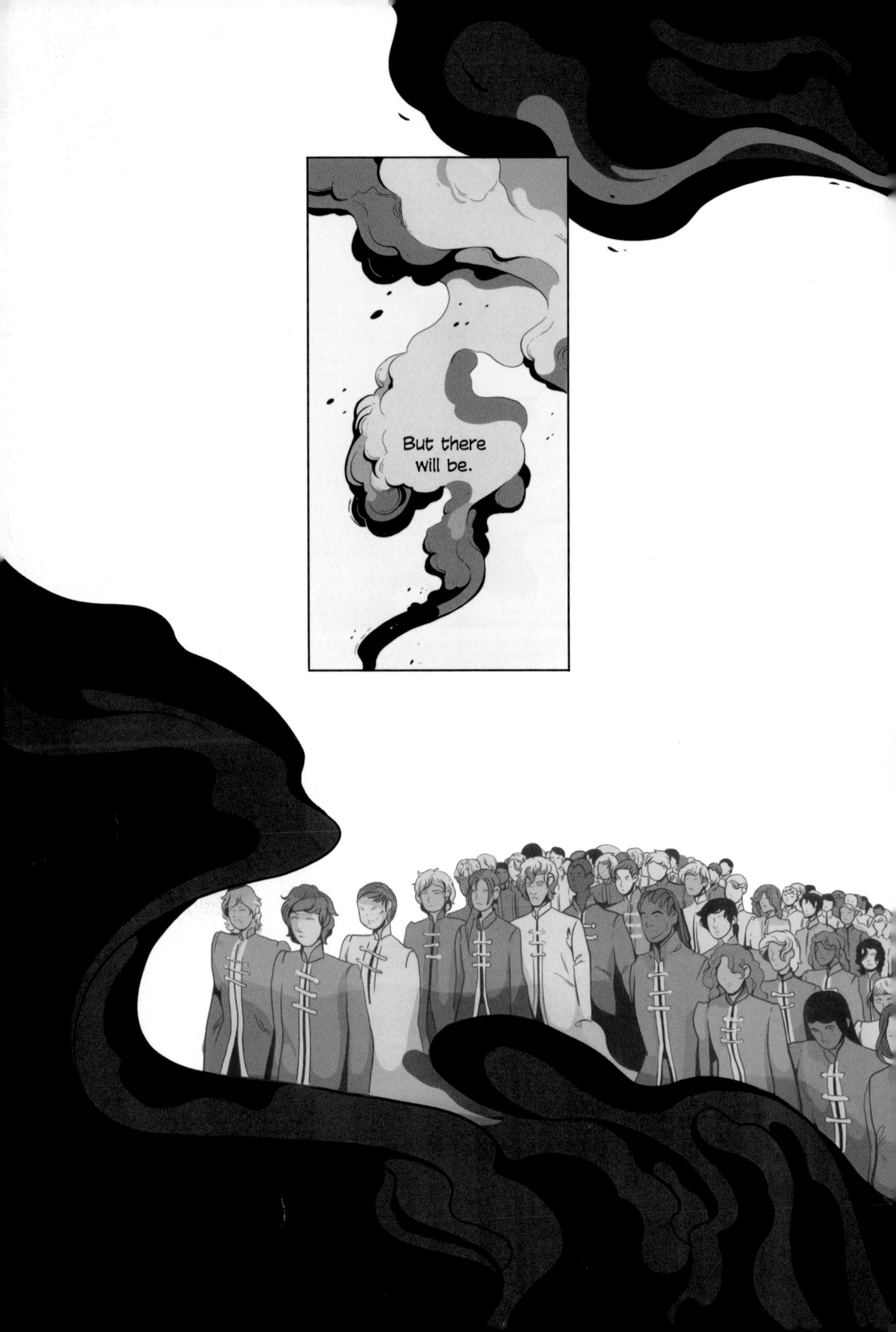
But there will be.

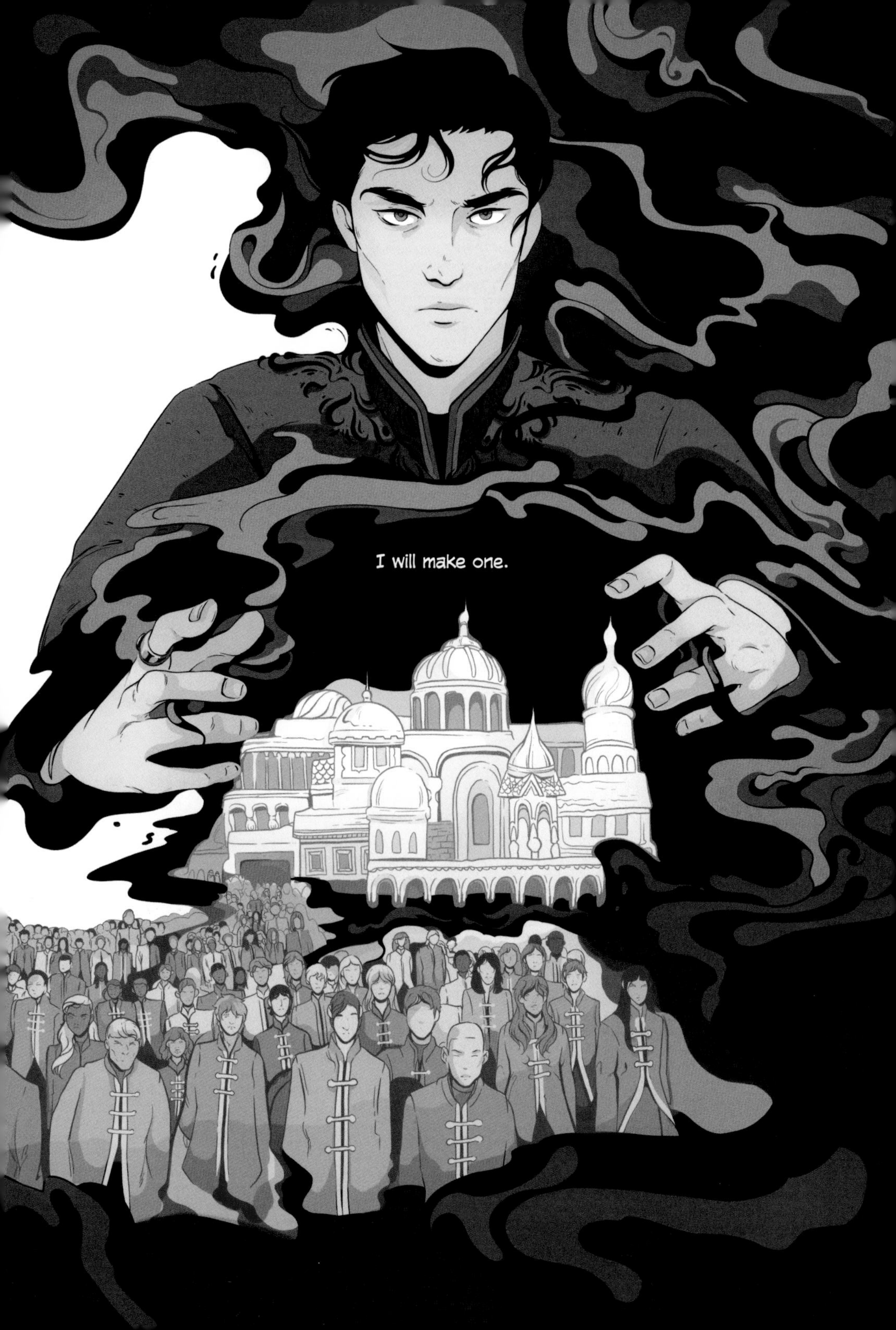
I will make one.

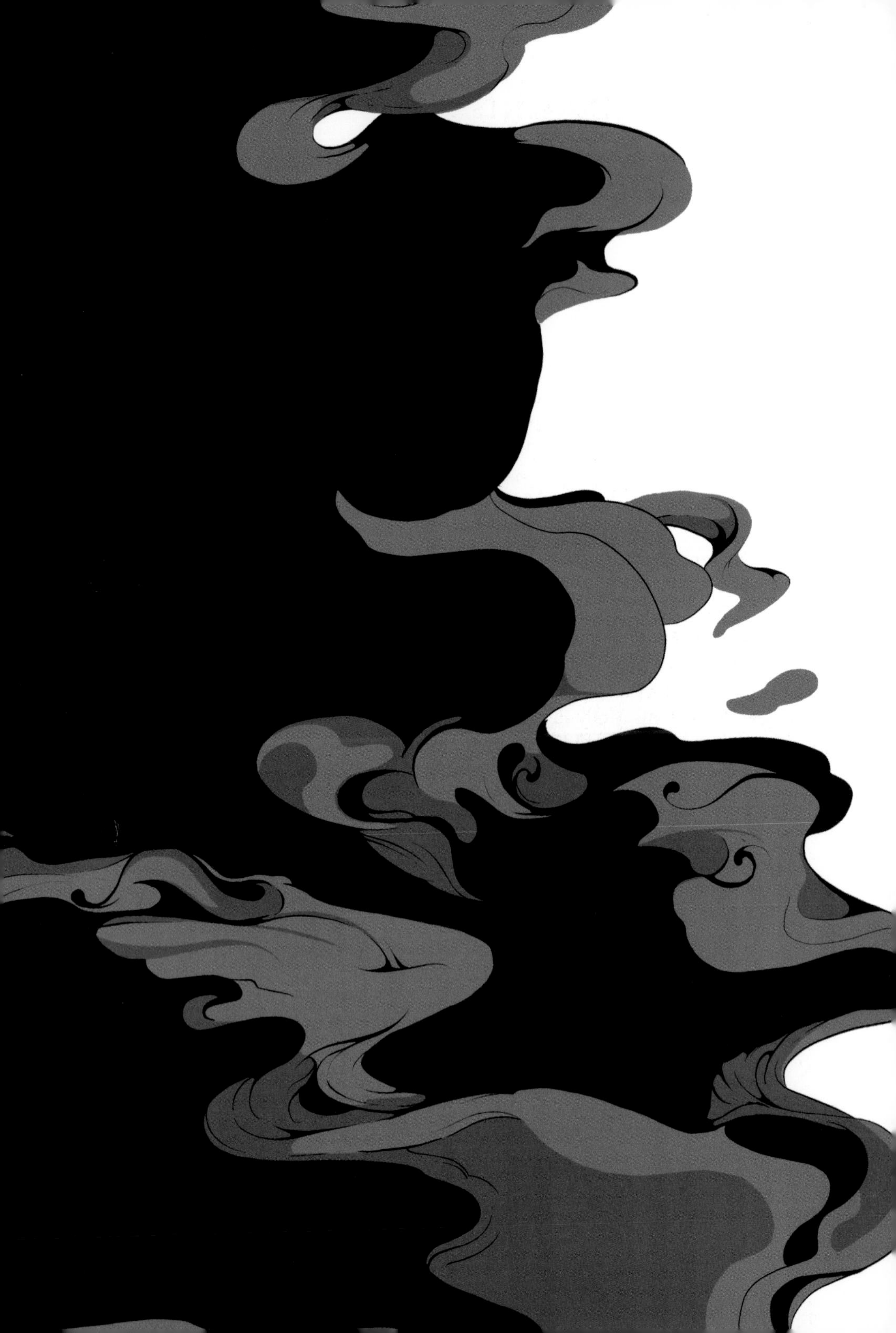

ACKNOWLEDGMENTS

I wrote this story sometime in 2013, during the lead-up to the release of *Ruin and Rising*, the final book in the Shadow and Bone trilogy. Is it a hero's origin story or a villain's? I've never been able to see Aleksander as purely one or the other. He is a survivor who dreams of safety for his people. He is a tyrant who brutalizes and exploits those who trust him most. If Ravka were a different country, if he'd been raised by a different mother, if his mother had been raised by a different mother . . . well, who knows what might have been?

I want to thank some of the many people who saw this story through from the start: First, Dani Pendergast, who brought these characters and this world to life with such originality, emotion, and talent. Dani, I am forever grateful.

Noa Wheeler edited the original short story. Erin Stein, Natalie Souza, and especially John Morgan and Kyla Vanderklugt were fundamental in transforming this story into a real script. Kate Meltzer shepherded us through our revisions with precision and patience. Many thanks to Allison Verost and Jen Besser, as well as the wonderful marketing, publicity, and subrights teams at MCPG: Mariel Dawson, who made a trip to the Grishaverse feel truly real; Kathryn Little, Melissa Zar, Teresa Ferraiolo, Julia Gardiner, Kristen Luby, Melissa Croce, Kristin Dulaney, Kaitlin Loss, Jordan Winch, and the ever-marvelous Molly Ellis and Morgan Kane. And a huge thank-you to the remarkable sales team of Jennifer Edwards, Jessica Brigman, Jasmine Key, Jennifer Golding, Mark Von Bargen, Matthew Mich, Rebecca Schmidt, Sofrina Hinton, and Taylor Armstrong. Also to Jon Yaged, who didn't fit into any of these lists.

My New Leaf Literary family has been with me from the start. Thank you to Hilary Pecheone, Veronica Grijalva, Victoria Hendersen, Meredith Barnes, Abigail Donoghue, Jenniea Carter, Katherine Curtis, Kate Sullivan, the brilliant and sharp-eyed Jordan Hill, the never-say-die Pouya Shahbazian, and my agent, Joanna Volpe, who has entertained my every wild scheme with humor, grace, and a sizable dose of "hell yeah."

All the love and gratitude to my family: Mom, Christine, Sam, Emily, Ryan, and Fredward. And, E, it doesn't matter how many stars we see, there's no one else I'd rather look up with.

—LEIGH BARDUGO

Working on this book was an extraordinary experience for me, and I wouldn't have been able to do it without the support and kindness of the people who held me up throughout the project. A million thank-yous to my family, who always cheered me on, and who have shown me what it means to work hard to achieve your dreams. Thank you to the team at Roaring Book Press and everyone who helped bring this book to life. Thank you to my editor, Kate Meltzer, and Kirk Benshoff for being joys to work with. A huge thank-you to Thao Le, who I am so lucky to call my agent. Big thanks to Geoff for his tireless support and for taking care of our home when I was so often tucked away drawing. And finally, a special thank-you to Leigh. I will be forever grateful for your trust and the opportunity to interpret your story visually. Your words inspire me.

—DANI PENDERGAST

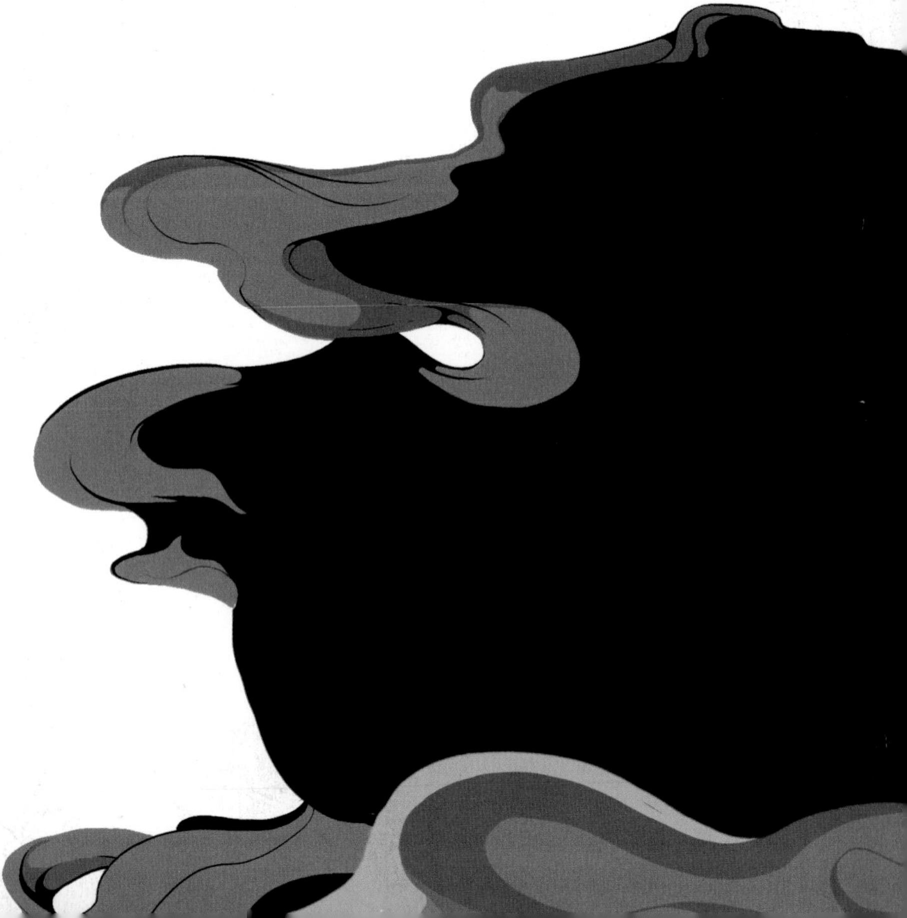

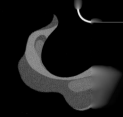

GRISHAVERSE
SHADOW AND BONE
LEIGH BARDUGO

GRISHAVERSE
SIEGE AND STORM
LEIGH BARDUGO

GRISHAVERSE
RUIN AND RISING
LEIGH BARDUGO

LEIGH BARDUGO
SIX OF CROWS

LEIGH BARDUGO
CROOKED KINGDOM

KING OF SCARS
LEIGH BARDUGO

RULE OF WOLVES
LEIGH BARDUGO

THE LANGUAGE OF THORNS
LEIGH BARDUGO

THE LIVES OF SAINTS
NETFLIX
LEIGH BARDUGO

THE SEVERED MOON
LEIGH BARDUGO

GRISHAVERSE
DEMON IN THE WOOD
A SHADOW AND BONE GRAPHIC NOVEL
LEIGH BARDUGO &
DANI PENDERGAST

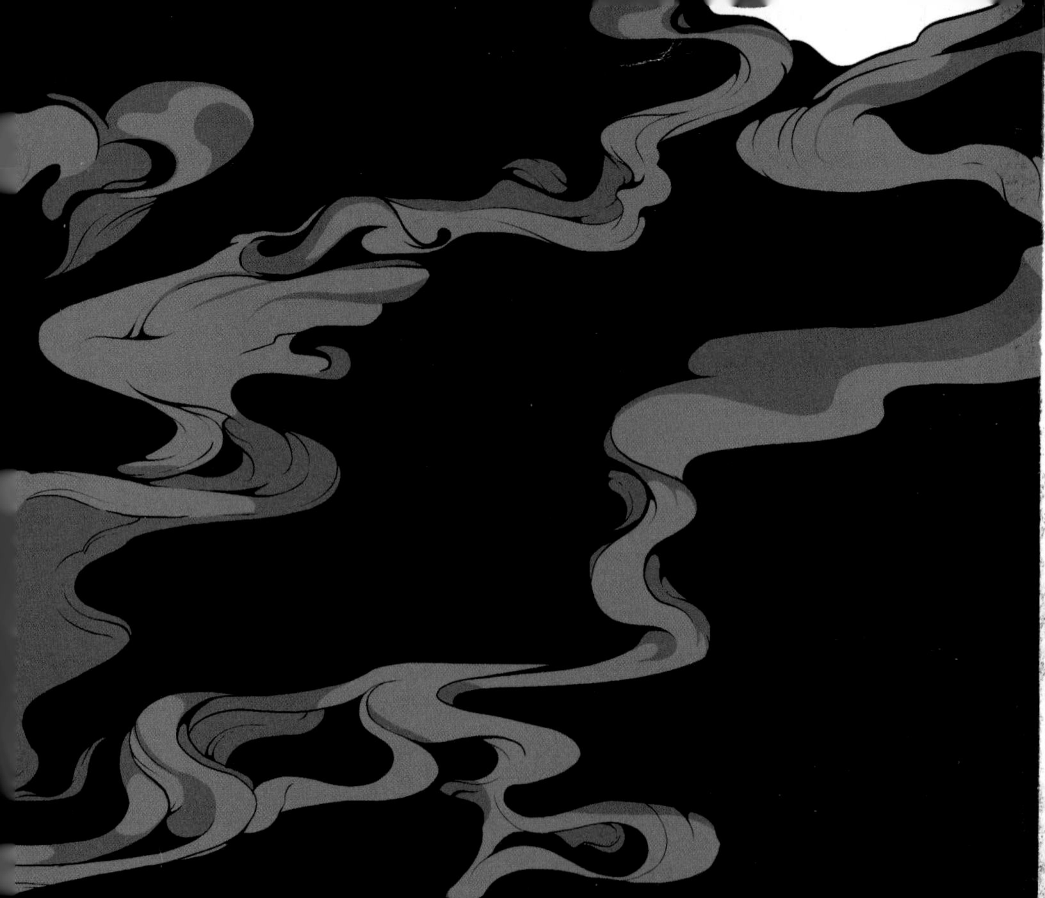

Published by Roaring Brook Press
Roaring Brook Press is a division of Holtzbrinck Publishing Holdings Limited Partnership
120 Broadway, New York, NY 10271 • fiercereads.com

Illustrations by Dani Pendergast.

Our books may be purchased in bulk for promotional, educational, or business use. Please contact your local bookseller or the Macmillan Corporate and Premium Sales Department at (800) 221-7945 ext. 5442 or by email at MacmillanSpecialMarkets@macmillan.com.

Library of Congress Control Number 2022907093

First edition, 2022
The text was set in Comicrazy, Aeneas, and Linotype Syntax Serif. The book was edited by Kate Meltzer, art directed by Kirk Benshoff, and designed by Sunny Lee. The production editor was Taylor Pitts, and the production managers were Raymond Colon and Alexa Blanco.
Penciled digitally in Photoshop with a Cintiq Pro 24. Inked and colored in Procreate on an iPad Pro (12.9)